KASIA BODDY teaches in the English Department at University College London. She is the author of *Boxing: A Cultural History* (2008) and co-editor (with Ali Smith and Sarah Wood) of *Brilliant Careers: The Virago Book of Twentieth-Century Fiction* (2000). She has also contributed an introduction to the Penguin Modern Classics edition of Carson McCullers, *The Heart is a Lonely Hunter*.

ALI SMITH was born in Inverness in 1962 and lives in Cambridge. She is the author of *Free Love* (1995), *Like* (1997), *Other Stories and Other Stories* (1999), *Hotel World* (2001), which was shortlisted for both the Orange Prize and the Booker Prize, *The Whole Stories and Other Stories* (2003), *The Accidental* (2005), which was shortlisted for both the Orange and the Booker and won the Whitbread Novel Prize 2005, *Girl Meets Boy* (2007) and *The First Person and Other Stories* (2008). Ali Smith also writes for the *Guardian*, the *Scotsman* and the *TLS*.

SARAH WOOD is an artist filmmaker and film curator.

D0231187

Let's Call the Whole Thing Off

Love Quarrels from Anton Chekhov to ZZ Packer

Selected by
Kasia Boddy
Ali Smith
Sarah Wood

PENGUIN BOOKS

PENGUIN CLASSICS

Published by the Penguin Group
Penguin Books Ltd, 80 Strand, London WC2R 0RL, England
Penguin Group (USA) Inc., 375 Hudson Street, New York, New York 10014, USA
Penguin Group (Canada), 90 Eglinton Avenue East, Suite 700, Toronto, Ontario,
Canada M4P 2Y3 (a division of Pearson Penguin Canada Inc.)
Penguin Ireland, 25 St Stephen's Green, Dublin 2, Ireland
(a division of Penguin Books Ltd)
Penguin Group (Australia), 250 Camberwell Road, Camberwell, Victoria 3124,
Australia (a division of Pearson Australia Group Pty Ltd)
Penguin Books India Pvt Ltd, 11 Community Centre, Panchsheel Park,
New Delhi – 110 017, India
Penguin Group (NZ), 67 Apollo Drive, Rosedale, North Shore 0632, New Zealand
(a division of Pearson New Zealand Ltd)
Penguin Books (South Africa) (Pty) Ltd, 24 Sturdee Avenue, Rosebank,
Johannesburg 2196, South Africa

Penguin Books Ltd, Registered Offices: 80 Strand, London WC2R 0RL, England

www.penguin.com

This selection first published in Penguin Modern Classics 2009

1

Selection copyright © Kasia Boddy, Ali Smith and Sarah Wood, 2009
Introduction copyright © Kasia Boddy, 2009
Pages 305–8 constitute an extension of this copyright page
All rights reserved

The moral right of the editors and the copyright holders has been asserted

Set in 10pt Imprint MT
Typeset by Palimpsest Book Production Limited, Grangemouth, Stirlingshire
Printed in England by Clays Ltd, St Ives plc

ISBN: 978–0–141–19022–8

www.greenpenguin.co.uk

For our loved ones, with whom we *never* quarrel,
and in memory of the doyenne of arguments,
Grace Paley (1922–2007)

Contents

Contents

The Best Part of Breaking Up

No Regrets?

Acknowledgements

With many thanks to everyone we talked to about lovers' quarrels: Janet Boddy, Christina Büchmann, Kate Daniels, Lindiwe Dovey, Nicky Haire, Philip Horne, Jackie Kay, Robin Krauze, Alison Light, Charlotte Mitchell, Helen Oyeyemi, Barbara Placido and David Trotter.

Thanks to everyone at Penguin, especially Mariateresa Boffo, and to Kristina Blagojevitch. A big thank-you to Tracy Bohan.

Introduction

Imagine a world in which lovers didn't quarrel. Would pop music still exist? Opera? Ballet? Hollywood would certainly suffer. What would be the point of *Shall We Dance* if Fred and Ginger didn't dispute 'tomayto' or 'tomahto' as they roller-skated through Central Park? Would you queue to see a remake of *Bringing Up Baby* in which Cary Grant and Katharine Hepburn simply agreed to disagree? A literature without amorous disputes would also be a sorry thing. Imagine Shakespeare without lovers' complaints, without 'jealous' Oberon and 'proud' Titania squabbling in the moonlight, without Antony's sexy 'sport' with his 'wrangling queen', Cleopatra, without Beatrice's and Benedick's 'merry war'.

BENEDICK: What, my dear Lady Disdain! Are you yet living?
BEATRICE: Is it possible Disdain should die while she hath such meet
    food to feed it as Signior Benedick? Courtesy itself must convert
    to Disdain if you come in her presence.

Lovers' quarrels might be 'much ado about nothing', but they are the much ado that art thrives upon.

So what do lovers, and ex-lovers and wannabe-lovers, quarrel about? Pretty much anything. A 'silly argument about where things hang in the wardrobe' is just one sign that Hilary and Ruth are on the verge of splitting up in Jackie Kay's 'You Go When You Can No Longer Stay', but such petty altercations are not confined to the end of the affair. No sooner is love declared than loving struggle begins. A new bride challenges her husband 'Did you really like my veil?' in Dorothy Parker's 'Here We Are'; in Lydia Davis's 'Disagreement', he wants the screen door open and she wants it shut. 'We see things differently,' the narrator's wife tells him in A. M. Homes's 'Do Not Disturb'; 'meaning she's right, I'm wrong', he adds.

Seeing things differently is, of course, the necessary condition for contestation. In Jhumpa Lahiri's 'This Blessed House', Sanjeev and Twinkle have been married for two months, but he doesn't think he knows what love is. Initially they 'concurred' on many things – an 'adolescent but still persistent fondness for Wodehouse novels, and their dislike for the sitar' – but soon great chasms of taste emerge. Sanjeev likes Bach and Twinkle 'hectic jazz'; he thinks their home should be elegantly understated and she revels in a 'treasure trove' of Christian kitsch. New couples like these worry a lot about their differences; they want, narcissistically, to be the same. The narrator of Harold Brodkey's 'The Quarrel' is delighted to see himself in fellow student Duncan Leggert: 'It seemed to me he was saying everything I had always thought and never expressed.' But when the boys go travelling together the illusion of sameness vanishes. As their differences emerge so too does their mutual affection, although neither can stand anything the other does. One night they sleep next to a stable where the smell of horses mingles with that of roses. The odours are 'oddly complementary', something the boys are perhaps still too young to appreciate.

The idea that the personalities, and even the appearance, of lovers should complement one another goes back a long way, at least as far as Plato's *Symposium*, where Aristophanes argued that the pursuit of love was really the pursuit of unity. The ideal couple, on this model, balanced each other out perfectly to create a harmonious whole, a 'vision of completeness' in George Eliot's phrase. But if many writers imagined true love as a kind of merging, or even annihilation, of individual identities – 'I *am* Heathcliff,' declares Cathy in *Wuthering Heights* – still others have insisted on the impossibility of fusion. How might one remain true to oneself and yet love and be loved? In Jackie Kay's story, Hilary and Ruth have been 'in it so long' that they have 'grown to look the same, wear similar clothes and have almost identical expressions' on their faces. Then Hilary starts changing everything from the way she looks to her taste in wine and books. 'You become far too similar,' she scolds an uncomprehending Ruth, 'especially two women. It's like looking in the mirror. You need a bit of difference to feel real passion.' In some stories, quarrelling not only leads to sex, but also seems to be a form of sex. 'Instead of fucking we fight,' says the beleaguered husband in Homes's 'Do Not Disturb': 'It's the same sort of thing, dramatic, draining.' In Joyce Carol Oates's 'The Quarrel', N. and S. no longer make love nor quarrel, and S. 'could not have said which he missed more'. The two activities are intimately connected in Zora Neale Hurston's 'The Gilded Six-Bits'. Every Saturday afternoon, Joe initiates a 'play-fight' with his wife, Missie May, by throwing his wages through the front door. Happiness depends on some 'rough and tumble', and 'banter that pretended to deny affection but in reality flaunted it'. How different these 'mock battles' are from any real dispute.

But if the sparking of opposites – think of 'blond boy' Andrew and 'dark boy' Nathan in David Leavitt's 'Dedicated', or Pink and Blue in Frances Gapper's fable – can lead to a happy sexual reunification it can also produce further discord. The tension between fighting and fusion has preoccupied many writers, but perhaps no one as much as D. H. Lawrence. In *Women in Love*, Birkin becomes disgusted and frightened by his love for Ursula, finding the very idea of 'this horrible fusion of two beings' to be 'nauseous and horrible'. They stay together but continue to avoid nauseous fusion by quarrelling through to the novel's final paragraph. In the story included here, 'Two Blue Birds', Lawrence presents a separated wife's unhappiness with the comfortable life her novelist husband has established with his devoted secretary. It is not that she's jealous – she's been enjoying numerous 'gallant affairs' – rather that she doesn't think that having 'nobody and nothing to contradict him' is good either for him or his writing. She sees it as her wifely duty to reintroduce the 'silent ceaseless tension' of marriage into his life. Two blue tits battle for love at the novelist's feet, but although his wife and secretary both don blue silk dresses, theirs is no contest of equals. Lawrence describes the wife, admiringly and repeatedly, as a wolf.

Early twentieth-century fiction liked to present the 'love-antics and dances' of people in bird and animal metaphors. Darwin's discussion of the numerous 'love battles' waged in the natural world was often evoked to support the idea that quarrelling was natural, even instinctive. But the representation of lovers as birds has a long history. Andrew Marvell, trying to argue his coy mistress into bed, speaks of 'am'rous birds of prey', and the narrator of Robert Browning's 'A Woman's Last Word' reflects on a past 'debate' by comparing her husband and herself to hawks. 'What so wild as words are?' she asks. These aggressive birds are in deliberate contrast to the turtle-dove, said to have pulled Venus's chariot and the traditional emblem of pure, gentle and faithful love. An alternative, not altogether ironic, view of this creature is given in Katherine Mansfield's 'Mr and Mrs Dove'. The story begins with cats and dogs. Reggie leaves behind his 'mater' and her pair of repulsive Pekinese to declare his love to Anne. But Anne, who has firm ideas about romance, can only laugh at a marriage proposal from a man whose bow tie reminds her of a cartoon cat. The problem, she says, is how exactly they resemble her pet doves. 'The one in front, she's Mrs Dove. She looks at Mr Dove and gives that little laugh and runs forward, and he follows her, bowing and bowing. And that makes her laugh again.' The comparison Anne evokes is unassailable, but when Reggie prepares to leave, she is not happy. 'Come back, Mr Dove,' she calls out, laughing. Perhaps she and Reggie can be love-birds after all.

In Mansfield's story, the imaginative transformation of Reggie and Anne into birds threatens a relationship that has not yet begun. In 'Lappin and Lapinova', by Mansfield's friend and rival Virginia Woolf, fantasy is all that holds the relationship together. The only way that Rosalind can 'get used' to her new husband – a 'spruce, muscular young man' called Ernest – is to turn him into something less threatening. The story begins, on their honeymoon, when Ernest twitches his nose in a rabbit-like way and she names him King Lappin. He reciprocates by casting her as a small, grey hare called Lapinova. By the time the couple have returned home, they possess a 'private world', a mutually sustaining fantasy designed to protect them from 'the rest of the world' and from their own adult selves. It's a way of avoiding disagreement, for a while at least.

Near the end of *Much Ado About Nothing*, Benedick says to Beatrice, 'Thou and I are too wise to woo peaceably.' Their wisdom, it seems, lies in the realization that their 'skirmishes of wit' are a kind of testing of love that serves only to strengthen its bond. 'Lovers' quarrels are love's renewal' is the most common translation of a much-quoted phrase from *Andria* by the Roman playwright Terence. *Amantium irae amoris integratio est* was among Winston Churchill's favourite mottoes – he telegraphed it to Franklin D. Roosevelt after one of their many disagreements threatened the Special Relationship. The phrase crops up in all sorts of literary makings-up. In Milton's *Samson Agonistes*, Samson reassures Delilah that, 'Love-quarrels oft in pleasing concord end;/ Not wedlock-treachery', a theme which Tennyson developed in 'The Princess':

> We fell out, my wife and I,
> O we fell out I know not why,
>   And kiss'd again with tears.
> And blessings on the falling out
>   That all the more endears,
> When we fall out with those we love
>   And kiss again with tears!

To assume that breaking up leads to making up is to believe that lovers' quarrels belong to the genre of comedy. That's an assumption that the dastardly Robert Lovelace makes in Samuel Richardson's *Clarissa*. In letters to his friend John Belford, he tries to present his relationship with Clarissa as a piece of comic drama which he entitles *The Quarrelsome Lovers*. Surely, Lovelace says, again paraphrasing Terence, 'lovers falling out occasions lovers falling in; and a better understanding of course'. This doesn't work in their case, however, because, as he notes, 'we fall out so often, without falling in once; and a second quarrel so generally happens before a first is made up that it's hard to guess what event our loves will be attended with'. Perhaps the real problem is that Clarissa views the affair less as a comedy than a potential tragedy. When Lovelace eventually rapes her, it becomes apparent that Richardson supports her interpretation.

The present collection tends more often to comedy than tragedy, but even here it's a risky strategy to assume that the calling-off will, at the midnight hour, be called off. 'Am I supposed to come over there and sweep your enraged self into my arms?' Dina asks her never-quite lover, Heidi, in ZZ Packer's 'Drinking Coffee Elsewhere'. 'Like in the movies? Is this the part where we're both so mad we kiss each other?' Dina and Heidi don't kiss and they don't make up. Alice Thorpe, in Arnold Bennett's 'One of Their Quarrels', cannot imagine how her marital quarrel will end, but she never doubts that it will end and that the ending will be 'delicious'. Alice reflects upon the argument as if it were a story she was writing, with 'a fine artistic interest', and calmly contemplates its development and 'different dodges for concluding it'. But the unpredictability of the quarrel's progress and the arbitrary nature of its conclusion is what Bennett's story is all about.

The nature of the quarrel partly depends on how well the lovers know each other, and so we've divided up the collection along those lines. We begin at the beginning, with the misunderstandings of those new to each other. Parker's couple are a mere two hours twenty-six minutes into their marriage. Like their clothes, they're still 'stiff with novelty' and feel that every word they tentatively utter is open to misinterpretation. 'I mean, I mean' is their uneasy refrain.

The everyday quarrels of established couples have less to do with uncertainty and more to do with the confidence that comes with intimacy; that is, each partner comes to know just what to say to annoy the other. Bickering can be the ultimate expression of togetherness; showing each other, and the world, how safe you feel together. The quarrel, Roland Barthes once said, is the ultimate lovers' luxury, precisely because 'it does not leave a mark, it does not sully'. 'Isn't general incivility,' Elizabeth Bennett remarks in *Pride and Prejudice*, 'the very essence of love?' Austen's heroes must work hard to deserve what Elinor Dashwood, in *Sense and Sensibility*, calls 'the compliment of rational opposition'. And it is a compliment, although not always recognized as such. In Tove Jansson's 'B-Western', Jonna would rather watch her favourite cowboy movies without interruption, but Mari stays close to needle her affectionately. The repetitive pleasure we get from genres like the Western, Jansson suggests, has a lot in common with the repetitive pleasures of quarrelsome love. In these stories, and elsewhere, love is defined as caring enough to answer back. The eponymous 'he and I' of Natalia Ginzburg's piece have agreed on nothing for decades and seem set to drive each other crazy into perpetuity. How different, the narrator thinks, from twenty years ago, when they'd just met and were ready both 'to judge one another with kind impartiality' and to say goodbye for ever. Love is never impartial.

Yet often more is at stake than the subject ostensibly under discussion. 'Protest March', by the Depression-era Welsh writer Kate Roberts, begins with Bronwen setting off to demonstrate against the Means Test while her young husband, Idris, lies 'coiled like a cat' on the bed. 'She still had hope. His had turned sour.' The story weighs up these points of view, but ends with a sense that, whoever's right or wrong, they're in it together. That's not always the case. Negotiations about power lie in the shadows of many seemingly less consequential disputes. In Lydia Davis's story, the real issue is not how to get rid of the flies that buzz around the door but whether she's disagreeing with him or he's disagreeing with her – not a trivial matter at all. The very title of Arnold Bennett's story, 'One of Their Quarrels', suggests the everyday nature of arguing for yet another pair of 'married belligerents', Alice and Jim Thorpe. 'Like all their quarrels, it had arisen out of almost nothing, and a word, even a tone, might have stifled it at birth.' Both recognize that they are being 'idiots' but both also have an overly developed 'sense of dignity'. Can anything break the impasse?

The third section features stories in which the quarrel threatens to, and indeed sometimes does, get out of hand. Erich Segal famously said that love means never having to say you're sorry, but often it's a stubborn refusal to apologize that endangers the relationship. And if love really means acting contrite (even when you're not), it also requires a willingness to let your partner have the last word, as Homes's 'Do Not Disturb' so compassionately shows. Homes's narrator and his wife both accept that they're 'a really bad match', but as he points out, 'we're such a good bad match it seems impossible to let it go'. A similar weariness informs Alasdair Gray's 'Pillow Talk'; sometimes breaking up is just not worth the trouble.

A rather different problem faces the protagonists of Andrey Platonov's 'The Return' – beginning again after a long separation, when they should know and trust each other but have forgotten how. Four years of the Second World War have passed since Captain Ivanov has seen his wife, Lyubov, and their children. His train home is delayed and on the platform he meets a young woman called Masha. Without the army, both feel 'orphaned' and are drawn together. Staying with Masha for a couple of days, Ivanov does not understand why he has put off the 'joyful and anxious moment of reunion with his family'. When he does get home, he finds to his dismay that his young son has taken charge and that his wife has been unfaithful. They do nothing but argue.

The final section includes stories that explore the aftermath of the quarrel, whether just a few days or many years have passed since its fires raged. What D. H. Lawrence calls the 'awful unspoken intimacy of the once married' is a common theme. Even after decades apart, exes retain the power to hurt, to make just the right 'narrow remark which, like a plumber's snake, could work its way through the ear down the throat, halfway to [the] heart', as Grace Paley so vividly puts it. But love too often remains, and with it, regret and acceptance. 'I shouldn't have let Kathy go,' the narrator of Alan Sillitoe's 'The Fishing-boat Picture' chastises himself. 'You no longer hope to "bring me back to the fold"; I don't count on ever converting you,' concludes Colette's letter to her 'dear Valentine'. 'I don't argue when there's real disagreement,' decides Paley's sensible narrator when she bumps into her still-ready-to-bicker ex-husband.

We've decided not to include poems or extracts from novels or plays in this anthology but to concentrate on short stories. In many ways, the short story and the quarrel are a match made in heaven. The confined space of the short-story form ideally suits the presentation of a single dramatic scene, a crisis point, with past tensions and future consequences merely implied. Many of the stories here present such scenes in a few pages or less; Lydia Davis needs only a single paragraph to stage her 'Disagreement'. 'Here We Are', by the accomplished screenwriter Dorothy Parker, places its just-married couple on the train that is taking them, line by nervous line, ever closer to their much-anticipated wedding night. Joyce Carol Oates presents the crisis point of 'The Quarrel' in a police station where N. and S. fail to agree on a single fact concerning the doorstep attack on N. by a would-be thief. As the police officers look on, the lovers quarrel 'quietly, yet wildly . . . unable to stop'. Later they are horrified and never again will they 'risk another scene like that terrible scene'.

'The House with the Mezzanine', by Anton Chekhov, locates the scene within a complete, if ambiguous, play. The story is divided into four parts with the decisive quarrel taking place in the third. Subtitled 'An Artist's Story', it initially seems to be the nostalgic recollection of a young landscape painter who spent a summer in the company of two beguiling sisters six or seven years earlier. The vagueness about the time-frame is the first of many uncertainties in this tale. Was the narrator in love with Zhenya, who both openly liked him and seemed to be like him? There was no squabbling between this pair. He greatly admired her, and in particular the way she gazed 'so tenderly and admiringly' at him. Or did that love disguise another, for Zhenya's beautiful and bossy elder sister, Lida, with whom he argued vehemently about the value of social reform and politically engaged art? Did their passion stem from their firm convictions, or did their firm convictions mask their passion? Does the narrator, looking back, even now know his own heart?

'The House with the Mezzanine' is one of many stories in which a lovers' quarrel extends beyond the expected *pas de deux*. Sometimes the third party exists only as a topic of jealous dispute – talk of a 'knock-out' bridesmaid detains Parker's honeymooners; an imaginary ideal husband stands between Mansfield's Reggie and Anne – but sometimes the third party actually gets into bed and the relationship, as Princess Diana put it, becomes 'crowded'. In David Leavitt's 'Dedicated', it is Nathan's jealousy of Andrew's affair with the 'famous activist Joel Miller' that adds heat to their debate about Gay Pride. In William Trevor's 'Access to the Children', Malcolmson drinks to the day when his 'happy marriage could continue', even as his ex-wife plans her wedding to another man.

Some quarrels need an audience in order to get started while others need one in order to end. In 'Dedicated', Celia relishes her role at the heart of the 'battleground' between Andrew and Nathan. Only later does she come to recognize 'that her happiness with Nathan and Andrew depended on Andrew and Nathan being unhappy with one another'. This is not how the children of quarrelling parents think. When, in 'The Return', Ivanov tells his son that he does not 'understand' adult affairs, Petya replies with great ferocity, 'It's you who don't understand. There's work to do, we have to go on living, and you two are quarrelling like stupid fools.' A fresh perspective can change everything: whether it's offered by a child, a friend, a shrink, or a stranger. It is only when Sanjeev, in Lahiri's story, is able to view Twinkle through the eyes of his party guests that he understands that she's not irritating but totally 'wow'.

Fresh perspectives are also what anthologies offer, not least because they are always in dispute with themselves, as one piece bumps up against another, to qualify or contradict its unfamiliar neighbours. And the contention is not simply internal. Anthologies provoke disagreement as well as agreement in their readers and, sometimes, between their editors. Ali, Sarah and I have had some really good quarrels about what to include and what to leave out of this book. We hope you enjoy reading, and perhaps disputing, our selection. What is incontestable, though, is that love, as Shakespeare says, often approaches 'armed in arguments'.

Kasia Boddy

We've Only Just Begun

argue, *v.t.* To attentively consider with the tongue.

Ambrose Bierce

DOROTHY PARKER
Here We Are

The young man in the new blue suit finished arranging the glistening luggage in tight corners of the Pullman compartment. The train had leaped at curves and bounced along straightaways, rendering balance a praiseworthy achievement and a sporadic one; and the young man had pushed and hoisted and tucked and shifted the bags with concentrated care.

Nevertheless, eight minutes for the settling of two suitcases and a hat-box is a long time.

He sat down, leaning back against bristled green plush, in the seat opposite the girl in beige. She looked as new as a peeled egg. Her hat, her fur, her frock, her gloves were glossy and stiff with novelty. On the arc of the thin, slippery sole of one beige shoe was gummed a tiny oblong of white paper, printed with the price set and paid for that slipper and its fellow, and the name of the shop that had dispensed them.

She had been staring raptly out of the window, drinking in the big weathered signboards that extolled the phenomena of codfish without bones and screens no rust could corrupt. As the young man sat down, she turned politely from the pane, met his eyes, started a smile and got it about half done, and rested her gaze just above his right shoulder.

'Well!' the young man said.

'Well!' she said.

'Well, here we are,' he said.

'Here we are,' she said. 'Aren't we?'

'I should say we were,' he said. 'Eeyop. Here we are.'

'Well!' she said.

'Well!' he said. 'Well. How does it feel to be an old married lady?'

'Oh, it's too soon to ask me that,' she said. 'At least – I mean. Well, I mean, goodness, we've only been married about three hours, haven't we?'

The young man studied his wrist-watch as if he were just acquiring the knack of reading time.

3

'We have been married,' he said, 'exactly two hours and twenty-six minutes.'

'My,' she said. 'It seems like longer.'

'No,' he said. 'It isn't hardly half-past six yet.'

'It seems like later,' she said. 'I guess it's because it starts getting dark so early.'

'It does, at that,' he said. 'The nights are going to be pretty long from now on. I mean. I mean – well, it starts getting dark early.'

'I didn't have any idea what time it was,' she said. 'Everything was so mixed up, I sort of don't know where I am, or what it's all about. Getting back from the church, and then all those people, and then changing all my clothes, and then everybody throwing things, and all. Goodness, I don't see how people do it every day.'

'Do what?' he said.

'Get married,' she said. 'When you think of all the people, all over the world, getting married just as if it was nothing. Chinese people and everybody. Just as if it wasn't anything.'

'Well, let's not worry about people all over the world,' he said. 'Let's don't think about a lot of Chinese. We've got something better to think about. I mean. I mean – well, what do we care about them?'

'I know,' she said. 'But I just sort of got to thinking of them, all of them, all over everywhere, doing it all the time. At least, I mean – getting married, you know. And it's – well, it's sort of such a big thing to do, it makes you feel queer. You think of them, all of them, all doing it just like it wasn't anything. And how does anybody know what's going to happen next?'

'Let them worry,' he said. 'We don't have to. We know darn well what's going to happen next. I mean. I mean – well, we know it's going to be great. Well, we know we're going to be happy. Don't we?'

'Oh, of course,' she said. 'Only you think of all the people, and you have to sort of keep thinking. It makes you feel funny. An awful lot of people that get married, it doesn't turn out so well. And I guess they all must have thought it was going to be great.'

'Come on, now,' he said. 'This is no way to start a honeymoon, with all this thinking going on. Look at us – all married and everything done. I mean. The wedding all done and all.'

'Ah, it was nice, wasn't it?' she said. 'Did you really like my veil?'

'You looked great,' he said. 'Just great.'

'Oh, I'm terribly glad,' she said. 'Ellie and Louise looked lovely, didn't they? I'm terribly glad they did finally decide on pink. They looked perfectly lovely.'

'Listen,' he said. 'I want to tell you something. When I was standing up there in that old church waiting for you to come up, and I saw those two bridesmaids, I thought to myself, I thought, "Well, I never knew Louise could look like that!" Why, she'd have knocked anybody's eye out.'

'Oh, really?' she said. 'Funny. Of course, everybody thought her dress and hat were lovely, but a lot of people seemed to think she looked sort of tired. People have been saying that a lot, lately. I tell them I think it's awfully mean of them to go around saying that about her. I tell them they've got to remember that Louise isn't so terribly young any more, and they've got to expect her to look like that. Louise can say she's twenty-three all she wants to, but she's a good deal nearer twenty-seven.'

'Well, she was certainly a knock-out at the wedding,' he said. 'Boy!'

'I'm terribly glad you thought so,' she said. 'I'm glad someone did. How did you think Ellie looked?'

'Why, I honestly didn't get a look at her,' he said.

'Oh, really?' she said. 'Well, I certainly think that's too bad. I don't suppose I ought to say it about my own sister, but I never saw anybody look as beautiful as Ellie looked today. And always so sweet and unselfish, too. And you didn't even notice her. But you never pay attention to Ellie, anyway. Don't think I haven't noticed it. It makes me feel just terrible. It makes me feel just awful, that you don't like my own sister.'

'I do like her!' he said. 'I'm crazy for Ellie. I think she's a great kid.'

'Don't think it makes any difference to Ellie!' she said. 'Ellie's got enough people crazy about her. It isn't anything to her whether you like her or not. Don't flatter yourself she cares! Only, the only thing is, it makes it awfully hard for me you don't like her, that's the only thing. I keep thinking, when we come back and get in that apartment and everything, it's going to be awfully hard for me that you won't want my own sister to come and see me. It's going to

5

make it awfully hard for me that you won't ever want my family around. I know how you feel about my family. Don't think I haven't seen it. Only, if you don't ever want to see them, that's your loss. Not theirs. Don't flatter yourself!'

'Oh, now, come on!' he said. 'What's all this talk about not wanting your family around? Why, you know how I feel about your family. I think your old lady – I think your mother's swell. And Ellie. And your father. What's all this talk?'

'Well, I've seen it,' she said. 'Don't think I haven't. Lots of people they get married, and they think it's going to be great and everything, and then it all goes to pieces because people don't like people's families, or something like that. Don't tell me! I've seen it happen.'

'Honey,' he said, 'what is all this? What are you getting all angry about? Hey, look, this is our honeymoon. What are you trying to start a fight for? Ah, I guess you're just feeling sort of nervous.'

'Me?' she said. 'What have I got to be nervous about? I mean. I mean, goodness, I'm not nervous.'

'You know, lots of times,' he said, 'they say that girls get kind of nervous and yippy on account of thinking about – I mean. I mean – well, it's like you said, things are all so sort of mixed up and everything, right now. But afterwards, it'll be all right. I mean. I mean – well, look, honey, you don't look any too comfortable. Don't you want to take your hat off? And let's don't ever fight, ever. Will we?'

'Ah, I'm sorry I was cross,' she said. 'I guess I did feel a little bit funny. All mixed up, and then thinking of all those people all over everywhere, and then being sort of 'way off here, all alone with you. It's so sort of different. It's sort of such a big thing. You can't blame a person for thinking, can you? Yes, don't let's ever, ever fight. We won't be like a whole lot of them. We won't fight or be nasty or anything. Will we?'

'You bet your life we won't,' he said.

'I guess I will take this darned old hat off,' she said. 'It kind of presses. Just put it up on the rack, will you, dear? Do you like it, sweetheart?'

'Looks good on you,' he said.

'No, but I mean,' she said, 'do you really like it?'

'Well, I'll tell you,' he said. 'I know this is the new style and everything like that, and it's probably great. I don't know anything about things like that. Only I like the kind of a hat like that blue hat you had. Gee, I liked that hat.'

'Oh, really?' she said. 'Well, that's nice. That's lovely. The first thing you say to me, as soon as you get me off on a train away from my family and everything, is that you don't like my hat. The first thing you say to your wife is you think she has terrible taste in hats. That's nice, isn't it?'

'Now, honey,' he said, 'I never said anything like that. I only said –'

'What you don't seem to realize,' she said, 'is this hat cost twenty-two dollars. Twenty-two dollars. And that horrible old blue thing you think you're so crazy about, that cost three ninety-five.'

'I don't give a darn what they cost,' he said. 'I only said – I said I liked that blue hat. I don't know anything about hats. I'll be crazy about this one as soon as I get used to it. Only it's kind of not like your other hats. I don't know about the new styles. What do I know about women's hats?'

'It's too bad,' she said, 'you didn't marry somebody that would get the kind of hats you'd like. Hats that cost three ninety-five. Why didn't you marry Louise? You always think she looks so beautiful. You'd love her taste in hats. Why didn't you marry her?'

'Ah, now, honey,' he said. 'For heaven's sakes!'

'Why didn't you marry her?' she said. 'All you've done, ever since we got on this train, is talk about her. Here I've sat and sat, and just listened to you saying how wonderful Louise is. I suppose that's nice, getting me all off here alone with you, and then raving about Louise right in front of my face. Why didn't you ask her to marry you? I'm sure she would have jumped at the chance. There aren't so many people asking her to marry them. It's too bad you didn't marry her. I'm sure you'd have been much happier.'

'Listen, baby,' he said, 'while you're talking about things like that, why didn't you marry Joe Brooks? I suppose he could have given you all the twenty-two-dollar hats you wanted, I suppose!'

'Well, I'm not so sure I'm not sorry I didn't,' she said. 'There! Joe Brooks wouldn't have waited until he got me all off alone and then sneered at my taste in clothes. Joe Brooks wouldn't ever hurt my feelings. Joe Brooks has always been fond of me. There!'

'Yeah,' he said. 'He's fond of you. He was so fond of you he didn't even send a wedding present. That's how fond of you he was.'

'I happen to know for a fact,' she said, 'that he was away on business, and as soon as he comes back he's going to give me anything I want, for the apartment.'

'Listen,' he said. 'I don't want anything he gives you in our apartment. Anything he gives you, I'll throw right out the window. That's what I think of your friend Joe Brooks. And how do you know where he is and what he's going to do, anyway? Has he been writing to you?'

'I suppose my friends can correspond with me,' she said. 'I didn't hear there was any law against that.'

'Well, I suppose they can't!' he said. 'And what do you think of that? I'm not going to have my wife getting a lot of letters from cheap traveling salesmen!'

'Joe Brooks is not a cheap traveling salesman!' she said. 'He is not! He gets a wonderful salary.'

'Oh yeah?' he said. 'Where did you hear that?'

'He told me so himself,' she said.

'Oh, he told you so himself,' he said. 'I see. He told you so himself.'

'You've got a lot of right to talk about Joe Brooks,' she said. 'You and your friend Louise. All you ever talk about is Louise.'

'Oh, for heaven's sakes!' he said. 'What do I care about Louise? I just thought she was a friend of yours, that's all. That's why I ever even noticed her.'

'Well, you certainly took an awful lot of notice of her today,' she said. 'On our wedding day! You said yourself when you were standing there in the church you just kept thinking of her. Right up at the altar. Oh, right in the presence of God! And all you thought about was Louise.'

'Listen, honey,' he said, 'I never should have said that. How does anybody know what kind of crazy things come into their heads when they're standing there waiting to get married? I was just telling you that because it was so kind of crazy. I thought it would make you laugh.'

'I know,' she said. 'I've been all sort of mixed up today, too. I told you that. Everything so strange and everything. And me all the time thinking about all those people all over the world, and now us here all alone, and everything. I know you get all mixed up. Only I did think, when you kept talking about how beautiful Louise looked, you did it with malice and forethought.'

'I never did anything with malice and forethought!' he said. 'I just told you that about Louise because I thought it would make you laugh.'

'Well, it didn't,' she said.

'No, I know it didn't,' he said. 'It certainly did not. Ah, baby, and we ought to be laughing, too. Hell, honey lamb, this is our honeymoon. What's the matter?'

'I don't know,' she said. 'We used to squabble a lot when we were going together and then engaged and everything, but I thought everything would be so different as soon as you were married. And now I feel so sort of strange and everything. I feel so sort of alone.'

'Well, you see, sweetheart,' he said, 'we're not really married yet. I mean. I mean – well, things will be different afterwards. Oh, hell. I mean, we haven't been married very long.'

'No,' she said.

'Well, we haven't got much longer to wait now,' he said. 'I mean – well, we'll be in New York in about twenty minutes. Then we can have dinner, and sort of see what we feel like doing. Or I mean. Is there anything special you want to do tonight?'

'What?' she said.

'What I mean to say,' he said, 'would you like to go to a show or something?'

'Why, whatever you like,' she said. 'I sort of didn't think people went to theaters and things on their – I mean, I've got a couple of letters I simply must write. Don't let me forget.'

'Oh,' he said. 'You're going to write letters tonight?'

'Well, you see,' she said. 'I've been perfectly terrible. What with all the excitement and everything. I never did thank poor old Mrs Sprague for her berry spoon, and I never did a thing about those book ends the McMasters sent. It's just too awful of me. I've got to write them this very night.'

'And when you've finished writing your letters,' he said, 'maybe I could get you a magazine or a bag of peanuts.'

'What?' she said.

'I mean,' he said, 'I wouldn't want you to be bored.'

'As if I could be bored with you!' she said. 'Silly! Aren't we married? Bored!'

'What I thought,' he said, 'I thought when we got in, we could go right up to the Biltmore and anyway leave our bags, and maybe have a little dinner in the room, kind of quiet, and then do whatever we wanted. I mean. I mean – well, let's go right up there from the station.'

'Oh, yes, let's,' she said. 'I'm so glad we're going to the Biltmore. I just love it. The twice I've stayed in New York we've always stayed there, Papa and Mamma and Ellie and I, and I was crazy about it. I always sleep so well there. I go right off to sleep the minute I put my head on the pillow.'

'Oh, you do?' he said.

'At least, I mean,' she said. 'Way up high it's so quiet.'

'We might go to some show or other tomorrow night instead of tonight,' he said. 'Don't you think that would be better?'

'Yes, I think it might,' she said.

He rose, balanced a moment, crossed over and sat down beside her.

'Do you really have to write those letters tonight?' he said.

'Well,' she said, 'I don't suppose they'd get there any quicker than if I wrote them tomorrow.'

There was a silence with things going on in it.

'And we won't ever fight any more, will we?' he said.

'Oh, no,' she said. 'Not ever! I don't know what made me do like that. It all got so sort of funny, sort of like a nightmare, the way I got thinking of all those people getting married all the time; and so many of them, everything spoils on account of fighting and everything. I got all mixed up thinking about them. Oh, I don't want to be like them. But we won't be, will we?'

'Sure we won't,' he said.

'We won't go all to pieces,' she said. 'We won't fight. It'll all be different, now we're married. It'll all be lovely. Reach me down my hat, will you, sweetheart? It's time I was putting it on. Thanks. Ah, I'm so sorry you don't like it.'

'I do so like it!' he said.

'You said you didn't,' she said. 'You said you thought it was perfectly terrible.'

'I never said any such thing,' he said. 'You're crazy.'

'All right, I may be crazy,' she said. 'Thank you very much. But that's what you said. Not that it matters – it's just a little thing. But it makes you feel pretty funny to think you've gone and married some-body that says you have perfectly terrible taste in hats. And then goes and says you're crazy, beside.'

'Now, listen here,' he said. 'Nobody said any such thing. Why, I love that hat. The more I look at it the better I like it. I think it's great.'

'That isn't what you said before,' she said.

'Honey,' he said. 'Stop it, will you? What do you want to start all this for? I love the damned hat. I mean, I love your hat. I love anything you wear. What more do you want me to say?'

'Well, I don't want you to say it like that,' she said.

'I said I think it's great,' he said. 'That's all I said.'

'Do you really?' she said. 'Do you honestly? Ah, I'm so glad. I'd hate you not to like my hat. It would be – I don't know, it would be sort of such a bad start.'

'Well, I'm crazy for it,' he said. 'Now we've got that settled, for heaven's sakes. Ah, baby. Baby lamb. We're not going to have any bad starts. Look at us – we're on our honeymoon. Pretty soon we'll be regular old married people. I mean. I mean, in a few minutes we'll be getting in to New York, and then we'll be going to the hotel, and then everything will be all right. I mean – well, look at us! Here we are married! Here we are!'

'Yes, here we are,' she said. 'Aren't we?'

JHUMPA LAHIRI

This Blessed House

They discovered the first one in a cupboard above the stove, beside an unopened bottle of malt vinegar.

'Guess what I found.' Twinkle walked into the living room, lined from end to end with taped-up packing boxes, waving the vinegar in one hand and a white porcelain effigy of Christ, roughly the same size as the vinegar bottle, in the other.

Sanjeev looked up. He was kneeling on the floor, marking, with ripped bits of a Post-it, patches on the baseboard that needed to be retouched with paint. 'Throw it away.'

'Which?'

'Both.'

'But I can cook something with the vinegar. It's brand-new.'

'You've never cooked anything with vinegar.'

'I'll look something up. In one of those books we got for our wedding.'

Sanjeev turned back to the baseboard, to replace a Post-it scrap that had fallen to the floor. 'Check the expiration. And at the very least get rid of that idiotic statue.'

'But it could be worth something. Who knows?' She turned it upside down, then stroked, with her index finger, the minuscule frozen folds of its robes. 'It's pretty.'

'We're not Christian,' Sanjeev said. Lately he had begun noticing the need to state the obvious to Twinkle. The day before he had to tell her that if she dragged her end of the bureau instead of lifting it, the parquet floor would scratch.

She shrugged. 'No, we're not Christian. We're good little Hindus.' She planted a kiss on top of Christ's head, then placed the statue on top of the fireplace mantel, which needed, Sanjeev observed, to be dusted.

By the end of the week the mantel had still not been dusted; it had, however, come to serve as the display shelf for a sizable collection of Christian paraphernalia. There was a 3-D postcard of Saint

Francis done in four colors, which Twinkle had found taped to the back of the medicine cabinet, and a wooden cross key chain, which Sanjeev had stepped on with bare feet as he was installing extra shelving in Twinkle's study. There was a framed paint-by-number of the three wise men, against a black velvet background, tucked in the linen closet. There was also a tile trivet depicting a blond, unbearded Jesus, delivering a sermon on a mountaintop, left in one of the drawers of the built-in china cabinet in the dining room.

'Do you think the previous owners were born-agains?' asked Twinkle, making room the next day for a small plastic snow-filled dome containing a miniature Nativity scene, found behind the pipes of the kitchen sink.

Sanjeev was organizing his engineering texts from MIT in alphabetical order on a bookshelf, though it had been several years since he had needed to consult any of them. After graduating, he moved from Boston to Connecticut, to work for a firm near Hartford, and he had recently learned that he was being considered for the position of vice president. At thirty-three he had a secretary of his own and a dozen people working under his supervision who gladly supplied him with any information he needed. Still, the presence of his college books in the room reminded him of a time in his life he recalled with fondness, when he would walk each evening across the Mass. Avenue bridge to order Mughlai chicken with spinach from his favorite Indian restaurant on the other side of the Charles, and return to his dorm to write out clean copies of his problem sets.

'Or perhaps it's an attempt to convert people,' Twinkle mused.

'Clearly the scheme has succeeded in your case.'

She disregarded him, shaking the little plastic dome so that the snow swirled over the manger.

He studied the items on the mantel. It puzzled him that each was in its own way so silly. Clearly they lacked a sense of sacredness. He was further puzzled that Twinkle, who normally displayed good taste, was so charmed. These objects meant something to Twinkle, but they meant nothing to him. They irritated him. 'We should call the Realtor. Tell him there's all this nonsense left behind. Tell him to take it away.'

'Oh, Sanj.' Twinkle groaned. 'Please. I would feel terrible throwing them away. Obviously they were important to the people who used to live here. It would feel, I don't know, sacrilegious or something.'

'If they're so precious, then why are they hidden all over the house? Why didn't they take them with them?'

'There must be others,' Twinkle said. Her eyes roamed the bare off-white walls of the room, as if there were other things concealed behind the plaster. 'What else do you think we'll find?'

But as they unpacked their boxes and hung up their winter clothes and the silk paintings of elephant processions bought on their honeymoon in Jaipur, Twinkle, much to her dismay, could not find a thing. Nearly a week had passed before they discovered, one Saturday afternoon, a larger-than-life-sized watercolor poster of Christ, weeping translucent tears the size of peanut shells and sporting a crown of thorns, rolled up behind a radiator in the guest bedroom. Sanjeev had mistaken it for a window shade.

'Oh, we must, we simply must put it up. It's too spectacular.' Twinkle lit a cigarette and began to smoke it with relish, waving it around Sanjeev's head as if it were a conductor's baton as Mahler's Fifth Symphony roared from the stereo downstairs.

'Now, look. I will tolerate, for now, your little biblical menagerie in the living room. But I refuse to have this,' he said, flicking at one of the painted peanut-tears, 'displayed in our home.'

Twinkle stared at him, placidly exhaling, the smoke emerging in two thin blue streams from her nostrils. She rolled up the poster slowly, securing it with one of the elastic bands she always wore around her wrist for tying back her thick, unruly hair, streaked here and there with henna. 'I'm going to put it in my study,' she informed him. 'That way you don't have to look at it.'

'What about the housewarming? They'll want to see all the rooms. I've invited people from the office.'

She rolled her eyes. Sanjeev noted that the symphony, now in its third movement, had reached a crescendo, for it pulsed with the telltale clashing of cymbals.

'I'll put it behind the door,' she offered. 'That way, when they peek in, they won't see. Happy?'

He stood watching her as she left the room, with her poster and her cigarette; a few ashes had fallen to the floor where she'd been standing. He bent down, pinched them between his fingers, and deposited them in his cupped palm. The tender fourth movement, the *adagietto*, began. During breakfast, Sanjeev had read in the liner notes that Mahler had proposed to his wife by sending her the manuscript of this portion of the score. Although there were elements of tragedy and struggle in the Fifth Symphony, he had read, it was principally music of love and happiness.

He heard the toilet flush. 'By the way,' Twinkle hollered, 'if you want to impress people, I wouldn't play this music. It's putting me to sleep.'

Sanjeev went to the bathroom to throw away the ashes. The cigarette butt still bobbed in the toilet bowl, but the tank was refilling, so he had to wait a moment before he could flush it again. In the mirror of the medicine cabinet he inspected his long eyelashes – like a girl's, Twinkle liked to tease. Though he was of average build, his cheeks had a plumpness to them; this, along with the eyelashes, detracted, he feared, from what he hoped was a distinguished profile. He was of average height as well, and had wished ever since he had stopped growing that he were just one inch taller. For this reason it irritated him when Twinkle insisted on wearing high heels, as she had done the other night when they ate dinner in Manhattan. This was the first weekend after they'd moved into the house; by then the mantel had already filled up considerably, and they had bickered about it in the car on the way down. But then Twinkle had drunk four glasses of whiskey in a nameless bar in Alphabet City, and forgot all about it. She dragged him to a tiny bookshop on St Mark's Place, where she browsed for nearly an hour, and when they left she insisted that they dance a tango on the sidewalk in front of strangers.

Afterward, she tottered on his arm, rising faintly over his line of vision, in a pair of suede three-inch leopard-print pumps. In this manner they walked the endless blocks back to a parking garage on Washington Square, for Sanjeev had heard far too many stories about the terrible things that happened to cars in Manhattan. 'But I do nothing all day except sit at my desk,' she fretted when they were driving home, after he had mentioned that her shoes looked uncomfortable and suggested that perhaps she should not wear them. 'I can't exactly wear heels when I'm typing.' Though he abandoned the argument, he knew for a fact that she didn't spend all day at her desk; just that afternoon, when he got back from a run, he found her inexplicably in bed, reading. When he asked why she was in bed in the middle of the day she told him she was bored. He had wanted to say to her then, You could unpack some boxes. You could sweep the attic. You could retouch the paint on the bathroom windowsill, and after you do it you could warn me so that I don't put my watch on it. They didn't bother her, these scattered, unsettled matters. She seemed content with whatever clothes she found at the front of the closet, with whatever magazine was lying around, with whatever song was on the radio – content yet curious. And now all of her curiosity centered around discovering the next treasure.

A few days later when Sanjeev returned from the office, he found Twinkle on the telephone, smoking and talking to one of her girl-friends in California even though it was before five o'clock and the long-distance rates were at their peak. 'Highly devout people,' she was saying, pausing every now and then to exhale. 'Each day is like a treasure hunt. I'm serious. This you won't believe. The switch plates in the bedrooms were decorated with scenes from the Bible. You know, Noah's Ark and all that. Three bedrooms, but one is my study. Sanjeev went to the hardware store right away and replaced them, can you imagine, he replaced every single one.'

Now it was the friend's turn to talk. Twinkle nodded, slouched on the floor in front of the fridge, wearing black stirrup pants and a yellow chenille sweater, groping for her lighter. Sanjeev could smell something aromatic on the stove, and he picked his way carefully across the extra-long phone cord tangled on the Mexican terra-cotta tiles. He opened the lid of a pot with some sort of reddish brown sauce dripping over the sides, boiling furiously.

'It's a stew made with fish. I put the vinegar in it,' she said to him, interrupting her friend, crossing her fingers. 'Sorry, you were saying?' She was like that, excited and delighted by little things, crossing her fingers before any remotely unpredictable event, like tasting a new flavor of ice cream, or dropping a letter in a mailbox. It was a quality he did not understand. It made him feel stupid, as if the world contained hidden wonders he could not anticipate, or see. He looked at her face, which, it occurred to him, had not grown out of its girl-hood, the eyes untroubled, the pleasing features unfirm, as if they still had to settle into some sort of permanent expression. Nicknamed after a nursery rhyme, she had yet to shed a childhood endearment. Now, in the second month of their marriage, certain things nettled him – the way she sometimes spat a little when she spoke, or left her undergarments after removing them at night at the foot of their bed rather than depositing them in the laundry hamper.

They had met only four months before. Her parents, who lived in California, and his, who still lived in Calcutta, were old friends, and across continents they had arranged the occasion at which Twinkle and Sanjeev were introduced – a sixteenth birthday party for a daughter in their circle – when Sanjeev was in Palo Alto on business. At the restaurant they were seated side by side at a round table with a revolving platter of spareribs and egg rolls and chicken wings, which, they concurred, all tasted the same. They had concurred too on their adolescent but still persistent fondness for Wodehouse novels, and their dislike for the sitar, and later Twinkle confessed that she was charmed by the way Sanjeev had dutifully refilled her teacup during their conversation.

And so the phone calls began, and grew longer, and then the visits, first he to Stanford, then she to Connecticut, after which Sanjeev would save in an ashtray left on the balcony the crushed cigarettes she had smoked during the weekend – saved them, that is, until the next time she came to visit him, and then he vacuumed the apartment, washed the sheets, even dusted the plant leaves in her honor. She was twenty-seven and recently abandoned, he had gathered, by an American who had tried and failed to be an actor; Sanjeev was lonely, with an excessively generous income for a single man, and had never been in love. At the urging of their matchmakers, they married in India, amid hundreds of well-wishers whom he barely remembered from his childhood, in incessant August rains, under a red and orange tent strung with Christmas tree lights on Mandeville Road.

'Did you sweep the attic?' he asked Twinkle later as she was folding paper napkins and wedging them by their plates. The attic was the only part of the house they had not yet given an initial cleaning.

'Not yet. I will, I promise. I hope this tastes good,' she said, planting the steaming pot on top of the Jesus trivet. There was a loaf of Italian bread in a little basket, and iceberg lettuce and grated carrots tossed with bottled dressing and croutons, and glasses of red wine. She was not terribly ambitious in the kitchen. She bought preroasted chickens from the supermarket and served them with potato salad prepared who knew when, sold in little plastic containers. Indian food, she complained, was a bother; she detested chopping garlic, and peeling ginger, and could not operate a blender, and so it was Sanjeev who, on weekends, seasoned mustard oil with cinnamon sticks and cloves in order to produce a proper curry.

He had to admit, though, that whatever it was that she had cooked today, it was unusually tasty, attractive even, with bright white cubes of fish, and flecks of parsley, and fresh tomatoes gleaming in the dark brown-red broth.

'How did you make it?'

'I made it up.'

'What did you do?'

'I just put some things into the pot and added the malt vinegar at the end.'

'How much vinegar?'

She shrugged, ripping off some bread and plunging it into her bowl.

'What do you mean you don't know? You should write it down. What if you need to make it again, for a party or something?'

'I'll remember,' she said. She covered the bread basket with a dishtowel that had, he suddenly noticed, the Ten Commandments printed on it. She flashed him a smile, giving his knee a little squeeze under the table. 'Face it. This house is blessed.'

The housewarming party was scheduled for the last Saturday in October, and they had invited about thirty people. All were Sanjeev's acquaintances, people from the office, and a number of Indian couples in the Connecticut area, many of whom he barely knew, but who had regularly invited him, in his bachelor days, to supper on Saturdays. He often wondered why they included him in their circle. He had little in common with any of them, but he always attended their gatherings, to eat spiced chickpeas and shrimp cutlets, and gossip and discuss politics, for he seldom had other plans. So far, no one had met Twinkle; back when they were still dating, Sanjeev didn't want to waste their brief weekends together with people he associated with being alone. Other than Sanjeev and an ex-boyfriend who she believed worked in a pottery studio in Brookfield, she knew no one in the state of Connecticut. She was completing her master's thesis at Stanford, a study of an Irish poet whom Sanjeev had never heard of.

Sanjeev had found the house on his own before leaving for the wedding, for a good price, in a neighborhood with a fine school system. He was impressed by the elegant curved staircase with its wrought-iron banister, and the dark wooden wainscoting, and the solarium overlooking rhododendron bushes, and the solid brass 22, which also happened to be the date of his birth, nailed impressively to the vaguely Tudor facade. There were two working fireplaces, a two-car garage, and an attic suitable for converting into extra bedrooms if, the Realtor mentioned, the need should arise. By then Sanjeev had already made up his mind, was determined that he and Twinkle should live there together, forever, and so he had not bothered to notice the switch plates covered with biblical stickers, or the transparent decal of the Virgin on the half shell, as Twinkle liked to call it, adhered to the window in the master bedroom. When, after moving in, he tried to scrape it off, he scratched the glass.

The weekend before the party they were raking the lawn when he heard Twinkle shriek. He ran to her, clutching his rake, worried that she had discovered a dead animal, or a snake. A brisk October breeze stung the tops of his ears as his sneakers crunched over brown and yellow leaves. When he reached her, she had collapsed on the grass, dissolved in nearly silent laughter. Behind an overgrown forsythia bush was a plaster Virgin Mary as tall as their waists, with a blue painted hood draped over her head in the manner of an Indian bride. Twinkle grabbed the hem of her T-shirt and began wiping away the dirt staining the statue's brow.

'I suppose you want to put her by the foot of our bed,' Sanjeev said.

She looked at him, astonished. Her belly was exposed, and he saw that there were goose bumps around her navel. 'What do you think? Of course we can't put this in our bedroom.'

'We can't?'

'No, silly Sanj. This is meant for outside. For the lawn.'

'Oh God, no. Twinkle, no.'

'But we must. It would be bad luck not to.'

'All the neighbors will see. They'll think we're insane.'

'Why, for having a statue of the Virgin Mary on our lawn? Every other person in this neighborhood has a statue of Mary on the lawn. We'll fit right in.'

'We're not Christian.'

'So you keep reminding me.' She spat onto the tip of her finger and started to rub intently at a particularly stubborn stain on Mary's chin. 'Do you think this is dirt, or some kind of fungus?'

He was getting nowhere with her, with this woman whom he had known for only four months and whom he had married, this woman with whom he now shared his life. He thought with a flicker of regret of the snapshots his mother used to send him from Calcutta, of prospective brides who could sing and sew and season lentils without consulting a cookbook. Sanjeev had considered these women, had even ranked them in order of preference, but then he had met Twinkle. 'Twinkle, I can't have the people I work with see this statue on my lawn.'

'They can't fire you for being a believer. It would be discrimination.'

'That's not the point.'

'Why does it matter to you so much what other people think?'

'Twinkle, please.' He was tired. He let his weight rest against his rake as she began dragging the statue toward an oval bed of myrtle, beside the lamppost that flanked the brick pathway. 'Look, Sanj. She's so lovely.'

He returned to his pile of leaves and began to deposit them by handfuls into a plastic garbage bag. Over his head the blue sky was cloudless. One tree on the lawn was still full of leaves, red and orange, like the tent in which he had married Twinkle.

He did not know if he loved her. He said he did when she had first asked him, one afternoon in Palo Alto as they sat side by side in a darkened, nearly empty movie theater. Before the film, one of her favorites, something in German that he found extremely depressing, she had pressed the tip of her nose to his so that he could feel the flutter of her mascara-coated eyelashes. That afternoon he had replied, yes, he loved her, and she was delighted, and fed him a piece of popcorn, letting her finger linger an instant between his lips, as if it were his reward for coming up with the right answer.

Though she did not say it herself, he assumed then that she loved him too, but now he was no longer sure. In truth, Sanjeev did not know what love was, only what he thought it was not. It was not, he had decided, returning to an empty carpeted condominium each night, and using only the top fork in his cutlery drawer, and turning away politely at those weekend dinner parties when the other men eventually put their arms around the waists of their wives and girlfriends, leaning over every now and again to kiss their shoulders or necks. It was not sending away for classical music CDs by mail, working his way methodically through the major composers that the catalogue recommended, and always sending his payments in on time. In the months before meeting Twinkle, Sanjeev had begun to realize this. 'You have enough money in the bank to raise three families,' his mother reminded him when they spoke at the start of each month on the phone. 'You need a wife to look after and love.' Now he had one, a pretty one, from a suitably high caste, who would soon have a master's degree. What was there not to love?

That evening Sanjeev poured himself a gin and tonic, drank it and most of another during one segment of the news, and then approached Twinkle, who was taking a bubble bath, for she announced that her limbs ached from raking the lawn, something she had never done before. He didn't knock. She had applied a bright blue mask to her face, was smoking and sipping some bourbon with ice and leafing through a fat paperback book whose pages had buckled and turned gray from the water. He glanced at the cover; the only thing written on it was the word 'Sonnets' in dark red letters. He took a breath, and then he informed her very calmly that after finishing his drink he was going to put on his shoes and go outside and remove the Virgin from the front lawn.

'Where are you going to put it?' she asked him dreamily, her eyes closed. One of her legs emerged, unfolding gracefully, from the layer of suds. She flexed and pointed her toes.

'For now I am going to put it in the garage. Then tomorrow morning on my way to work I am going to take it to the dump.'

'Don't you dare.' She stood up, letting the book fall into the water, bubbles dripping down her thighs. 'I hate you,' she informed him, her eyes narrowing at the word 'hate'. She reached for her bathrobe, tied it tightly about her waist, and padded down the winding staircase, leaving sloppy wet footprints along the parquet floor. When she reached the foyer, Sanjeev said, 'Are you planning on leaving the house that way?' He felt a throbbing in his temples, and his voice revealed an unfamiliar snarl when he spoke.

'Who cares? Who cares what way I leave this house?'

'Where are you planning on going at this hour?'

'You can't throw away that statue. I won't let you.' Her mask, now dry, had assumed an ashen quality, and water from her hair dripped onto the caked contours of her face.

'Yes I can. I will.'

'No,' Twinkle said, her voice suddenly small. 'This is our house. We own it together. The statue is a part of our property.' She had begun to shiver. A small pool of bathwater had collected around her ankles. He went to shut a window, fearing that she would catch cold. Then he noticed that some of the water dripping down her hard blue face was tears.

'Oh God, Twinkle, please, I didn't mean it.' He had never seen her cry before, had never seen such sadness in her eyes. She didn't turn away or try to stop the tears; instead she looked strangely at peace. For a moment she closed her lids, pale and unprotected compared to the blue that caked the rest of her face. Sanjeev felt ill, as if he had eaten either too much or too little.

She went to him, placing her damp toweled arms about his neck, sobbing into his chest, soaking his shirt. The mask flaked onto his shoulders.

In the end they settled on a compromise: the statue would be placed in a recess at the side of the house, so that it wasn't obvious to passersby, but was still clearly visible to all who came.

The menu for the party was fairly simple: there would be a case of champagne, and samosas from an Indian restaurant in Hartford, and big trays of rice with chicken and almonds and orange peels, which Sanjeev had spent the greater part of the morning and afternoon preparing. He had never entertained on such a large scale before and, worried that there would not be enough to drink, ran out at one point to buy another case of champagne just in case. For this reason he burned one of the rice trays and had to start it over again. Twinkle swept the floors and volunteered to pick up the samosas; she had an appointment for a manicure and a pedicure in that direction, anyway. Sanjeev had planned to ask if she would consider clearing the menagerie off the mantel, if only for the party, but she left while he was in the shower. She was gone for a good three hours, and so it was Sanjeev who did the rest of the cleaning. By five-thirty the entire house sparkled, with scented candles that Twinkle had picked up in Hartford illuminating the items on the mantel, and slender stalks of burning incense planted into the soil of potted plants. Each time he passed the mantel he winced, dreading the raised eyebrows of his guests as they viewed the flickering ceramic saints, the salt and pepper shakers designed to resemble Mary and Joseph. Still, they would be impressed, he hoped, by the lovely bay windows, the shining parquet floors, the impressive winding staircase, the wooden wainscoting, as they sipped champagne and dipped samosas in chutney.

Douglas, one of the new consultants at the firm, and his girlfriend Nora were the first to arrive. Both were tall and blond, wearing matching wire-rimmed glasses and long black overcoats. Nora wore a black hat full of sharp thin feathers that corresponded to the sharp thin angles of her face. Her left hand was joined with Douglas's. In her right hand was a bottle of cognac with a red ribbon wrapped around its neck, which she gave to Twinkle.

'Great lawn, Sanjeev,' Douglas remarked. 'We've got to get that rake out ourselves, sweetie. And this must be . . .'

'My wife. Tanima.'

'Call me Twinkle.'

'What an unusual name,' Nora remarked.

Twinkle shrugged. 'Not really. There's an actress in Bombay named Dimple Kapadia. She even has a sister named Simple.'

Douglas and Nora raised their eyebrows simultaneously, nodding slowly, as if to let the absurdity of the names settle in. 'Pleased to meet you, Twinkle.'

'Help yourself to champagne. There's gallons.'

'I hope you don't mind my asking,' Douglas said, 'but I noticed the statue outside, and are you guys Christian? I thought you were Indian.'

'There are Christians in India,' Sanjeev replied, 'but we're not.'

'I love your outfit,' Nora told Twinkle.

'And I adore your hat. Would you like the grand tour?'

The bell rang again, and again and again. Within minutes, it seemed, the house had filled with bodies and conversations and unfamiliar fragrances. The women wore heels and sheer stockings, and short black dresses made of crepe and chiffon. They handed their wraps and coats to Sanjeev, who draped them carefully on hangers in the spacious coat closet, though Twinkle told people to throw their things on the ottomans in the solarium. Some of the Indian women wore their finest saris, made with gold filigree that draped in elegant pleats over their shoulders. The men wore jackets and ties and citrus-scented aftershaves. As people filtered from one room to the next, presents piled onto the long cherry-wood table that ran from one end of the downstairs hall to the other.

It bewildered Sanjeev that it was for him, and his house, and his wife, that they had all gone to so much care. The only other time in his life that something similar had happened was his wedding day, but somehow this was different, for these were not his family, but people who knew him only casually, and in a sense owed him nothing. Everyone congratulated him. Lester, another coworker, predicted that Sanjeev would be promoted to vice president in two months maximum. People devoured the samosas, and dutifully admired the freshly painted ceilings and walls, the hanging plants, the bay windows, the silk paintings from Jaipur. But most of all they admired Twinkle, and her brocaded *salwar-kameez*, which was the shade of a persimmon with a low scoop in the back, and the little string of white rose petals she had coiled cleverly around her head, and the pearl choker with a sapphire at its center that adorned her throat. Over hectic jazz records, played under Twinkle's supervision, they laughed at her anecdotes and observations, forming a widening circle around her, while Sanjeev replenished the samosas that he kept warming evenly in the oven, and getting ice for people's drinks, and opening more bottles of champagne with some difficulty, and explaining for the fortieth time that he wasn't Christian. It was Twinkle who led them in separate groups up and down the winding stairs, to gaze at the back lawn, to peer down the cellar steps. 'Your friends adore the poster in my study,' she mentioned to him triumphantly, placing her hand on the small of his back as they, at one point, brushed past each other.

Sanjeev went to the kitchen, which was empty, and ate a piece of chicken out of the tray on the counter with his fingers because he thought no one was looking. He ate a second piece, then washed it down with a gulp of gin straight from the bottle.

'Great house. Great rice.' Sunil, an anesthesiologist, walked in, spooning food from his paper plate into his mouth. 'Do you have more champagne?'

'Your wife's wow,' added Prabal, following behind. He was an unmarried professor of physics at Yale. For a moment Sanjeev stared at him blankly, then blushed; once at a dinner party Prabal had pronounced that Sophia Loren was wow, as was Audrey Hepburn. 'Does she have a sister?'

Sunil picked a raisin out of the rice tray. 'Is her last name Little Star?'

The two men laughed and started eating more rice from the tray, plowing through it with their plastic spoons. Sanjeev went down to the cellar for more liquor. For a few minutes he paused on the steps, in the damp, cool silence, hugging the second crate of champagne to his chest as the party drifted above the rafters. Then he set the reinforcements on the dining table.

'Yes, everything, we found them all in the house, in the most unusual places,' he heard Twinkle saying in the living room. 'In fact we keep finding them.'

'No!'

'Yes! Every day is like a treasure hunt. It's too good. God only knows what else we'll find, no pun intended.'

That was what started it. As if by some unspoken pact, the whole party joined forces and began combing through each of the rooms, opening closets on their own, peering under chairs and cushions, feeling behind curtains, removing books from bookcases. Groups scampered, giggling and swaying, up and down the winding staircase.

'We've never explored the attic,' Twinkle announced suddenly, and so everybody followed.

'How do we get up there?'

'There's a ladder in the hallway, somewhere in the ceiling.'

Wearily Sanjeev followed at the back of the crowd, to point out the location of the ladder, but Twinkle had already found it on her own. 'Eureka!' she hollered.

Douglas pulled the chain that released the steps. His face was flushed and he was wearing Nora's feather hat on his head. One by one the guests disappeared, men helping women as they placed their strappy high heels on the narrow slats of the ladder, the Indian women wrapping the free ends of their expensive saris into their waistbands. The men followed behind, all quickly disappearing, until Sanjeev alone remained at the top of the winding staircase. Footsteps thundered over his head. He had no desire to join them. He wondered if the ceiling would collapse, imagined, for a split second, the sight of all the tumbling drunk perfumed bodies crashing, tangled, around him. He heard a shriek, and then rising, spreading waves of laughter in discordant tones. Something fell, something else shattered. He could hear them babbling about a trunk. They seemed to be struggling to get it open, banging feverishly on its surface.

He thought perhaps Twinkle would call for his assistance, but he was not summoned. He looked about the hallway and to the landing below, at the champagne glasses and half-eaten samosas and napkins smeared with lipstick abandoned in every corner, on every available surface. Then he noticed that Twinkle, in her haste, had discarded her shoes altogether, for they lay by the foot of the ladder, black patent-leather mules with heels like golf tees, open toes, and slightly soiled silk labels on the instep where her soles had rested. He placed them in the doorway of the master bedroom so that no one would trip when they descended.

He heard something creaking open slowly. The strident voices had subsided to an even murmur. It occurred to Sanjeev that he had the house all to himself. The music had ended and he could hear, if he concentrated, the hum of the refrigerator, and the rustle of the last leaves on the trees outside, and the tapping of their branches against the windowpanes. With one flick of his hand he could snap the ladder back on its spring into the ceiling, and they would have no way of getting down unless he were to pull the chain and let them. He thought of all the things he could do, undisturbed. He could sweep Twinkle's menagerie into a garbage bag and get in the car and drive it all to the dump, and tear down the poster of weeping Jesus, and take a hammer to the Virgin Mary while he was at it. Then he would return to the empty house; he could easily clear up the cups and plates in an hour's time, and pour himself a gin and tonic, and eat a plate of warmed rice and listen to his new Bach CD while reading the liner notes so as to understand it properly. He nudged the ladder slightly, but it was sturdily planted against the floor. Budging it would require some effort.

'My God, I need a cigarette,' Twinkle exclaimed from above.

Sanjeev felt knots forming at the back of his neck. He felt dizzy. He needed to lie down. He walked toward the bedroom, but stopped short when he saw Twinkle's shoes facing him in the doorway. He thought of her slipping them on her feet. But instead of feeling irritated, as he had ever since they'd moved into the house together, he felt a pang of anticipation at the thought of her rushing unsteadily down the winding staircase in them, scratching the floor a bit in her path. The pang intensified as he thought of her rushing to the bathroom to brighten her lipstick, and eventually rushing to get people their coats, and finally rushing to the cherry-wood table when the last guest had left, to begin opening their housewarming presents. It was the same pang he used to feel before they were married, when he would hang up the phone after one of their conversations, or when he would drive back from the airport, wondering which ascending plane in the sky was hers.

'Sanj, you won't believe this.'

She emerged with her back to him, her hands over her head, the tops of her bare shoulder blades perspiring, supporting something still hidden from view.

'You got it, Twinkle?' someone asked.

'Yes, you can let go.'

Now he saw that her hands were wrapped around it: a solid silver bust of Christ, the head easily three times the size of his own. It had a patrician bump on its nose, magnificent curly hair that rested atop a pronounced collarbone, and a broad forehead that reflected in miniature the walls and doors and lampshades around them. Its expression was confident, as if assured of its devotees, the unyielding lips sensuous and full. It was also sporting Nora's feather hat. As Twinkle descended, Sanjeev put his hands around her waist to balance her, and he relieved her of the bust when she had reached the ground. It weighed a good thirty pounds. The others began lowering themselves slowly, exhausted from the hunt. Some trickled downstairs in search of a fresh drink.

She took a breath, raised her eyebrows, crossed her fingers. 'Would you mind terribly if we displayed it on the mantel? Just for tonight? I know you hate it.'

He did hate it. He hated its immensity, and its flawless, polished surface, and its undeniable value. He hated that it was in his house, and that he owned it. Unlike the other things they'd found, this contained dignity, solemnity, beauty even. But to his surprise these qualities made him hate it all the more. Most of all he hated it because he knew that Twinkle loved it.

'I'll keep it in my study from tomorrow,' Twinkle added. 'I promise.'

She would never put it in her study, he knew. For the rest of their days together she would keep it on the center of the mantel, flanked on either side by the rest of the menagerie. Each time they had guests Twinkle would explain how she had found it, and they would admire her as they listened. He gazed at the crushed rose petals in her hair, at the pearl and sapphire choker at her throat, at the sparkly crimson polish on her toes. He decided these were among the things that made Prabal think she was wow. His head ached from gin and his arms ached from the weight of the statue. He said, 'I put your shoes in the bedroom.'

'Thanks. But my feet are killing me.' Twinkle gave his elbow a little squeeze and headed for the living room.

Sanjeev pressed the massive silver face to his ribs, careful not to let the feather hat slip, and followed her.

ZZ PACKER

Drinking Coffee Elsewhere

Orientation games began the day I arrived at Yale from Baltimore. In my group we played heady, frustrating games for smart people. One game appeared to be charades reinterpreted by existentialists; another involved listening to rocks. Then a freshman counselor made everyone play Trust. The idea was that if you had the faith to fall backward and wait for four scrawny former high school geniuses to catch you, just before your head cracked on the slate sidewalk, then you might learn to trust your fellow students. Russian roulette sounded like a better way to go.

'No way,' I said. The white boys were waiting for me to fall, holding their arms out for me, sincerely, gallantly. 'No fucking way.'

'It's all cool, it's all cool,' the counselor said. Her hair was a shade of blond I'd seen only on *Playboy* covers, and she raised her hands as though backing away from a growling dog. 'Sister,' she said, in an I'm-down-with-the-struggle voice, 'you don't have to play this game. As a person of color, you shouldn't have to fit into any white, patriarchal system.'

I said, 'It's a bit too late for that.'

In the next game, all I had to do was wait in a circle until it was my turn to say what inanimate object I wanted to be. One guy said he'd like to be a gadfly, like Socrates. 'Stop me if I wax Platonic,' he said. I didn't bother mentioning that gadflies weren't inanimate – it didn't seem to make a difference. The girl next to him was eating a rice cake. She wanted to be the Earth, she said. Earth with a capital E.

There was one other black person in the circle. He wore an Exeter T-shirt and his overly elastic expressions resembled a series of facial exercises. At the end of each person's turn, he smiled and bobbed his head with unfettered enthusiasm. 'Oh, that was good,' he said, as if the game were an experiment he'd set up and the results were turning out better than he'd expected. 'Good, good, good!'

When it was my turn I said, 'My name is Dina, and if I had to be any object, I guess I'd be a revolver.' The sunlight dulled as if on cue. Clouds passed rapidly overhead, presaging rain. I don't know why I said it. Until that moment I'd been good in all the ways that were meant to matter. I was an honor roll student – though I'd learned long ago not to mention it in the part of Baltimore where I lived. Suddenly I was hard-bitten and recalcitrant, the kind of kid who took pleasure in sticking pins into cats; the kind who chased down smart kids to spray them with Mace.

'A revolver,' a counselor said, stroking his chin, as if it had grown a rabbinical beard. 'Could you please elaborate?'

The black guy cocked his head and frowned, as if the beakers and Erlenmeyer flasks of his experiment had grown legs and scurried off.

'You were just kidding,' the dean said, 'about wiping out all of mankind. That, I suppose, was a joke.' She squinted at me. One of her hands curved atop the other to form a pink, freckled molehill on her desk.

'Well,' I said, 'maybe I meant it at the time.' I quickly saw that this was not the answer she wanted. 'I don't know. I think it's the architecture.'

Through the dimming light of the dean's office window, I could see the fortress of the old campus. On my ride from the bus station to the campus, I'd barely glimpsed New Haven – a flash of crumpled building here, a trio of straggly kids there. A lot like Baltimore. But everything had changed when we reached those streets hooded by gothic buildings. I imagined how the college must have looked when it was founded, when most of the students owned slaves. I pictured men wearing tights and knickers, smoking pipes.

'The architecture,' the dean repeated. She bit her lip and seemed to be making a calculation of some sort. I noticed that she blinked less often than most people. I sat there, intrigued, waiting to see how long it would be before she blinked again.

My revolver comment won me a year's worth of psychiatric counseling, weekly meetings with Dean Guest, and – since the parents of the roommate I'd never met weren't too hip on the idea of their Amy sharing a bunk bed with a budding homicidal loony – my very own room.

Shortly after getting my first C ever, I also received the first knock on my door. The female counselors never knocked. The dean had spoken to them; I was a priority. Every other day, right before dinnertime, they'd look in on me, unannounced. 'Just checking up,' a counselor would say. It was the voice of a suburban mother in training. By the second week, I had made a point of sitting in a chair in front of the door, just when I expected a counselor to pop her head around. This was intended to startle them. I also made a point of being naked. The unannounced visits ended.

The knocking persisted. Through the peephole I saw a white face, distorted and balloonish.

'Let me in.' The person looked like a boy but it sounded like a girl. 'Let me in,' the voice repeated.

'Not a chance,' I said. I had a suicide single, and I wanted to keep it that way. No roommates, no visitors.

Then the person began to sob, and I heard a back slump against the door. If I hadn't known the person was white from the peephole, I'd have known it from a display like this. Black people didn't knock on strangers' doors, crying. Not that I understood the black people at Yale. Most of them were from New York and tried hard to pretend that they hadn't gone to prep schools. And there was something pitiful in how cool they were. Occasionally one would reach out to me with missionary zeal, but I'd rebuff the person with haughty silence.

'I don't have anyone to talk to!' the person on the other side of the door cried.

'That is correct.'

'When I was a child,' the person said, 'I played by myself in a corner of the schoolyard all alone. I hated dolls and I hated games, animals were not friendly and birds flew away. If anyone was looking for me I hid behind a tree and cried out "I am an orphan –"'

I opened the door. It was a she.

'Plagiarist!' I yelled. She had just recited a Frank O'Hara poem as though she'd thought it up herself. I knew the poem because it was one of the few things I'd been forced to read that I wished I'd written myself.

The girl turned to face me, smiling weakly, as though her triumph was not in getting me to open the door but in the fact that she was able to smile at all when she was so accustomed to crying. She was

ZZ Packer

large but not obese, and crying had turned her face the color of raw chicken. She blew her nose into the waist end of her T-shirt, revealing a pale belly.

'How do you know that poem?'

She sniffed. 'I'm in your Contemporary Poetry class.'

She said she was Canadian and her name was Heidi, although she said she wanted people to call her Henrik. 'That's a guy's name,' I said. 'What do you want? A sex change?'

She looked at me with so little surprise that I suspected she hadn't discounted this as an option. Then her story came out in teary, hiccup-like bursts. She had sucked some 'cute guy's dick' and he'd told everybody and now people thought she was 'a slut'.

'Why'd you suck his dick? Aren't you a lesbian?'

She fit the bill. Short hair, hard, roach-stomping shoes. Dressed like an aspiring plumber. And then there was the name Henrik. The lesbians I'd seen on TV were wiry, thin strips of muscle, but Heidi was round and soft and had a moonlike face. Drab henna-colored hair. And lesbians had cats. 'Do you have a cat?' I asked.

Her eyes turned glossy with new tears. 'No,' she said, her voice quavering, 'and I'm not a lesbian. Are you?'

'Do I look like one?' I said.

She didn't answer.

'OK,' I said. 'I could suck a guy's dick, too, if I wanted. But I don't. The human penis is one of the most germ-ridden objects there is.' Heidi looked at me, unconvinced. 'What I meant to say,' I began again, 'is that I don't like anybody. Period. Guys or girls. I'm a misanthrope.'

'I am, too.'

'No,' I said, guiding her back through my door and out into the hallway. 'You're not.'

'Have you had dinner?' she asked. 'Let's go to Commons.'

I pointed to a pyramid of ramen noodle packages on my window-sill. 'See that? That means I never have to go to Commons. Aside from class, I have contact with no one.'

'I hate it here, too,' she said. 'I should have gone to McGill, eh.'

'The way to feel better,' I said, 'is to get some ramen and lock yourself in your room. Everyone will forget about you and that guy's

32

dick and you won't have to see anyone ever again. If anyone looks for you –'

'I'll hide behind a tree.'

'A revolver?' Dr Raeburn said, flipping through a manila folder. He looked up at me as if to ask another question, but he didn't.

Dr Raeburn was the psychiatrist. He had the gray hair and whiskers of a Civil War general. He was also a chain smoker with beige teeth and a navy wool jacket smeared with ash. He asked about the revolver at the beginning of my first visit. When I was unable to explain myself, he smiled, as if this were perfectly reasonable.

'Tell me about your parents.'

I wondered what he already had on file. The folder was thick, though I hadn't said a thing of significance since Day One.

'My father was a dick and my mother seemed to like him.'

He patted his pockets for his cigarettes. 'That's some heavy stuff,' he said. 'How do you feel about Dad?' The man couldn't say the word 'father'. 'Is Dad someone you see often?'

'I hate my father almost as much as I hate the word "Dad".'

He started tapping his cigarette.

'You can't smoke in here.'

'That's right,' he said, and slipped the cigarette back into the packet. He smiled, widening his eyes brightly. 'Don't ever start.'

I thought that that first encounter would be the last of Heidi or Henrik, or whatever, but then her head appeared in a window of Linsly-Chit during my Chaucer class. A few days later, she swooped down a flight of stairs in Harkness, following me. She hailed me from across Elm Street and found me in the Sterling Library stacks. After one of my meetings with Dr Raeburn, she was waiting for me outside Health Services, legs crossed, cleaning her fingernails.

'You know,' she said, as we walked through Old Campus, 'you've got to stop eating ramen. Not only does it lack a single nutrient but it's full of MSG.'

I wondered why she even bothered, and was vaguely flattered she cared, but I said, 'I like eating chemicals. It keeps the skin radiant.'

'There's also hepatitis.' She knew how to get my attention – mention a disease.

'You get hepatitis from unwashed lettuce,' I said. 'If there's anything safe from the perils of the food chain, it's ramen.'

'But do you refrigerate what you don't eat? Each time you reheat it, you're killing good bacteria, which then can't keep the bad bacteria in check. A guy got sick from reheating Chinese noodles, and his son died from it. I read it in the *Times*.' With this, she put a jovial arm around my neck. I continued walking, a little stunned. Then, just as quickly, she dropped her arm and stopped walking. I stopped, too.

'Did you notice that I put my arm around you?'

'Yes,' I said. 'Next time, I'll have to chop it off.'

'I don't want you to get sick,' she said. 'Let's eat at Commons.'

In the cold air, her arm had felt good.

The problem with Commons was that it was too big; its ceiling was as high as a cathedral's, but below it there were no awestruck worshippers, only eighteen-year-olds at heavy wooden tables, chatting over veal patties and Jell-O.

We got our food, tacos stuffed with meat substitute, and made our way through the maze of tables. The Koreans had a table. Each singing group had a table. The crew team sat at a long table of its own. We passed the black table. Heidi was so plump and moonfaced that the sheer quantity of her flesh accentuated just how white she was. The black students gave me a long, hard stare.

'How you doing, sista?' a guy asked, his voice full of accusation, eyeballing me as though I were clad in a Klansman's sheet and hood. 'I guess we won't see you till graduation.'

'If,' I said, 'you graduate.'

The remark was not well received. As I walked past, I heard protests, angry and loud as if they'd discovered a cheat at their poker game. Heidi and I found an unoccupied table along the periphery, which was isolated and dark. We sat down. Heidi prayed over her tacos.

'I thought you didn't believe in God,' I said.

'Not in the God depicted in the Judeo-Christian Bible, but I do believe that nature's essence is a spirit that –'

'All right,' I said. I had begun to eat, and cubes of diced tomato fell from my mouth when I spoke. 'Stop right there. Tacos and spirits don't mix.'

'You've always got to be so flip,' she said. 'I'm going to apply for another friend.'

'There's always Mr Dick,' I said. 'Slurp, slurp.'

'You are so lame. So unbelievably lame. I'm going out with Mr Dick. Thursday night at Atticus. His name is Keith.'

Heidi hadn't mentioned Mr Dick since the day I'd met her. That was more than a month ago and we'd spent a lot of that time together. I checked for signs that she was lying; her habit of smiling too much, her eyes bright and cheeks full so that she looked like a chipmunk. But she looked normal. Pleased, even, to see me so flustered.

'You're insane! What are you going to do this time?' I asked. 'Sleep with him? Then when he makes fun of you, what? Come pound your head on my door reciting the collected poems of Sylvia Plath?'

'He's going to apologize for before. And don't call me insane. You're the one going to the psychiatrist.'

'Well, I'm not going to suck his dick, that's for sure.'

She put her arm around me in mock comfort, but I pushed it off, and ignored her. She touched my shoulder again, and I turned, annoyed, but it wasn't Heidi after all; a sepia-toned boy dressed in khakis and a crisp plaid shirt was standing behind me. He thrust a hot-pink square of paper toward me without a word, then briskly made his way toward the other end of Commons, where the crowds blossomed. Heidi leaned over and read it: 'Wear Black Leather – the Less, the Better.'

'It's a gay party,' I said, crumpling the card. 'He thinks we're fucking gay.'

Heidi and I signed on to work at the Saybrook dining hall as dish-washers. The job consisted of dumping food from plates and trays into a vat of rushing water. It seemed straightforward, but then I learned better. You wouldn't believe what people could do with food until you worked in a dish room. Lettuce and crackers and soup would be bullied into a pulp in the bowl of some bored anorexic; ziti would be mixed with honey and granola; trays would appear heaped with mashed potato snow women with melted choco-late ice cream for hair. Frat boys arrived at the dish-room window, en masse. They liked to fill glasses with food, then seal them, airtight, onto their trays. If you tried to prize them off, milk,

35

Worcestershire sauce, peas, chunks of bread vomited onto your dish-room uniform.

When this happened one day in the middle of the lunch rush, for what seemed like the hundredth time, I tipped the tray toward one of the frat boys as he turned to walk away, popping the glasses off so that the mess spurted onto his Shetland sweater.

He looked down at his sweater. 'Lesbo bitch!'

'No,' I said, 'that would be your mother.'

Heidi, next to me, clenched my arm in support, but I remained motionless, waiting to see what the frat boy would do. He glared at me for a minute, then walked away.

'Let's take a smoke break,' Heidi said.

I didn't smoke, but Heidi had begun to, because she thought it would help her lose weight. As I hefted a stack of glasses through the steamer, she lit up.

'Soft packs remind me of you,' she said. 'Just when you've smoked them all and you think there's none left, there's always one more, hiding in that little crushed corner.' Before I could respond she said, 'Oh, God. Not another mouse. You know whose job that is.'

By the end of the rush, the floor mats got full and slippery with food. This was when mice tended to appear, scurrying over our shoes; more often than not, a mouse got caught in the grating that covered the drains in the floor. Sometimes the mouse was already dead by the time we noticed it. This one was alive.

'No way,' I said. 'This time you're going to help. Get some gloves and a trash bag.'

'That's all I'm getting. I'm not getting that mouse out of there.'

'Put on the gloves,' I ordered. She winced, but put them on. 'Reach down,' I said. 'At an angle, so you get at its middle. Otherwise, if you try to get it by its tail, the tail will break off.'

'This is filthy, eh.'

'That's why we're here,' I said. 'To clean up filth. Eh.'

She reached down, but would not touch the mouse. I put my hand around her arm and pushed it till her hand made contact. The cries from the mouse were soft, songlike. 'Oh, my God,' she said. 'Oh, my God, ohmigod.' She wrestled it out of the grating and turned her head away.

'Don't you let it go,' I said.

'Where's the food bag? It'll smother itself if I drop it in the food bag. Quick,' she said, her head still turned away, her eyes closed. 'Lead me to it.'

'No. We are not going to smother this mouse. We've got to break its neck.'

'You're one heartless bitch.'

I wondered how to explain that if death is unavoidable it should be quick and painless. My mother had died slowly. At the hospital, they'd said it was kidney failure, but I knew, in the end, it was my father. He made her so scared to live in her own home that she was finally driven away from it in an ambulance.

'Breaking its neck will save it the pain of smothering,' I said. 'Breaking its neck is more humane. Take the trash bag and cover it so you won't get any blood on you, then crush.'

The loud jets of the steamer had shut off automatically and the dish room grew quiet. Heidi breathed in deeply, then crushed the mouse. She shuddered, disgusted. 'Now what?'

'What do you mean, "now what?" Throw the little bastard in the trash.'

At our third session, I told Dr Raeburn I didn't mind if he smoked. He sat on the sill of his open window, smoking behind a jungle screen of office plants.

We spent the first ten minutes discussing the Iliad, and whether or not the text actually states that Achilles had been dipped in the River Styx. He said it did, and I said it didn't. After we'd finished with the Iliad, and with my new job in what he called 'the scullery', he asked questions about my parents. I told him nothing. It was none of his business. Instead, I talked about Heidi. I told him about that day in Commons, Heidi's plan to go on a date with Mr Dick, and the invitation we'd been given to the gay party.

'You seem preoccupied by this soirée.' He arched his eyebrows at the word 'soirée'.

'Wouldn't you be?'

'Dina,' he said slowly, in a way that made my name seem like a song title, 'have you ever had a romantic interest?'

'You want to know if I've ever had a boyfriend?' I said. 'Just go ahead and ask if I've ever fucked anybody.'

This appeared to surprise him. 'I think that you are having a crisis of identity,' he said.

'Oh, is that what this is?'

His profession had taught him not to roll his eyes. Instead, his exasperation revealed itself in a tiny pursing of his lips, as though he'd just tasted something awful and was trying very hard not to offend the cook.

'It doesn't have to be, as you say, someone you've fucked, it doesn't have to be a boyfriend,' he said.

'Well, what are you trying to say? If it's not a boy, then you're saying it's a girl –'

'Calm down. It could be a crush, Dina.' He lit one cigarette off another. 'A crush on a male teacher, a crush on a dog, for heaven's sake. An interest. Not necessarily a relationship.'

It was sacrifice time. If I could spend the next half hour talking about some boy, then I'd have given him what he wanted.

So I told him about the boy with the nice shoes.

I was sixteen and had spent the last few coins in my pocket on bus fare to buy groceries. I didn't like going to the Super Fresh two blocks away from my house, plunking government food stamps into the hands of the cashiers.

'There she go reading,' one of them once said, even though I was only carrying a book. 'Don't your eyes get tired?'

On Greenmount Avenue you could read schoolbooks – that was understandable. The government and your teachers forced you to read them. But anything else was antisocial. It meant you'd rather submit to the words of some white dude than shoot the breeze with your neighbors.

I hated those cashiers, and I hated them seeing me with food stamps, so I took the bus and shopped elsewhere. That day, I got off the bus at Govans, and though the neighborhood was black like my own – hair salon after hair salon of airbrushed signs promising arabesque hair styles and inch-long fingernails – the houses were neat and orderly, nothing at all like Greenmount, where every other house had at least one shattered window. The store was well swept, and people quietly checked long grocery lists – no screaming kids, no loud cashier-customer altercations. I got the groceries and left the store.

I decided to walk back. It was a fall day, and I walked for blocks.

Then I sensed someone following me. I walked more quickly, my arms around the sack, the leafy lettuce tickling my nose. I didn't want to hold the sack so close that it would break the eggs or squash the hamburger buns, but it was slipping, and as I looked behind me a boy my age, maybe older, rushed toward me.

'Let me help you,' he said.

'That's all right.' I set the bag on the sidewalk. Maybe I saw his face, maybe it was handsome enough, but what I noticed first, splayed on either side of the bag, were his shoes. They were nice shoes, real leather, a stitched design like a widow's peak on each one, or like birds' wings, and for the first time in my life I understood what people meant when they said 'wing-tip shoes'.

'I watched you carry them groceries out that store, then you look around, like you're lost, but like you liked being lost, then you walk down the sidewalk for blocks and blocks. Rearranging that bag, it almost gone to slip, then hefting it back up again.'

'Uh-huh,' I said.

'And then I passed my own house and was still following you. And then your bag really look like it was gone crash and everything. So I just thought I'd help.' He sucked in his bottom lip, as if to keep it from making a smile. 'What's your name?' When I told him, he said, 'Dina, my name is Cecil.' Then he said, 'D comes right after C.'

'Yes,' I said, 'it does, doesn't it.'

Then, half question, half statement, he said, 'I could carry your groceries for you? And walk you home?'

I stopped the story there. Dr Raeburn kept looking at me. 'Then what happened?'

I couldn't tell him the rest: that I had not wanted the boy to walk me home, that I didn't want someone with such nice shoes to see where I lived.

Dr Raeburn would only have pitied me if I'd told him that I ran down the sidewalk after I told the boy no, that I fell, the bag slipped, and the eggs cracked, their yolks running all over the lettuce. Clear amniotic fluid coated the can of cinnamon rolls. I left the bag there on the sidewalk, the groceries spilled out randomly like cards loosed from a deck. When I returned home, I told my mother that I'd lost the food stamps.

'Lost?' she said. I'd expected her to get angry, I'd wanted her to get angry, but she hadn't. 'Lost?' she repeated. Why had I been so clumsy and nervous around a harmless boy? I could have brought the groceries home and washed off the egg yolk, but instead I'd just left them there. 'Come on,' Mama said, snuffing her tears, pulling my arm, trying to get me to join her and start yanking cushions off the couch. 'We'll find enough change here. We got to get something for dinner before your father gets back.'

We'd already searched the couch for money the previous week, and I knew there'd be nothing now, but I began to push my fingers into the couch's boniest corners, pretending that it was only a matter of time before I'd find some change or a lost watch or an earring. Something pawnable, perhaps.

'What happened next?' Dr Raeburn asked again. 'Did you let the boy walk you home?'

'My house was far, so we went to his house instead.' Though I was sure Dr Raeburn knew that I was making this part up, I continued. 'We made out on his sofa. He kissed me.'

Dr Raeburn lit his next cigarette like a detective. Cool, suspicious. 'How did it feel?'

'You know,' I said. 'Like a kiss feels. It felt nice. The kiss felt very, very nice.'

Raeburn smiled gently, though he seemed unconvinced. When he called time on our session, his cigarette had become one long pole of ash. I left his office, walking quickly down the corridor, afraid to look back. It would be like him to trot after me, his navy blazer flapping, just to get the truth out of me. *You never kissed anyone.* The words slid from my brain, and knotted in my stomach.

When I reached my dorm, I found an old record player blocking my door and a Charles Mingus LP propped beside it. I carried them inside and then, lying on the floor, I played the Mingus over and over again until I fell asleep. I slept feeling as though Dr Raeburn had attached electrodes to my head, willing into my mind a dream about my mother. I saw the lemon meringue of her skin, the long bone of her arm as she reached down to clip her toenails. I'd come home from a school trip to an aquarium, and I was explaining the differences between baleen and sperm whales according to the size of their heads, the range of their habitats, their feeding patterns.

I awoke remembering the expression on her face after I'd finished my dizzying whale lecture. She looked like a tourist who'd asked for directions to a place she thought was simple enough to get to only to hear a series of hypothetical turns, alleys, one-way streets. Her response was to nod politely at the perilous elaborateness of it all; to nod and save herself from the knowledge that she would never be able to get where she wanted to go.

The dishwashers always closed down the dining hall. One night, after everyone else had punched out, Heidi and I took a break, and though I wasn't a smoker, we set two milk crates upside down on the floor and smoked cigarettes.

The dishwashing machines were off, but steam still rose from them like a jungle mist. Outside in the winter air, students were singing carols in their groomed and tailored singing-group voices. The Whiffenpoofs were back in New Haven after a tour around the world, and I guess their return was a huge deal. Heidi and I craned our necks to watch the year's first snow through an open window.

'What are you going to do when you're finished?' Heidi asked. Sexy question marks of smoke drifted up to the windows before vanishing.

'Take a bath.'

She swatted me with her free hand. 'No, silly. Three years from now. When you leave Yale.'

'I don't know. Open up a library. Somewhere where no one comes in for books. A library in a desert.'

She looked at me as though she'd expected this sort of answer and didn't know why she'd asked in the first place.

'What are you going to do?' I asked her.

'Open up a psych clinic. In a desert. And my only patient will be some wacko who runs a library.'

'Ha,' I said. 'Whatever you do, don't work in a dish room ever again. You're no good.' I got up from the crate. 'C'mon. Let's hose the place down.'

We put out our cigarettes on the floor, since it was our job to clean it anyway. We held squirt guns in one hand and used the other to douse the floors with the standard-issue, eye-burning cleaning solution. We hosed the dish room, the kitchen, the serving line, sending the water and crud and suds into the drains. Then we hosed them again so the solution wouldn't eat holes in our shoes as we left. Then I had an idea. I unbuckled my belt.

'What the hell are you doing?' Heidi said.

'Listen, it's too cold to go outside with our uniforms all wet. We could just take a shower right here. There's nobody but us.'

'What the fuck, eh?'

I let my pants drop, then took off my shirt and panties. I didn't wear a bra, since I didn't have much to fill one. I took off my shoes and hung my clothes on the stepladder.

'You've flipped,' Heidi said. 'I mean, really, psych-ward flipped.'

I soaped up with the liquid hand soap until I felt as glazed as a ham. 'Stand back and spray me.'

'Oh, my God,' she said. I didn't know whether she was confused or delighted, but she picked up the squirt gun and sprayed me. She was laughing. Then she got too close and the water started to sting.

'God damn it!' I said. 'That hurt!'

'I was wondering what it would take to make you say that.'

When all the soap had been rinsed off, I put on my regular clothes and said, 'OK. You're up next.'

'No way,' she said.

'Yes way.'

She started to take off her uniform shirt, then stopped.

'What?'

'I'm too fat.'

'You goddam right.' She always said she was fat. One time I'd told her that she should shut up about it, that large black women wore their fat like mink coats. 'You're big as a house,' I said now. 'Frozen yogurt may be low in calories, but not if you eat five tubs of it. Take your clothes off. I want to get out of here.'

She began taking off her uniform, then stood there, hands cupped over her breasts, crouching at the pubic bone.

'Open up,' I said, 'or we'll never get done.'

Her hands remained where they were. I threw the bottle of liquid soap at her, and she had to catch it, revealing herself as she did.

I turned on the squirt gun, and she stood there, stiff, arms at her side, eyes closed, as though awaiting mummification. I began with the water on low, and she turned around in a full circle, hesitantly, letting the droplets from the spray fall on her as if she were submitting to a death by stoning.

42

When I increased the water pressure, she slipped and fell on the sudsy floor. She stood up and then slipped again. This time she laughed and remained on the floor, rolling around on it as I sprayed.

I think I began to love Heidi that night in the dish room, but who is to say that I hadn't begun to love her the first time I met her? I sprayed her and sprayed her, and she turned over and over like a large beautiful dolphin, lolling about in the sun.

Heidi started sleeping at my place. Sometimes she slept on the floor; sometimes we slept sardinelike, my feet at her head, until she complained that my feet were 'taunting' her. When we finally slept head to head, she said, 'Much better.' She was so close I could smell her toothpaste. 'I like your hair,' she told me, touching it through the darkness. 'You should wear it out more often.'

'White people always say that about black people's hair. The worse it looks, the more they say they like it.'

I'd expected her to disagree, but she kept touching my hair, her hands passing through it till my scalp tingled. When she began to touch the hair around the edge of my face, I felt myself quake. Her fingertips stopped for a moment, as if checking my pulse, then resumed.

'I like how it feels right here. See, mine just starts with the same old texture as the rest of my hair.' She found my hand under the blanket and brought it to her hairline. 'See,' she said.

It was dark. As I touched her hair, it seemed as though I could smell it, too. Not a shampoo smell. Something richer, murkier. A bit dead, but sweet, like the decaying wood of a ship. She guided my hand.

'I see,' I said. The record she'd given me was playing in my mind, and I kept trying to shut it off. I could also hear my mother saying that this is what happens when you've been around white people: things get weird. So weird I could hear the stylus etching its way into the flat vinyl of the record. 'Listen,' I said finally, when the bass and saxes started up. I heard Heidi breathe deeply, but she said nothing.

We spent the winter and some of the spring in my room – never hers – missing tests, listening to music, looking out my window to comment on people who wouldn't have given us a second thought.

We read books related to none of our classes. I got riled up by *The Autobiography of Malcolm X* and *The Chomsky Reader*; Heidi read aloud passages from *The Anxiety of Influence*. We guiltily read mysteries and *Clan of the Cave Bear*, then immediately threw them away. Once we looked up from our books at exactly the same moment, as though trapped at a dinner table with nothing to say. A pleasant trap of silence.

Then one weekend I went back to Baltimore and stayed with my father. He asked me how school was going, but besides that, we didn't talk much. He knew what I thought of him. I stopped by the Enoch Pratt Library, where my favorite librarian, Mrs Ardelia, cornered me into giving a little talk to the after-school kids, telling them to stay in school. They just looked at me like I was crazy; they were only nine or ten, and it hadn't even occurred to them to bail.

When I returned to Yale – to a sleepy, tree-scented spring – a group of students were holding what was called 'Coming Out Day'. I watched it from my room.

The emcee was the sepia boy who'd given us the invitation months back. His speech was strident but still smooth and peppered with jokes. There was a speech about AIDS, with lots of statistics: nothing that seemed to make 'coming out' worth it. Then the women spoke. One girl pronounced herself 'out' as casually as if she'd announced the time. Another said nothing at all: she came to the microphone with a woman who began cutting off her waist-length, bleached-blond hair. The woman doing the cutting tossed the shorn hair in every direction as she cut. People were clapping and cheering and catching the locks of hair.

And then there was Heidi. She was proud that she liked girls, she said when she reached the microphone. She loved them, wanted to sleep with them. She was a dyke, she said repeatedly, stabbing her finger to her chest in case anyone was unsure to whom she was referring. She could not have seen me. I was across the street, three stories up. And yet, when everyone clapped for her, she seemed to be looking straight at me.

Heidi knocked. 'Let me in.'

It was like the first time I met her. The tears, the raw pink of her face.

We hadn't spoken in weeks. Outside, pink-and-white blossoms hung from the Old Campus trees. Students played Hacky Sack in T-shirts and shorts. Though I was the one who'd broken away after she went up to that podium, I still half expected her to poke her head out a window in Linsly-Chit, or tap on my back in Harkness, or even join me in the Commons dining hall, where I'd asked for my dish-room shift to be transferred. She did none of these.

'Well,' I said, 'what is it?'

She looked at me. 'My mother,' she said.

She continued to cry, but seemed to have grown so silent in my room I wondered if I could hear the numbers change on my digital clock.

'When my parents were getting divorced,' she said, 'my mother bought a car. A used one. An El Dorado. It was filthy. It looked like a huge crushed can coming up the street. She kept trying to clean it out. I mean –'

I nodded and tried to think what to say in the pause she left behind. Finally I said, 'We had one of those,' though I was sure ours was an Impala.

She looked at me, eyes steely from trying not to cry. 'Anyway, she'd drive me around in it and although she didn't like me to eat in it, I always did. One day I was eating cantaloupe slices, spitting the seeds on the floor. Maybe a month later, I saw this little sprout, growing right up from the car floor. I just started laughing and she kept saying what, what? I was laughing and then I saw she was so –'

She didn't finish. So what? So sad? So awful? Heidi looked at me with what seemed to be a renewed vigor. 'We could have gotten a better car, eh?'

'It's all right. It's not a big deal,' I said.

Of course, that was the wrong thing to say. And I really didn't mean it to sound the way it had come out.

I told Dr Raeburn about Heidi's mother having cancer and how I'd said it wasn't a big deal, though I'd wanted to say the opposite. I told Dr Raeburn how I meant to tell Heidi that my mother had died, that I knew how one eventually accustoms oneself to the physical world's lack of sympathy: the buses that are still running late, the kids who still play in the street, the clocks that won't stop ticking for the person who's gone.

'You're pretending,' Dr Raeburn said, not sage or professional, but a little shocked by the discovery, as if I'd been trying to hide a pack of his cigarettes behind my back.

'I'm pretending?' I shook my head. 'All those years of psych grad,' I said. 'And to tell me *that*?'

'What I mean is that you construct stories about yourself and dish them out – one for you, one for you –' Here he reenacted this process, showing me handing out lies as if they were apples.

'Pretending. I believe the professional name for it might be denial,' I said. 'Are you calling me gay?'

He pursed his lips noncommittally, then finally said, 'No, Dina. I don't think you're gay.'

I checked his eyes. I couldn't read them.

'No. Not at all,' he said, sounding as if he were telling a subtle joke. 'But maybe you'll finally understand.'

'Understand what?'

'Oh, just that constantly saying what one doesn't mean accustoms the mouth to meaningless phrases.' His eyes narrowed. 'Maybe you'll understand that when you finally need to express something truly significant your mouth will revert to the insignificant nonsense it knows so well.' He looked at me, his hands sputtering in the air in a gesture of defeat. 'Who knows?' he asked with a glib, psychiatric smile I'd never seen before. 'Maybe it's your survival mechanism. Black living in a white world.'

I heard him, but only vaguely. I'd hooked on to that one word, pretending. Dr Raeburn would never realize that 'pretending' was what had got me this far. I remembered the morning of my mother's funeral. I'd been given milk to settle my stomach; I'd pretended it was coffee. I imagined I was drinking coffee elsewhere. Some Arabic-speaking country where the thick coffee served in little cups was so strong it could keep you awake for days.

Heidi wanted me to go with her to the funeral. She'd sent this message through the dean. 'We'll pay for your ticket to Vancouver,' the dean said.

These people wanted you to owe them for everything. 'What about my return ticket?' I asked the dean. 'Maybe the shrink will chip in for that.'

The dean looked at me as though I were an insect she'd like to squash. 'We'll pay for the whole thing. We might even pay for some lessons in manners.'

So I packed my suitcase and walked from my suicide single dorm to Heidi's room. A thin wispy girl in ragged cutoffs and a shirt that read 'LSBN!' answered the door. A group of short-haired girls in thick black leather jackets, bundled up despite the summer heat, encircled Heidi in a protective fairy ring. They looked at me critically, clearly wondering if Heidi was too fragile for my company.

'You've got our numbers,' one said, holding on to Heidi's shoulder. 'And Vancouver's got a great gay community.'

'Oh, God,' I said. 'She's going to a funeral, not a Save the Dykes rally.'

One of the girls stepped in front of me.

'It's OK, Cynthia,' Heidi said. Then she ushered me into her bedroom and closed the door. A suitcase was on her bed, half packed.

'I could just uninvite you,' Heidi said. 'How about that? You want that?' She folded a polka-dotted T-shirt that was wrong for any occasion and put it in her suitcase. 'Why haven't you talked to me?' she said, looking at the shirt instead of me. 'Why haven't you talked to me in two months?'

'I don't know,' I said.

'*You don't know*,' she said, each syllable steeped in sarcasm. 'You don't know. Well, *I* know. You thought I was going to try to sleep with you.'

'Try to? We slept together all winter!'

'If you call smelling your feet sleeping together, you've got a lot to learn.' She seemed thinner and meaner; every line of her body held me at bay.

'So tell me,' I said. 'What can you show me that I need to learn?' But as soon as I said it I somehow knew she still hadn't slept with anyone. 'Am I supposed to come over there and sweep your enraged self into my arms?' I said. 'Like in the movies? Is this the part where we're both so mad we kiss each other?'

She shook her head and smiled weakly. 'You don't get it,' she said. 'My mother is dead.' She closed her suitcase, clicking shut the old-fashioned locks. 'My mother is dead,' she said again, this time reminding herself. She set her suitcase upright on the floor and sat on it. She looked like someone waiting for a train.

'Fine,' I said. 'And she's going to be dead for a long time.' Though it sounded stupid, I felt good saying it. As though I had my own locks to click shut.

Heidi went to Vancouver for her mother's funeral. I didn't go with her. Instead, I went back to Baltimore and moved in with an aunt I barely knew. Every day was the same: I read and smoked outside my aunt's apartment, studying the row of hair salons across the street, where girls in denim cutoffs and tank tops would troop in and come out hours later, a flash of neon nails, coifs the color and sheen of patent leather. And every day I imagined Heidi's house in Vancouver. Her place would not be large, but it would be clean. Flowery shrubs would line the walks. The Canadian wind would whip us about like pennants. I'd be visiting her in some vague time in the future, deliberately vague, for people like me, who realign past events to suit themselves. In that future time, you always have a chance to catch the groceries before they fall; your words can always be rewound and erased, rewritten and revised.

Then I'd imagine Heidi visiting me. There are no psychiatrists or deans, no boys with nice shoes or flip cashiers. Just me in my single room. She knocks on the door and says, 'Open up.'

HAROLD BRODKEY
The Quarrel

I came to Harvard from St Louis in the fall of 1948. I had a scholarship and a widowed mother and a reputation for being a good,
hardworking boy. What my scholarship didn't cover, I earned working
Wednesday nights and Saturdays, and I strenuously avoided using
any of my mother's small but adequate income. During the summer
between my freshman and sophomore years, my grandmother died
and willed me five thousand dollars. I quit my part-time job and
bought a gray flannel suit and a pair of white buck shoes, and I got
on the editorial board of the college literary magazine. I met Duncan
Leggert at the first editorial meeting I attended. He had been an
editor for a full year, and this particular night he was infuriated by
a story, which everyone wanted to print, about an unhappy, sensitive
child. 'Why shouldn't that child be unhappy?' Duncan shouted.
'He's a bore.' The story was accepted, and Duncan stalked out of
the meeting.

Two nights later, as I was walking along Massachusetts Avenue
in the early dusk, I saw Duncan peering into the window of a record
store at a display of opera albums. He was whistling 'Piangi, piangi',
from *La Traviata*, and he looked, as usual, wan, handsome, and
unapproachable. I stood beside him until he looked up, and then I
told him I thought he'd been right about the story.

'Of course I was right,' he said, looking down at me from his
patient, expectant eyes. 'Those people confuse being sordid with
being talented.'

We went to a tavern and sat in a booth that was illuminated by
one of those glowing juke-box things in which you deposit a nickel
and push a button, and the Wurlitzer, a mile away, plays the tune.
At first, I was nearly asphyxiated with shyness, but I asked Duncan
what he was planning to be when he graduated (substituting 'graduated' for 'grown up' at the last minute), and he said 'Nothing.' I
looked blank, and he took his cigarette and stared at the glowing
coal for a moment and then said quietly, with a good deal of sadness
in his voice, 'I'm rich.' Then he raised his head, looked me in the

eye – he was half smiling – and added, 'Filthy rich.' I was utterly charmed. I asked him how rich. He said, airily, 'Oh, a couple million if the market holds.' The idea of talking to someone that rich pleased me so much I burst into idiotic laughter. He asked me why I was laughing, but I didn't tell him.

We talked warily at first, as men – or, rather, as boys imitating men – will; but then, impelled by the momentum of some deep and inexplicable sympathy, we went on talking until one o'clock. Duncan said the college literary magazine was a mere journal of self-pity, and those parts of it that weren't amateurish were grubby. He firmly believed, he said, that most unhappiness was a pose. 'It's a way of getting out of being interesting.'

Even at his most arrogant, Duncan always had a note of despair in his voice. 'People get what they deserve,' he said. 'Why should I believe in tragedy? I've never seen any. Stories ought to have happy endings; people ought to be more interesting; everyone ought to have better taste.

'The important thing,' he said as he slouched in his corner of the booth and sketched faces in the sugar he had poured on the table, 'is to have quality. No one cares if your mother loved you or not if you're dull. And most people are dull,' he added sadly.

'This is a democracy,' he said later. 'I'm supposed to consider everyone my equal. Well, I don't. Dull people give me a pain. I think Whitman is a lousy poet and Willa Cather is feeble-minded, and old Huckleberry Twain gives me the creeps. What's more, if there's anything I can't stand, it's a lot of pointless good nature.' I quenched my smile.

It seemed to me he was saying everything I had always thought and never expressed.

From that first night, we were friends. I suppose any friendship must have a core of mutual need. I was tired of what I had been. I was full of Midwestern optimism about my ability to change. From that very first night, I fully intended to live my life in line with the doctrine Duncan was expounding. But it wasn't his ideas that I admired and wanted. What I wanted was his Eastern Shore of Maryland manner, and his honesty, and his faith that what he thought was important. And I wanted to look like him. He was very tall. He had a wan, smooth face, elongated and arrogant. He walked with a slouch and often sat for hours among people without saying a word, sometimes without an expression crossing his handsome countenance. But then he might suddenly begin to talk, especially if there was a discussion going on, and he would talk overexcitedly, gesticulate, occasionally not even making sense, and then later he would be inconsolable because he thought he had made a fool of himself. I thought he was charming at those moments. What did dismay me was the way he had of being rendered speechless by a color, or a pretty woman's gesture of welcome, or an automobile, or the way a girl's hair blew. He would stand, quite tense and excited, held by a kind of surprised rapture. When he had these quiet transports, I was embarrassed – for myself, because I was unable to share a friend's emotion. But as I knew Duncan longer, the beauty that seemed to electrify him touched me, too. Duncan was always showing me shapes in the clouds.

Everything he said explained me to myself or else put a weapon in my hand, and his bitterness struck me like a surge of sunlight, bringing crispness and definition, drenched as I was in the foggy optimism of my home. I was discarding my traditions as fast as I could, but it was difficult work; I had first to locate the roots and then to get them up. And Duncan's disillusion – any disillusion, in fact – was infinitely helpful. I did my best to speak as Duncan did, with frequent, entrancing pauses, and with small curlicues of contempt.

Yet if Duncan felt it was a moment for kindness, his entire soul and bank account, his car, his wardrobe, his time were yours. I used to worry about people taking advantage of him; but although he had a terrible memory for telephone numbers and people's names, he never forgot how much he spent, where, and with whom.

Girls fell in love with him often. They seemed to find his mixture of melancholy and arrogance irresistible. At first, Duncan would be overwhelmingly chivalrous to them, light their cigarettes, take them out when they asked him. But sooner or later he would begin to feel cornered; he'd cease lighting cigarettes; he'd stop answering the telephone.

The number of people we saw that year steadily dwindled as we decided they were doomed to be ordinary or as they disagreed with us; and they were struck from our list of acquaintances. He and I both believed that if we were careful and did the right thing, we could escape turning out as our elders had. 'They give you advice,'

Duncan pointed out, 'and never stop to think of what you think of what they turned out to be.' We thought if you traveled far enough and long enough, you would come to a place where everyone liked the things you liked and talked the way you talked, where everyone knew your value without your having to get undignified and nervous in proving it. In this place that we were looking for, you would never have to boast or to make conversation out of pity for an ugly girl or to feel sorry for your parents. One January night when Duncan and I were walking along the Charles – it was cold and foggy – we swore never to hide the truth from each other, always to admit our faults, to admire each other's virtues, to become men of stature, true stature, and to go to Europe together that summer for a year, leaving college, no matter what our parents said or did about it. We would take bicycles and be frugal and healthy, and we would deepen our culture and our refinement.

My mother objected violently when I told her I was going to Europe with Duncan. She said I was wasting my inheritance and going to the bad out of sheer obstinacy, and that it was all Duncan's bad example. Duncan said that, of course, she was right. I got drunk and told Duncan that my mother could go to hell, and he watched me, as I recall, with eyes glassy with admiration. How could my mother compete with Duncan? All I wanted, that year, was to be like him.

We sailed from Halifax in June, on the Aquitania, for Southampton. Almost as soon as the green hills around Halifax receded and the ship was in open water, Duncan said to me, 'I think you ought to write your mother a good letter. You were quite unpleasant to her over the phone. That's one of your faults,' he added, and he grimaced to show that he didn't like to talk this way but that he had to, in accordance with our vow. 'You have so little tact. On the other hand, you're much more dynamic than I am. I wish I were more like you.'

'But you're not,' I said, candid at any cost. 'You mustn't worry about it,' I went on quickly, 'because I like you very much the way you are now . . .'

We were free from college and observation; we were molding each other, protecting each other from being ordinary. Duncan put his hand on my shoulder briefly and smiled, and then we paced each other around the deck of the ship to get our exercise in before dinner. The statured figure had to be physically attractive, too.

We stayed in England just long enough to see the Tower of London, the National Gallery, and Scott's, and to decide the food was inedible, and then we took the channel steamer from Newhaven. Standing at the rail, we saw the shores of France rise from the waves, green and promising.

When we landed in Dieppe, my delight – let me say that my delight rose like a flock of startled birds. Everything I saw or heard – the whole pastel city, the buildings as serene and placid as the green water of the harbor – touched off another flutter of the white wings. At one wharf, a group of fishing boats huddled in a confusion of masts, the hulls green and black and purple, arched like slices of melon. Along the waterfront was a row of buildings, with here and there a gap and a pile of rubble or a portion of a wall. But these were the colors of the buildings: pale green and mauve, light yellow like wispy sunlight, faded pink, gentle bluish gray. And then, perched on a hillside, the immemorial hulk of a castle.

Duncan's gaze moved lovingly around the scene. 'Every town should have a castle,' he said.

Our hotel room was old, with a sloping floor and a single, huge brass bed. There were no rugs on the wooden floor and no curtains on the high French windows, which wouldn't quite close, because of their crooked frames. Outside our window, three streets converged and formed a triangular island, planted with plane trees and patterned beds of yellow flowers. Workmen in gray clothes and thick boots were sitting on stone benches and drinking wine. The fronts of the houses along the street were decorated with heavy lintels and occasionally with stringy caryatids, at once frivolous and orderly. In the distance an elegant spire rose, and the sound of bells floated down to us. We washed our faces and brushed our teeth and changed our clothes, singing the entire time – and then, since we were in France, we set out to find some women.

First, we walked along the beach and saw the collection of Grand and Univers and Windsor hotels; they were shattered, and workmen scurried in and out of their rubbled interiors carrying bricks. Other workmen were fitting dumpy concrete columns into the balustrade that ran along the street, separating it from the rocky beach; as the workmen finished one section, another crew of workmen, with large pneumatic machines, came along and drilled holes in the columns, chipped the edges, and scarred the fluting. Duncan and I stared, fascinated, and then realized that they were making the balustrade look old. Within a few years, people would forget that the balustrade had been repaired after the war; they would see it ancient-looking and indestructible and a tie to an earlier time.

Duncan and I picked our way over the upper beach, which was mostly rock, and down to the narrow ridge of sand that bordered the ocean. The beach was almost empty, but a few groups of people sat or lay on blankets. The people seemed strangely solid and fleshy. The only sound was that of the pneumatic machines busily restoring time.

The channel was gray and empty of ships; it was rather like a border of sky in a faded tapestry. Duncan said that as soon as we shipped our trunk to Paris we ought to set out on our bicycles to see Mont-Saint-Michel. 'It's quite a small island,' he said. 'They've been working on it for a long time. It must be quite perfect by now.'

On our way back to the hotel, we passed many women. Only one girl was pretty, and she was running, with her thin print dress whipping around her muscular figure and her arms pumping, and nothing short of a pistol shot would have stopped her.

In a moment of self-assertion, I said I had no particular interest in Mont-Saint-Michel and it was out of the way, to boot; I didn't want Duncan to know I was his follower. To my surprise, he gave in, and the next morning, on our bicycles, we set off for Paris. We each had two knapsacks and a sleeping bag. We rode through Arques-la-Bataille and Neufchatel, through Forges-les-Eaux and Gournay-en-Bray. The countryside was green, and we passed the dried-lavender granite spires of old, weather-beaten churches. Duncan told hideously funny, embarrassing stories about himself as a child. One he told me as we swam in a small pond near the road. I laughed so loud a farmer with a seamed face and huge dusty hands came to see who we were.

At Pontoise, we sat on a terrace above the Oise and watched the rockets of Bastille Day in the night sky over Paris. The day we entered Paris, we spent hours bicycling through endless suburbs, and then at noon, at last, we burst into the Place de la Concorde, with the fountains playing and the gardens of the Tuileries in bloom. And one morning we wakened in a wheat field, surrounded by pale stalks of spiked wheat, and saw on the horizon, shadowy and dim, the spires of Chartres. And at Beaugency we spent a whole day idling on a sandbar in the Loire with a family of seven girls, all of them blond, all of them charming, all of them in love with Duncan. ('You will write to us, yes?')

I don't know exactly when we each decided that the other wasn't worthy of this paradise. What I do remember is that it became increasingly difficult to decide which hotel we would stay at, which restaurant we would eat in, which road we would take.

The moments multiplied when one of us would draw his breath and turn away, confront the scenery and remark, 'Well, whatever you want . . .' Against the sound of strained politeness in the background, I remember the sunset at Blois flooding crimson through the sky, and the long allées at Chambord; in such a manner I remember two swallows skimming low over the Loire, chirruping and beating their bent pointed wings. I remember Duncan's voice at Chenonceaux – the sky was filled with domed white clouds – saying, 'I don't care really . . . I suppose we ought . . .' and his voice quivered with resentment.

We had decided to see the west of France – mostly it was my idea – because there would be fewer Americans there. But actually I had another reason. So far as I knew, it was barren of difficult places like Chartres. At Chartres, I'd had all the wrong reactions. Who would have known that the thing to do with the cathedral was to go into a pâtisserie and buy a bag full of chocolate éclairs and cherry tarts and then sit down on the grass plot in front of the entrance and stare at the towers while eating oneself into a chocolate coma? Duncan didn't like it when I said the cathedral was beautiful; you were supposed to feel these things so deeply you couldn't express yourself, and wouldn't even *want* to express yourself.

Duncan enjoyed Pernod. It made me sick. Duncan hated talking to people. I talked to everyone. My French vocabulary was better than Duncan's. His pronunciation was better than mine. I became terribly adept at not irritating Duncan before breakfast. I couldn't see that he appreciated any of this, or that he responded with any similar awareness. For the fiftieth time, I thought him unfair. The moment came when I could no longer stand the sound of his voice, or his ideas. After traveling with him day and night, without a break, for fifty-three days, I felt my senses suffocating in an awareness of Duncan.

We rode through the flat Vendéen landscape, with its bright-yellow marsh grasses and wheat and green meadows, its white farmhouses, and its tiny drawbridges over canals and streams – two college boys, sun-tanned and healthy, in T-shirts and shorts, so angry with each other that we rode our bicycles ten or fifteen feet apart. When an infrequent car passed us, I would wonder if Duncan would see it in time, but he always did.

There was a moist, sticky quality in the air. The villages were far apart, and when we came to one, the houses were shuttered and unfriendly. The French were barricaded in their cool, high-ceilinged rooms, cutting into ripe pears with tiny pearl-handled knives, while we bicycled the hot and dusty streets, only to emerge, on the other side of the gray church and white stucco café, back in the flat open country.

The heat was unbearable. At Luçon, we turned off the main road and headed toward the sea again, to a village on the map called La Tranche, which turned out to be three or four buildings along the highway. Just beyond La Tranche, our road climbed to the top of a ridge, and we saw that the flat, grassy countryside humped into the ridge we were on and then flowed into the Bay of Biscay, with no beach, or wall of rocks. The grass of the meadows, green and glowing, waved in the salt sea breezes and melted into the water. One could see the grass continuing underwater out of sight, probably to the rim of the low tide. Cows squooshed through their pasture; around their hoofs bubbles clung like necklaces. French boys and girls, their bicycles lying in the grass, swam over the submerged meadow. A few yards offshore, fishing boats with blue and yellow painted hulls swung to and fro at their moorings.

I stopped and called to Duncan, who continued a few yards and then stopped. I walked toward him, wheeling my bicycle. 'It's really lovely, isn't it –' I began.

Duncan turned to me, and in a voice shaking with fury he said, 'Do you always have to say something? Do you feel it's like dropping a coin in the box at church?'

We rode the rest of the day in silence. At sunset, we stopped in

La Rochelle, where the old Huguenot fortifications still surround the tiny harbor, and we found a room in a strange old hotel near the railroad station. Our bedroom had two huge brass beds with swollen mattresses, which rustled whenever we moved. The back of the building contained a stable. The smell of horses permeated our room, and there was a vast rose trellis outside our window. The roses were blooming. All night long, we drifted on the ebb and flow of the oddly complementary odors; and every hour or so we could hear a train arriving or departing.

The next day, we bicycled on to Bordeaux. By midafternoon, we were racing, with neither slowing down or asking to rest. We reached Bordeaux at seven in the evening, and we went at once to a café and ordered a bottle of wine and began to quarrel. Several times, the waiter, a fat, black-browed Basque, came running on his toes, one pink round finger to his lips, and we nodded and said, '*Pardon, pardon*,' and lowered our voices.

It seemed that Duncan could not stand the way I whistled when I shaved, the way I talked to waiters, the fact that even when I felt bad I smiled. 'Is it something the corn belt does to the disposition?' he asked.

I told Duncan, at the top of my lungs, that he was childish, an arty son of a bitch, and a snob.

'You're ill-bred,' he said. 'You're yelling in a café.'

He said that he'd always thought of me as an intelligent vulgarian but he'd had no idea how really ill-bred I was.

'All right,' I said, rising to my feet. 'That's it! That's *it*! Let's fight.'

Solemnly we walked out of the café. The waiter ran after us and waved his bill in our faces. We had to figure out the bill and pay it; as usual, we were overcharged. I hadn't realized until that minute how dear Duncan was to me or how much he'd taught me. It also occurred to me that Duncan outweighed me by fifteen pounds.

We walked along, wheeling our bicycles. 'All my friends have turned out to be no good.' Duncan said bitterly, at one point. And then later he said, under his breath, 'Once, I wanted to be like you –' I thought he was lying just to make me feel worse.

We came to a deserted street lined with warehouses. Duncan leaned his bicycle against a wall. I threw mine to the pavement. We faced each other and advanced. 'I'm so angry that I'm going to try to hit your face,' Duncan said.

We traded five or six blows, and then our eyes met. Shamefacedly, we backed away, and our hands dropped. Duncan sat down on the curb and pulled out his cigarettes and offered me one.

'You hurt my feelings,' I said.

'I meant to.'

'You meant what you said?'

'Of course,' he said. 'Didn't you?'

'Of course.'

We agreed that we would have to separate.

'Where will I meet you in Biarritz?' Duncan asked; we had shipped our clothes there, in a trunk.

'At the railroad station,' I said.

'When?'

I got out my map and tried to figure how long it would take us. 'The hell with it,' I said, finally. 'It's too hard to figure out. We'll bicycle there together.'

'Oh!' Duncan was disappointed. 'Well, whatever you say . . .'

We rose from the curb and got our bicycles.

'Your knapsack is loose,' Duncan said politely.

'Thank you,' I said.

We were much too depressed to find our way by our Michelins, and Bordeaux, like Paris, is afflicted with endless suburbs. At one o'clock in the morning, we were still hopelessly lost, and we were worn out with the strain of our emotional predicament. Finally, after giving up hope that we might find an open field to sleep in, we settled in the graveyard of a church, next to a flowering hedge and beneath a small apple tree. We spread our sleeping bags and lay down. In a few moments, we began to itch. I suppose we were lying on an anthill. At any rate, in no time at all our sleeping bags were swarming with insect life. We talked about getting up and moving on, but the thought of bicycling was too much for us both. We lay inert, now and then scratching ourselves, immersed in the odor of the flowers, the silence of the graveyard, the buzz of insects. Above us loomed the church. Out on the street, an occasional truck would lumber by, but they were diesel mostly, and diesels rumble with a pleasant noise.

Finally, Duncan began to talk. He said that now, since we were going to part, he could tell me that he hadn't meant anything at the meeting of the literary magazine. He had been ashamed of never saying anything at the meetings; he'd thought up a line of argument and his little witticism, and he'd planned to use it no matter what might be under discussion. He'd been very pleased when I agreed with him, but he had found it a little stifling trying to live up to my admiration. 'I find it difficult to think,' he told me. Anyway, he'd always thought his snobbery was something psychological, which he would have cured in time, and it upset him to have me always taking it so seriously and turning it into a doctrine. Much of what he said, he told me, he said just to be saying something. 'You can't be silent all the time.' It bothered him, he said, that I hadn't seen through him. It convinced him that I was a fool. He felt both guilty and superior. He was sorry if he'd misled me, but actually he had wanted to come to Europe mostly to get away from schoolwork, which bored him. He was sorry that we had come to hate each other so much, but he guessed it was inevitable, because he was so worthless a person.

A truck rumbled by on the cobble-stones, backfiring strenuously. Through the filigree of tree branches above me I could see the stars.

I told him I forgave him. He said he was grateful, and he added that he was sorry if he'd hurt my feelings. He was sure my habit of talking in front of a piece of scenery or a national monument would undoubtedly please most of the people I'd have to deal with in my life.

I called him a bastard, under my breath.

We wound up confessing that we were both irretrievably dishonest, incapable of a true relationship, faulty as people. Finally, after a long silence, I spoke up and said we ought to try to get along, but I couldn't persuade him. Alternately he would berate himself and insult me. It was amazing, though, how much affection was in the air, how sad we both felt, how hopeless it all seemed.

The next morning, we found our way out of the city by daylight, both of us depressed and silent. I discovered that there is a kind of embarrassment that has no boundary. Every hour revealed new and hitherto unexplored regions. At lunch, in a small café set beneath trees at a crossroads, we drank two bottles of wine, and our constraint broke enough for us to talk – but with difficulty and a great many migrant smiles, and without ever really looking each other in the face.

We clambered onto our bicycles and began to ride, weaving back and forth in our drunkenness. The road was crowded with trucks carrying young Bordelais to the seashore for the weekend. Their faces were fresh and unsuspecting, sharp-nosed, bright-eyed. They leaned from the back of their trucks and clutched at our shirts, so that their trucks would pull us up hills, and they roared with excited laughter when they discovered I was ticklish. When Duncan sang all of 'Le Poisson dans l'Eau', which he'd learned from an old Trenet record, the French youths, crammed in their open trucks under the hot August southern sky, applauded, yelling, '*C'est joli, ça!*'

On one long hill, my shirt tore. We had fallen behind, from truck to truck; this was the last truck in the procession. My shirt was almost ripped off my back, the truck grunted up the long hill and disappeared over the crest, and Duncan and I were alone in the middle of a birchwood. I looked at Duncan and was disappointed that I was there with him. The birchwood was lovely. Through the pale and fragile leaves, beams of sunlight fell in all directions. As I wobbled from one side of the road to the other, it seemed the trees leaned toward me, brushed my face with the tips of their branches, and then swung away; or, going downhill, I thought the trees leaned backward like a child's drawing of speed. Around a curve the trees seemed to take off, soar upward at the sky. Suddenly we were in the midst of a horde of yellow butterflies; they filled the air; their wings beat and trembled; they were everywhere. They beat on our foreheads and on our eyelids, tangled in our clothes, died on the wheels of our bicycles. With horror, Duncan stopped his bicycle and then slowly began to thread his way through the yellow cloud. 'Try not to touch them,' he said. 'Their wings won't work if you touch them; they die.' I was too drunk even to be able to slow my bicycle. I rode blindly through the butterflies, blinking my eyes, cursing when one lit on the wheel and was crushed. At the very last, a butterfly blundered against my eye, and my eye remained open with abrupt pity; between it and the sky was a yellow film laced with airy veins; the film beat, came apart. I closed my eyes and rode blindly into a tree.

Duncan helped me up, silently. We rode side by side, still drunk, but not as drunk as we had been. Occasionally, our bicycles lurched into each other. Duncan's hand was cut where it had scraped against my handle bars on one of the lurches. My torn shirt flapped in the wind.

At four, we reached Arcachon. It was a small resort with several public beaches and miles of tiny villas. We could smell the sea, the stiff, salty odors from the bay, the wisteria, the pinewoods on the surrounding hills. We rode through the village and came to a large red brick villa, square and Victorian, with a large glass conservatory facing southward, by the sea. Its garden was filled with gardenia bushes and small lemon trees. We lifted our bicycles over a low wall, made our way through some trees, and climbed over another wall to the white beach.

I sank on the sand, and Duncan, beside me, muttered, 'A resort is a resort is a resort.' The beach curved outward from us to a sandspit, where there was a picnic party, and southward out of our vision. Up the beach from us, a few people were sprawled beneath a pink-and-yellow umbrella. I said, 'Do you want to swim out to the spit and see if we can join the party?' Duncan looked at me, frightened. He began to tremble. I turned away.

The waves of the bay were sparkling and blue. Small sailboats with tinted sails swooped about in the wide waters. The tide was out, and stranded on the sand lay, seemingly, hundreds of small craft, some with masts, some without, some the size of dinghies, some good-sized, with the rounded, almost voluptuously shaped hull of shallow-water craft.

Duncan was so embarrassed that he began to build a sand castle. I reached into the pouch on the back of my bicycle and took out a pad of paper and began a letter to my mother.

Dear Mother,
    We have just come to Arcachon, a small French town which is a resort and very interesting. Duncan and I are having a wonderful time and learning a good deal which is what I told you would happen and why I wanted to come to Europe. You see, I was right about the trip and—

I threw the pad down and crawled over to Duncan and started to help him build his castle. He still wouldn't look me in the eye. I got

on my bicycle and rode into the village and brought back ham sandwiches, two bottles of Evian water, and two bottles of *vin ordinaire*.
We had to get through the evening somehow.

The party on the spit packed up their hampers and disappeared.
The pink-and-yellow umbrella was folded up and whisked away. We
were alone on the beach. Duncan scooped out a place for his shoulders and piled the sand in a mound behind his head, so that he
could watch the boats on the water. We drank steadily, pausing only
now and then to run into the water and swim a few strokes, through
the seaweed that was close to the surface at low tide. We decided
that that – the low tide – was the reason the beach was so empty.

'Oh God!' Duncan said suddenly. 'This is sheer hell!' In desperation, we began to work on the sand castle. The towers multiplied,
the moats and bridges; spires arose, Babylonian ziggurats, Egyptian
pyramids, Mayan pyramids, Christian steeples, and Moslem mina-
rets. Our castle became a city. The city began to spread over the
beach, foot by foot, more and more grandiose, more and more
wistful.

In the cool of the evening, a small blond boy came out of the red
brick villa and began to play by himself in the garden. He was
wearing a blue sailor blouse and short pants and a tiny pair of
sandals.

Duncan was admiring the castle. We were quite drunk again. 'It's
really a nice castle,' he said sadly. 'If I had a camera, I'd take a
picture. It's worth saving, don't you think?'

I felt that it was a wonderful castle, but I was damned if I knew
what to do with it. 'We could throw rocks at it,' I suggested.

The little boy wandered down the wall and peered at us through
the gate; one arm encircled one of the iron bars and the other arm
lay over the top. He hung there, occasionally drawing lines with the
tip of his sandal in the sand that had blown into the garden. He saw
the castle; his eyes grew round. He and Duncan stared at each other.
Then the little boy turned away and sat down behind the wall. We
could see only a portion of his leg.

'He's bored,' Duncan said desperately. 'He's unhappy. I can't
stand it.'

I remember we tiptoed – we must have confused the little boy
with the butterflies – to the wall and stuck our heads over it.

'Hi,' Duncan said.

'*Bonjour,*' the child said.

'I can't remember any French,' Duncan said to me. He leaned over the wall anxiously. '*Voulez-vous* – What's the word for play?' he cried, turning to me. I didn't know. I was leaning on the wall for support.

The little boy looked at us; he was polite, unfrightened, and mystified. Finally, Duncan reached down and lifted the child over the wall. The little boy's face went pale. '*Les brigands?*' he asked, in a tiny voice. Duncan didn't hear; he carried the little boy over to the castle-city and placed him in front of it. 'Yours,' he said grandly. 'All yours.' The little boy looked at Duncan and then gave him a wan smile. 'Go ahead,' Duncan said patiently. 'Play with the castle. Wreck it if you want. I don't care.'

The child's head, cocked to one side, stayed motionless. The small hands grasped each other. Duncan fell to his knees and, with a face suffused with emotion, said, 'I don't frighten you, do I? I'm a coward. I can't frighten you. Can I?'

'*Comment, Monsieur?*' the little boy said. He was quite close to tears.

Duncan gently took the child's hand and patted one of the ziggurats. A few grains of sand crumbled off. Duncan pointed to the little boy, then to the castle. Then, still holding the little boy's hand, he walked him all around the castle. The little boy began to smile. He looked up at Duncan.

'*Oui,*' Duncan said excitedly. 'For you. *Votre,*' he shouted in triumph. '*Pour vous, s'il vous plaît,* or whatever.'

'*Pour moi, Monsieur?*'

'*Oui,*' Duncan said. '*Oui.*'

'*Tout château? Vraiment?*' The child clapped his hands.

A little later, just as we were finishing a new super three-way tunnel, just as Duncan was asking me, 'He's happy now, isn't he? I haven't hurt his feelings, have I?' we heard a woman's voice. The little boy cried out in reply, and a woman came running – a tall, fair woman, with large, intent, genteel blue eyes. She swept down on the little boy and scooped him up, and when he was safe in her arms, she turned and glared suspiciously at us. We were drunk and unshaven, with bloodshot eyes and dirty clothes. Duncan made a bow of sorts, and explained that we were Americans. The woman exclaimed, and then a smile came over her face. She stepped forward and shook Duncan's hand. '*Enchanté, Monsieur*,' she said brusquely, and then, '*Enchanté*,' as she shook my hand, too. She stood a moment, holding her child, talking to us slowly and kindly, in careful French. She asked us where in America we came from, and nodded at our replies. She asked us if we planned to be in France long, and when we said a year, she nodded her head again and said we were *très sage*. Her voice was both grave and soft, and at first Duncan and I stared at her; Duncan caught himself up, and sent me a dirty glance, and then we both, shyly, stared at the ground. If we needed water, she said, we could come to the back door and get it. She had to cook dinner for the boy's grandparents. Her husband was working late in Bordeaux. She shook hands with us again, and then, still carrying the child, she went back into the garden. She was wearing a light-blue skirt that blew back and forth against the iron bars of the gate as she closed it.

Our wine was gone. The sunset was beginning, its pink splendor reflected in Duncan's bony kneecaps. He sat back on the sand, talking, piling the sand over his legs. 'You know what makes their figures so beautiful? Work. They don't use these lousy labor-saving devices. They bend, they walk, they ride bicycles. Did you see how small her waist was? There's no use pretending that American women are as charming.'

'That's not true,' I said. 'France is fine, but –' All around me the air was perfumed, and the sunset was unraveling its tinted streamers across the sky. 'You know. We're seeing it for the first time. I'm sure America –'

Duncan grew quite fierce. He told me I was being stubborn, defensive. Just because I didn't fit. After all, I hadn't even said a word to the woman.

'That's true,' I admitted lazily. 'But that's because I was so impressed I couldn't speak.' I propped myself on my elbow and looked at him. I was smiling – a little uncertainly, it's true, as one does at an elder brother, or at someone inexpressibly dear, whose approval one longs for. Duncan gave me a sidelong glance. Then, several seconds after I'd spoken, we both laughed, as if I'd been quite witty.

The shadows, blue, liquid, were gathering across the beach. There we were, the two of us, with all of our fears and flaws, and our hopes that we didn't really believe in, and our failures; there we were, nineteen and twenty. From one of the houses along the beach came the strains of a phonograph playing 'La Vie en Rose'. Duncan began to hum the song. The kindness of France spread around us like the incoming night. I listened to Duncan and the distant phonograph and the dreamlike rush of the waves, and I knew I would survive my youth and be forgiven.

KATHERINE MANSFIELD

Mr and Mrs Dove

Of course he knew – no man better – that he hadn't a ghost of a chance, he hadn't an earthly. The very idea of such a thing was preposterous. So preposterous that he'd perfectly understand it if her father – well, whatever her father chose to do he'd perfectly understand. In fact, nothing short of desperation, nothing short of the fact that this was positively his last day in England for God knows how long, would have screwed him up to it. And even now . . . He chose a tie out of the chest of drawers, a blue and cream check tie, and sat on the side of his bed. Supposing she replied, 'What impertinence!' would he be surprised? Not in the least, he decided, turning up his soft collar and turning it down over the tie. He expected her to say something like that. He didn't see, if he looked at the affair dead soberly, what else she could say.

Here he was! And nervously he tied a bow in front of the mirror, jammed his hair down with both hands, pulled out the flaps of his jacket pockets. Making between £500 and £600 a year on a fruit farm in – of all places – Rhodesia. No capital. Not a penny coming to him. No chance of his income increasing for at least four years. As for looks and all that sort of thing, he was completely out of the running. He couldn't even boast of top-hole health, for the East Africa business had knocked him out so thoroughly that he'd had to take six months' leave. He was still fearfully pale – worse even than usual this afternoon, he thought, bending forward and peering into the mirror. Good heavens! What had happened? His hair looked almost bright green. Dash it all, he hadn't green hair at all events. That was a bit too steep. And then the green light trembled in the glass; it was the shadow from the tree outside. Reggie turned away, took out his cigarette case, but remembering how the mater hated him to smoke in his bedroom, put it back again and drifted over to the chest of drawers. No, he was dashed if he could think of one blessed thing in his favour, while she . . . Ah! . . . He stopped dead, folded his arms, and leaned hard against the chest of drawers.

And in spite of her position, her father's wealth, the fact that she

66

was an only child and far and away the most popular girl in the neighbourhood; in spite of her beauty and her cleverness – cleverness! – it was a great deal more than that, there was really nothing she couldn't do; he fully believed, had it been necessary, she would have been a genius at anything – in spite of the fact that her parents adored her, and she them, and they'd as soon let her go all that way as . . . In spite of every single thing you could think of, so terrific was his love that he couldn't help hoping. Well, was it hope? Or was this queer, timid longing to have the chance of looking after her, of making it his job to see that she had everything she wanted, and that nothing came near her that wasn't perfect – just love? How he loved her! He squeezed hard against the chest of drawers and murmured to it, 'I love her, I love her!' And just for the moment he was with her on the way to Umtali. It was night. She sat in a corner asleep. Her soft chin was tucked into her soft collar, her gold-brown lashes lay on her cheeks. He doted on her delicate little nose, her perfect lips, her ear like a baby's and the gold-brown curl that half covered it. They were passing through the jungle. It was warm and dark and far away. Then she woke up and said, 'Have I been asleep?' and he answered, 'Yes. Are you all right? Here, let me –' And he leaned forward to . . . He bent over her. This was such bliss that he could dream no further. But it gave him the courage to bound downstairs, to snatch his straw hat from the hall, and to say as he closed the front door, 'Well, I can only try my luck, that's all.'

But his luck gave him a nasty jar, to say the least, almost immediately. Promenading up and down the garden path with Chinny and Biddy, the ancient Pekes, was the mater. Of course Reginald was fond of the mater and all that. She – she meant well, she had no end of grit, and so on. But there was no denying it, she was rather a grim parent. And there had been moments, many of them, in Reggie's life, before Uncle Alick died and left him the fruit farm, when he was convinced that to be a widow's only son was about the worst punishment a chap could have. And what made it rougher than ever was that she was positively all that he had. She wasn't only a combined parent, as it were, but she had quarrelled with all her own and the governor's relations before Reggie had won his first trouser pockets. So that whenever Reggie was homesick out there, sitting on his dark veranda by starlight, while the gramophone cried, 'Dear, what is Life but Love?' his only vision was of the mater, tall and stout, rustling down the garden path, with Chinny and Biddy at her heels . . .

The mater, with her scissors outspread to snap the head of a dead something or other, stopped at the sight of Reggie.

'You are not going out, Reginald?' she asked, seeing that he was.

'I'll be back for tea, mater,' said Reggie weakly, plunging his hands into his jacket pockets.

Snip. Off came a head. Reggie almost jumped.

'I should have thought you could have spared your mother your last afternoon,' said she.

Silence. The Pekes stared. They understood every word of the mater's. Biddy lay down with her tongue poked out; she was so fat and glossy she looked like a lump of half-melted toffee. But Chinny's porcelain eyes gloomed at Reginald, and he sniffed faintly as though the whole world were one unpleasant smell. Snip, went the scissors again. Poor little beggars; they were getting it!

'And where are you going, if your mother may ask?' asked the mater.

It was over at last, but Reggie did not slow down until he was out of sight of the house and half-way to Colonel Proctor's. Then only he noticed what a top-hole afternoon it was. It had been raining all the morning, late summer rain, warm, heavy, quick, and now the sky was clear, except for a long tail of little clouds, like ducklings, sailing over the forest. There was just enough wind to shake the last drops off the trees; one warm star splashed on his hand. Ping! – another drummed on his hat. The empty road gleamed, the hedges smelled of briar, and how big and bright the hollyhocks glowed in the cottage gardens. And here was Colonel Proctor's – here it was already. His hand was on the gate, his elbow jogged the syringa bushes, and petals and pollen scattered over his coat sleeve. But wait a bit. This was too quick altogether. He'd meant to think the whole thing out again. Here, steady. But he was walking up the path, with the huge rose bushes on either side. It can't be done like this. But his hand had grasped the bell, given it a pull, and started it pealing wildly, as if he'd come to say the house was on fire. The house-maid must have been in the hall, too, for the front door flashed open, and Reggie was shut in the empty drawing-room before that confounded bell had stopped ringing. Strangely enough, when it did, the big room, shadowy, with someone's parasol lying on top of the grand piano, bucked him up – or rather, excited him. It was so quiet, and yet in one moment the door would open, and his fate be decided. The feeling was not unlike that of being at the dentist's; he was almost reckless. But at the same time, to his immense surprise, Reggie heard himself saying, 'Lord, Thou knowest, Thou hast not done *much* for me . . .' That pulled him up; that made him realize again how dead serious it was. Too late. The door handle turned. Anne came in, crossed the shadowy space between them, gave him her hand, and said, in her small, soft voice, 'I'm so sorry, father is out. And mother is having a day in town, hat-hunting. There's only me to entertain you, Reggie.'

Reggie gasped, pressed his own hat to his jacket buttons, and stammered out, 'As a matter of fact, I've only come . . . to say goodbye.'

'Oh!' cried Anne softly – she stepped back from him and her grey eyes danced – 'what a *very* short visit!'

Then, watching him, her chin tilted, she laughed outright, a long soft peal, and walked away from him over to the piano, and leaned against it, playing with the tassel of the parasol.

'I'm so sorry,' she said, 'to be laughing like this. I don't know why I do. It's just a bad ha-habit.' And suddenly she stamped her grey shoe, and took a pocket-handkerchief out of her white woolly jacket. 'I really must conquer it, it's too absurd,' said she.

'Good heavens, Anne,' cried Reggie, 'I love to hear you laughing! I can't imagine anything more –'

But the truth was, and they both knew it, she wasn't always laughing; it wasn't really a habit. Only ever since the day they'd met, ever since that very first moment, for some strange reason that Reggie wished to God he understood, Anne had laughed at him. Why? It didn't matter where they were or what they were talking about. They might begin by being as serious as possible, dead serious – at any rate as far as he was concerned – but then suddenly, in the middle of a sentence, Anne would glance at him, and a little quick quiver passed over her face. Her lips parted, her eyes danced, and she began laughing.

Another queer thing about it was, Reggie had an idea she didn't herself know why she laughed. He had seen her turn away, frown, suck in her cheeks, press her hands together. But it was no use. The long, soft peal sounded, even while she cried, 'I don't know why I'm laughing.' It was a mystery . . .

Now she tucked the handkerchief away. 'Do sit down,' said she. 'And smoke, won't you? There are cigarettes in that little box beside you. I'll have one too.' He lighted a match for her, and as she bent forward he saw the tiny flame glow in the pearl ring she wore. 'It is tomorrow that you're going, isn't it?' said Anne.

'Yes, tomorrow as ever is,' said Reggie, and he blew a little fan of smoke. Why on earth was he so nervous? Nervous wasn't the word for it.

'It's – it's frightfully hard to believe,' he added.

'Yes – isn't it?' said Anne softly, and she leaned forward and rolled the point of her cigarette round the green ash-tray. How beautiful she looked like that! – simply beautiful – and she was so small in that immense chair. Reginald's heart swelled with tenderness, but it was her voice, her soft voice, that made him tremble. 'I feel you've been here for years,' she said.

Reginald took a deep breath of his cigarette. 'It's ghastly, this idea of going back,' he said.

'*Coo-roo-coo-coo-coo,*' sounded from the quiet.

'But you're fond of being out there, aren't you?' said Anne. She hooked her finger through her pearl necklace. 'Father was saying only the other night how lucky he thought you were to have a life of your own.' And she looked up at him. Reginald's smile was rather wan. 'I don't feel fearfully lucky,' he said lightly.

'*Roo-coo-coo-coo,*' came again. And Anne murmured, 'You mean it's lonely.'

'Oh, it isn't the loneliness I care about,' said Reginald, and he stumped his cigarette savagely on the green ash-tray. 'I could stand any amount of it, used to like it even. It's the idea of –' Suddenly, to his horror, he felt himself blushing.

'*Roo-coo-coo-coo! Roo-coo-coo-coo!*'

Anne jumped up. 'Come and say goodbye to my doves,' she said. 'They've been moved to the side veranda. You do like doves, don't you, Reggie?'

'Awfully,' said Reggie, so fervently that as he opened the french window for her and stood to one side, Anne ran forward and laughed at the doves instead.

To and fro, to and fro over the fine red sand on the floor of the dove house, walked the two doves. One was always in front of the other. One ran forward, uttering a little cry, and the other followed, solemnly bowing and bowing. 'You see,' explained Anne, 'the one in front, she's Mrs Dove. She looks at Mr Dove and gives that little laugh and runs forward, and he follows her, bowing and bowing. And that makes her laugh again. Away she runs, and after her,' cried Anne, and she sat back on her heels, 'comes poor Mr Dove, bowing and bowing . . . and that's their whole life. They never do anything else, you know.' She got up and took some yellow grains out of a bag on the roof of the dove house. 'When you think of them, out in Rhodesia, Reggie, you can be sure that is what they will be doing . . .'

Reggie gave no sign of having seen the doves or of having heard a word. For the moment he was conscious only of the immense effort it took to tear his secret out of himself and offer it to Anne. 'Anne, do you think you could ever care for me?' It was done. It was over. And in the little pause that followed Reginald saw the garden open to the light, the blue quivering sky, the flutter of leaves on the veranda poles, and Anne turning over the grains of maize on her palm with one finger. Then slowly she shut her hand, and the new world faded as she murmured slowly, 'No, never in that way.' But he had scarcely time to feel anything before she walked quickly away, and he followed her down the steps, along the garden path, under the pink rose arches, across the lawn. There, with the gay herbaceous border behind her, Anne faced Reginald. 'It isn't that I'm not awfully fond of you,' she said. 'I am. But' – her eyes widened – 'not in the way' – a quiver passed over her face – 'one ought to be fond of –' Her lips parted, and she couldn't stop herself. She began laughing. 'There, you see, you see,' she cried, 'it's your check t-tie. Even at this moment, when one would think one really would be solemn, your tie reminds me fearfully of the bow-tie that cats wear in pictures! Oh, please forgive me for being so horrid, please!'

Reggie caught hold of her little warm hand. 'There's no question of forgiving you,' he said quickly. 'How could there be? And I do believe I know why I make you laugh. It's because you're so far above me in every way that I am somehow ridiculous. I see that, Anne. But if I were to –'

'No, no.' Anne squeezed his hand hard. 'It's not that. That's all wrong. I'm not far above you at all. You're much better than I am. You're marvellously unselfish and . . . and kind and simple. I'm none of those things. You don't know me. I'm the most awful character,' said Anne. 'Please don't interrupt. And besides, that's not the point. The point is' – she shook her head – 'I couldn't possibly marry a man I laughed at. Surely you see that. The man I marry –' breathed Anne softly. She broke off. She drew her hand away, and looking at Reggie she smiled strangely, dreamily. 'The man I marry –'

And it seemed to Reggie that a tall, handsome, brilliant stranger stepped in front of him and took his place – the kind of man that Anne and he had seen often at the theatre, walking on to the stage from nowhere, without a word catching the heroine in his arms, and after one long, tremendous look, carrying her off to anywhere . . .

Reggie bowed to his vision. 'Yes, I see,' he said huskily.

'Do you?' said Anne. 'Oh, I do hope you do. Because I feel so horrid about it. It's so hard to explain. You know I've never –' She stopped. Reggie looked at her. She was smiling. 'Isn't it funny?' she said. 'I can say anything to you. I always have been able to from the very beginning.'

He tried to smile, to say 'I'm glad.' She went on. 'I've never known anyone I like as much as I like you. I've never felt so happy with anyone. But I'm sure it's not what people and what books mean when they talk about love. Do you understand? Oh, if you only knew how horrid I feel. But we'd be like . . . like Mr and Mrs Dove.'

That did it. That seemed to Reginald final, and so terribly true that he could hardly bear it. 'Don't drive it home,' he said, and he turned away from Anne and looked across the lawn. There was the gardener's cottage, with the dark ilex-tree beside it. A wet, blue thumb of transparent smoke hung above the chimney. It didn't look real. How his throat ached! Could he speak? He had a shot. 'I must be getting along home,' he croaked, and he began walking across the lawn. But Anne ran after him. 'No, don't. You can't go yet,' she said imploringly. 'You can't possibly go away feeling like that.' And she stared up at him frowning, biting her lip.

'Oh, that's all right,' said Reggie, giving himself a shake. 'I'll . . . I'll –' And he waved his hand as much as to say 'get over it'.

'But this is awful,' said Anne. She clasped her hands and stood in front of him. 'Surely you do see how fatal it would be for us to marry, don't you?'

'Oh, quite, quite,' said Reggie, looking at her with haggard eyes.

'How wrong, how wicked, feeling as I do. I mean, it's all very well for Mr and Mrs Dove. But imagine that in real life – imagine it!'

'Oh, absolutely,' said Reggie, and he started to walk on. But again Anne stopped him. She tugged at his sleeve, and to his astonishment, this time, instead of laughing, she looked like a little girl who was going to cry.

'Then why, if you understand, are you so un-unhappy?' she wailed. 'Why do you mind so fearfully? Why do you look so aw-awful?'

Reggie gulped, and again he waved something away. 'I can't help it,' he said, 'I've had a blow. If I cut off now, I'll be able to –'

'How can you talk of cutting off now?' said Anne scornfully. She stamped her foot at Reggie; she was crimson. 'How can you be so cruel? I can't let you go until I know for certain that you are just as happy as you were before you asked me to marry you. Surely you must see that, it's so simple.'

But it did not seem at all simple to Reginald. It seemed impossibly difficult.

'Even if I can't marry you, how can I know that you're all that way away, with only that awful mother to write to, and that you're miserable, and that it's all my fault?'

'It's not your fault. Don't think that. It's just fate.' Reggie took her hand off his sleeve and kissed it. 'Don't pity me, dear little Anne,' he said gently. And this time he nearly ran, under the pink arches, along the garden path.

'*Roo-coo-coo-coo! Roo-coo-coo-coo!*' sounded from the veranda. 'Reggie, Reggie,' from the garden.

He stopped, he turned. But when she saw his timid, puzzled look, she gave a little laugh.

'Come back, Mr Dove,' said Anne. And Reginald came slowly across the lawn.

ANTON CHEKHOV

The House with the Mezzanine

(An Artist's Story)

I

About six or seven years ago I was staying in a district of T—
province, on the estate of a young landowner by the name of
Belokurov – a very early riser who sported a peasant jerkin, drank
beer in the evenings and who was always complaining to me that
no one, anywhere, really appreciated him. He had a cottage in the
garden, while I lived in the old manor house, in a vast colonnaded
ballroom which, apart from the wide sofa on which I slept and a
table where I played patience, was devoid of furniture. Even in
calm weather there was always a peculiar droning in the ancient
Amos stoves and during thunderstorms the whole house shook as
if it were splitting into small pieces. It was rather frightening,
especially at night when the ten big windows were suddenly all
aglow in the lightning.

Doomed to perpetual idleness, I didn't do a thing and would gaze
for hours on end through the windows at the sky, birds, avenues; I
would read everything that came with the post – and I slept.
Sometimes I would go out and wander around until late evening.

Once, as I was returning home, I happened to stray into the
grounds of a manor house that was unfamiliar to me. The sun was
already sinking and the evening shadows lay across the flowering
rye. Two rows of closely planted, towering fir trees stood like solid,
unbroken walls, forming a handsome, sombre avenue. I easily
climbed the fence and walked down the avenue, slipping on pine
needles that lay about two inches deep on the ground. It was quiet
and dark – only high up in the tree tops a vivid golden light quivered here and there and transformed spiders' webs into shimmering
rainbows. The smell of resin from the firs was almost stifling. Then
I turned into a long avenue of lime trees. And here too all was
neglect and age. Last year's leaves rustled sadly underfoot and in

the dusk shadows lurked between the trees. In the old fruit orchard to the right an oriole sang feebly, reluctantly, most probably because he too was old. But then the limes ended. I went past a white house with a terrace and a kind of mezzanine or attic storey – and suddenly a vista opened up: a courtyard, a large pond with bathing place, a clump of green willows, and a village on the far bank, with a slender, tall bell-tower whose cross glittered in the setting sun. For one fleeting moment I felt the enchantment of something very close and familiar to me, as though I had once seen this landscape as a child.

At the white stone gates that led from the courtyard into open country – sturdy, old-fashioned gates surmounted by lions – two young girls were standing. One of them – the elder, who was slim, pale and very pretty, with a mass of auburn hair and a small stubborn mouth – wore a stern expression and hardly looked at me. But the other girl, still very young – no more than seventeen or eighteen – similarly slim and pale, with large mouth and big eyes, looked at me in astonishment as I passed by. She said something in English and seemed embarrassed. And it seemed that I had long known these two charming faces. I returned home with the feeling that it had all been a lovely dream.

Soon afterwards when I was strolling with Belokurov one day around noon by the house, a light sprung carriage suddenly drove into the yard, rustling over the grass: in it was one of the girls – the elder. She was collecting money for some villagers whose houses had burnt down. Without looking at us she gave a serious, detailed report about how many houses had burnt down in the village of Siyanov, how many women and children had been left homeless and what immediate measures the relief committee (to which she now belonged) was proposing to take. After getting us to sign the list she put it away and immediately started saying goodbye.

'You've quite forgotten us, Pyotr Petrovich,' she told Belokurov as she gave him her hand. 'Please come and see us – and if Monsieur N— (she mentioned my name) would like to see some admirers of his work and fancies paying us a visit, Mama and I would be really delighted.' I bowed.

When she had driven off Pyotr Petrovich started telling me about her. He said that the girl was of good family and that her name was Lidiya Volchaninov. The estate on which she lived with her mother and sister – like the large village on the other side of the pond – was called Shelkovka. Her father had once held an important post in Moscow and was a high-ranking civil servant when he died. Although they were very well-off, the Volchaninovs never left their estate, summer or winter. Lidiya taught in their own rural school in Shelkovka, at a monthly salary of twenty-five roubles. She spent nothing else besides this money on herself and was proud of earning her own living.

'An interesting family,' said Belokurov. 'We'll go and visit them one day if you like. They'd be delighted to see you.'

One day after dinner (it was some sort of holiday) we remembered the Volchaninovs and went over to see them at Shelkovka. The mother and her two daughters were at home. Yekaterina Pavlovna, the mother, obviously once very pretty but now plump for her age, sad, short-winded and absent-minded, tried to entertain me with talk about painting. Having learnt from her daughter that I might be coming to see them at Shelkovka she hurriedly mentioned two or three of my landscapes that she had seen at Moscow exhibitions, and now she asked me what I wanted to express in them. Lidiya – or Lida as she was called at home – talked more to Belokurov than to me. Serious and unsmiling, she asked him why he wasn't on the local council and had so far never attended a single meeting.

'It's not right!' she said reproachfully. 'It's not right. You should be ashamed of yourself.'

'That's true, perfectly true,' her mother agreed. 'It's just not right!'

'The whole district is under Balagin's thumb,' Lida continued, turning to me. 'He himself is chairman of the council, he's handed out all the jobs in the district to his nephews and sons-in-law, and he does just what he likes. We must take a stand. The young people must form a pressure group, but you can see for yourself what our young people are like. You ought to be ashamed of yourself, Pyotr Petrovich!'

While we were discussing the local council, Zhenya, the younger sister, said nothing. She never took part in serious conversations: in that family she wasn't considered grown-up at all – just as if she were a little girl they called her Missy, the name she had given her governess as a child. The whole time she kept looking at me inquisitively and when I was examining the photographs in the album she explained: 'That's Uncle . . . that's my godfather . . .' and she ran her finger over the photographs, touching me with her shoulder like a child, so that I had a close view of her delicate, undeveloped bosom, her slender shoulders, her plait and her slim, tight-belted waist.

We played croquet and tennis, strolled in the garden, drank tea, after which we had a leisurely supper. After that vast, empty colon-naded ballroom I somehow felt at home in that small, cosy house where there were no oleographs on the walls and where the servants were spoken to politely. Thanks to Lida and Missy, everything seemed so pure and youthful: it was all so civilized. Over supper Lida again talked to Belokurov about the council, about Balagin and school libraries. She was a vivacious, sincere girl with strong views. And it was fascinating listening to her, although she said a lot, and in a loud voice – perhaps because that was how she was used to speaking in school. On the other hand my friend Pyotr Petrovich, who still retained the student habit of turning everything into an argument, spoke boringly, listlessly and longwindedly – he was obvi-ously most anxious to appear advanced and clever. He waved his arms about and upset a sauceboat with his sleeve, so that a large pool of gravy formed on the tablecloth. But I was the only one who seemed to notice it.

It was quiet and dark when we returned.

'Good breeding isn't that you don't upset gravy on tablecloths, but that you don't notice when someone else does it,' sighed Belokurov. 'Yes, they're a splendid, cultured family. I'm out of touch with refined people – ever so badly out of touch! Nothing but work, work, work!'

He spoke of all the work involved in being a model farmer. But I thought to myself: what an unpleasant, lazy fellow! Whenever he spoke about anything serious he would laboriously drag out his words with a great deal of 'er's and 'erring'. And he worked as he spoke – slowly, always late, always missing deadlines. I had little confidence in his efficiency, if only because he carried around for weeks on end in his pockets the letters I'd given him to post.

'The hardest thing,' he muttered as he walked beside me, 'is not having your work appreciated by anyone! You get no thanks at all!'

II

I became a regular visitor at the Volchaninovs. Usually I would sit on the bottom step of the terrace, depressed by feelings of dissatisfaction with myself, regretting that my life was passing so quickly, so uninterestingly. I kept thinking how marvellous it would be if I could somehow tear my heart, which felt so heavy, out of my chest. Just then they were talking on the terrace and I could hear the rustle of dresses, the sound of someone turning over pages in a book. I soon became used to Lida receiving the sick and handing out books during the day. Often she would go off to the village with a parasol over her bare head, while in the evenings she would hold forth in a loud voice about councils and schools. Whenever the conversation turned to serious matters, that slim, pretty, invariably severe young lady with her small, finely modelled mouth, would coldly tell me:

'That's of no interest to you.'

I did not appeal to her at all. She did not like me because I was a landscape painter who did not portray the hardships of the common people in my canvases and because – so she thought – I was indifferent to all her deepest beliefs. I remember, when I was once travelling along the shores of Lake Baikal I met a young Buryat girl on horseback, wearing a smock and cotton trousers. I asked her to sell me her pipe, but while we were talking she looked contemptuously at my European face and hat. All of a sudden she became tired of talking and galloped off, uttering wild yells. And in the same way Lida looked down on me, because we were from different worlds. She didn't express her dislike openly, but I could sense it. Sitting on the bottom step of the terrace I felt irritated and told her that dishing out treatment to peasants without being a doctor was a fraud: it was easy enough to play the Good Samaritan when one had five thousand acres of one's own.

But her sister Missy didn't have a care in the world. Like me, she lived a life of complete idleness. The moment she got up in the morning she would take a book and sit reading in a deep armchair on the terrace with her feet barely touching the ground; or she would escape with her book to the lime-tree avenue, or go beyond the gates into the open fields. She would read all day long, eagerly poring over her book and one could only tell from her occasionally tired and glazed look, and her extreme pallor, how taxing this really was for her. When I came she would blush slightly on seeing me, put down her book, look into my face with her big eyes and tell me enthusiastically what had been happening – for example, that the chimney in the servants' quarters had caught fire, or that a workman had hooked a large fish in the pond. On weekdays she usually went around in a brightly coloured blouse and navy blue skirt. We would go for walks together, pick cherries for jam or go boating and whenever she jumped up to reach the cherries or plied the oars her thin, delicate arms showed through her full sleeves. Occasionally, I would sketch while she stood beside me, looking on admiringly.

One Sunday at the end of July I went over to the Volchaninovs at about nine in the morning and I walked through the park, keeping as far as I could away from the house, looking for white mushrooms which were plentiful that summer and putting down markers so that I could return later with Zhenya to pick them. A warm breeze was blowing. I saw Zhenya and her mother, both in bright Sunday dresses, coming back from church. Zhenya was holding onto her hat in the wind. Then I could hear them having breakfast on the terrace.

For a carefree person like myself, forever trying to find an excuse for his perpetual idleness, these Sunday mornings on our estates in summer always had a particular charm. When the green garden, still wet with dew, gleams in the sun and seems to be rejoicing; when there is the scent of mignonette and oleander by the house; when the young people have just returned from church and are having breakfast in the garden; when everyone is dressed so charmingly and is so gay; when you know that all these healthy, well-fed, handsome people will be doing nothing all day long – then one wishes life to be always like that. And these were my thoughts as I walked through the garden, ready to wander just like this, idly and aimlessly, all day, all summer.

Zhenya came out with a basket and she looked as if she knew or sensed she would find me in the garden. We gathered mushrooms and when she asked me something she would go on ahead, so that she could see my face.

'There was a miracle in our village yesterday,' she said. 'That lame Pelageya's been ill the whole year, no doctors or medicine did her any good. But yesterday an old woman recited a spell and she got better.'

'That's nothing much,' I said. 'You shouldn't look for miracles only among the sick and old women. Isn't health a miracle? And life itself? Anything we can't understand is a miracle.'

'But aren't you scared of things you don't understand?'

'No, I face up to phenomena I don't understand boldly and I don't allow myself to be intimidated. I'm on a higher level than them. Man should consider himself superior to lions, tigers, stars – to everything in nature – even those things he doesn't understand and thinks of as miraculous. Otherwise he's not a man but a mouse, afraid of everything.'

Zhenya thought that, as I was an artist, I must know a great deal and could accurately guess what I didn't know. She wanted me to lead her into the realm of the eternal and beautiful, into that loftier world in which, she fancied, I was quite at home. And she spoke to me of God, of immortality, of the miraculous. I refused to admit that I and my imagination would perish for ever after death. 'Yes, people are immortal. Yes, eternal life awaits us,' I replied. And she listened and believed – and she did not ask for proof.

When we were going back to the house she suddenly stopped and said: 'Lida's a remarkable person, isn't she? I love her dearly and I would readily sacrifice my life for her. But tell me,' Zhenya continued, touching my sleeve with her finger, 'tell me why you're always arguing with her? Why do you get so exasperated?'

'Because she's in the wrong.'

Zhenya shook her head and tears came into her eyes. 'I just don't understand,' she murmured.

Lida had just returned from somewhere and she stood by the front porch, crop in hand, graceful and beautiful in the sunlight; she was giving orders to one of the workmen. Talking very loudly, she hurriedly saw two or three patients and then, with a preoccupied, busy look, marched through the rooms, opening one cupboard after the other, after which she went up to the attic storey. For a long time they looked for her, to tell her dinner was ready, and by the time she came down we were already finishing our soup. I remember and cherish all these little details and I vividly remember the whole of that day, although it wasn't particularly eventful. After dinner Zhenya lay in a deep armchair reading, while I sat on the bottom step of the terrace. We said nothing. The sky was overcast and a fine drizzle had set in. It was hot, the wind had long dropped and it seemed the day would never end. Yekaterina Pavlovna came out onto the terrace with a fan – she looked half asleep.

'Oh, Mama!' Zhenya said, kissing her hand. 'It's not healthy sleeping during the day.'

They adored each other. When one went into the garden, the other would be standing on the terrace looking towards the trees, calling out: 'Hullo, Zhenya!' or 'Mama, where are you?' They always prayed together, both shared the same faith and they understood one another perfectly, even when they said nothing. And they both had the same attitude towards people. Yekaterina Pavlovna also took to me in no time at all and when I didn't appear for two or three days she would send someone over to inquire if I was well. She would also gaze admiringly at my sketches and would rattle away about all the latest news – just as readily as Missy; and she often confided family secrets to me.

She revered her elder daughter. Lida never made up to her and would only discuss serious matters with her. She lived a life apart and for her mother and sister she was godlike, something of an enigma, just like an admiral who never leaves his cabin.

'Our Lida's a remarkable person, isn't she?' her mother would often say.

And now, as the drizzle came down, we talked about Lida.

'She's a remarkable person,' her mother said, adding in a muted, conspiratorial tone as she glanced anxiously over her shoulder: 'You don't find many like her. Only I'm getting rather worried, you know. The school, the dispensaries, books – all that's most commendable, but why go to such extremes? After all, she's twenty-three, it's time she thought seriously about herself. What with all those books and dispensaries her life will be over before she even notices it . . . it's time she got married.'

Pale from reading, her hair in disarray, Zhenya raised her head a little, looked at her mother and said as if to herself: 'Mama, everything depends on God's will.'

And once again she buried herself in her book.

Belokurov arrived in his peasant jerkin and embroidered smock. We played croquet and tennis. And then, after dark, we enjoyed a leisurely supper. Again Lida talked about schools and that Balagin, who had the whole district under his thumb. As I left the Volchaninovs that evening I took away with me an impression of a long, idle day

– and the sad realization that everything in this world comes to an end, however long it may appear. Zhenya saw us to the gates and, perhaps because she had spent the whole day with me from morning to night, I felt that without her everything was such a bore and I realized how dear this whole charming family was to me. And for the first time that summer I had the urge to paint.

'Tell me, why do you lead such a boring, drab life?' I asked Belokurov as we went back. 'My own life is boring, difficult, monotonous, because I'm an artist. I'm an odd kind of chap; since I was young I've been plagued by feelings of hatred, by frustration with myself, by lack of belief in my work. I've always been poor, I'm a vagrant. But as for you – you're a normal, healthy man, a landowner, a squire. So why do you lead such a boring life? Why do you take so little from it? For instance, why have you never fallen in love with Lida or Zhenya?'

'You're forgetting that I love another woman,' Belokurov replied.

He was talking of his companion Lyubov Ivanovna, who lived in the cottage with him. Every day I saw that plump, podgy, self-important woman – rather like a fattened goose – strolling around the garden in a traditional beaded folk costume, always carrying a parasol. The servants were always calling her in for a meal, or for tea. Three years ago she had rented one of the holiday cottages and had simply stayed on to live with Belokurov – for ever, it seemed. She was about ten years older than him and ruled him with a rod of iron – so much so that he had to ask permission whenever he wanted to go somewhere. She often sobbed in a deep, masculine voice and then I would send word that I would move out of the flat if she didn't stop. And stop she did.

When we were back Belokurov sat on my couch with a pensive frown, while I paced the room, feeling a gentle excitement, as if I were in love. I wanted to talk about the Volchaninovs.

'Lida could only fall in love with a council worker who is as devoted as she is to hospitals and schools,' I said. 'Oh, for a girl like her one would not only do welfare work but even wear out a pair of iron boots, like the girl in the fairy-tale! And there's Missy. Isn't she charming, this Missy!'

Belokurov embarked on a long-winded discussion about the malady of the age – pessimism – dragging out those 'er's. He spoke confidently and his tone suggested that I was quarrelling with him.

Hundreds of miles of bleak, monotonous, scorched steppe can never be so utterly depressing as someone who just sits and chatters away – and you have no idea when he's going to leave you in peace.

'Pessimism or optimism have nothing to do with it,' I said, irritably. 'The point is, ninety-nine people out of a hundred have no brains.'

Belokurov took this personally and left in a huff.

III

'The prince is staying in Malozyomovo and sends his regards,' Lida told her mother. She had just come in from somewhere and was removing her gloves. 'He had many interesting things to tell us . . . He promised to raise the question of a clinic for Malozyomovo with the council again, but stressed that there was little hope.' Turning to me she said: 'I'm sorry, I keep forgetting that kind of thing's of no interest to you.'

This really got my back up.

'Why isn't it interesting?' I asked, shrugging my shoulders. 'You don't want to know my opinion, but I assure you that the question interests me a great deal.'

'Really?'

'Yes, really. In my opinion they don't need a clinic at Malozyomovo.'

My irritation was infectious. She looked at me, screwed up her eyes and asked: 'What do they need then? Landscape paintings?'

'They don't need landscapes either. They don't need anything.'

She finished taking off her gloves and unfolded the paper that had just been collected from the post office. A minute later she said quietly, as if trying to control herself: 'Last week Anna died in childbirth. If there'd been a clinic near her she'd be alive now. And I really do think that our fine gentlemen landscape painters should have some opinions on that score.'

'I have very definite views on that score, I assure you,' I replied – and she hid behind her paper as if she didn't want to listen. 'To my mind, with things as they are, clinics, schools, libraries, dispensaries only serve to enslave people. The peasants are weighed down by a great chain and instead of breaking this chain you're only adding new links – that's what I think.'

She raised her eyes and smiled ironically as I continued, trying to catch the main thread of my argument:

'What matters is not Anna dying in childbirth, but that all these peasant Annas, Mavras and Pelageyas toil away from dawn to dusk and that this unremitting labour makes them ill. All their lives they go in fear and trembling for their sick and hungry children, dreading death and illness. All their lives they're being treated for some illness. They fade away before their time and die in filth and stench. And as their children grow up it's the same old story. And so the centuries pass and untold millions of people live worse than animals, wondering where their next meal will come from, hounded by constant fear. The whole horror of their situation is that they have no time to think of their souls, no time to remember that they were created in the image and likeness of their Creator. Famine, irrational fears, unceasing toil – these are like avalanches, blocking all paths to spiritual activity, which is precisely what distinguishes man from beast and makes life worth living. You come to their aid with hospitals and schools, but this doesn't free them from their shackles: on the contrary, you enslave them even more since, by introducing fresh prejudices you increase the number of their needs – not to mention the fact that they have to pay the council for their plasters and books – and so they have to slave away even harder.'

'I'm not going to argue with you,' Lida said, putting down her paper. 'I've heard it all before. But I'll say one thing: you can't just sit twiddling your thumbs. True, we're not the saviours of humanity and perhaps we make lots of mistakes, but we are doing what we can and we are right. The loftiest, most sacred task for any civilized man is to serve his neighbours – and we try to serve them as best we can. You don't like it, but there's no pleasing everyone.'

'True, Lida, that's true,' her mother said.

In Lida's presence she was always rather timid, glancing nervously at her when she spoke and afraid of saying something superfluous or irrelevant. And she never contradicted her:

'True, Lida, that's true,' she always agreed.

'Teaching peasants to read and write, books full of wretched maxims and sayings, clinics, cannot reduce either ignorance or the death-rate, just as the light from your windows cannot illuminate this huge garden,' I said. 'You contribute nothing by meddling in these people's lives, you're simply creating new needs and even more reasons for them to slave away.'

'Oh, God! Surely something has to be done,' Lida said irritably and from her tone I gathered that she considered my arguments trivial and beneath contempt.

'The people must be freed from heavy physical work,' I said. 'We must lighten their yoke, they must have breathing-space, so that they don't have to spend all their lives at the stove, wash-tub and in the fields, so that they have time to think of their souls, of God and thus develop their spiritual lives. Man's true vocation is the life of the spirit, the constant search for truth, for the meaning of life. Liberate them from this rough, brutish labour, let them feel they are free – then you'll see what a farce these dispensaries and books really are. Once a man recognizes his true vocation, only religion, science, art can satisfy him – not all this nonsense of yours.'

'Free them from labour!' Lida laughed. 'Can that be possible?'

'It can. You must take some of their labour on your own shoulders. If all of us town and country dwellers unanimously agreed to divide among ourselves the labour that is normally expended by humanity on the satisfaction of its physical needs, then each of us would probably have to work no more than two or three hours a day. Just imagine if all of us, rich and poor, worked only two or three hours a day and had the rest of the time to ourselves. Imagine if we invented labour-saving machines and tried to reduce our needs to the absolute minimum so as to be less dependent on our bodies and to be able to work even less. We would harden ourselves and our children so that they would no longer fear hunger or cold. We wouldn't be constantly worrying about their health, unlike Anna, Mavra and Pelageya. Imagine if we no longer doctored ourselves, didn't maintain dispensaries, tobacco factories, distilleries – how much more leisure time we'd finally have at our disposal! All of us, working together, would be able to devote our leisure to science and art. Just as peasants sometimes mend roads, working as a community, so all of us, as one big community, would search for the truth and the meaning of life: and the truth would be discovered very quickly, man would rid himself of this constant, agonizing, oppressive fear of death – and even from death itself – of that I'm convinced.'

'But you're contradicting yourself,' Lida said. 'You keep going on about science and art, yet you yourself reject literacy.'

'The kind of literacy, when a man has nothing else to read except pub signs and sometimes books he doesn't understand, has been with us since Ryurik's time. Gogol's Petrushka's been able to read for absolutely ages, whereas our villages are exactly the same as they were in Ryurik's time. It isn't literacy that we need, but freedom to develop our spiritual faculties as widely as possible. We don't need schools – we need universities.'

'And you reject medicine as well?'

'Yes. Medicine might be necessary for the study of diseases as natural phenomena, but not for their treatment. If you want to cure people you shouldn't treat the illness but its cause. Take away the main cause – physical labour – and there won't be any more diseases. I don't recognize the healing arts,' I continued excitedly. 'Genuine science and art don't strive towards temporary, personal ends, but towards the universal and eternal: they seek truth and the meaning of life, they seek God, the soul. But if you reduce them to the level of everyday needs, to the mundane, to dispensaries and libraries, they only complicate life and make it more difficult. We have loads of doctors, pharmacists, lawyers, lots of people who can read and write, but there's a complete lack of biologists, mathematicians, philosophers and poets. One's entire intellect, one's entire spiritual energy has been used up satisfying transient, temporary needs. Scholars, writers and artists are working away – thanks to them life's comforts increase with every day. Our physical needs multiply, whereas the truth is still far, far off and man still remains the most predatory and filthy of animals and everything conspires towards the larger part of mankind degenerating and losing its vitality. In such conditions an artist's life has no meaning and the more talented he is the stranger and more incomprehensible his role, since, on closer inspection, it turns out that, by supporting the existing order, he's working for the amusement of this rapacious, filthy animal. I don't want to work . . . and I *shan't*! I don't need a thing, the whole world can go to hell!'

'Missy dear, you'd better leave the room,' Lida told her sister, evidently finding my words harmful for such a young girl.

Zhenya sadly looked at her sister and mother and went out.

'People who want to justify their own indifference usually come out with such charming things,' Lida said. 'Rejecting hospitals and schools is easier than healing people or teaching.'

'That's true, Lida, that's true,' her mother agreed.

'Now you're threatening to give up working,' Lida continued. 'It's obvious you value your painting very highly! But let's stop arguing. We'll never see eye to eye, since I value the most imperfect of these libraries or dispensaries – of which you spoke so contemptuously just now – more highly than all the landscapes in the world.' Turning to her mother she immediately continued in an entirely different tone of voice: 'The prince has grown much thinner, he's changed dramatically since he was last with us. They're sending him to Vichy.'

She told her mother about the prince to avoid talking to me. Her face was burning and to hide her agitation she bent low over the table as if she were short-sighted, and pretended to be reading the paper. My company was disagreeable for them. I said goodbye and went home.

IV

It was quiet outside. The village on the far side of the pond was already asleep. Not a single light was visible, only the pale reflections of the stars faintly glimmered on the water. Zhenya stood motionless at the gates with the lions, waiting to see me off.

'Everyone's asleep in the village,' I told her, trying to make out her face in the gloom – and I saw those dark, mournful eyes fixed on me. 'The innkeeper and horse thieves are peacefully sleeping, while we respectable people quarrel and annoy one another.'

It was a sad August night – sad because there was already a breath of autumn in the air. The moon was rising, veiled by a crimson cloud and casting a dim light on the road and the dark fields of winter corn along its sides. There were many shooting stars. Zhenya walked along the road by my side, trying not to see the shooting stars, which frightened her for some reason.

'I think you're right,' she said, trembling from the damp night air. 'If people would only work together, if they could give themselves up to the life of the spirit they would soon know everything.'

'Of course, we're superior beings and if in fact we did recognize the full power of human genius and lived only for some higher end, then in the long run we'd all come to be like gods. But that will never happen – mankind will degenerate and not a trace of genius will remain.'

When we could no longer see the gates Zhenya stopped and hurriedly shook hands with me.

'Good night,' she said with a shudder. Only a thin blouse covered her shoulders and she huddled up from the cold. 'Please come tomorrow!'

I was horrified at the prospect of being left alone and felt agitated and unhappy with myself and others. And I too tried not to look at the shooting stars.

'Please stay a little longer,' I said. 'Please do!'

I loved Zhenya. I loved her – perhaps – for meeting me and seeing me off, for looking so tenderly and admiringly at me. Her pale face, her slender neck, her frailty, her idleness, her books – they were so moving in their beauty! And what about her mind? I suspected that she was extremely intelligent. The breadth of her views enchanted me, perhaps because she thought differently from the severe, pretty Lida, who disliked me. Zhenya liked me as an artist. I had won her heart with my talent and I longed to paint for her alone. I dreamt of her as my little queen who would hold sway with me over these trees, fields, this mist, sunset, over this exquisite, magical nature where I had so far felt hopelessly lonely and unwanted.

'Please stay a little longer,' I asked. 'Please stay!'

I took off my coat and covered her chilled shoulders. Afraid that she might look silly and unattractive in a man's coat, she threw it off – and then I embraced her and started showering her face, shoulders and arms with kisses.

'Till tomorrow!' she cried.

For about two minutes after that I could hear her running. I didn't feel like going home and I had no reason for going there anyway. I stood and reflected for a moment and then slowly made my way back to have another look at that dear, innocent old house that seemed to be staring at me with its attic windows as if they were all-comprehending eyes. I walked past the terrace and sat down on a bench in the darkness under the old elm by the tennis court. In the windows of the attic storey where she slept a bright light suddenly shone, turning soft green when the lamp was covered with a shade. Shadows stirred. I was full of tenderness, calm and contentment – contentment because I had let myself be carried away and had fallen in love. And at the same time I was troubled by the thought that only a few steps away Lida lived in one of the rooms of that house – Lida, who disliked and possibly even hated me. I sat waiting for Zhenya to come out. I listened hard and people seemed to be talking in the attic storey.

About an hour passed. The green light went out and the shadows vanished. The moon stood high now over the house and illuminated the sleeping garden, the paths. Dahlias and roses in the flowerbeds in front of the house were clearly visible and all of them seemed the same colour. It became very cold. I left the garden, picked up my coat from the path and unhurriedly made my way home.

Next day, when I arrived at the Volchaninovs after dinner, the French windows into the garden were wide open. I sat for a while on the terrace, expecting Zhenya to appear any minute behind the flowerbed by the tennis court, or on one of the avenues – or her voice to come from one of the rooms. Then I went through the drawing-room and dining-room. There wasn't a soul about. From the dining-room I walked down a long corridor to the hall and back. In the corridor there were several doors and through one of them I could hear Lida's voice.

'God sent a crow . . .' she was saying in a loud, deliberate voice – probably dictating – 'God sent a crow a piece of cheese . . . Who's there?' she suddenly called out, hearing my footsteps.

'It's me.'

'Oh, I'm sorry, but I can't come out now. I'm busy with Dasha.'

'Is Yekaterina Pavlovna in the garden?'

'No. She went this morning with my sister to her aunt's in Penza. This winter they'll probably go abroad,' she added after a pause.

'Go-od se-ent a crow a pi-iece of che-eese. Have you written that down?'

I went into the hall and stared vacantly at the pond and the village. And I could hear her voice: 'A pi-iece of che-eese . . . Go-od sent the crow . . .'

And I left the grounds the same way I had first come: from the courtyard into the garden, past the house, then along the lime-tree avenue. Here a boy caught up with me and handed me a note.

'I've told my sister everything and she insists we break up,' I read. 'I could never upset her by disobeying. May God grant you happiness. I'm sorry. If you only knew how bitterly Mama and I are crying.'

Then came the dark fir avenue, the broken-down fence. On that same field where once I had seen the flowering rye and heard the quails calling, cows and hobbled horses were now grazing. Here and there on the hills were the bright green patches of winter corn. A sober, humdrum mood came over me and I felt ashamed of all I had said at the Volchaninovs. And I was as bored as ever with life. When I got home I packed and left for St Petersburg that same evening.

I never saw the Volchaninovs again. Not long ago, however, I met Belokurov on the train when I was travelling to the Crimea. He was still wearing that peasant jerkin and embroidered smock, and when I inquired about his health he replied that he was well – thank you very much! We started talking. He had sold his estate and bought a smaller one in Lyubov Ivanovna's name. He told me Lida was still living in Shelkovka and teaching in the school. Gradually she'd managed to gather around her a circle of congenial spirits, a pressure group, and at the last local election they'd 'blackballed' Balagin, who up to then had his hands on the whole district. As for Zhenya, Belokurov only told me that she wasn't living at home and that he didn't know where she was.

I'm already beginning to forget that old house with the mezzanine and only occasionally, when I'm painting or reading, do I suddenly remember – for no apparent reason – that green light in the window; or the sound of my footsteps as I walked home across the fields at night, in love, rubbing my hands in the cold. And even more rarely, when I am sad at heart and afflicted with loneliness, do I have dim memories. And gradually I come to feel that I haven't been forgotten either, that she is waiting for me and that we'll meet again . . .

Missy, where are you?

Translated from the Russian by Ronald Wilks

Just Another Day

A day without an argument is like an egg without salt.

Angela Carter

LYDIA DAVIS

Disagreement

He said she was disagreeing with him. She said no, that was not true, he was disagreeing with her. This was about the screen door. That it should not be left open was her idea, because of the flies; his was that it could be left open first thing in the morning, when there were no flies on the deck. Anyway, he said, most of the flies came from other parts of the building: in fact, he was probably letting more of them out than in.

JOYCE CAROL OATES
The Quarrel

Mornings, early, in most weathers, N. jogged around the reservoir, a distance of approximately two miles, while S. made coffee, started breakfast, had his first cigarette of the day sitting in a window alcove of the kitchen reading through *The New York Times*; glancing up repeatedly to follow N.'s progress around the reservoir, knowing now by instinct where N. would appear, at which curve of shore he would disappear, and where, along the sandy strip of shore facing the house, he would again appear, in warm weather in a white T-shirt, through much of the autumn in a red-checked woolen shirt they called his hunter's shirt, jogging easily, in no haste, with no appearance of self-consciousness though he knew that S. was watching, sipping his coffee, smoking his cigarette with a bitter sort of pleasure, thinking, There is my life. What remains of my life.

Once, years ago, his and N.'s love for each other had glowed like phosphorescent fire on the surfaces of their bodies, making them objects of beauty (and perhaps of terror) in others' eyes; now the fire seemed to have retreated . . . invisible, wholly interior, residing in the marrow of their bones. They rarely made love now, and they rarely quarreled now, and S., who would be fifty-six years old on his next birthday, N.'s elder by five years, could not have said which he missed more.

It happened that, one wintry morning, when N. returned from jogging, he was attacked by an intruder, a stranger, evidently a would-be thief, hiding in the garage (which was in the ground floor of the old house – the house itself was built into a hill): before N. knew what was happening the man had rushed him, struck him a numbing blow to the side of the head, and N. would have fallen except by instinct he'd grabbed his attacker, shouting for S., for help . . . in the confusion of the moment trying to retain him and not, as of course he should have done, letting him go. There came, however, almost at once, S. from the rear door, shouting too, 'Stop! Get away! Who are you! Get away!' – badly frightened, as he would confess afterward, for what if the man had had a gun – and the

94

intruder gave N. a final powerful blow, knocking him against the right front fender of the station wagon, parked there in the sandy-graveled driveway, and turned, and ran up the driveway to the road, and was gone. Like all such astonishing incidents the encounter had happened more swiftly than it could be absorbed, far more swiftly than it would ever be explained, and whether S. had scared off the intruder, and, in a manner of speaking, saved N., or whether the man was preparing to flee anyway, as soon as he freed himself of N.'s inexplicable (and imprudent) grasp, could not be said. Both men were badly agitated: S. helped N. to his feet, N.'s fingers came away from his face covered in blood, 'My God what *is* this,' he said, amazed, 'is this my *blood*?' His attacker had razor-slashed him without either man having seen the razor in his hand.

So N. was treated in the emergency room of the nearest hospital, eight deft stitches, a stinging sort of pain, and afterward, at police headquarters, police officers questioned N. and S. separately – which was, evidently, standard police procedure: N. carefully described his attacker as a 'light-skinned black' in his late twenties, weighing approximately two hundred pounds, about six feet, two inches tall, with a narrow moustache, deep-set bloodshot eyes 'like a dog's', wearing a soiled sheepskin jacket, work trousers, and a dark green wool-knit cap pulled down low on his forehead; S. carefully described the man as Caucasian, with a sallow, coarse, 'possibly pitted' skin, between thirty and thirty-five years old, weighing approximately one hundred seventy or eighty pounds, wearing a nondescript jacket, and jeans, and a navy blue wool-knit cap pulled down low on his forehead. N. described the man's voice as low and guttural while S. was positive the man had not spoken once, at least in his hearing . . . but then of course he'd been so excited, and had been shouting himself, it was impossible to remember.

Since the men's descriptions of N.'s attacker were so different, the police decided against having a composite drawing attempted, nor was there much point in their considering photographs of possible suspects, though they did so, doggedly, stubbornly, for the remainder of the morning, peering at the photostatted images of men who might reasonably be identified as light-skinned blacks or sallow-skinned Caucasians, but the effort seemed futile, the faces began to blur and jumble, and though they tried to maintain an air of absolute civility with each other, N. said, at last, in an embittered voice, 'You're doing this to humiliate me, aren't you? – contradicting every damn thing I *saw*.' S. stared at him, astonished, and N. added, 'Every damn thing I saw with my own eyes.' S. said, 'To humiliate you? But why? What on earth do you mean?' and suddenly they were quarreling, quietly, yet wildly, not minding that one of the police detectives was listening, or, if minding, if marginally aware of the fact, unable to stop, N.'s heavy face appearing heavier with blood, darkening, and his eyes angrily bright, S.'s heart beating hard, fast, erratic. One said, 'I got a good close look at the man and I know what I saw,' and the other said, '*I* got a perfectly good look at him and *I* know what I saw,' and added, in a spiteful whisper, 'Don't be ridiculous, please: you are making yourself ridiculous in public.' The other said, staring, 'I can't believe you would do this to me, *you!* do this to *me!*' and the other shot back, '*I* can't believe you would do this to *me!*' as the youngish police officer tried not too obviously to listen, embarrassed, or perhaps amused, and afterward, ah afterward he would entertain his buddies by mimicking in high-pitched breathless voices N. and S.'s quarrel which like a brushfire flared up as if from a single spark and ran and ran, wild, terrible, searing, until at last it burned itself out and S. was wiping his mouth with a handkerchief, badly trembling, and N. had slammed shut his book of photostatted pictures saying he'd come back another time, maybe another time would be best, this wasn't a good time right now, he didn't think. On their way out of the police station S. tried to soothe things over with a joke, asking one of the detectives if 'this sort of thing happens often', and he and N. saw the man think hard, think frowningly hard, wondering what exactly S. meant by 'this sort of thing' – the discrepancy in the descriptions of the wanted man, or the subsequent quarrel – before he answered, politely, perhaps condescendingly, 'All the time, yes sure it happens all the time, eyewitnesses are never reliable,' smiling at S. and N. as if to reassure them, '– almost never reliable.'

'How could you do that to me, – I mean, simply, how could you.'
    'How could you do that to *me*? And quarreling in front of –'
    'Which you began.'
    'Which *you* began. With such evident, such – palpable – pleasure.'

'The pleasure was all yours.'
'There was no pleasure! It was *yours*.'
'And in front of −'
'That isn't how I remember it!'
'That isn't how I remember it!'

They returned to the splendid century-old five-gabled brown-shingled house overlooking the reservoir, S. driving the station wagon, N. furious and silent beside him, compulsively touching the bandage on his cheek, until, unable to contain himself, S. whispered, 'Please *don't*.' For the remainder of that very long day the men were icily civil with each other, for the remainder of that week they were stiff, cautious, circumspect, knowing that the terrible quarrel still smoldered underground like a peat fire and they dared not stir it, provoke it, give it air, for had not S. seen the loathing in N.'s face, there in the police station? and had not N. seen the mockery in S.'s face, like a child grimacing into a mirror? − even as both men well knew that the outburst of a mere moment, particularly in such strained, heightened circumstances, does not really count. Several times S. prepared to say, in a little speech, 'You must realize don't you that I hurt a number of people badly for your sake,' but could not bring himself to utter the first syllable, and several times N. prepared to say, in the tone he'd used during those years when, intermittently, he had choreographed difficult dance sequences for a New York City troupe, sometimes with conspicuous success, sometimes not, and the dancers, some of whom were very young, had needed not merely to hear but to understand, 'You must realize that *life is a serious affair*.'

And weeks passed. And months. And then it was six months, and they never heard any longer from the police, about whom they joked, bitterly, but always cautiously: how ineffectual they'd been about 'that thing that had happened back in November', how little you can rely upon them really. At least in such minor matters. And in time the hairbreadth of a scar on N.'s right cheek came to seem hardly more than a curious sort of downward crease in the skin (which was beginning rather more seriously to crease along other, horizontal fault lines) about which they never spoke. And then, one spring evening, when the men were entertaining friends at dinner, S. told of the incident − 'our mysterious little adventure' − but his delivery was impeccably light, his tone light, as a popular lecturer at the small liberal arts college at which he'd taught for the past twenty years (S.'s specialty was twentieth-century Europe 'post-and prewar') he knew how crucial it was to keep one's tone light, and the thing that had happened back in November, the thing in the driveway, the thing between the two men that had frightened them so, became, now, an anecdote . . . a tale meant to amuse . . . its upshot being not that he and N. had disagreed so violently nor even that N. had been permanently scarred (no mention was made of the scar) but that the police, for all their seeming professionalism, had done so remarkably little. Had anything been taken from the garage or the house, the men were asked, and the answer was no, nothing, that was the puzzle, the mystery, why had the man been there and what had he intended, the entire episode, S. concluded, was inexplicable, sui generis, but of course they kept their doors and windows locked at all times now even during the day even when they were both home, and so on and so forth, and eventually the conversation shifted to other crimes in the area, solved or unsolved, comical or serious or frankly tragic: the rape of an eleven-year-old girl in the next township; the death, by cardiac arrest, of an elderly widow whom some of the company knew, when a never apprehended burglar had broken into her house in the middle of the night.

So the episode became, in a sense, public; published. And now the men were free to allude to it if they wished, though always in anecdotal terms, with wry expressions, the central theme, indeed the only theme, being police incompetence and unreliability. And the years passed, and the years. And never did they risk another scene like that terrible scene in the police station. And they never wept, at least to each other's knowledge. And they never quarreled again.

ARNOLD BENNETT
One of Their Quarrels

I

The yacht *Alice II*, a ketch of one hundred and eight tons, with auxiliary engine and a crew of nine, was just leaving the small haven of the Rotterdam Yacht Club, whose hospitality she and her owner, James Thorpe, had been enjoying for two days. The haven was studded with many mooring posts, to each of which a yacht was tied up; so that there was little room to spare for the manœuvring of a biggish, beamy, and sluggish craft like *Alice II* – easily the most important vessel in the cove.

Now Rotterdam is one of the greatest river ports of the whole world, and it is certainly the most feverish and busy of all European ports whatever. At the open mouth of the haven the mighty tide of the Maas streamed past at a speed of four or five knots, and the rushing water thereof was covered with tugs, motor-barges, sailing-barges, passenger steamers, sailing-ships, terrific ferries, and Atlantic liners – not to mention dredgers and such monstrosities as floating cranes. But chiefly tugs, of which scores and scores rushed to and fro, navigated by their skippers with more than the nonchalance of taxi-drivers navigating taxis along the Strand.

The wind was fresh; flags and burgees stood out pretty straight. The much-disturbed water was lolloping and splashing against the banks of the haven; a few rats as big as rabbits were to be seen foraging on the deep sides of the banks; sirens and whistles were sounding menaces everywhere; steam-cranes were creaking as they raised huge burdens of barrels, cheeses, and grain out of the holds of ships or off wharves, and flung them down again like toys. And railway bridges and road bridges were swinging high gigantic arms on steel joists to let trains and lorries and people go across or to let ships go through.

In brief, the scene was bewildering to an extreme degree, and Captain Abbott, who possessed the two finest qualities of a skipper

– to wit, a strong sense of danger and a gloomy outlook upon the future – was glad that he had a Dutch pilot on board. Captain Abbott and the pilot between them were moving the *Alice II* out of the haven stern foremost. The dinghy, with a crew of two, was afloat carrying ropes to mooring posts and generally executing shouted orders from the poop – orders of which details need not be given here, as this story is in essence domestic and of a purely family nature.

The family, now leaning critically against the rail on the port quarter and watching the operations, consisted of efficient James Thorpe, his efficient wife Alice, and their daughter, who was usually addressed as Alice II. The yacht had been called *Alice II* because the name of Jim's previous yacht, a mere fifty-tonner with a crew of only four, was *Alice*. The increase in the size of Jim's yacht was a measure of the increase in his prosperity since the earlier days of *Alice*. Real yachtsmen are always selling the smaller for the larger if they are getting on in the world, or selling the larger for the smaller if they are not. The Thorpe family were beyond doubt real yachtsmen. They lived for yachting, and occasional sea-sickness never daunted them. As for Alice II, aged four, she had had a narrow escape of being actually born on *Alice*. (*Alice II* was acquired after the birth of Alice II. It may sound complicated, but is not.)

Right at the mouth of the yacht-haven was a station for tugs, and just as *Alice II* was feeling her way out backwards, a tug swayed casually to a berth, and her nose stopped about a yard from *Alice II*'s stern. The skipper, not used to such circus performances, was alarmed, but neither the Dutch pilot nor the Dutch captain of the tug showed any sign of fever, though the two men in the dinghy certainly did. And the family, while outwardly tranquil, were aware of qualms.

'Come along, darling,' said Mrs Thorpe. 'Time for your afternoon snoozelet.'

'Is it, daddy?'

Jim Thorpe, tall, with a tendency to bulk, glanced at his little, slim girl of a wife (aged thirty-three, but not looking it) with a secret appeal.

'It is,' said Alice Thorpe, staring down her mass of a husband. So that was that. Mother and daughter disappeared below.

When Alice returned to the deck there was a considerable noise of voices both on the yacht and in the dinghy, and the engine-room bell was ringing a new order about every thirty seconds.

'Look out for that dinghy,' cried Alice, leaning over. Jim Thorpe was making the same cry, but only in his mind. He was not like Alice, of whom it might be said that, as a rule, whatever came into her mind went out through her lips.

'Shut up,' Jim remonstrated. 'Don't confuse them. They know exactly what they're doing.'

'Do they? Well, they'll have the dinghy nipped between the yacht and that post in half a minute.'

'Not they!'

But in about exactly half a minute the dinghy did get nipped, just as the tiresome Alice had predicted, and the general outcry was multiplied.

'Good gracious!' Alice exclaimed, with all her efficiency. 'I never saw such clumsiness. And why is Pete in the dinghy at all?'

The post was immovable, and the hundred tons of the yacht uncontrollably and ruthlessly moved towards the post; and then there was a startling sound of crushed wood.

'A dinghy smashed!' said the skipper under his breath, gloomily justified of his pessimism.

Then one side of the dinghy rose up on the post and the dinghy suddenly filled with water; and the two men sprang out of her, clutched madly at the mizzen shrouds, and somehow got aboard the yacht. Jim had seen panic and the fear of death upon their bronzed faces. The yacht forged safely ahead, dragging after her the nearly submerged dinghy, in which oars and other gear were floating. A rope attached to the mooring post was tightening as the yacht moved.

'Ye'll have to cut that rope, Alf!' the skipper shouted to the mate. 'Get your knife ready and cut it!' he repeated, savagely.

The rope was cut, and the tail of it left hanging round the post, a memorial to all Rotterdam of the inefficiency of British seamanship. The yacht was now safely away in the stream.

But there had been an accident, and the drowned dinghy dragging astern was the awful desolating proof of it. Alice had never before seen a marine mess, and she was outraged by this one. When the dinghy had been salved, and hauled up on its davits and emptied of a ton or so of water, it looked better, for not much damage had been done, the wretched boat having slipped under the yacht's quarter instead of being squeezed to matchwood. But red-headed Pete was now lying on deck, feeling his ankle and having his ankle felt. The man could not stand.

'Carry him down into the port-cabin. He'll be more comfortable there,' Jim Thorpe ordered curtly.

'But Alice is asleep there. It's her cabin,' said Mrs Jim, tensely.

'Take Alice out, then, and put her in your cabin – or mine,' said Jim, still more curtly. 'There's no room for a crippled man in the forecastle. He must be made comfortable, and he can't be comfortable in that box-room of a forecastle with eight other men and a kitchen in it.'

II

'Jim,' said Alice, quietly, when she had finished, with considerable efficiency, putting a cold compress, surrounded with flannel, upon the severely sprained ankle of Pete, 'I want just two words with you.'

They were in the narrow corridor, at the door of the port-cabin, which Alice had closed, and she led the way into Jim's own cabin, which was on the starboard side; and, having got him within, she closed the door of that cabin also. The yacht was breasting the densely-populated stream of the Maas, and on deck the excitement of the accident had died down. But below, between the pair in Jim's cabin, the shut-in atmosphere vibrated to unseen forces more dangerous than electricity. The big man and the small woman, who till that moment had talked together (in the presence of others) with an admirable sweet reasonableness, were now formidably glaring. Their bodies almost touched, for the cabin was not quite as large as a drawing-room on a liner, and Jim's high head was bent a little to avoid a beam in the ceiling of his private apartment.

'Well, child?' growled Jim.

'You made me look very silly just now in front of the captain and the mate and all of them, insisting on Pete being put in Alice's cabin when you knew I strongly objected to it.'

'Not a bit,' Jim replied. 'I was perfectly polite. So were you, as far as that goes. Also, I carried the kid out myself, and she's asleep now all right. Where's the harm done?'

'The harm is this. This yacht is our summer home. Am I the mistress of the house, or am I not? I never interfere on deck –'

'Oh, yes, you do, my girl.'

'I do *not* – and I don't expect you to interfere in the cabins.'

'Oh, don't you?'

'No, I certainly do not. Imagine that great hulking fellow in little Alice's cabin! It's simply disgusting. If a dustman slipped on the front steps at home and hurt himself, would you bring him into the flat and put him into Alice's bed *there*?'

'No, I shouldn't.'

'Why not?'

'Because the kid's bed there is only a cot, and Pete wouldn't hold in it.'

Mrs Jim stamped her foot, but she could not stamp hard because she was wearing indiarubber soles.

'Moreover,' Jim continued, 'the two cases are not quite on all fours. This is a –'

'They are exactly the same,' Mrs Jim insisted. 'And there's another thing. It was all Pete's fault. I asked you before: Why was he in the dinghy at all? He isn't in the dinghy's crew. He's steward, and of course he only gets into a muddle in the dinghy.'

'Pardon me. Pete's as handy a man as anybody aboard the vessel. He was in the dinghy because he likes to vary his work sometimes – surely that's natural! This isn't the Royal Navy.'

'Then he must take the consequences, like anybody else. You always favour him. And if there's any difficulty between him and me you always take his side. I shan't forget the trouble I had in the old yacht.'

The first honeymoon quarrel between the married pair had indeed happened in *Alice*, and apropos of precisely red-headed Pete.

'Anyhow, Pete was quite innocent then.'

'I absolutely insist on him being taken to the forecastle, where he ought to be. You understand – absolutely.'

'That's your ultimatum, is it?' said Jim, darkly. He was reflecting that if he allowed himself to be defeated in this battle he would lose all moral authority for ever. 'Well, my heated darling, I'll just tell you two things. First, you're a horrid little piece, and a snob, and entirely without the milk of human kindness. Why on earth *shouldn't* the poor fellow be treated decently, as a fellow-creature, for once?

Second, that he is not going to be moved back to the forecastle – not if I know it! Is that clear?'

It is astonishing with what perilous foolishness married people can behave to one another when prestige seems to be at stake; but somehow they will do it.

'Very well,' said Mrs Jim, raising her chin.

At that moment a hopping noise was heard in the corridor. Jim opened the door to see what was happening. It was happening that Pete, feeling ill at ease in the solitary splendour of the port-cabin, had arisen from his bunk and was hopping through the saloon towards the forecastle, his natural home. Mrs Jim watched his retreating figure, and saw his great dirty hands imperilling the beautiful upholstery of the saloon as he balanced his way on one leg over the floor of the heaving vessel.

'Of course, his bandage will all come loose,' she observed, dryly. 'A lot of use it was me taking so much trouble over him!'

III

The episode would have ended at this point if the married belligerents had had as much common sense as the rest of mankind. Pete's independent and instinctive action had given Alice a clear, notable triumph in the affray, and yet a triumph which could not humiliate Jim. But with all their efficiency and all their mutual affection and other fine qualities, the married belligerents suffered from a lack of common sense. In the supply of that precious commodity they were our inferiors. And therefore the episode did not by any means end with the vanishing of red-headed Pete into the forecastle and the evacuation of Alice II's cabin. The personal dignity of the parties had been engaged, and the question of personal dignity had been the source of nearly all their marital differences. Each wanted to laugh lightly and make peace, but personal dignity prevented either of them from laughing.

'As usual, you've been very inconsiderate to me,' said Mrs Jim. 'And, of course, I shall expect you to apologize.'

To which Jim replied:

'Expect – by all means. Keep on expecting with all your might, my child.' His tone was cold and cutting as a razor.

'And seeing how carefully I've looked after the ankle of that man,' said Mrs Jim, following her own thought and ignoring Jim's, 'I don't quite see the point of your saying that I've no kindness in me. However –'

And yet that night at dinner, which in the regretted absence of Pete was served by the second steward, the atmosphere was as smooth as the canals and rivers upon which *Alice II* was so beautifully sailing in a fair wind. The most penetrating of stewards could not have detected a false note, much less a rift within the lute. And little Alice, upon whom both parents were lavishing all sweetness, was present at the soup stage of the meal as a special treat. Mrs Jim had suggested this departure from the routine of discipline, and Jim had agreed to it with positive ardour. The fact was, of course, that the belligerents desired to be alone as little as possible.

'About where shall we be tomorrow afternoon, Jim?' Mrs Jim inquired, graciously.

'I should think not so awfully far from Flushing, my pet,' Jim graciously replied, stroking his offspring's golden hair.

'Then I think I *shall* take the steamer to Folkestone,' said Mrs Jim. 'With all those urgent things to see to at the flat . . . And Alice had better go with me, hadn't she?'

For a moment Jim, with all his acuteness, was at a loss to understand what Mrs Jim was at, for there had been no previous suggestion whatever that Mrs Jim should return to the flat, or that there was anything urgently needing her attention at the flat. Then he comprehended. He had not apologized to her, and never would apologize (deeming himself, of course, to have been entirely in the right in this dispute); she had therefore determined to show her displeasure, and prove her unconquerable mind, by leaving him alone in the yacht and taking Alice II with her. But she wanted to achieve her purpose smoothly, and without giving any hint to the child or to the little world of the yacht that a serious state of war existed. Hence she was displaying her remarkable skill in the art of acting. But Jim also could act, and Jim's mind also was unconquerable.

He said, charmingly:

'I think you're quite right, my dear, though I shall be very sorry to lose my two darlings. Of course if you'd like me to come with you –'

'Oh, no! You must finish the cruise, dear.'

'Very well, then. We'll keep going all night. You can take the train at Vlake and you'll be in plenty of time to catch the steamer at Flushing.'

And so it came to pass. Early the next morning he helped her to pack, and Alice II felt obliged also to help her mamma to pack; he gave her money; he saw them both off at Vlake station; and very trim, neat, charming, and efficient mother and daughter looked as they leaned their heads out of the carriage window and waved good-bye to daddy. It was a lovely morning. But for some twenty hours husband and wife had not exchanged one word save in the presence of others.

'Women are staggering,' Jim reflected, naïvely. 'Absolutely staggering.' Just as if he hadn't been married for six years or so. He did, however, show some gleam of an appreciation of the fact that men also are staggering, when he asked himself: 'I wonder why I didn't apologize to her? It would have cost me nothing.' Then he resumed his masculine bias by adding: 'No! Not on your life! It would have cost me my position in the home.'

IV

Alice and Alice II sat together side by side in a red-velvet-covered compartment of the train to Flushing. It was a boat-train, sure enough, but a boat-train that stopped at every station. So that as she gazed casually at cows, dykes, steeples, barges apparently sailing through fields, maids and matrons in high-waisted 'native' costume with gold-ornamented head-pieces, station-gardens, and windmills, and explained the various phenomena of the journey to Alice II, Alice had plenty of opportunity to reflect upon the quarrel. Like all their quarrels, it had arisen out of almost nothing, and a word, even a tone, might have stifled it at birth. The important thing, however, was not the originating cause, but the nature of the issue engaged. And the issue in this particular quarrel was about the same as in all their previous quarrels – namely, the rights and dignity of man and the rights and dignity of woman.

'Jim is an idiot,' thought Alice; and then 'I am an idiot too!'

But idiots are apt to have a powerful sense of dignity, the same as the wise. Alice could not imagine how the quarrel would end, but of course it would end; and the end would be delicious, as the ends of all their quarrels always were. In the meantime Alice felt a fine artistic interest in the quarrel, and contemplated calmly its growth, and conceived different dodges for concluding it with advantage to herself – an advantage which, having won it, she would cheerfully throw away as soon as the affair was over. She contemplated also, with satisfaction, the vision of Jim alone in the yacht. Put on what proud, careless air he might, he would certainly be rather miserable that evening!

She liked the thought of his misery; and she assured herself that *she* would not be miserable – and the assurance was not the least in the world convincing. Certainly she had Alice II, whereas Jim had nobody except his silly old captain and his sillier old red-headed Pete.

Alice II had begun by being prim, more prim than her mother. But soon Alice II grew tired of dangling her legs a dozen inches off the floor, and she slipped down and carried out a complete inspection of the compartment, and fell violently once when the train stopped with a jerk. Being very like her parents, she did not cry over her fall; she had a full share of pride. Then she climbed on to her mother's lap, and hugged her mother with much love.

'You're very demonstrative this morning, my pet,' observed Alice.

Strange that Alice II knew precisely the meaning of that long word which she had never heard before.

'Mummy, won't daddy be awful sad all by himself?'

'Mummy, when's daddy coming home?'

'Mummy, why didn't daddy kiss you at the station?'

'Well, he was very busy with the luggage,' Alice answered the last question uneasily. Nothing could be hidden from the child. The child knew as well as anybody that trouble was in the air. Nevertheless the demeanour of both the child's parents in her presence had been unexceptionable in its show of friendliness and affection. Alice ought to have made Jim kiss her. She hated nothing more than to give away the fact of a family quarrel to the innocent child. They, idiots both of them, were gods to the child. In another minute Alice II was fast asleep, and Alice could feel through her thin frock the warm, regular breathing of infancy. And she squeezed the child and woke her.

The train had seemingly no intention of ever arriving at Flushing; but it did arrive. And there was a Flemish horse on the platform dragging bits of luggage about at the end of a long chain: a spectacle which made Alice II shriek with glee. Alice arranged matters efficiently with a porter and walked off the platform and turned to the left in obedience to printed instructions for boarding the steamer. And then she heard a call in Dutch-English:

'This way for passports, please.'

At first she had an idea that the Dutch authorities were going to present her with a passport for the purpose of returning to England, and she tripped forward until she came to a wide gap with the view of a steamboat in the middle distance. Just at this gap was a table, with a bald-headed official seated thereat. He at once perceived that Alice was English, and he addressed her in her own language:

'Your passport, please, madam.'

'But – but I haven't got a passport,' Alice replied. A dreadful truth vaguely took shape in her mind.

'But it is forbidden to go on board the steamer without a passport.'

Now she saw the dreadful truth very clearly. With Jim she had gone to various foreign countries in the yacht, which, belonging to an officially recognized yacht club, flew the blue ensign of the Royal Naval Reserve. On arriving in a foreign port Customs officers had come aboard for a formal inspection, but no officer had ever asked for passports. She and Jim had just walked ashore, and no questions put and no demand made. Similarly for re-embarkation. And similarly on the return to Britain. Yachting people were exempt from all passport complications. But on the present occasion Alice was no longer a yachting person. She was a mere common traveller. She explained matters to the urbane official, whose urbanity, however, proved to be of no help to her.

'But what am I to do ?' she asked plaintively. In her war-days that celebrated efficiency of hers was habituated to dealing successfully with every crisis that arose, but now her efficiency failed her.

'Ah!' exclaimed the official suddenly. 'Here is a gentleman from the office of the British Consul here. Good afternoon, sir,' he greeted a young man who had put down a passport on the table. 'You are going to England, sir?'

'On leave,' said the young Englishman, who, indeed, was dressed in holiday style and had a bright face to match.

But immediately the Dutch official began to state the case of

Alice, and Alice joined in with explanatory remarks, the young man's face hardened into the face which he wore in the Consular office. He was well used to petitioners who had foolishly omitted formalities, and, moreover, on the very threshold of his holiday, he objected to being worried with professional affairs. He was most definitely off duty. He said, finally:

'If you go to Rotterdam, or to the British Legation at The Hague, and fill up the proper forms and furnish references, you will be able to obtain a temporary passport, but you wouldn't get it under four or five days at the earliest . . . Where is this yacht of yours, madam?'

'Near Vlake.'

'Anybody on board who could help you?'

'My husband, the owner.'

'Well, then, madam, I think your best course would be to go back at once to your husband.' And, his own passport having been inspected, he raised his hat and vanished away in the direction of the steamer.

Alice very unjustly considered him to be a rather unpleasant young man. 'Return to your husband!' 'Return to your husband!' The young man had not the slightest notion of the horror implied in his words. Go back – ignominiously! Go back – defeated! She cursed men in her heart, and particularly the ex-Kaiser Wilhelm, author of wars and therefore of passports.

'Darling,' she said, sweetly, bending down to Alice II, 'we must go back to daddy.' And the thoughtless child clapped her hands.

'There's a train –' the helpful official was beginning.

'Can you tell me where I can hire a car?' she asked, and to herself: 'Anyhow, it shall cost him as much as possible.'

But supposing the yacht had already left her moorings!

V

That same afternoon, which happened to be full of sunshine, Jim Thorpe, the august owner of the one-hundred-and-eight-ton auxiliary ketch *Alice II*, sat on his deck with a book in front of him. But he was not reading and could not read. For he was in a state of nervous apprehension surpassing anything in his experience since the other war – the Great War. The same thought ran round and

round in his mind. 'What a Hades of a row when we do meet!' Then
he heard the noise of an automobile approaching on the long, tree-
shaded, straight road that skirted the canal. He jumped up, and in
the distance saw in the car two figures that looked like his womenkind,
together with certain luggage, the aspect of which seemed familiar.

'By Jove!' he exclaimed to the captain, who came aft to meet him.
'They've come back. I wonder what's happened?' He acted as well
as he could, but not too well.

'I thought it was them, sir,' said the captain, anxiously, and glad
of an occasion for anxiety.

The car stopped on the quay alongside the yacht.

'Hello! Hello!' cried Jim, despite his notorious manliness almost
shaking with fright. 'What's this, my children?'

'Missed the steamer,' called Alice, nicely, and with a calm
smile.

The chauffeur lifted down the baby whom Jim and the captain
passed across the abyss that separated the quay wall from the yacht's
side. Alice stopped the chauffeur from unloading the luggage.

'We were just waiting for the lock to open to put to sea. How
lucky you had the idea of hiring a car!' The first statement was
misleading, for Jim had no intention of putting to sea.

'Jim!' said Alice, persuasively, 'just come here for a moment, will
you?'

He obeyed, saying to himself: 'She's playing with me like a cat
with a mouse. What an idiot I was to let her go off like that!'

The assembling crew, aroused from torpor by the unexpected
contretemps, saw the car turn and drive off with Mr and Mrs James
Thorpe, while Alice II ran forward to her friend, red-headed Pete,
who was stretched on deck near the forecastle-hatch.

'Jim,' began Alice, in the speeding car – the chauffeur could not
possibly hear for the loud rustling of the trees – 'I wanted to have
a bit of a chat with you, and I thought this was the best way. There's
no more privacy on a hundred-ton ship than there used to be on a
fifty-tonner. I was wrong to run off like that, and when *I*'m wrong
I prefer to say so frankly. I don't agree at all with the attitude you
took about that cabin, but I can see now you were acting for the
best, and you honestly thought you were right, and so, of course,
you couldn't conscientiously apologize.'

'Oh, my child!' said Jim. 'Please! Please! I dare say I was wrong,

though I didn't think so, as you say.' His heart was magically light-
ened. For once he had been lucky. She hadn't been near the steamer.
She hadn't found out about the passport snag. She had just taken
fright at the enormity of her rash foolishness in leaving him in a
tantrum, and had turned tail. And she had had such fear of missing
the yacht that she had hired a car. She had simply flown back to
him.

'*But*,' she continued, and Jim's heart was heavy once more –
heavier than ever, 'why did you let me and Alice II go away when
you knew perfectly well that we couldn't get on to the steamer
without a passport?'

'I – I –' the coward stammered.

'Did you know or didn't you know? Do be straight and tell me
the truth.'

'Yes, I knew.'

'I suppose you thought it would be a lesson to me?'

'Well, I did,' said Jim, shortly, intimidated by the formidableness
of her tone, and wishing to Heaven he had never had the notion of
teaching her a lesson.

'Well, it *will* be a lesson to me. But not the lesson you think. I'll
never trust you again. You aren't a man, and you aren't a husband.
You're a horrible brute. That was what I wanted to say to you, and
I'll never forgive you.'

She touched the chauffeur in the middle of the back, and motioned
to him to return to the yacht.

'Of course,' she proceeded, 'I'm in your power. You know it, and
I admit it fully. I couldn't get away from you, no matter how much
money and pluck I had. I'm fast, simply because I haven't a passport.
I shall have to fall in with your wishes, and there's nothing more to
be said. So I won't say another word. But I must say this –' She
went on talking until the car was once again alongside the yacht.

'The whole thing is perfectly silly. It's infantile,' Jim muttered.

'You may think so, but I don't,' said Alice.

They stepped on to the yacht. The crew got the luggage
aboard.

'You'd better pay him, dearest,' said Alice, silkily, for the benefit
of the crew.

'Pilot!' Jim shouted. 'Find out how much that fellow wants, will
you? And you pay him, skipper.'

'Lock's opening, sir,' said the skipper.

'All right. Get her through.'

Jim planted himself on the deck, feet wide apart and hands deep in his pockets, a statue of ferocious gloom. Up forward baby Alice II was pretending to bandage Pete's ankle. And she was absurdly like her mother at the task, though she had never seen her mother bandaging Pete's ankle. The resemblance was wonderful, incredible, very touching. Even while they were casting-off the crew gave side-long glances at the sight and smiled; and as for the engineer, he could scarcely bring himself to descend into the engine-room, so spellbound was he by the group of red-headed Pete and Alice II.

Alice herself smiled.

Only Jim would not smile. He went below and dropped disgust-edly on his bunk and glowered at the ceiling, cursing himself and cursing Alice, and resolving to sell the rotten yacht. Then Alice invaded his cabin.

'Oh, lor'!' thought Jim. 'More to come!'

'You great silly!' murmured Alice bending over him and kissing him. 'You great silly!' And she kissed him again. 'Now kiss me. A good one.'

He kissed her. All was light. In an instant of time all was happi-ness. But in the secrecy of his soul Jim stoutly maintained that you never knew where you were with women. When they seemed to be most serious they really weren't serious at all. And if she hadn't happened to be touched and flattered by the sight of Alice II imitating her Red Cross work upon Pete . . .

DAVID LEAVITT
Dedicated

Celia is treading the lukewarm blue water of Nathan's parents' swimming pool. It is a cloudless Sunday in late June, the sun high and warm. She is watching the shadows which the waves she makes cast on the bottom of the pool – pulses of light and darkness whose existence is frenzied and brief, so different from the calm, lapping waves they reflect. Celia is at the center. The waves radiate out from where she treads, her arms and legs moving as instinctively as those of a baby held up in the air. Near the French doors to the library, Nathan and Andrew, her best friends, are dancing to a song with a strong disco beat and lyrics in German which emanates from a pair of two-foot-high speakers at either end of the library. The speakers remind Celia of the canvas bases her mother uses for her macramé wall hangings, but she knows that in spite of their simplicity, or because of it, they are worth thousands of dollars each, and represent a state-of-the-art technology. Nathan has told her this several times in the course of the weekend; he worries that she or Andrew might knock one of the speakers over, or carelessly topple a precious vase, or spill Tab on one of the leather sofas. They are not rich, he tells them jokingly; they do not know about these things. (The expensiveness of his parents' house is, by both necessity and design, easy to overlook, but Celia's eye for what she does not have has already rooted out the precious, notices that there are fresh bowls of roses in every room and that the gray parachute-cloth sofas are actually made of silver silk.)

The song changes. 'Oh, I love this,' Andrew says. He is an enthusiastic and uncontrolled dancer. He twists and jolts, and lunges forward accidentally, nearly colliding with one of the speakers. 'Will you be careful?' Nathan shouts, and Andrew jumps back onto the patio. 'Relax,' he says. 'I'm not going to break anything.'

Celia kicks her legs, pulls her neck back, and gracefully somersaults into the water; suddenly the music is gone, Nathan and Andrew are gone, though she can see their distorted reflections above the pool's surface. She breathes out a steady stream of bubbles, pulls herself head over heels, and emerges once again, sputtering water. The music pounds. They are still fighting. 'Andrew, if you don't calm down,' Nathan says, 'I'm going to turn off the music. I swear.'

'Go to hell,' Andrew says, and Celia takes another dive, this time headfirst, pulling herself deep into the pool's brightness. She can hear nothing but the sound of the pool cleaning itself – a wet buzz. When she reaches the bottom, she turns around and looks up at the sun refracted through the prisms of the water. She is striped by bars of light. She would stay underwater a long time, but soon she's feeling that familiar pressure, that near-bursting sensation in her lungs, and she has to push off the bottom, swim back up toward the membrane of the water's surface. When she breaks through, she gulps air and opens her eyes wide. The music has been turned off, Andrew is gone, and Nathan is sitting on the chaise next to the pool, staring at his knees.

'You were sitting on the bottom of the pool,' he says to Celia.

'What happened? Where's Andrew?' she asks, wiping the chlorine off her lips.

'He stormed off,' Nathan says. 'Nothing unusual.'

'Oh,' Celia says. She looks at her legs, which move like two eels under the water. 'I wish I knew what to tell you,' she says.

'There's nothing to tell.'

Celia keeps her head bowed. Her legs seem to be rippling out of existence, swimming away with the tiny waves.

Celia has spent every free moment, this weekend, in the water. She lusts after Nathan's tiled swimming pool, and the luminous crystal liquid which inhabits it. In the water, Celia's body becomes sylph-like, a floating essence, light; she can move with ease, even with grace. On land, she lumbers, her body is heavy and ungainly and must be covered with dark swatches of fabric, with loose skirts and saris. Celia is twenty-three years old, and holds the position of assistant sales director at a publishing company which specializes in legal textbooks. Of course, Nathan and Andrew always encourage her to quit her job and apply for a more creative position somewhere, to move downtown and leave behind her tiny apartment and terrible neighborhood. But Andrew is blessed, and Nathan is rich. They don't understand that things like that don't work out so easily for other people.

Here are Andrew and Nathan, as someone who hasn't known them for very long might see them: blond boy and dark boy, WASP and Jew, easy opposites. They work for rival advertising companies, but work seems to be just about the only thing they don't fight about. Nathan has dark, pitted skin, curly hair, a face always shadowed by the beginnings of a beard, while Andrew is fine-boned and fair, with a spindly, intelligent nose, and a body which in another century might have been described as 'slight'. He likes to say that he belongs in another century, the nineteenth, in the tea-drinking circle of Oscar Wilde; Nathan is invincibly devoted to present-day. They live on opposite poles of Manhattan – Nathan on the Lower East Side, Andrew in an East Ninety-sixth Street tenement on the perilous border of Harlem. From his window, Andrew can see the point where the 'ground ruptures and the train tracks out of Grand Central emerge into open air. Three blocks down Park Avenue he can see Nathan's parents' apartment building. Sometimes he runs into Nathan's mother at D'Agostino's, and they chat about the price of tomatoes, and Nathan's mother, who knows nothing, tells Andrew that he really must come to dinner sometime. Publicly, they are ex-lovers and enemies; privately (but everyone guesses) current lovers and (occasionally) friends. As for Celia, she floats between them, suspended in the strange liquid of her love for them – a love, she likes to think, that dares not speak its name.

That is what they look like to their friends from work, to the people they eat dinner with and sleep with, to all those acquaintances who find them interesting and likeable, but have other concerns in their lives.

And what, Celia wonders now, floating in the pool, is she doing here this weekend, when she has sworn time and again never to travel alone with them anywhere, not even to a restaurant? She always ends up in the middle of their battleground, the giver of approval, the spoils which they fight over, forget, and abandon. She tells herself she is here because it is over a hundred degrees in Manhattan, because her super has confided that the old woman across the hall from her apartment hasn't opened the door for days, and he's getting worried. She tells herself she is here because Nathan's parents are in Bermuda, the maid is on vacation, there is the swimming pool and the garden with fresh basil growing in it. And it's true, they've had a good time. Friday, sticky with Penn Station grime, they walked along the beach, ran in the tide, let the dry, hot wind blow against their faces. Saturday, they went into East Hampton, and looked at all the pretty people on the beach, and Celia decided it really wasn't all that surprising that those people should be rich and happy, while she was poor and miserable. They ate salad and watched a rerun of *The Love Boat*, and then Nathan and Andrew tucked Celia into Nathan's parents' big bed and disappeared together to another part of the house. She closed her eyes and cursed herself for feeling left out, for being alone, for having come out here in the first place. She tried, and failed, to imagine what they looked like making love. She tried to hear them. Now, Sunday morning, they have begun fighting because the fact that they still sleep together is a source of shame to both of them. And why not? Even Celia is ashamed. She is not supposed to know that Nathan and Andrew still sleep together, but Andrew calls her every time it happens. 'I don't even like him,' he tells Celia, his voice hoarse and strained. 'But he has this power over me which he has to keep reasserting for the sake of his own ego. Well, no more. I'm not going to give in to him anymore.' But even as he says these words, she can hear his voice grow hesitant with doubt, desire, love.

Celia swims to the pool ladder and hoists herself onto the deck. She has been in the water so long that her hands and feet have wrinkled and whitened. She wraps a towel around herself, suddenly ashamed of how her thighs bounce out of water, lies down on an empty chaise, and picks up a magazine called *Army Slave* from the patio table between her and Nathan. Andrew bought the magazine as a belated birthday present for Nathan, but neither of them has shown much interest in it this weekend. Now Celia thumbs through the pages – a man in green fatigues sitting on a bunk bed, clutching his groin; then a few shots of the man fornicating with another man, in officer's garb. In the last pages, a third figure shows up, dressed in leather chaps, and looks on from the sidelines. 'Do you like it?' Nathan asks. 'Does it turn you on?'

'I don't understand what's so erotic about army bases and locker rooms,' Celia says. 'I mean, I suppose I understand that these are very male places. But still, they're very anti-gay places. I mean, do you find this erotic? Did you find locker rooms erotic when you were growing up? And this guy in the leather –'

Nathan thrusts out his hips and purses his lips. 'Oh, don't let's talk about whips and leather. Let's talk about Joan Crawford!' He makes little kissing gestures at Celia.

'Be serious,' Celia says. 'I was wondering because I want to know, to understand, genuinely.'

'From a sociological perspective?' Nathan asks, returning to a normal posture.

'You could call it that,' Celia says.

'I'll tell you this,' Nathan says. 'When draft registration was reintroduced, I saw a magazine with a picture on the cover of it of this very big hairy guy in a torn-up army uniform, staring out at you very lewdly. And underneath him it said, "The Gay Community salutes the return of the military draft." It was really very funny.'

Celia's eyes light up. 'Oh, that's great!' she says. 'That's reclamation!'

Nathan doesn't respond, so she returns to the magazine. She picks up a pencil from the table and starts to scribble something in the margin when Andrew appears, seemingly from nowhere, before her and Nathan. 'I'm mad,' he says. 'But I'm not going to play your stupid game and just run away and hide out and sulk. I want to face things.'

'Andrew,' Nathan says, 'explain to Celia why that magazine is a turn-on. Note I do not use the word "erotic".'

'Oh, Christ, Celia,' Andrew says, 'I can't talk about that with you.'

'I should've figured you'd be prudish about things like this when I found out you slept in pajamas,' Celia says.

'Andrew doesn't want to spoil the integrity of his double life,' Nathan says. 'He doesn't want you to know that though by day he is your average preppie fashion-conscious fag, by night he goes wild – leather, cowboy hats, water sports. You name it, he's into it.'

'Speak for yourself,' Andrew says. 'You're the one with the double life.' He glances significantly at the pool.

'This isn't sociology. This isn't objective curiosity,' Celia says. 'You should know that by now.'

They both look at her, puzzled. She closes her eyes. The sun beats down, and Celia imagines that the temperature has risen ten degrees in the last ten minutes. She opens her eyes again. Andrew has sat down on the end of Nathan's chaise and is berating him.

In a single, swift lunge, Celia pulls herself up and hurls herself into the water.

Celia, Nathan, and Andrew have known each other since their freshman year in college, when they were all in the same introductory English class. For most of that year, however, Nathan and Andrew recognized each other only as 'Celia's other friend'; they had no relationship themselves. She recalls the slight nausea she experienced the day when she learned Nathan was gay. Up until that point, she had never known a homosexual, and she felt ashamed for having liked him, shyly as she did, so shyly that she phrased her feelings like that: 'I like him,' she confided to her roommate, who played varsity hockey. Celia felt ashamed as well for not having known better, and she feared her naïve affection might seem like an insult to Nathan, and turn him against her. Nathan was something new to Celia; she idolized him because he had suffered for being different, and because his difference gave him access to whole realms of experience she knew nothing of. Celia had never had many friends in school, had never been terribly popular, and this had always seemed just to her: She was fat and shy, and she was constantly being reprimanded for being fat and shy. She never considered that she might be 'different' in the intense, romantic way Nathan was. She was simply alone, and where Nathan's aloneness was something that ennobled him, hers was something to regret.

At first, Nathan accepted Celia's gestures of affection toward him because she would listen – endlessly, it seemed – and talk to him, respond, as well. She was fascinated by the stories that he told her so willingly, stories about mysterious sexual encounters in men's rooms, adolescent fumblings in changing rooms. Her curiosity grew; she read every book and article she could find on the subject of homosexuality, including explicit diaries of nights spent cruising the docks and beaches, the bars and bathhouses of New York and LA and Paris. She read all of Oscar Wilde, and most of Hart Crane. She started to speak up more, to interrupt in class, and found in her underused vocal cords her mother's powerful, Bronx-born timbre, capable of instantly bringing crowds to attention. At their college, it was quite common for women in certain majors – women with long hair and purple clothes and a tendency to talk loudly and quickly and a lot – to spend most of their time in the company of gay men.

Celia became the prime example of this accepted social role, so much so that some people started referring to her as the 'litmus paper test', and joking that one had only to introduce her to a man to determine his sexual preference. It was not a kind nickname, implying that somehow she drove them to it, but Celia bore it stoically, and worse nicknames as well. She joked that she was the forerunner of a new breed of women who emitted a strange pheromone which turned men gay, and would eventually lead to the end of the human race. All the time she believed herself to be better off for the company she kept. What Celia loved in her gay friends was their willingness to commit themselves to endless analytical talking. Over dinner, over coffee, late at night, they talked and talked, about their friends, their families, about books and movies, about 'embodying sexual difference', and always being able to recognize people in the closet. This willingness to talk was something no man Celia had ever known seemed to possess, and she valued it fiercely. Indeed, she could go on forever, all night, and invariably it would be Nathan who would finally drag himself off her flabby sofa and say, 'Excuse me, Celia, it's four a.m. I've got to get to bed.' After he left, she would lie awake for hours, unable to cease in her own mind the conversation which had finally exhausted him.

As their friendship intensified, she wanted still to probe more deeply, to learn more about Nathan. She knew that he (and, later, Andrew) had a whole life which had nothing, could have nothing to do with her – a life she heard about only occasionally, when she was brave enough to ask (the subject embarrassed Nathan). This life took place primarily in bars – mysterious bastions of maleness which she imagined as being filled with yellow light creeping around dark corners, cigarettes with long fingers of ash always about to crumble, and behind every door, more lewdness, more sexuality, until finally, in her imagination, there was a last door, and behind it – here she drew a blank. She did not know. Of course Nathan scoffed at her when she begged him to take her to a bar. 'They're boring, Celia, totally banal,' he said. 'You'd be disappointed the same way I was.' They were just out of college, and Nathan was easily bored by most things.

A few weeks later Andrew arrived in the city. The night he got in he and Celia went to the Village for dinner, and as they walked down Greenwich Avenue she watched his eyes grow wide, and his head turn, as they passed through the cluster of leather-jacketed men sporting together in front of Uncle Charlie's. The next night he asked Celia to accompany him to another bar he was scared to go to alone (he'd never actually been to a gay bar), and she jumped at the opportunity. At the steel doors of the bar, which was located on a downtown side street, the bouncer looked her over and put out his arm to bar their entrance. 'Sorry,' he said, 'no women allowed' – pronouncing each syllable with dental precision, as if she were a child or a foreigner, someone who barely understood English. No women: There was the lure of the unknown, the unknowable. She could catch riffs of disco music from inside, and whiffs of a strange fragrance, like dirty socks, but slightly sweet. Here she was at the threshold of the world of the men she loved, and she was not being allowed in, because that world would fall apart, its whole structure of exclusive fantasy would be disrupted if she walked into it. 'No women,' the bouncer said again, as if she hadn't heard him. 'It's nothing personal, it's just policy.'

'When all the men you love can only love each other,' Celia would later tell people – a lot of people – 'you can't help but begin to wonder if there's something wrong with being a woman. Even if it goes against every principle you hold, you can't help but wonder.' That night she stood before those closed steel doors and shut her eyes and wished, the way a small child wishes, that she could be freed from her loose skirts, her make-up and jewels, her interfering breasts and buttocks. If she could only be stripped and pared, made sleek and svelte like Nathan and Andrew, then she might slip between those doors as easily as the men who hurried past her that night, their hands in their pockets; she might be freed of the rank and untrustworthy baggage of femininity. But all she could do was turn away. Andrew remained near the door. 'Well,' he said. 'Well, what?' Celia asked. 'Would you mind terribly much if I went in myself, anyway?' he asked. She saw in his eyes that desperate, hounded look she recognized from the times they'd walked together, and passed good-looking men in the streets; that look she realized was probably on her face tonight as well. There was something behind those doors which was stronger than his love for her, much stronger. She didn't say anything, but walked away into the street, vowing never to go downtown again. On the subway, riding home, she watched a bag lady endlessly and meticulously rearrange her few possessions, and she decided that she would become bitter and ironic, and talk about

herself in witticisms, and live alone always. 'For most
she decided she'd say, 'falling in love with a gay mar
passage. For me it became a career.' Then she would
no, a drag – from her cigarette (she would of course h,
smoking). And laugh. And toss it off.

Celia has made Andrew and Nathan eggs, and garnished each plate
with a sprig of watercress and a little tuft of alfalfa sprouts. Now,
balancing the plates on her arm, she walks toward the library, where
they've retreated from the sun for the afternoon. When she enters
the library, she sees Andrew leaning against the windowsill, and
Nathan lying with his legs slung over the leather sofa, his head
resting on the floor.

'Lunch,' Celia says.

'Sundays are always horrible,' Andrew says. 'No matter what.
Especially Sundays in summer.'

Nathan does a backflip off the sofa, and makes a loud groaning
noise. 'Such depression!' he says. 'What to do, what to do. We could
go tea dancing! That's a lovely little Sunday afternoon tradition at
the River Club. Thumping disco, live erotic dancers . . .'

'I'm not going back to the city one more minute before I have
to,' Celia says.

'Yes,' Andrew says. 'I'm sure Celia would just love it if we went
off tea dancing.'

Celia looks at him.

'I'm surprised at you, Andrew,' Nathan says. 'You usually enjoy
dancing tremendously. You usually seem to have a really euphoric
time dancing.'

'Enough, Nathan,' Andrew says.

'Yes, watching Andrew dance is like – it's like – how to describe
it? I think we see in Andrew's dancing the complete realization of
the mind–body dualism.'

He stands up, walks around the sofa, and hoists himself over its
back, resuming his upside-down position. 'The body in abandon,'
Nathan continues. 'Total unself-consciousness. Nothing which has
anything to do with thought.'

Celia gives Nathan a glance of disapproval. It is unnecessary;
Andrew is on the defensive himself today. 'I find your hypocrisy
laughable,' he says. 'One minute you're telling me, "Why don't you

stop analyzing everything to death?" and the next you're accusing me of not thinking. Get your attacks straight, Nathan.'

'Ah,' Nathan says, lifting up his head and cocking it (as best he can) at Andrew, 'but I'm not criticizing your dancing, Andrew! I'm just extrapolating! Can you imagine what it would be like to never, ever think, really? I think it would be wonderful! You'd just sort of trip along, not particularly enjoying yourself but never having a bad time, either! Never feeling anguish or jealousy – too complicated, too tiring. I know people who are really like that. You see, Celia, Andrew thinks I'm dishonest. He thinks I run scared from the full implications of my sexual choice. He would like my friends, the Peters. Lovers, Celia. They're both named Peter, and they live together, but they're completely promiscuous, and if one has an affair, the other isn't bothered. Peter just has to tell Peter all about it and it's as if Peter's had the affair, too. But they're happy. They've fully integrated their gayness into their lives. Isn't that what we're supposed to do, Andrew?'

He hoists himself up, and sits down again on the sofa, this time normally.

'Don't be ridiculous,' Andrew says. 'People like that aren't even people.'

Celia, sitting cross-legged on the floor, has finished her eggs. Now she reaches for Nathan's plate and picks the watercress off it. Nathan has eaten only a few spoonfuls. At restaurants, Celia often finds herself picking food off other people's plates, completely unintentionally, as if she's lost control over her eating.

Nathan, his head right side up, is humming the tune to the Pete Seeger song 'Little Boxes'. Now he glances up at Celia. 'Shall we sing, my dear?' he asks.

'You can,' she says. 'I don't ever want to sing that song again.' Nathan sings:

> 'Little faggots in the Village,
> And they're all made out of ticky-tacky,
> Yes, they're all made out of ticky-tacky,
> And they all look just the same.
> There's a cowboy and a soldier and a UCLA wrest-i-ler,
> And they're all made out of ticky-tacky,
> And they all look just the same.'

Andrew bursts out laughing. 'That's funny,' he says. 'When did you make that up?'

'*I* made it up,' Celia says. 'Walking down the street one night.' She smiles, rather bitterly, remembering the evening they walked arm in arm, very drunk, past Uncle Charlie's Downtown and sang that song. Nathan suddenly became very self-conscious, very guilty, and pulled away from Celia. He had a sudden horror of being mistaken for half of a heterosexual couple, particularly here, in front of his favorite bar. 'Just remember,' he had said to Celia. 'I'm not your boyfriend.'

'Why do I even speak to you?' Celia had answered. It was right after Andrew had abandoned her outside that other bar. That summer Andrew and Nathan, singly and collectively, stood her up at least fourteen times; twice Nathan, who was living at his parents' place, asked to use her apartment to meet people and she let him. She didn't think she was worth more than that. She was fat, and she was a litmus test. The only men she cared about were gay, and she didn't seem to know many women. She was Typhoid Celia. But finally she got angry, one Sunday, when she was at Jones Beach with Andrew. 'Answer me this,' she said to him, as they settled down on that stretch of the beach which is the nearly exclusive domain of Puerto Rican families. Andrew wasn't even looking at her; he couldn't keep his head from pulling to the left, straining to catch a glimpse of the gay part of the beach, where Celia had refused to sit. 'Answer me this,' Celia said again, forcing him to look at her. 'A nice hypothetical question along the lines of, would you rather be blind or deaf? Why is it that no matter how much you love your friends, the mere possibility of a one-night stand with someone you probably won't ever see again is enough to make you stand them up, lock them out, pretend they don't exist when you pass them in the street? Why do we always so willingly give up a beloved friend for any lover?'

Even now she could see Andrew's head drifting just slightly to the left. Then he looked at her, pointed a finger at her face, and said, 'There's a tea leaf lodged between your front teeth.'

Celia doesn't realize until she's doing it that she is eating the last of the alfalfa sprouts off Andrew's plate. In horror, she throws them down. She slaps her hand and swears she won't do it again.

'When are your parents getting back?' Andrew asks.

'Not until tonight,' Nathan says. 'They're due in at seven.'

'I spoke to my parents last week. They said they'd look for me in the TV coverage of the Pride March next week. It really touched me, that they'd say that. I didn't even have to mention that there was going to be a Pride March, they already knew.'

Silence from Nathan. Celia gathers her hands into fists.

'Are you going to march this year, Nathan?'

Nathan stands up and walks over to the stereo. 'No,' he says. He puts a recording of Ravel on the turntable.

'That's too bad,' Andrew says.

Celia considers screaming, insisting that they stop right here. Andrew knows that Nathan has never marched, will never march, in the annual Gay Pride Parade, ostensibly because he considers such public displays 'stupid', but really because he lives in fear of his parents discovering his homosexuality. The last time she visited him here Nathan and his father sat in the library and talked about stocks. All night he was the perfect son, the obedient little boy, but on the train ride back he bit his thumbnail and would not speak. 'Do you want to talk about it?' Celia asked him, and he shook his head. He would hide from them always. The happy relationship Andrew enjoys with his liberal, accepting parents is probably his most powerful weapon against Nathan, and the one which he withholds until the last minute, for the final attack.

'I'm carrying the alumni group banner in the march this year,' Andrew says.

'Good,' says Nathan.

'I really wish you'd come. You'd like it. Everyone will be there, and it's a lot of fun to march.'

'Drop it, Andrew,' Nathan says. 'You know how I feel. I think that kind of public display doesn't do any good to anyone. It's ridiculous.'

'It does the marchers a lot of good. It does the world a lot of good to see people who aren't ashamed of who they are.'

'That's not who *I* am,' Nathan says. 'Maybe it's part of *what* I am. But not who.' He turns and looks at the rose garden outside the window. 'Don't you see,' he says, 'that it's a question of privacy?'

'In any battle for freedom of identity there can be no distinction between the private and the political.'

'Oh, great, quote to me from the manual,' Nathan says. 'That helps. You know what's wrong with your party-line political correctness? Exactly what's wrong with your march. It homogenizes gay people. It doesn't allow for personal difference. It doesn't recognize that maybe for some people what's politically correct is personally impossible, emotionally impossible. And for a politics which is supposed to be in favor of difference, it certainly doesn't allow for much difference among the "different".' His pronunciation of this word brings to their minds the voices of elementary school teachers.

'I think you're underselling politics, Nathan,' Andrew says.

'Oh, just give me a break, Andrew, give me a break,' Nathan says. 'You know the only reason you ever found politics was because you had a crush on what's-his-name – Joel Miller – senior year. You had a huge crush on him and you were scared little Andrew and you were afraid to use the word "gay". I remember distinctly all the little ways you had of talking around that word. "I'm joining the widening circle," was all you could say to Celia. I remember that. "The widening circle." Where in hell you came up with that phrase is beyond me. And then there's hunky Joel Miller who'll only sleep with you if you wear a lavender armband and talk about "pre-Stonewall" and "post-Stonewall" every chance you get and suddenly our little Andrew is Mr Big Political Activist. Jesus. You're right about your politics, about there being no separation between the private and the political.'

He turns away from Andrew, clearly disgusted, picks up the jacket of the Ravel record, and begins to read the liner notes furiously.

'I can't stand this anymore,' Celia says, then sits down on the sofa. Neither of them seems to have heard her. Nathan looks as if he might start crying any second – he cries easily – and a slick smile is beginning to emerge on Andrew's face.

'Nathan,' he says, 'do I detect a note of jealousy in your voice?'

'Go to hell,' Nathan says, and storms out of the room.

'That's right, that's right, run away,' says Andrew, marching after him to the library door. 'Just go cry on Daddy's lap, why don't you, you just go tell him all about it.'

'Stop it,' Celia says. He turns around, and she is in front of him, her face wrathful. 'Jesus Christ,' she says, 'you two are children. He overreacts to you, and the minute he's vulnerable, you just go for the balls, don't you? You just hit him right where it hurts?'

'Give me a break, Celia,' Andrew says. 'He's been asking for it, he's been taunting me all weekend. I'm sorry, but I'm not going to be his little punching bag, not anymore. I'm the stronger one. What just happened proves it.'

'All it proves is that you can be as cruel to him as he can be to you,' Celia says. 'Big shit.'

'He knows I'm sensitive about dancing, so he goes after me about it. He treats me like a heedless fool whose only purpose in life is to break all his parents' precious possessions. Well, I'm not a fool, Celia, I'm a hell of a lot better put-together person than he is.'

'All the more reason why you shouldn't hurt him,' Celia says. 'You know all that stuff about the march, about his parents, you know what a sore subject that is for him. Not to mention Joel Miller.'

'And all that time I was seeing Joel, did he say a word to me? Did he even talk to me? No! That time, Celia, he hurt me more than I could ever possibly have hurt him.'

Celia laughs, then – a hard, shrill laugh. 'Let's add up points,' she says. 'Let's see who's been hurt the most.'

Nathan and Andrew became lovers in Florence, the summer after junior year. It happened only a few days before their scheduled rendezvous with Celia in Rome. That summer, like every summer, Nathan was a wanderer, a rich boy, one of hordes of backpack-bearing students trying to make the most of their Eurail passes. Andrew was in Europe under more impressive auspices; he had won a fellowship to study the influence of Mannerism on the Baroque, using as his chief example the statuary of several late-sixteenth-century Italian gardens. Celia's journey began later and ended earlier than her friends' because she didn't have much money, and had to get back to slave at a secretarial job in order to earn funds for her next year in college. She had never been to Europe before, and when she met her friends in Rome, she was exuberant with stories to tell them about her travels in England and France. In particular she wanted to tell them about a tiny town in Wales which had a wall and a moat, and how – big and uncoordinated as she was – she had climbed to the top of the old stone wall and marched its perimeter, as guardian knights had done in the thirteenth century. From the top of the wall, she could see the town – snug houses crammed together, and ruins of a castle, and the bay where fishermen caught salmon at high tide. And there, above it all, was Celia. She felt a rare self-confidence, and for once she liked the way she imagined she looked to other people – smart and self-assured, aware of how to travel right, able to drink in the pleasures of Europe without falling prey to its pitfalls and inconveniences. Indeed, arriving in Italy, Celia was so distracted by herself that it took her a few days to figure out what was going on between Nathan and Andrew. She talked and talked, and they sat across from her, their hands in front of them, and listened politely. Then, on the third day of their week together, the two of them insisted on keeping the double room they were sharing, and keeping Celia in an expensive single, even though a cheaper triple had opened up. She wondered why, and knew. That afternoon they walked out to the Catacombs, and on the way they played a game called In My Grandmother's Trunk. 'In my grandmother's trunk,' Nathan began, 'I found an addlepated aardvark.' Now it was Andrew's turn. 'In my grandmother's trunk,' he declaimed, 'I found an addlepated aardvark and a bellicose bovine.' Celia twisted her hair around her pinky and thought about it. 'In my grandmother's trunk, I found an addlepated aardvark, a bellicose bovine, and a crenellated chry-santhemum,' she said at last, smiling, proud of her answer. Nathan didn't even look at her, though he had laughed at Andrew's response. She realized they were in love as well as lovers then – recognizing, she supposes now, a certain secretiveness in the way they spoke, the way they listened for each other's answers, as if they were talking in code. They offered each other enervated earwigs and truncated turnips as if they were precious gifts, until the game became some-thing which had no place for Celia. Andrew was not out of the closet, then, and as far as she knew, he and Nathan knew each other only through her. The meeting among the three of them had been arranged spontaneously over one of the dinners the three of them had together. 'Let's say, July twenty-fourth, in front of the Pantheon,' said Nathan, who knew Rome (he claimed) as well as he knew New York. Andrew and Celia, neither of whom had been to Europe before, both marveled that it was even possible to plan here, in the New World, for actual rendezvous in the strange Old World of Marcus Aurelius and Isabella Sforza and Eleanora de Toledo. And Nathan, too, enjoyed his status as expert, as experienced traveler. He would show them everything, he told them. He would be a marvelous tour guide. Falling asleep that night, Celia had thought of books she had read as a child in which trios of children went on adventures together in distant lands and on other worlds. But apparently, Nathan and Andrew had made some other plans without telling her, to meet earlier, and alone; apparently they had been seeing each other without her, and without her knowing; apparently, she realized, walking away from Rome, they were no longer hers, but each other's.

Celia finally confronted them over Orzata at a café on the Piazza Navona. 'I want you to know that I'm aware of what's going on,' she said, 'and I think we should talk about it.' In fact, Nathan did all the talking, while Andrew wriggled, embarrassed and terrified. What Celia remembers most vividly about that afternoon is the overwhelming desire to bolt and run which took her over. She thought longingly of her town in Wales, and of the old, crumbling wall, and of herself atop it, and she wished she could transport herself back there, just for an instant, and regain – now, when she needed it – that rare feeling of freedom, of having surpassed the needy world.

She congratulated them (and thought, how stupid, as if it's an achievement); said she was happy for them (and thought, why am I so unhappy for myself?); agreed willingly to stay in her single room. But should she stay at all? Wouldn't it be better if she left, and left the two of them alone? No, never! Of course they wanted her, she must stay. So she did. A few days later, they visited the garden of the Villa d'Este at Tivoli. Andrew was doing his research, taking furious notes about certain bas-reliefs of men turning into fishes. Andrew read to Nathan from his notebook:

It is the final act of reclamation that moss is destroying their faces. What's thematized here is an endless battle between nature and art. On one level, nature subjugates the men by turning them into lower forms of life, but really art is subjugating nature. The fishes' mouths are part of the drainage system – a technical wonder in the sixteenth century – which allows the fountain water to ceaselessly recirculate, by means of a number of pumps. Only now is nature taking its revenge, by destroying these fish faces, a little at a time, year after year. Wearing them down, growing them over with moss. Moss and wind and time. How long can Tivoli last?

Triumphantly he closed the blue notebook, which was printed with the insignia of their university. 'Well?' he said.

'How poetic,' said Nathan.

Andrew looked at him. 'What do you mean?' he asked.

'I mean,' Nathan said, 'it's all lovely and sensitive, but I really can't believe you're making all these claims when you have no basis in historical fact. How can you know that what you say is going on is what was intended?'

'Historical fact,' Andrew said, 'is the historicist's fiction. I don't pretend I can know anyone's intention. I'm doing a *reading* of the garden.'

It went on from there. Andrew accused Nathan of being a pedant, and Nathan accused Andrew of evading the rigors of scholarship. Already Celia understood more about them than they did about themselves: Andrew was impulsive, Nathan cautious; Andrew had a reason to be in Europe, Nathan had none (and was jealous). She found the matter altogether tedious, so she wandered away from them and fell in with a tour group from Oklahoma. The group was standing in front of the statue of Diana of Ephesus, her twelve breasts spouting water into an ancient urn, and the guide was talking about the Goddess being a symbol of natural fertility. 'Some say she is related to Vishnu,' he said solemnly, 'the God with the thirteen hands.'

'I'll bet her husband was the guy with the thirteen hands!' a woman with a beehive hairdo bellowed, and everyone roared, and Celia – standing among them – realized suddenly that she, too, was laughing, and that she had to leave.

She went the next morning. At the train station, Nathan and Andrew pleaded with her, begged her to stay, but she was decided. She got on an all-night train to Calais, and a ferry back to England, and another train to London. And after a single night in a hostel in Knightsbridge she took all the money she had left and bought a round-trip ticket to her beloved little town in Wales. Almost as soon as she got there she checked into a bed-and-breakfast and went to look at the old stone wall. There was a group of children no more than nine or ten years old being led around it, children from some industrial town in the Midlands, with Mohawk haircuts and dirty black vinyl jackets on. They were fighting with each other over candy, pretending to push each other off the wall. Then they started yelling things at her – obscenities she could hardly understand – and she hurriedly walked away and stood on the grass of the town green and closed her eyes. The air was fresh with the smell of recent rain, as well as the smell of biscuits baking nearby. An old man sitting on a stone bench hobbled over to her, and started speaking to her, but his Welsh accent was so strong that she thought he was speaking in another language, Finnish or Dutch. 'Slower, please, slower,' she said, until she finally realized he was asking her why she was crying. 'Crying?' she said, and put her hands to her eyes, which were moist with tears.

Across a continent, Nathan and Andrew were not even thinking about her.

Although they've knocked repeatedly on his door, Nathan has apparently resolved not to acknowledge the presence of his friends this afternoon, and so, around three o'clock, Andrew and Celia take a walk to the beach. Celia is determined to spend most of the day outdoors, with or without Nathan. He has brooded too long, and she is losing patience with him. Andrew, on the other hand, cannot stop worrying about his friend; his brief triumph has left in its wake a weighty sense of guilt. 'I guess I won,' he tells Celia, 'and it felt so good. But now I wish I'd lost. I don't like this feeling. You know, he's won practically every argument we've ever had.'

'Don't be too upset about him,' Celia says. 'You know how he is. He broods. Anyway, I thought you were so happy to have put him in his place.'

'But that's just it,' Andrew says. 'I'm not supposed to put him in his place. I'm not supposed to do that.'

'Andrew, that's ridiculous,' Celia says. 'Things change in relationships, and maybe this means you're breaking out of the old pattern.'

Andrew shakes his head violently, and pushes a mosquito out of his face. 'It just doesn't work that way,' he says. 'For years I've had this idea of who he was and who I was. I knew I was more politically aware and had a healthier attitude toward sex and toward being gay. And I knew he was politically backward and closeted and conservative and torn apart because the fact that he liked to sleep with men contradicted everything he was raised to be. But all that time, he still had this power over me because he was the first person I slept with. He'll never let go of the fact that I was a scared little boy and he knew exactly what he was doing.'

'I'm not so sure that's true,' Celia says.

'But he did that for me, Celia. That first night we met in Florence, we were so scared, we both knew what we were there for, why we'd come, but we couldn't even seem to talk about it. Every gesture – every mention of anything having to do with being gay – seemed very courageous, because I still believed, on some level, that he'd be horrified if he found out I wanted to sleep with him, and say something like, "How could you think I'd want to do that?" I mean, I really didn't know about Nathan. I was going on instinct. And then, finally, we were both in the room in the *pensione*, and we were sitting on his bed, and he wouldn't do anything. We just sat there, and five minutes went by, and not a word. I couldn't move.'

'Why?'

'You see, it was understood that he was more experienced. And that he would make the first move. I can't explain why, but it just was. And then he started coughing. Oh, God, I was scared. And I patted him on the back. And I just didn't move my hand away again.

'He said, "You're very suave," and then I hoisted my legs up on the bed – I was sitting and he was lying – and in the middle of getting up on the bed I got this terrible charley horse and started screaming and he just laughed. He bent me over and sort of wrenched my leg into shape again. And then – well, we made love. It was very greedy. No subtlety, no technique. But it was still very definitely "making love", not just sex.' He laughs. 'I remember there were these two drunk Americans who came into the room next to ours late that night from the Red Garter singing "Superfreak". And then around three one of them must have had a nightmare because he ran out into the hall and started screaming, and then crying. The other one tried to shut him up, but he just wailed and wailed. I remember exactly what his friend said. He said. "Hey, man, chill out, don't freak." Nathan was asleep, and we were wrapped around each other in an incredibly complicated way. I could feel all the hairs on his body, and his breath, and his heartbeat. I lay awake all night.'

For several minutes they have been walking by the ocean without realizing it. The beach is almost empty except for a single sunbather, and a woman swimming laterally alongside the shore.

'The next day,' Andrew says, 'we ran into this girl I knew from my botany class the semester before. Charlotte Mallory, you remember her? We had dinner with her. Nathan had his leg pressed against mine under the table the whole time. It was a wonderful secret, something to look forward to, what we'd try that night, everything I had to learn.'

He stops, smiles, and turns to face Celia. 'This isn't fair of me, is it?' he says. 'Imposing this all on you.'

'Oh, don't start on that,' Celia says. 'Andrew, I just wonder why you and Nathan feel you have to keep this thing up. I mean, sure, it was nice once, but it always turns out like it did today. You two know too well how to hurt each other. The memory's precious, but look what it's given rise to, look at yourselves now.'

They are walking again, away from the beach, back toward Nathan's parents' house. Andrew has his hands in his pockets, and keeps his eyes on the ground in front of him. 'Celia,' he says, 'there's something you've got to understand about me and Nathan. He taught me things.'

'Taught you what?'

'Growing up a fag is a strange thing. You never learn about boys' bodies because you're afraid of what you will feel and you never learn about girls' bodies because you're afraid of what you won't feel. And so the first time you sleep with someone, it's like the first time you've ever noticed a body. I watched everything. I remember I was amazed to see the way his diaphragm moved up and down when he slept because I'd never watched anyone sleep before. And for showing me that, because of that, I'll always love him, even if he acts the way he does. I'll never forget the way he looked, sleeping.'

They keep walking. Celia doesn't say anything.

'It's because of that,' Andrew says, after a few seconds, 'that he'll always have an advantage on me. You know what I was just remembering? How that whole summer we stayed in *pensiones*, and usually there were two single beds in the rooms we were given. And in the morning, Nathan always insisted we unmake the bed we hadn't slept in. And I always assumed, and he always assumed, that the unslept-in bed was mine.'

They are in the garden now. Celia looks at the tilled earth beneath her feet, raw end-of-season, everything picked. No sign of Nathan.

'Oh, Celia,' Andrew says, 'this is mean of me.'

'What?'

'It's cruel of me. It must make you feel like you aren't a part of it. But you are. You're very dear to us both.'

'You sound like I'm your adopted child,' Celia says.

'I'm sorry. I don't mean to. It's just – well, I think you should know. Nathan's always thought you were in love with him on some level, and that's why you've stuck around with us.'

Celia looks up at him, startled, and her eyes narrow. She tells herself that she knows what he is doing. He is trying to get her on his side. Nothing unusual. Even so, the revelation, which is no revelation at all, hits her hard, in the stomach.

She looks away from him. 'Why I've stuck around with you?' she says. 'I've stuck around with you because I love you both. I'm devoted to you both. But if Nathan thinks I've just been panting after him all these years, he's flattering himself.'

Andrew laughs, and she curses the slight timbre of resentment in her voice. She does not want to satisfy him by seeming recriminating. Yet she is thinking, why, after all? And she thinks, has it finally arrived, the day when she must confront herself? It has almost arrived many times, and there has always been a reprieve.

'He's just an egotist, I guess,' Andrew says. 'I mean, he thinks of himself as being like those thousand-dollar speakers of his parents. You have to be so careful around him, though God knows he's willing to hurt everyone else.' He smiles affectionately. 'Poor Nathan,' he says. 'You know where he is now? He's in his parents' bedroom, all curled up like a little kid, and he's just lying there, on that huge bed. That's where he goes when he feels small; somewhere where he is small.'

They are at the front door now. Andrew turns and looks down at Celia, and suddenly he seems much taller than he did an hour ago. 'Would you mind terribly if I went in to him for a little while?' he asks. 'Just lie there with him? You can wait in the library, or by the pool. We'll all be ready to leave on the six forty-five.'

Celia wraps her arms around her chest. 'Sure,' she says. 'Fine.' She does not look at Andrew, but at the maple trees, the vines twining up the sides of the house, the fragrant bunches of wisteria.

'I'll see you soon, then,' Andrew says. Then there is the sound of his footsteps, the sound of the screen door as it slaps the house.

It is, Celia realizes, a kind of reprieve to be forgotten.

One night, late in the spring of senior year when they were both drunk on big, deceptive rum-and-fruit concoctions, Nathan told Celia the story of the first time he and Andrew slept together. He told it more cheerfully, and he did not mention the unused bed, though he dwelled with loving attention on the painful conversations they had had that night at dinner. 'Our feet touched once,' Nathan said, 'and we both sort of jumped, as if we had given each other an electric shock. The second time our feet touched we just sort of left them there. I kept thinking, If he says anything, I could just say I thought I was resting my foot against a part of the table.' And of course, Nathan wasn't asleep either. He remembered the boys next door singing 'Superfreak', and the exact words with which the one comforted the other: 'Hey, man, chill out, don't freak.'

'The thing was,' Nathan said, 'I had Andrew convinced that I was Mr Suave, very experienced. And it's true, I was more experienced than he was, but I was a nervous wreck anyway. I mean, being the seducer is a very different thing from knowing how to be seduced. Anyway, when we were alone in the room, I just decided to be brave. So I walked over to Andrew – he was unbuttoning his shirt – and I said, "Why don't you let me do that?" He just froze. And then I kissed him.'

He smiled. Celia knew better than to believe his version, recognizing even then that there were situations in which Nathan had to change the truth, to fit an image of himself which was just a bit wrong, a size too small or too large. After all, Andrew's affair with Joel Miller was at its apex. Nathan was terribly jealous, and it was important to him to prove himself to Celia, since she provided the only link between them. All that year Celia had been insisting that she wanted time to herself, time to pursue her own social life, but almost from the first day Andrew and Nathan wouldn't leave her alone. They wanted her to take sides in the fight they were having. The argument she had witnessed at the Villa d'Este, it seemed, had continued and festered after she left them. They bickered and lashed out at each other until finally, in Paris, Andrew packed his backpack in a fury and, in the middle of the night, stormed out of their little room in the Latin Quarter and boarded a train for Salzburg. By the time he arrived his anger had cooled, and he got on another train back to Paris, but when he got back to their *auberge*, Nathan had checked out and left no forwarding address.

Andrew was seized with panic, for now he was alone, absolutely alone, and there was no way he could find Nathan unless they happened upon each other by chance. Their itinerary was vague, but they had more or less planned to go to Cannes, so Andrew went there, and for two days walked the town tirelessly, scanning the streets and beaches for Nathan, planning what he'd say when he saw him, how aloof and distant he'd be and how he'd draw forgiveness from him. He found it hard to sleep alone again, and he couldn't get out of his nostrils that clean smell of soap and cologne and Nathan. But he never found Nathan in Cannes, or anywhere else in Europe. He continued traveling. By the time he got back to the States, his longing had hardened into something like hatred. And Nathan was angry, too. It was hard to say, after all, who had abandoned whom first, who was to blame for what had happened.

At school they could hardly talk to each other, and so they talked to Celia instead, each giving her his version of what happened in Paris, and trying to win her over to his side. It was the only time, Celia reflected, that two men were rivals for her affections.

She told herself that her position was difficult. At first she had to make sure that Nathan never saw her with Andrew, or vice versa; they insisted on pumping her for information about one another. Then she began to arrange accidental meetings between them; they couldn't help but talk to each other – silence would have seemed too stilted a response, and they both prided themselves on their originality. Finally Andrew called Celia at three o'clock one morning, in tears; she couldn't understand what he was saying, but she managed to get him to tell her where he was, and she put on her coat and trudged out after him. It was just beginning to feel wintry out, and the sky was fringed with blue, as if it were dawn or dusk, and not the middle of the night; and since it was Sunday morning, and just after midterms, there were a few drunk football players still out, tromping around and causing trouble. Celia found Andrew sitting on the post of an old fence, wrapped in a coat he had bought at the Salvation Army, inert. She walked him back to her room, brewed some tea, and sat down in front of him, settling her still-gloved hands comfortably on his knees.

'Now,' she said, 'what's wrong?'

He started crying almost immediately; she let him cry, hugging him, until his body shivered and his teeth chattered, and, stuttering, he said exactly what she expected him to say: 'He doesn't want me. And I love him.'

Celia tracked Nathan down the next day, in the library. As soon as she mentioned Andrew's name, he shushed her, and pointed to his roommate – a tall young man smoking a pipe a few feet away – and hurried her off to a nearby cubicle. There he explained that he had had absolutely enough of Andrew's impulsiveness and silliness. To first simply run away in the middle of the night, stranding Nathan in Paris, and now, after two months, to show up suddenly in his room – thank God his roommate hadn't been home! – and start blubbering about not wanting to keep up the charade, about wanting to talk, about feeling hurt and intimidated by Nathan's behavior toward him in Paris. All of this, naturally, was too much, considering it was Andrew who had all but abandoned Nathan, and to cap it off, he had to be loud about it. So Nathan told him to get out, it was over, he was making a mountain out of a molehill. Of course, even then, sitting in the library cubicle, Celia knew better than to take Nathan's version of things at face value. She realized Nathan was angry, but also, that he was frightened by Andrew's willingness to make a passionate display over matters Nathan felt best left in the bedroom. Where Nathan's skill lay in small, private insults, Andrew's great tactic was, and would always be, display. Probably Nathan realized that his friend was, as Celia would put it, about to shoot out of the closet like a cannonball, and this was more than his ingrained sense of propriety would allow him to accept. Fear lay behind that sense of propriety. Little Andrew, for all his innocence, was turning out to be the one thing Nathan never could be: He was turning out to be brave. So Nathan chose not to forgive Andrew his actions in Paris, and dropped him.

Shortly thereafter, people started seeing Andrew in the company of the famous activist Joel Miller, and the rest was fairly predictable. Joel Miller had done it before, with other apparently uncorruptible young men, and they always emerged from the affairs card-carrying members of the lavender left. Ostensibly, Nathan shouldn't have cared, but Celia could see what was in his eyes when he spied Andrew and Joel eating together in a dining hall. Nathan couldn't stay silent very long about it. 'What's he doing spending so much time with that Joel Miller person?' he'd say to Celia, figuring she'd leak information, but Celia made it a new policy not to talk about Andrew with Nathan, or vice versa. Soon the affair became a public phenomenon, and Nathan's discomfort increased. He slunk away whenever he saw them, and usually left the parties they attended together. ('They walk into the room like they're the football captain and the homecoming queen,' he'd tell Celia.) As for Andrew, he was in bliss; Joel was a genius; he wanted to marry Joel. Celia could afford to be happy for him, because she had her hands full taking care of Nathan, who showed up at her door at all hours. She pitied Nathan; he could never admit that he was terribly intimidated by Joel Miller, or that he might have loved Andrew. Still, she had him. He was there all the time – at her door, waiting for her in the dining hall, in the library. She controlled what he and Andrew heard about one another, and she, of course, knew everything about both of them. One night she would listen to Nathan's anxieties, his claims to misery and loneliness; the next night, to Andrew's praises of the wonders of love, the transcendence of gender roles, and the lovely, dark hair which curled over Joel Miller's shoulder blades.

It did not occur to Celia until a long time later – when she was able to gain some perspective on that year, in which things had been the most intense between them – that her happiness with Nathan and Andrew depended on Nathan and Andrew being unhappy with each other.

Around dusk, Nathan and Andrew emerge from the house. They are dressed in different clothes from the ones they were wearing earlier, and they are talking animatedly, eagerly, occasionally laughing. As soon as she sees them, Celia closes her eyes. She is lying by the pool, the copy of *Army Slave* open on her lap, and all around her fireflies are exploding with light, crickets screeching. 'Come on, Celia, get ready to go,' Nathan says. She opens her eyes and he is leaning over her, smiling. 'My parents may be back any second, and I don't want to be here when they arrive.' He pats her knee, and heads back to the patio, where Andrew is waiting. 'Oh,' he says, turning around, 'and don't forget to bring the magazine.' She lifts up her head, but in the dusk light, she can just barely make out their faces. 'I guess you're feeling better,' she says.

'Yes,' Nathan says. 'Much better.'

She nods, and gets up to pack her things. It is about a ten-minute walk to the train station, and when they get there, the platform is already full of tired-looking people in shorts, all yawning and opening up their newspapers. When the train pulls in, it's already crowded; there are no sets of three seats together. Andrew sits with Celia, and Nathan sits alone, two rows behind them, but the arrangement is entirely for her benefit. Something has happened between Nathan and Andrew this afternoon: They appear to have forgiven each other. Why else would they be thinking about her?

She lies back, watches the pleasurable journey from the scum of Penn Station to the beautiful Hamptons run backward; now they are in the famous suburbs of the Guyland (as Nathan calls it), now in the nether regions of Queens. When they pass the exact border between New York City and the rest of the world, Nathan cannot resist walking up to point it out to them.

Then they are in the tunnel under the East River, and under the famous city where they spend their lives.

They get off the train. Penn Station has no air-conditioning, and is packed with people. Celia wipes the sweat off her brow, and rearranges her bags between her legs. She will take the Broadway local to the Upper West Side, while Nathan and Andrew must walk across town to catch the East Side subway, and ostensibly ride it in opposite directions. She has no doubt but that they will spend tonight, and perhaps tomorrow night, together; and she wonders if they will eat dinner out, see a movie, talk about her, and shake their heads. It will last a few days; then, she is confident, they will fight. One of them will call her, or both of them will call her. Or perhaps they will decide to move in together, and never call her again.

'I've got to catch my train,' Celia says, when it becomes clear that they're not going to invite her out with them. She offers them each her cheek to kiss as if to give her blessing. They look at her a little awkwardly, a little guiltily, and she can't believe they're acting guilty now, when it's been like this for so many years between them. Besides, there really isn't anything anyone can apologize for. Celia begins to walk away, and Nathan calls out her name. She turns, and he is next to her, a big smile plastered on his face. 'You know,' he says, 'you're wonderful. When I write my book, I'm dedicating it to you.'

She smiles back, and laughs. He said the same thing the day she left them at Termini station in Rome and boarded a train for Calais. All that night the couchette car in which she slept was added on and taken off of other strings of lit cars, passed among the major trains and in this way, like a changeling infant, carried singly to the coast. She shared a cabin with two Englishwomen on their way back from holiday and a Swiss man who was going to Liverpool to buy a spare part for his car. Like college roommates, the four of them lay in their bunk beds and talked late into the night. The wheels rumbled against the tracks, the train moved on; every minute she was closer to England. Then she fell asleep, wondering to herself what kind of book Nathan could ever possibly write.

KATE ROBERTS

Protest March

After she finished buttoning her coat, Bronwen looked at her feet.
Then she turned her head over her shoulder to see was there a hole
in her stocking, and raised her heel to see how long her shoe would
hold out without being heeled. Then she looked at the place that
had worn thin around the pocket of her coat. She was doing all this
in the manner of someone conscious of her poverty and wanting to
look neat.

Idris, her husband, was sitting on a hard chair on the hearth, with
his head down, looking into the fire the way men do who are on the
outs with the whole world. That was to be seen in his profile and
in his posture. In talking to his wife he would address the spot where
she was standing or the fireplace, not her.

Bronwen was setting out to march with the United Front against
the Means Test, her husband having refused to come. She still had
hope. His had turned sour. The couple were only twenty-five years
old, and they hadn't seen a halfpenny of wages since they'd been
married. They were living in an underground kitchen, a kitchen that
had once belonged to the house above, and their bedroom was the
kitchen pantry. For this they were paying six shillings a week in
rent. Bronwen was anxious as she said what she'd always say on
leaving the house.

'Well, I'm going, then.'

'Yes, I'll bet you are; you're stupid enough to listen to the fools.
I'm telling you that it's a fraud, the bloody lot of them, and you're
wasting your time and your shoe-leather to go listen to such rubbish.
United Front! United like hell! They'd like to break each other's
necks. Look at how the Labour Party's looking down their noses at
the Communists, and then they go accusing the Labour Party of
selling jobs for money, and if they'd half a chance to sell a job
themselves, they would. A lot of good your marching will do, I'll
tell you. And it's no use your coming back here with a headache
after listening to their screaming.'

He got up as he said the last sentence. He tightened the belt of the grey trousers that were too big for him and came down over his shoes. He gave himself another shake, turned on his heel and went past the curtain into the next room, and lay down on the bed.

Bronwen stood looking at him. She was close to taking off her coat and staying home. But when she thought of spending Sunday afternoon in this hole, her hope had a second boost. She looked at her husband lying in the black windowless hole that was called a bedroom. He lay coiled like a cat on top of a haystack, and to her the turn in his back was an expression of all his sourness and bitterness against life as a whole. She turned on her heel and walked out, and as she went further away from her husband she cheered up. As she went past the ash heaps and the clutter in the back street her hope was on the increase, and by the time she reached the high street with its larger and cleaner houses she was feeling staunch in her hope in the United Front.

It was a warm, tranquil day at the beginning of October, and its effect on people's hearts was like the effect of a day in Spring. There were many others walking ahead of her on their way to the same place, and she was hoping she wouldn't catch up with them so that she could create dreams of her future with Idris; work, wages, better clothes, a house like the ones that she was passing now, children. In a little while she reached the crest of the hill that separated Little Cwm Du from Big Cwm Du. She leaned on the wall to look at the two valleys – the row houses placed like regiments of soldiers along the sides of the hills, with their windows in the sunlight looking like bright buttons, the river between them like a narrow ditch. If the knowledge had been handed down to her by her family or her school she would have known that it was on this spot her great-grandfather and her great-grandmother stood seventy years before, to have the first look at the place that was home to them and their children the rest of their lives. There they had stood, after travelling in a cart from Carmarthenshire, their furniture and their children lying under sacks in the cart, getting their first look at the promised land they'd heard so much about while living in poverty as farmhands and servant-girls. Bronwen didn't know, as she fondled her own hopes now, anything of the hopes of her ancestors on the threshold of their new world. She knew nothing of their homesickness, their joy and their trials later, or she could have blended her dreams of her own future with those of the past. All she knew was that her own parents had

had a better time than she was having now. She couldn't see why better times shouldn't come again, and certainly, to her mind, protesting like this against the injustice of the Means Test was certain to lead somewhere. Things couldn't be like this forever.

She set off again, and walked light-heartedly past houses without signs of poverty on them. She couldn't stop herself from looking into them and gaping at the sideboards' mirrors that were reflecting the silver dishes on their tables. She too would have ones like that sometime. Her eyes turned at times to the trees that surrounded the manager's mansion. What struck her most were the colours of the trees and not the mansion. She didn't envy the manager because of his big house. It was in too lonely a place, and she, who was raised in the neighbourly warmth of Cwm Du, couldn't think of living apart like that. But the trees were pretty. A pity their leaves were falling. They whirled and spun into the corners as she turned into the high street of the other valley.

After reaching the field from which the march was supposed to start she saw a crowd of a size that she'd never seen. She imagined the whole population of the Valley was there, men, women, children, and dogs. It was like a sea in motion, and the talking like its monotonous murmur, except that the carefree laughter of the young sometimes interrupted it. In a little while, a number of men went on top of a dray, and one of them began addressing the crowd. A shiver went down Bronwen's back, that shiver which is an expression of something one can't define, when a person sees a great throng hanging on the words of one man. This man had a narrow chest, and there was a terrible strain on his body in addressing the crowd. His words were coming as though from the depths of his guts, and he was bending and raising his arms as if that would be a help to lift the words up. Every now and then a groan would come from the depths of his being at the tail-end of a word. He stood above the crowd, and he addressed it as though he were its father. Everyone was drinking in his words.

There wasn't as fatherly a look on the next speaker, or as many scars on his face. But the stream of his words ran on unbroken. They ran over Bronwen's head as well. She didn't know what he had to say, but evidently everyone thought the language of the gods was on his lips. The only word that stuck in her mind was the word 'proletariat', and she didn't know the meaning of that.

The crowd formed a procession, and pushed itself from the field to the street. Bronwen found herself marching side by side with a number of fat toothless women, much older than she was. They had one thing in common – poor clothing. But these women could laugh pleasantly. Perhaps their husbands were more contented than her husband, or perhaps they didn't have a husband. Her forehead wrinkled as she remembered Idris and the stubborn turn in his back. She forgot him in hearing the tramp of the feet on the hard road. She had a shiver of pleasure again in seeing the great crowd marching so united in its determination against that invisible thing that was responsible for all their poverty – the Government. A pity the Government wasn't seeing this crowd. She believed they would get what they were after, and more. These old pits would be opened again, and she'd have a house like her mother at least. They were going past similar houses now, but they were greyer than her mother's house ever was. And here were cellars again, like her house. Her anger turned for a moment from the Government to the man who placed the cellars in their row. He wasn't in this crowd, for sure. In thinking like this, she gave a kick unconsciously to the heels of the man who was walking in front of her. She steadied herself back, and her attention was drawn from the purpose of the procession to the procession itself. The man who'd been kicked by her had big feet that turned out, one to the east and the other to the west. On seeing him like this, she began laughing inside. Indeed, there were some amusing people in the procession as she looked around. The women in the same row with her were there to have a good time, obviously. Some others, in the row ahead of her, looked as though they were in earnest, and were, like herself, putting their hope in the results of the march. One of them was looking very serious, and she didn't speak a word to anyone else. She had better clothing than the others. She was pursing her lips tightly, and she was marching ostentatiously, picking out where to put her feet on the ground. This was very amusing to the women in Bronwen's row. They made fun of her walk, and went straight from that to the woman's record on women's committees of the political party to which she belonged. To Bronwen's mind they wouldn't have laughed at her way of walking if they hadn't had a bone to pick with her about her behaviour somewhere else; or why would they laugh at her and not at the man? Strange, the worlds she knew nothing about, the world of committees for example.

By now the sun was going down low on the horizon, and one side of the valley was black in its own shadow. It began to get cold, and Bronwen felt in need of food. Her feet were aching, and she felt the outer side of her heel turning more and more. She was feeling greatly in sympathy with the man with the big feet by this time, because obviously he had trouble walking, and she was kicking him more often. The humorous women were talking less. In the silence, she could hear the craving of her own hunger grumble in her side. As the talk decreased, the sound of the crowd marching became like the sound of sheep walking on a hard road. They kept on going, and by now the first part had crossed the bridge over the river and were walking back to the valley on the other side, until the crowd was in the shape of a U.

The crowd itself was looking like something absurd to Bronwen now, and depressing in its absurdity. She thought, if the Government were to see them now what they'd do was laugh at them. After all, what were they marching to?

When her row was within ten yards of the bridge her attention was caught by a woman in a row that was walking on the bridge that moment and so was before her eyes. She hadn't seen her before that. This woman had on an expensive coat of fur. This gave Bronwen a shock, and now the woman next to her was starting in.

'Well, great heavens! look at her in her fur coat. That's cost a penny or two, you can bet.'

'Yes, there's something better than catskin in that,' the other said.

Bronwen's heart fell lower, and when she understood from the conversation of the others that it was the Member of Parliament's wife who was wearing the fur coat, her heart dropped like a clock pendulum when its cord breaks.

She was in a hurry to leave the procession, and she did so when she had a chance. She wasn't looking forward to going home either. She knew something of Idris' feelings by now. But she couldn't bear to think of his sarcasm when she'd arrive; and the look that would say 'I told you'.

But she had to go. She was almost collapsing from hunger. Of course there wouldn't be a fire in the grate, and she had only bread-and-butter for tea. But there would have been a relish to that if the march had turned out as it began, and if she could have reported to Idris the enthusiasm and the eloquence. What if she should tell him about the fur coat! There'd be a double edge to his sarcasm. A pity her husband was so dreadfully embittered. She knew it was his back she'd see first after opening the door, and she couldn't bear to remember the meaning of that posture. Between fear and weakness and fatigue her legs were sagging by the time she reached the garden gate. She was glad it was beginning to get dark.

No indeed, Idris wasn't in bed. She could see him through the window, sitting by the fire. She went inside like a dog that had been killing sheep. She saw a clean cloth on the table, with tea things and a pot of jam. A small glowing fire had been made up in the grate, and Idris was toasting a slice of bread at it on the tip of a fork. He turned his eyes from the toast and looked into his wife's face. And those eyes were not without compassion.

Translated from the Welsh by Joseph P. Clancy

NATALIA GINZBURG
He and I

He always feels hot, I always feel cold. In the summer when it really is hot he does nothing but complain about how hot he feels. He is irritated if he sees me put a jumper on in the evening.

He speaks several languages well; I do not speak any well. He manages – in his own way – to speak even the languages that he doesn't know.

He has an excellent sense of direction, I have none at all. After one day in a foreign city he can move about in it as thoughtlessly as a butterfly. I get lost in my own city; I have to ask directions so that I can get back home again. He hates asking directions; when we go by car to a town we don't know he doesn't want to ask directions and tells me to look at the map. I don't know how to read maps and I get confused by all the little red circles and he loses his temper.

He loves the theatre, painting, music, especially music. I do not understand music at all, painting doesn't mean much to me and I get bored at the theatre. I love and understand one thing in the world and that is poetry.

He loves museums, and I will go if I am forced to but with an unpleasant sense of effort and duty. He loves libraries and I hate them.

He loves travelling, unfamiliar foreign cities, restaurants. I would like to stay at home all the time and never move.

All the same I follow him on his many journeys. I follow him to museums, to churches, to the opera. I even follow him to concerts, where I fall asleep.

Because he knows the conductors and the singers, after the performance is over he likes to go and congratulate them. I follow him down long corridors lined with the singers' dressing-rooms and listen to him talking to people dressed as cardinals and kings.

He is not shy; I am shy. Occasionally however I have seen him be shy. With the police when they come over to the car armed with a notebook and pencil. Then he is shy, thinking he is in the wrong.

And even when he doesn't think he is in the wrong. I think he has a respect for established authority. I am afraid of established authority, but he isn't. He respects it. There is a difference. When I see a policeman coming to fine me I immediately think he is going to haul me off to prison. He doesn't think about prison; but, out of respect, he becomes shy and polite.

During the Montesi trial, because of his respect for established authority, we had very violent arguments.

He likes tagliatelle, lamb, cherries, red wine. I like minestrone, bread soup, omelettes, green vegetables.

He often says I don't understand anything about food, that I am like a great strong fat friar – one of those friars who devour soup made from greens in the darkness of their monasteries; but he, oh he is refined and has a sensitive palate. In restaurants he makes long inquiries about the wines; he has them bring two or three bottles then looks at them and considers the matter, and slowly strokes his beard.

There are certain restaurants in England where the waiter goes through a little ritual: he pours some wine into a glass so that the customer can test whether he likes it or not. He used to hate this ritual and always prevented the waiter from carrying it out by taking the bottle from him. I used to argue with him about this and say that you should let people carry out their prescribed tasks.

And in the same way he never lets the usherette at the cinema direct him to his seat. He immediately gives her a tip but dashes off to a completely different place from the one she shows him with her torch.

At the cinema he likes to sit very close to the screen. If we go with friends and they look for seats a long way from the screen, as most people do, he sits by himself in the front row. I can see well whether I am close to the screen or far away from it, but when we are with friends I stay with them out of politeness; all the same it upsets me because I could be next to him two inches from the screen, and when I don't sit next to him he gets annoyed with me.

We both love the cinema, and we are ready to see almost any kind of film at almost any time of day. But he knows the history of the cinema in great detail; he remembers old directors and actors who have disappeared and been forgotten long ago, and he is ready to travel miles into the most distant suburbs in search of some ancient silent film in which an actor appears – perhaps just for a few seconds – whom he affectionately associates with memories of his early childhood. I remember one Sunday afternoon in London; somewhere in the distant suburbs on the edge of the countryside they were showing a film from the 1930s, about the French Revolution, which he had seen as a child, and in which a famous actress of that time appeared for a moment or two. We set off by car in search of the street, which was a very long way off; it was raining, there was a fog, and we drove for hour after hour through identical suburbs, between rows of little grey houses, gutters and railings; I had the map on my knees and I couldn't read it and he lost his temper; at last, we found the cinema and sat in the completely deserted auditorium. But after a quarter of an hour, immediately after the brief appearance of the actress who was so important to him, he already wanted to go; I on the other hand, after seeing so many streets, wanted to see how the film finished. I don't remember whether we did what he wanted or what I wanted; probably what he wanted, so that we left after a quarter of an hour, also because it was late – though we had set off early in the afternoon it was already time for dinner. But when I begged him to tell me how the film ended I didn't get a very satisfactory answer; because, he said, the story wasn't at all important, the only thing that mattered was those few moments, that actress's curls, gestures, profile.

I never remember actors' names, and as I am not good at remembering faces it is often difficult for me to recognize even the most famous of them. This infuriates him; his scorn increases as I ask him whether it was this one or that one; 'You don't mean to tell me,' he says, 'You don't mean to tell me that you didn't recognize William Holden!'

And in fact I didn't recognize William Holden. All the same, I love the cinema too; but although I have been seeing films for years I haven't been able to provide myself with any sort of cinematic education. But he has made an education of it for himself and he does this with whatever attracts his curiosity; I don't know how to make myself an education out of anything, even those things that I love best in life; they stay with me as scattered images, nourishing my life with memories and emotions but without filling the void, the desert of my education.

He tells me I have no curiosity, but this is not true. I am curious about a few, a very few, things. And when I have got to know them I retain scattered impressions of them, or the cadence of phrase, or a word. But my world, in which these completely unrelated (unless in some secret fashion unbeknown to me) impressions and cadences rise to the surface, is a sad, barren place. His world, on the other hand, is green and populous and richly cultivated; it is a fertile, well-watered countryside in which woods, meadows, orchards and villages flourish.

Everything I do is done laboriously, with great difficulty and uncertainty. I am very lazy, and if I want to finish anything it is absolutely essential that I spend hours stretched out on the sofa. He is never idle, and is always doing something; when he goes to lie down in the afternoons he takes proofs to correct or a book full of notes; he wants us to go to the cinema, then to a reception, then to the theatre – all on the same day. In one day he succeeds in doing, and in making me do, a mass of different things, and in meeting extremely diverse kinds of people. If I am alone and try to act as he does I get nothing at all done, because I get stuck all afternoon somewhere I had meant to stay for half an hour, or because I get lost and cannot find the right street, or because the most boring person and the one I least wanted to meet drags me off to the place I least wanted to go to.

If I tell him how my afternoon has turned out he says it is a completely wasted afternoon and is amused and makes fun of me and loses his temper; and he says that without him I am good for nothing.

I don't know how to manage my time; he does.

He likes receptions. He dresses casually, when everyone is dressed formally; the idea of changing his clothes in order to go to a reception never enters his head. He even goes in his old raincoat and crumpled hat; a woollen hat which he bought in London and which he wears pulled down over his eyes. He only stays for half an hour; he enjoys chatting with a glass in his hand for half an hour; he eats lots of *hors d'oeuvres*, and I eat almost none because when I see him eating so many I feel that I at least must be well-mannered and show some self-control and not eat too much; after half an hour, just as I am beginning to feel at ease and to enjoy myself, he gets impatient and drags me away.

I don't know how to dance and he does.

I don't know how to type and he does.

I don't know how to drive. If I suggest that I should get a licence too he disagrees. He says I would never manage it. I think he likes me to be dependent on him for some things.

I don't know how to sing and he does. He is a baritone. Perhaps he would have been a famous singer if he had studied singing.

Perhaps he would have been a conductor if he had studied music. When he listens to records he conducts the orchestra with a pencil. And he types and answers the telephone at the same time. He is a man who is able to do many things at once.

He is a professor and I think he is a good one.

He could have been many things. But he has no regrets about those professions he did not take up. I could only ever have followed one profession – the one I chose and which I have followed almost since childhood. And I don't have any regrets either about the professions I did not take up, but then I couldn't have succeeded at any of them.

I write stories, and for many years I have worked for a publishing house.

I don't work badly, or particularly well. All the same I am well aware of the fact that I would have been unable to work anywhere else. I get on well with my colleagues and my boss. I think that if I did not have the support of their friendship I would soon have become worn out and unable to work any longer.

For a long time I thought that one day I would be able to write screenplays for the cinema. But I never had the opportunity, or I did not know how to find it. Now I have lost all hope of writing screenplays. He wrote screenplays for a while, when he was younger. And he has worked in a publishing house. He has written stories. He has done all the things that I have done and many others too.

He is a good mimic, and does an old countess especially well. Perhaps he could also have been an actor.

Once, in London, he sang in a theatre. He was Job. He had to hire evening clothes; and there he was, in his evening clothes, in front of a kind of lectern; and he sang. He sang the words of Job; the piece called for something between speaking and singing. And I, in my box, was dying of fright. I was afraid he would get flustered, or that the trousers of his evening clothes would fall down.

He was surrounded by men in evening clothes and women in long dresses, who were the angels and devils and other characters in Job.

It was a great success, and they said that he was very good.

If I loved music I would love it passionately. But I don't understand it, and when he persuades me to go to concerts with him my mind wanders off and I think of my own affairs. Or I fall sound asleep.

I like to sing. I don't know how to sing and I sing completely out of tune; but I sing all the same – occasionally, very quietly, when I am alone. I know that I sing out of tune because others have told me so; my voice must be like the yowling of a cat. But I am not – in myself – aware of this, and singing gives me real pleasure. If he hears me he mimics me; he says that my singing is something quite separate from music, something invented by me.

When I was a child I used to yowl tunes I had made up. It was a long wailing kind of melody that brought tears to my eyes.

It doesn't matter to me that I don't understand painting or the figurative arts, but it hurts me that I don't love music, and I feel that my mind suffers from the absence of this love. But there is nothing I can do about it, I will never understand or love music. If I occasionally hear a piece of music that I like I don't know how to remember it; and how can I love something that I can't remember?

It is the words of a song that I remember. I can repeat words that I love over and over again. I repeat the tune that accompanies them too, in my own yowling fashion, and I experience a kind of happiness as I yowl.

When I am writing it seems to me that I follow a musical cadence or rhythm. Perhaps music was very close to my world, and my world could not, for whatever reason, make contact with it.

In our house there is music all day long. He keeps the radio on all day. Or plays records. Every now and again I protest a little and ask for a little silence in which to work; but he says that such beautiful music is certainly conducive to any kind of work.

He has bought an incredible number of records. He says that he owns one of the finest collections in the world.

In the morning when he is still in his dressing gown and dripping water from his bath, he turns the radio on, sits down at the type-writer and begins his strenuous, noisy, stormy day. He is superabundant in everything; he fills the bath to overflowing, and the same with the teapot and his cup of tea. He has an enormous number of shirts and ties. On the other hand he rarely buys shoes.

His mother says that as a child he was a model of order and precision; apparently once, on a rainy day, he was wearing white boots and white clothes and had to cross some muddy streams in the country – at the end of his walk he was immaculate and his clothes and boots had not one spot of mud on them. There is no trace in him of that former immaculate little boy. His clothes are always covered in stains. He has become extremely untidy.

But he scrupulously keeps all the gas bills. In drawers I find old gas bills, which he refuses to throw away, from houses we left long ago.

I also find old, shrivelled Tuscan cigars, and cigarette holders made from cherry wood.

I smoke a brand of king-size, filterless cigarettes called *Stop*, and he smokes his Tuscan cigars.

I am very untidy. But as I have got older I have come to miss tidiness, and I sometimes furiously tidy up all the cupboards. I think this is because I remember my mother's tidiness. I rearrange the linen and blanket cupboards and in the summer I reline every drawer with strips of white cloth. I rarely rearrange my papers because my mother didn't write and had no papers. My tidiness and untidiness are full of complicated feelings of regret and sadness. His untidiness is triumphant. He has decided that it is proper and legitimate for a studious person like himself to have an untidy desk.

He does not help me get over my indecisiveness, or the way I hesitate before doing anything, or my sense of guilt. He tends to make fun of every tiny thing I do. If I go shopping in the market he follows me and spies on me. He makes fun of the way I shop, of the way I weigh the oranges in my hand unerringly choosing, he says, the worst in the whole market; he ridicules me for spending an hour over the shopping, buying onions at one stall, celery at another and fruit at another. Sometimes he does the shopping to show me how quickly he can do it; he unhesitatingly buys everything from one stall and then manages to get the basket delivered to the house. He doesn't buy celery because he cannot abide it.

And so – more than ever – I feel I do everything inadequately or mistakenly. But if I once find out that he has made a mistake I tell him so over and over again until he is exasperated. I can be very annoying at times.

His rages are unpredictable, and bubble over like the head on beer. My rages are unpredictable too, but his quickly disappear whereas mine leave a noisy nagging trail behind them which must be very annoying – like the complaining yowl of a cat.

Sometimes in the midst of his rage I start to cry, and instead of quietening him down and making him feel sorry for me this infuriates him all the more. He says my tears are just play-acting, and perhaps he is right. Because in the middle of my tears and his rage I am completely calm.

I never cry when I am really unhappy.

There was a time when I used to hurl plates and crockery on the floor during my rages. But not any more. Perhaps because I am older and my rages are less violent, and also because I dare not lay a finger on our plates now; we bought them one day in London, in the Portobello Road, and I am very fond of them.

The price of those plates, and of many other things we have bought, immediately underwent a substantial reduction in his memory. He likes to think he did not spend very much and that he got a bargain. I know the price of that dinner service – it was £16, but he says £12. And it is the same with the picture of King Lear that is in our dining room, and which he also bought in the Portobello Road (and then cleaned with onions and potatoes); now he says he paid a certain sum for it, but I remember that it was much more than that.

Some years ago he bought twelve bedside mats in a department store. He bought them because they were cheap, and he thought he ought to buy them; and he bought them as an argument against me because he considered me to be incapable of buying things for the house. They were made of mud-coloured matting and they quickly became very unattractive; they took on a corpse-like rigidity and were hung from a wire line on the kitchen balcony, and I hated them. I used to remind him of them, as an example of bad shopping; but he would say that they had cost very little indeed, almost nothing. It was a long time before I could bring myself to throw them out – because there were so many of them, and because just as I was about to get rid of them it occurred to me that I could use them for rags. He and I both find throwing things away difficult; it must be a kind of Jewish caution in me, and the result of my extreme indecisiveness; in him it must be a defence against his impulsiveness and open-handedness.

He buys enormous quantities of bicarbonate of soda and aspirins.

Now and again he is ill with some mysterious ailment of his own; he can't explain what he feels and stays in bed for a day completely wrapped up in the sheets; nothing is visible except his beard and the tip of his red nose. Then he takes bicarbonate of soda and aspirins in doses suitable for a horse, and says that I cannot understand because I am always well, I am like those great fat strong friars who go out in the wind and in all weathers and come to no harm; he on the other hand is sensitive and delicate and suffers from mysterious ailments. Then in the evening he is better and goes into the kitchen and cooks himself tagliatelle.

When he was a young man he was slim, handsome and finely built; he did not have a beard but long, soft moustaches instead, and he looked like the actor Robert Donat. He was like that about twenty years ago when I first knew him, and I remember that he used to wear an elegant kind of Scottish flannel shirt. I remember that one evening he walked me back to the *pensione* where I was living; we walked together along the Via Nazionale. I already felt that I was very old and had been through a great deal and had made many mistakes, and he seemed a boy to me, light years away from me. I don't remember what we talked about on that evening walking along the Via Nazionale; nothing important, I suppose, and the idea that we would become husband and wife was light years away from me. Then we lost sight of each other, and when we met again he no longer looked like Robert Donat, but more like Balzac. When we met again he still wore his Scottish shirts but on him now they looked like garments for a polar expedition; now he had his beard and on his head he wore his ridiculous crumpled woollen hat; everything about him put you in mind of an imminent departure for the North Pole. Because, although he always feels hot, he has the habit of dressing as if he were surrounded by snow, ice and polar bears; or he dresses like a Brazilian coffee-planter, but he always dresses differently from everyone else.

If I remind him of that walk along the Via Nazionale he says he remembers it, but I know he is lying and that he remembers nothing;

and I sometimes ask myself if it was us, these two people, almost twenty years ago on the Via Nazionale; two people who conversed so politely, so urbanely, as the sun was setting; who chatted a little about everything perhaps and about nothing; two friends talking, two young intellectuals out for a walk; so young, so educated, so uninvolved, so ready to judge one another with kind impartiality; so ready to say goodbye to one another for ever, as the sun set, at the corner of the street.

Translated from the Italian by Dick Davis

TOVE JANSSON
B-Western

Jonna came in with a bottle of bourbon, a carafe of water, and a packet of Cortez cigarillos.

'Aha,' said Mari, 'the Wild West. A B-Western?'

'Yes. An early classic.'

The room was cold, and Mari wrapped herself in a blanket. 'What time?'

'Actually,' Jonna said. 'Actually, it would probably be better if I watched it alone.'

'I promise not to say a word.'

'Yes, but I'll know what you're thinking, and I can't concentrate.' Jonna poured them both a drink. 'You think Westerns repeat the same theme over and over. That may be. But you have to understand that Americans are in love with their history, which was so short and powerful, and they describe and depict it again and again . . . Are you in love with the Renaissance? What do you care about the ancient Egyptians? The Chinese?'

'Not much,' Mari said. 'They're just there. Or were.'

'Fine. Now don't assume that I'm defending B-Westerns, but think about it, try to imagine what it was like in the early days. Courage! Courage and patience. And pure curiosity. Imagine being among the very first to discover and conquer a new country, a new continent!'

'Conquer,' Mari repeated and pulled the blanket tighter.

'Yes, yes. Now don't go on about the Indians and all that stuff about cruelty and arrogance; those things happen on both sides. Great change always involves great intensity. That's just the way it is, right? Look at their desolate little towns in a completely empty landscape, and remember they lived in constant danger . . . They had to develop a strict, an implacable, sense of justice, they had to try to invent the Law for themselves, as best they could . . .' Jonna put down her cigarillo. 'It doesn't draw,' she said. 'It's the wrong kind.'

Mari remarked that perhaps the cigarillos had been lying around too long, and Jonna went on. 'It must be that lawlessness has its own laws. Of course mistakes occurred. They lived such violent lives that they simply didn't have time to reflect, that's what I think. But mistakes happen today, too, don't they? We hang the wrong guy, so to speak.'

Jonna leaned forward and looked at her friend earnestly. 'The sense of honour,' she announced. 'Believe me, the sense of honour has never been so strong. Friendship between men. You said the heroines were idiotic. Fine, they are idiotic. But take them away, forget them, and what do you find? Friendship between men who are unswervingly honourable toward one another. That's the concept of the Western.'

'I know,' Mari said. 'They have an honourable fist fight and then they're friends for life. Unless the noblest of them gets shot at the end, sacrificing his life to soft music.'

'Now you're just being mean,' said Jonna. She lifted aside the cloth that protected her television screen and turned to channel two.

'Anyway, I'm right,' Mari said. 'It's the same thing over and over. They ride past precisely the same mountain and the same waterfall and that Mexican church. And the saloon. And the oxcarts. Don't they ever get tired of it?'

'No,' Jonna answered. 'They never do. It's about recognition, about recognizing what you've imagined. People make dreams, don't they? The oxcarts that fight their way forward through unexplored territory, dangerous lands . . . Whether it's an A-Western or a B or even a C, they feel this is the way it must have been, just like this, and it makes them proud and maybe gives them a little comfort. I think.'

'Yes,' Mari said. 'Well, yes, maybe you're right . . .'

But Jonna couldn't stop. 'It's not fair of you to come and talk about repetition and the same thing over and over, and anyway your short stories are the same way, the same theme over and over again. Now close the curtains; it starts in three minutes.'

Mari dropped the blanket on the floor and announced, very slowly, 'I think . . . now I think I'll go to bed.'

She had a hard time falling asleep. Now they're galloping past the red mountain. Now they're playing poker in the saloon. Honky-tonk . . . They're shooting bottles in the bar, girls are screaming. Now the stairs to the second floor are crashing down . . .

A trumpet blast woke her up, and she knew the movie had come to the brave men in the final fort. Maybe they've more or less worked things out with the Indians – everyone forgives everyone, except maybe the ones who died – and now they're playing 'My Darling Clementine', which means she's finally figured out who she loved the whole time.

And now Jonna's turning off the television and rewinding the video. She's brushing her teeth and coming to bed and doesn't say a word.

Mari asked, 'Was it good?'

'No. But I'm saving it anyway.'

'Still, I liked "My Darling Clementine",' Mari said. 'They use that same song every time, but somehow it's right.'

Jonna got up and closed the window because the snow had begun to blow in. The room was very peaceful.

Before Mari fell asleep, she asked if they could watch this same B-Western some other evening, and Jonna said yes, she supposed they could.

Translated from the Swedish by Thomas Teal

The Best Part of Breaking Up

Love-quarrels oft in pleasing concord end.

John Milton

ZORA NEALE HURSTON
The Gilded Six-Bits

It was a Negro yard around a Negro house in a Negro settlement
that looked to the payroll of the G. and G. Fertilizer works for its
support.

But there was something happy about the place. The front yard
was parted in the middle by a sidewalk from gate to door-step, a
sidewalk edged on either side by quart bottles driven neck down
into the ground on a slant. A mess of homey flowers planted without
a plan but blooming cheerily from their helter-skelter places. The
fence and house were whitewashed. The porch and steps scrubbed
white.

The front door stood open to the sunshine so that the floor of
the front room could finish drying after its weekly scouring. It was
Saturday. Everything clean from the front gate to the privy house.
Yard raked so that the strokes of the rake would make a pattern.
Fresh newspaper cut in fancy edge on the kitchen shelves.

Missie May was bathing herself in the galvanized washtub in the
bedroom. Her dark-brown skin glistened under the soapsuds that
skittered down from her wash rag. Her stiff young breasts thrust
forward aggressively like broad-based cones with the tips lacquered
in black.

She heard men's voices in the distance and glanced at the dollar
clock on the dresser.

'Humph! Ah'm way behind time t'day! Joe gointer be heah 'fore
Ah git mah clothes on if Ah don't make haste.'

She grabbed the clean meal sack at hand and dried herself
hurriedly and began to dress. But before she could tie her slippers,
there came the ring of singing metal on wood. Nine times.

Missie May grinned with delight. She had not seen the big tall
man come stealing in the gate and creep up the walk grinning happily
at the joyful mischief he was about to commit. But she knew that
it was her husband throwing silver dollars in the door for her to
pick up and pile beside her plate at dinner. It was this way every
Saturday afternoon. The nine dollars hurled into the open door, he

scurried to a hiding place behind the cape jasmine bush and waited.

Missie May promptly appeared at the door in mock alarm.

'Who dat chunkin' money in mah do'way?' she demanded. No answer from the yard. She leaped off the porch and began to search the shrubbery. She peeped under the porch and hung over the gate to look up and down the road. While she did this, the man behind the jasmine darted to the china berry tree. She spied him and gave chase.

'Nobody ain't gointer be chunkin' money at me and Ah not do 'em nothin',' she shouted in mock anger. He ran around the house with Missie May at his heels. She overtook him at the kitchen door. He ran inside but could not close it after him before she crowded in and locked with him in a rough and tumble. For several minutes the two were a furious mass of male and female energy. Shouting, laughing, twisting, turning, tussling, tickling each other in the ribs; Missie May clutching onto Joe and Joe trying, but not too hard, to get away.

'Missie May, take yo' hand out mah pocket!' Joe shouted out between laughs.

'Ah ain't, Joe, not lessen you gwine gimme whateve' it is good you got in yo' pocket. Turn it go, Joe, do Ah'll tear yo' clothes.'

'Go on tear 'em. You de one dat pushes de needles round heah. Move yo' hand, Missie May.'

'Lemme git dat paper sack out yo' pocket. Ah bet it's candy kisses.'

'Tain't. Move yo' hand. Woman ain't got no business in a man's clothes nohow. Go way.'

Missie May gouged way down and gave an upward jerk and triumphed.

'Unhhunh! Ah got it. It 'tis so candy kisses. Ah knowed you had somethin' for me in yo' clothes. Now Ah got to see whut's in every pocket you got.'

Joe smiled indulgently and let his wife go through all of his pockets and take out the things that he had hidden there for her to find. She bore off the chewing gum, the cake of sweet soap, the pocket handkerchief as if she had wrested them from him, as if they had not been bought for the sake of this friendly battle.

'Whew! dat play-fight done got me all warmed up,' Joe exclaimed. 'Got me some water in de kittle?'

'Yo' water is on de fire and yo' clean things is cross de bed. Hurry up and wash yo'self and git changed so we kin eat. Ah'm hongry.' As Missie said this, she bore the steaming kettle into the bedroom.

'You ain't hongry, sugar,' Joe contradicted her. 'Youse jes' a little empty. Ah'm de one whut's hongry. Ah could eat up camp meetin', back off 'ssociation, and drink Jurdan dry. Have it on de table when Ah git out de tub.'

'Don't you mess wid mah business, man. You git in yo' clothes. Ah'm a real wife, not no dress and breath. Ah might not look lak one, but if you burn me, you won't git a thing but wife ashes.'

Joe splashed in the bedroom and Missie May fanned around in the kitchen. A fresh red and white checked cloth on the table. Big pitcher of buttermilk beaded with pale drops of butter from the churn. Hot fried mullet, crackling bread, ham hock atop a mound of string beans and new potatoes, and perched on the window-sill a pone of spicy potato pudding.

Very little talk during the meal but that little consisted of banter that pretended to deny affection but in reality flaunted it. Like when Missie May reached for a second helping of the tater pone. Joe snatched it out of her reach.

After Missie May had made two or three unsuccessful grabs at the pan, she begged, 'Aw, Joe gimme some mo' dat tater pone.'

'Nope, sweetenin' is for us men-folks. Y'all pritty lil frail eels don't need nothin' lak dis. You too sweet already.'

'Please, Joe.'

'Naw, naw. Ah don't want you to git no sweeter than whut you is already. We goin' down de road a lil piece t'night so you go put on yo' Sunday-go-to-meetin' things.'

Missie May looked at her husband to see if he was playing some prank. 'Sho nuff, Joe?'

'Yeah. We goin' to de ice cream parlor.'

'Where de ice cream parlor at, Joe?'

'A new man done come heah from Chicago and he done got a place and took and opened it up for a ice cream parlor, and bein' as it's real swell, Ah wants you to be one de first ladies to walk in dere and have some set down.'

'Do Jesus, Ah ain't knowed nothin' 'bout it. Who de man done it?'

'Mister Otis D. Slemmons, of spots and places – Memphis, Chicago, Jacksonville, Philadelphia and so on.'

'Dat heavy-set man wid his mouth full of gold teethes?'

'Yeah. Where did you see 'im at?'

'Ah went down to de sto' tuh git a box of lye and Ah seen 'im standin' on de corner talkin' to some of de mens, and Ah come on back and went to scrubbin' de floor, and he passed and tipped his hat whilst Ah was scourin' de steps. Ah thought Ah never seen *him* befo'.'

Joe smiled pleasantly. 'Yeah, he's up to date. He got de finest clothes Ah ever seen on a colored man's back.'

'Aw, he don't look no better in his clothes than you do in yourn. He got a puzzlegut on 'im and he so chuckle-headed, he got a pone behind his neck.'

Joe looked down at his own abdomen and said wistfully, 'Wisht Ah had a build on me lak he got. He ain't puzzle-gutted, honey. He jes' got a corperation. Dat make 'm look lak a rich white man. All rich mens is got some belly on 'em.'

'Ah seen de pitchers of Henry Ford and he's a spare-built man and Rockefeller look lak he ain't got but one gut. But Ford and Rockefeller and dis Slemmons and all de rest kin be as many-gutted as dey please, Ah'm satisfied wid you jes lak you is, baby. God took pattern after a pine tree and built you noble. Youse a pritty man, and if Ah knowed any way to make you mo' pritty still Ah'd take and do it.'

Joe reached over gently and toyed with Missie May's ear. 'You jes' say dat cause you love me, but Ah know Ah can't hold no light to Otis D. Slemmons. Ah ain't never been nowhere and Ah ain't got nothin' but you.'

Missie May got on his lap and kissed him and he kissed back in kind. Then he went on. 'All de womens is crazy 'bout 'im everywhere he go.'

'How you know dat, Joe?'

'He tole us so hisself.'

'Dat don't make it so. His mouf is cut cross-ways, ain't it? Well, he kin lie jes' lak anybody else.'

'Good Lawd, Missie! You womens sho is hard to sense into things. He's got a five-dollar gold piece for a stick-pin and he got a ten-dollar gold piece on his watch chain and his mouf is jes' crammed full of gold teethes. Sho wisht it wuz mine. And whut make it so cool, he got money 'cumulated. And womens give it all to 'im.'

'Ah don't see whut de womens see on 'im. Ah wouldn't give 'im a wink if de sheriff wuz after 'im.'

'Well, he tole us how de white womens in Chicago give 'im all dat gold money. So he don't 'low nobody to touch it at all. Not even put dey finger on it. Dey tole 'im not to. You kin make 'miration at it, but don't tetch it.'

'Whyn't he stay up dere where dey so crazy 'bout 'im?'

'Ah reckon dey done made 'im vast-rich and he wants to travel some. He say dey wouldn't leave 'im hit a lick of work. He got mo' lady people crazy 'bout him than he kin shake a stick at.'

'Joe, Ah hates to see you so dumb. Dat stray nigger jes' tell y'all anything and y'all b'lieve it.'

'Go 'head on now, honey and put on yo' clothes. He talkin' 'bout his pritty womens – Ah want 'im to see *mine*.'

Missie May went off to dress and Joe spent the time trying to make his stomach punch out like Slemmons' middle. He tried the rolling swagger of the stranger, but found that his tall bone-and-muscle stride fitted ill with it. He just had time to drop back into his seat before Missie May came in dressed to go.

On the way home that night Joe was exultant. 'Didn't Ah say ole Otis was swell? Can't he talk Chicago talk? Wuzn't dat funny whut he said when great big fat ole Ida Armstrong come in? He asted me, "Who is dat broad wid de forte shake?" Dat's a new word. Us always thought forty was a set of figgers but he showed us where it means a whole heap of things. Sometimes he don't say forty, he jes' say thirty-eight and two and dat mean de same thing. Know whut he tole me when Ah wuz payin' for our ice cream? He say, "Ah have to hand it to you, Joe. Dat wife of yours is jes' thirty-eight and two. Yessuh, she's forte!" Ain't he killin'?'

'He'll do in case of a rush. But he sho is got uh heap uh gold on 'im. Dat's de first time Ah ever seed gold money. It lookted good on him sho nuff, but it'd look a whole heap better on you.'

'Who, me? Missie May youse crazy! Where would a po' man lak me git gold money from?'

Missie May was silent for a minute, then she said, 'Us might find some goin' long de road some time. Us could.'

'Who would be losin' gold money round heah? We ain't even seen none dese white folks wearin' no gold money on dey watch chain. You must be figgerin' Mister Packard or Mister Cadillac goin' pass through heah.'

'You don't know whut been lost 'round heah. Maybe somebody way back in memorial times lost they gold money and went on off and it ain't never been found. And then if we wuz to find it, you could wear some 'thout havin' no gang of womens lak dat Slemmons say he got.'

Joe laughed and hugged her. 'Don't be so wishful 'bout me. Ah'm satisfied de way Ah is. So long as Ah be yo' husband. Ah don't keer 'bout nothin' else. Ah'd ruther all de other womens in de world to be dead than for you to have de toothache. Less we go to bed and git our night rest.'

It was Saturday night once more before Joe could parade his wife in Slemmons' ice cream parlor again. He worked the night shift and Saturday was his only night off. Every other evening around six o'clock he left home, and dying dawn saw him hustling home around the lake where the challenging sun flung a flaming sword from east to west across the trembling water.

That was the best part of life – going home to Missie May. Their white-washed house, the mock battle on Saturday, the dinner and ice cream parlor afterwards, church on Sunday nights when Missie out-dressed any woman in town – all, everything was right.

One night around eleven the acid ran out at the G. and G. The foreman knocked off the crew and let the steam die down. As Joe rounded the lake on his way home, a lean moon rode the lake in a silver boat. If anybody had asked Joe about the moon on the lake, he would have said he hadn't paid it any attention. But he saw it with his feelings. It made him yearn painfully for Missie. Creation obsessed him. He thought about children. They had been married more than a year now. They had money put away. They ought to be making little feet for shoes. A little boy child would be about right.

He saw a dim light in the bedroom and decided to come in through the kitchen door. He could wash the fertilizer dust off himself before presenting himself to Missie May. It would be nice for her not to know that he was there until he slipped into his place in bed and hugged her back. She always liked that.

He eased the kitchen door open slowly and silently, but when he went to set his dinner bucket on the table he bumped it into a pile of dishes, and something crashed to the floor. He heard his wife gasp in fright and hurried to reassure her.

'Iss me, honey. Don't git skeered.'

There was a quick, large movement in the bedroom. A rustle, a thud, and a stealthy silence. The light went out.

What? Robbers? Murderers? Some varmint attacking his helpless wife, perhaps. He struck a match, threw himself on guard and stepped over the door-sill into the bedroom.

The great belt on the wheel of Time slipped and eternity stood still. By the match light he could see the man's legs fighting with his breeches in his frantic desire to get them on. He had both chance and time to kill the intruder in his helpless condition – half in and half out of his pants – but he was too weak to take action. The shapeless enemies of humanity that live in the hours of Time had waylaid Joe. He was assaulted in his weakness. Like Samson awakening after his haircut. So he just opened his mouth and laughed.

The match went out and he struck another and lit the lamp. A howling wind raced across his heart, but underneath its fury he heard his wife sobbing and Slemmons pleading for his life. Offering to buy it with all that he had. 'Please, suh, don't kill me. Sixty-two dollars at de sto'. Gold money.'

Joe just stood. Slemmons looked at the window, but it was screened. Joe stood out like a rough-backed mountain between him and the door. Barring him from escape, from sunrise, from life.

He considered a surprise attack upon the big clown that stood there laughing like a chessy cat. But before his fist could travel an inch, Joe's own rushed out to crush him like a battering ram. Then Joe stood over him.

'Git into yo' damn rags, Slemmons, and dat quick.'

Slemmons scrambled to his feet and into his vest and coat. As he grabbed his hat, Joe's fury overrode his intentions and he grabbed at Slemmons with his left hand and struck at him with his right. The right landed. The left grazed the front of his vest. Slemmons was knocked a somersault into the kitchen and fled through the open door. Joe found himself alone with Missie May, with the golden watch charm clutched in his left fist. A short bit of broken chain dangled between his fingers.

Missie May was sobbing. Wails of weeping without words. Joe stood, and after awhile he found out that he had something in his hand. And then he stood and felt without thinking and without seeing with his natural eyes. Missie May kept on crying and Joe kept on feeling so much and not knowing what to do with all his feelings, he put Slemmons' watch charm in his pants pocket and took a good laugh and went to bed.

'Missie May, whut you cryin' for?'

'Cause Ah love you so hard and Ah know you don't love *me* no mo'.'

Joe sank his face into the pillow for a spell then he said huskily, 'You don't know de feelings of dat yet, Missie May.'

'Oh Joe, honey, he said he wuz gointer give me dat gold money and he jes' kept on after me –'

Joe was very still and silent for a long time. Then he said, 'Well, don't cry no mo', Missie May. Ah got yo' gold piece for you.'

The hours went past on their rusty ankles. Joe still and quiet on one bed-rail and Missie May wrung dry of sobs on the other. Finally the sun's tide crept upon the shore of night and drowned all its hours. Missie May with her face stiff and streaked towards the window saw the dawn come into her yard. It was day. Nothing more. Joe wouldn't be coming home as usual. No need to fling open the front door and sweep off the porch, making it nice for Joe. Never no more breakfast to cook; no more washing and starching of Joe's jumper-jackets and pants. No more nothing. So why get up?

With this strange man in her bed, she felt embarrassed to get up and dress. She decided to wait till he had dressed and gone. Then she would get up, dress quickly and be gone forever beyond reach of Joe's looks and laughs. But he never moved. Red light turned to yellow, then white.

From beyond the no-man's land between them came a voice. A strange voice that yesterday had been Joe's.

'Missie May, ain't you gonna fix me no breakfus'?'

She sprang out of bed. 'Yeah, Joe. Ah didn't reckon you wuz hongry.'

No need to die today. Joe needed her for a few more minutes anyhow.

Soon there was a roaring fire in the cook stove. Water bucket full and two chickens killed. Joe loved fried chicken and rice. She didn't deserve a thing and good Joe was letting her cook him some breakfast. She rushed hot biscuits to the table as Joe took his seat.

He ate with his eyes in his plate. No laughter, no banter.

'Missie May, you ain't eatin' yo' breakfus'.'

'Ah don't choose none, Ah thank yuh.'

His coffee cup was empty. She sprang to refill it. When she turned from the stove and bent to set the cup beside Joe's plate, she saw the yellow coin on the table between them.

She slumped into her seat and wept into her arms.

Presently Joe said calmly, 'Missie May, you cry too much. Don't look back lak Lot's wife and turn to salt.'

The sun, the hero of every day, the impersonal old man that beams as brightly on death as on birth, came up every morning and raced across the blue dome and dipped into the sea of fire every evening. Water ran down hill and birds nested.

Missie knew why she didn't leave Joe. She couldn't. She loved him too much, but she could not understand why Joe didn't leave her. He was polite, even kind at times, but aloof.

There were no more Saturday romps. No ringing silver dollars to stack beside her plate. No pockets to rifle. In fact the yellow coin in his trousers was like a monster hiding in the cave of his pockets to destroy her.

She often wondered if he still had it, but nothing could have induced her to ask nor yet to explore his pockets to see for herself. Its shadow was in the house whether or no.

One night Joe came home around midnight and complained of pains in the back. He asked Missie to rub him down with liniment. It had been three months since Missie had touched his body and it all seemed strange. But she rubbed him. Grateful for the chance. Before morning, youth triumphed and Missie exulted. But the next day, as she joyfully made up their bed, beneath her pillow she found the piece of money with the bit of chain attached.

Alone to herself, she looked at the thing with loathing, but look she must. She took it into her hands with trembling and saw first thing that it was no gold piece. It was a gilded half dollar. Then she knew why Slemmons had forbidden anyone to touch his gold. He trusted village eyes at a distance not to recognize his stick-pin as a gilded quarter, and his watch charm as a four-bit piece.

She was glad at first that Joe had left it there. Perhaps he was through with her punishment. They were man and wife again. Then another thought came clawing at her. He had come home to buy from her as if she were any woman in the long house. Fifty cents for her love. As if to say that he could pay as well as Slemmons. She slid the coin into his Sunday pants pocket and dressed herself and left his house.

Half way between her house and the quarters she met her husband's mother, and after a short talk she turned and went back home. Never would she admit defeat to that woman who prayed for it nightly. If she had not the substance of marriage she had the outside show. Joe must leave *her*. She let him see she didn't want his old gold four-bits too.

She saw no more of the coin for some time though she knew that Joe could not help finding it in his pocket. But his health kept poor, and he came home at least every ten days to be rubbed.

The sun swept around the horizon, trailing its robes of weeks and days. One morning as Joe came in from work, he found Missie May chopping wood. Without a word he took the ax and chopped a huge pile before he stopped.

'You ain't got no business choppin' wood, and you know it.'

'How come? Ah been choppin' it for de last longest.'

'Ah ain't blind. You makin' feet for shoes.'

'Won't you be glad to have a lil baby chile, Joe?'

'You know dat 'thout astin' me.'

'Iss gointer be a boy chile and de very spit of you.'

'You reckon, Missie May?'

'Who else could it look lak?'

Joe said nothing, but he thrust his hand deep into his pocket and fingered something there.

It was almost six months later Missie May took to bed and Joe went and got his mother to come wait on the house.

Missie May was delivered of a fine boy. Her travail was over when Joe came in from work one morning. His mother and the old women were drinking great bowls of coffee around the fire in the kitchen.

The minute Joe came into the room his mother called him aside.

'How did Missie May make out?' he asked quickly.

'Who, dat gal? She strong as a ox. She gointer have plenty mo'. We done fixed her wid de sugar and lard to sweeten her for de nex' one.'

Joe stood silent awhile.

'You ain't ast 'bout de baby, Joe. You oughter be mighty proud cause he sho is de spittin' image of yuh, son. Dat's yourn all right, if you never git another one, dat un is yourn. And you know Ah'm mighty proud too, son, cause Ah never thought well of you marryin' Missie May cause her ma used tuh fan her foot round right smart and Ah been mighty skeered dat Missie May wuz gointer git misput on her road.'

Joe said nothing. He fooled around the house till late in the day then just before he went to work, he went and stood at the foot of the bed and asked his wife how she felt. He did this every day during the week.

On Saturday he went to Orlando to make his market. It had been a long time since he had done that.

Meat and lard, meal and flour, soap and starch. Cans of corn and tomatoes. All the staples. He fooled around town for awhile and bought bananas and apples. Way after while he went around to the candy store.

'Hello, Joe,' the clerk greeted him. 'Ain't seen you in a long time.'

'Nope, Ah ain't been heah. Been round in spots and places.'

'Want some of them molasses kisses you always buy?'

'Yessuh.' He threw the gilded half dollar on the counter. 'Will dat spend?'

'Whut is it, Joe? Well, I'll be doggone! A gold-plated four-bit piece. Where'd you git it, Joe?'

'Offen a stray nigger dat come through Eatonville. He had it on his watch chain for a charm – goin' round making out iss gold money. Ha ha! He had a quarter on his tie pin and it wuz all golded up too. Tryin' to fool people. Makin' out he so rich and everything. Ha! Ha! Tryin' to tole off folkses wives from home.'

'How did you git it, Joe? Did he fool you, too?'

'Who, me? Naw suh! He ain't fooled me none. Know whut Ah done? He come round me wid his smart talk. Ah hauled off and knocked 'im down and took his old four-bits way from 'im. Gointer buy my wife some good ole lasses kisses wid it. Gimme fifty cents worth of dem candy kisses.'

'Fifty cents buys a mighty lot of candy kisses, Joe. Why don't you split it up and take some chocolate bars, too. They eat good, too.'

'Yessuh, dey do, but Ah wants all dat in kisses. Ah got a lil boy chile home now. Tain't a week old yet, but he kin suck a sugar tit and maybe eat one them kisses hisself.'

Joe got his candy and left the store. The clerk turned to the next customer. 'Wisht I could be like these darkies. Laughin' all the time. Nothin' worries 'em.'

Back in Eatonville, Joe reached his own front door. There was the ring of singing metal on wood. Fifteen times. Missie May couldn't run to the door, but she crept there as quickly as she could.

'Joe Banks, Ah hear you chunkin' money in mah do'way. You wait till Ah got mah strength back and Ah'm gointer fix you for dat.'

VIRGINIA WOOLF

Lappin and Lapinova

They were married. The wedding march pealed out. The pigeons fluttered. Small boys in Eton jackets threw rice; a fox-terrier sauntered across the path; and Ernest Thorburn led his bride to the car through that small inquisitive crowd of complete strangers which always collects in London to enjoy other people's happiness or unhappiness. Certainly he looked handsome and she looked shy. More rice was thrown, and the car moved off.

That was on Tuesday. Now it was Saturday. Rosalind had still to get used to the fact that she was Mrs Ernest Thorburn. Perhaps she never would get used to the fact that she was Mrs Ernest Anybody, she thought, as she sat in the bow window of the hotel looking over the lake to the mountains, and waited for her husband to come down to breakfast. Ernest was a difficult name to get used to. It was not the name she would have chosen. She would have preferred Timothy, Antony, or Peter. He did not look like Ernest either. The name suggested the Albert Memorial, mahogany sideboards, steel engravings of the Prince Consort with his family – her mother-in-law's dining-room in Porchester Terrace in short.

But here he was. Thank goodness he did not look like Ernest – no. But what did he look like? She glanced at him sideways. Well, when he was eating toast he looked like a rabbit. Not that anyone else would have seen a likeness to a creature so diminutive and timid in this spruce, muscular young man with the straight nose, the blue eyes, and the very firm mouth. But that made it all the more amusing. His nose twitched very slightly when he ate. So did her pet rabbit's. She kept watching his nose twitch; and then she had to explain, when he caught her looking at him, why she laughed.

'It's because you're like a rabbit, Ernest,' she said. 'Like a wild rabbit,' she added, looking at him. 'A hunting rabbit; a King Rabbit; a rabbit that makes laws for all the other rabbits.'

Ernest had no objection to being that kind of rabbit, and since it amused her to see him twitch his nose – he had never known that his nose twitched – he twitched it on purpose. And she laughed and laughed; and he laughed too, so that the maiden ladies and the fishing man and the Swiss waiter in his greasy black jacket all guessed right; they were very happy. But how long does such happiness last? they asked themselves; and each answered according to his own circumstances.

At lunch time, seated on a clump of heather beside the lake, 'Lettuce, rabbit?' said Rosalind, holding out the lettuce that had been provided to eat with the hard-boiled eggs. 'Come and take it out of my hand,' she added, and he stretched out and nibbled the lettuce and twitched his nose.

'Good rabbit, nice rabbit,' she said, patting him, as she used to pat her tame rabbit at home. But that was absurd. He was not a tame rabbit, whatever he was. She turned it into French. 'Lapin,' she called him. But whatever he was, he was not a French rabbit. He was simply and solely English – born in Porchester Terrace, educated at Rugby; now a clerk in His Majesty's Civil Service. So she tried 'Bunny' next; but that was worse. 'Bunny' was someone plump and soft and comic; he was thin and hard and serious. Still, his nose twitched. 'Lappin,' she exclaimed suddenly; and gave a little cry as if she had found the very word she looked for.

'Lappin, Lappin, King Lappin,' she repeated. It seemed to suit him exactly; he was not Ernest, he was King Lappin. Why? She did not know.

When there was nothing new to talk about on their long solitary walks – and it rained, as everyone had warned them that it would rain; or when they were sitting over the fire in the evening, for it was cold, and the maiden ladies had gone and the fishing man, and the waiter only came if you rang the bell for him, she let her fancy play with the story of the Lappin tribe. Under her hands – she was sewing, he was reading – they became very real, very vivid, very amusing. Ernest put down the paper and helped her. There were the black rabbits and the red; there were the enemy rabbits and the friendly. There were the wood in which they lived and the outlying prairies and the swamp. Above all there was King Lappin, who, far from having only the one trick – that he twitched his nose – became, as the days passed, an animal of the greatest character. Rosalind was always finding new qualities in him. But above all he was a great hunter.

'And what,' said Rosalind, on the last day of the honeymoon, 'did the King do to-day?'

In fact they had been climbing all day; and she had worn a blister on her heel; but she did not mean that.

'To-day,' said Ernest twitching his nose as he bit the end off his cigar, 'he chased a hare.' He paused; struck a match, and twitched again.

'A woman hare,' he added.

'A white hare!' Rosalind exclaimed, as if she had been expecting this. 'Rather a small hare; silver grey; with big bright eyes?'

'Yes,' said Ernest, looking at her as she had looked at him, 'a smallish animal; with eyes popping out of her head, and two little front paws dangling.' It was exactly how she sat, with her sewing dangling in her hands; and her eyes, that were so big and bright, were certainly a little prominent.

'Ah, Lapinova,' Rosalind murmured.

'Is that what she's called,' said Ernest, 'the real Rosalind?' He looked at her. He felt very much in love with her.

'Yes; that's what she's called,' said Rosalind: 'Lapinova.' And before they went to bed that night it was all settled. He was King Lappin; she was Queen Lapinova. They were the very opposite of each other; he was bold and determined; she wary and undependable. He ruled over the busy world of rabbits; her world was a desolate, mysterious place, which she ranged mostly by moonlight. All the same, their territories touched; they were King and Queen of the land of rabbits and hares.

Thus when they came back from their honeymoon they possessed a private world, inhabited, save for the one white hare, entirely by rabbits. No one guessed that there was such a place, and that of course made it all the more amusing. It made them feel, more even than most young married couples, in league together against the rest of the world. Often they looked slyly at each other when people talked about rabbits and woods and traps and shooting. Or they winked furtively across the table when Aunt Mary said that she could never bear to see a hare in a dish – it looked so like a baby; or when John, Ernest's sporting brother, told them what price rabbits were fetching that autumn in Wiltshire, skins and all. Sometimes when they wanted a gamekeeper, or a poacher or a Lord of the Manor, they amused themselves by distributing the parts among their friends. Ernest's mother, Mrs Reginald Thorburn, for example, fitted the part of the Squire to perfection. But it was all secret – that was the point of it; nobody save themselves knew that such a world existed.

Without that world, how, Rosalind wondered, could she ever have endured the golden-wedding party when all the Thorburns assembled at Porchester Terrace to celebrate the fiftieth anniversary of that union which had been so blessed – had it not produced Ernest Thorburn? – and so fruitful – had it not produced nine other sons and daughters into the bargain, many themselves married and also fruitful? She dreaded that party. But it was inevitable. As she walked upstairs she felt bitterly that she was an only child and an orphan at that; a mere drop among all those Thorburns assembled in the great drawing-room with the shiny satin wallpaper and the lustrous family portraits. The living Thorburns much resembled the painted; save that instead of painted lips they had real lips; out of which came jokes; jokes about schoolrooms, and how they had pulled the chair from under the governess; jokes about frogs and how they had put them between the virgin sheets of maiden ladies. As for herself, she had never even made an apple-pie bed. Holding her present in her hand, she advanced towards her mother-in-law, sumptuous in yellow satin; and towards her father-in-law, decorated with a rich yellow carnation. All round them on tables and chairs there were golden tributes, some nestling in cotton wool; others branching resplendent – candlesticks; cigar boxes; chains; each stamped with the goldsmith's proof that it was solid gold, hall-marked, authentic. But her present was only a little pinchbeck box pierced with holes; an old sand caster, an eighteenth-century relic, once used to sprinkle sand over wet ink. Rather a senseless present, she felt, in an age of blotting-paper; and as she proffered it, she saw in front of her the stubby black handwriting in which her mother-in-law, when they were engaged, had expressed the hope that 'My son will make you happy.' No, she was not happy. Not at all happy. She looked at Ernest, straight as a ramrod with a nose like all the noses in the family portraits, a nose that never twitched at all.

Then they went down to dinner. She was half hidden by the great chrysanthemums that curled their red and gold petals into large tight balls. Everything was gold. A gold-edged card with gold initials intertwined recited the list of all the dishes that would be set one after another before them. She dipped her spoon in a plate of clear golden soup. The raw white fog outside had been turned by the lamps into a golden mesh that blurred the edges of the plates and gave the pineapples a rough golden skin. Only she herself in her white wedding dress peering ahead of her with her prominent eyes seemed insoluble as an icicle.

As the dinner wore on, however, the room grew steamy with heat. Beads of perspiration stood out on the men's foreheads. She felt that her icicle was being turned to water. She was being melted; dispersed; dissolved into nothingness; and would soon faint. Then through the surge in her head and the din in her ears she heard a woman's voice exclaim, 'But of course they breed so!'

The Thorburns – yes; they breed so, she echoed; looking at all the round red faces that seemed doubled in the giddiness that overcame her; and magnified in the gold mist that enhaloed them. 'They breed so.' Then John bawled:

'Little devils! Shoot 'em! Jump on 'em with big boots! That's the only way to deal with 'em . . . rabbits!'

At that word, that magic word, she revived. Peeping between the chrysanthemums she saw Ernest's nose twitch. It rippled, it ran, with successive twitches. And at that a mysterious catastrophe befell the Thorburns. The golden table became a moor with the gorse in full bloom; the din of voices turned to one peal of lark's laughter ringing down from the sky. It was a blue sky – clouds passed slowly. And they had all been changed – the Thorburns. She looked at her father-in-law, a furtive little man with dyed moustaches. His foible was collecting things – seals, enamel boxes, trifles from eighteenth-century dressing-tables which he hid from his wife in the drawers of his desk. Now she saw him as he was – a poacher, stealing off with his coat bulging with pheasants and partridges to drop them stealthily into a three-legged pot in his smoky little cottage. That was her real father-in-law – a poacher. And Celia, the unmarried daughter, who always nosed out other people's secrets, the little things they wished to hide – she was a white ferret with pink eyes, and a nose clotted with earth from her horrid underground nosings and pokings. Slung round men's shoulders, in a net, and thrust down a hole – it was a pitiable life, Celia's; it was none of her fault. So she saw Celia. And then she looked at her mother-in-law – whom they dubbed The Squire. Flushed, coarse, a bully – she was all that, as she stood returning thanks, but now that Rosalind – that is Lapinova – saw her, she saw behind her the decayed family mansion, the plaster peeling off the walls, and heard her, with a sob in her voice, giving thanks to her children (who hated her) for a world that had ceased to exist. There was a sudden silence. They all stood with their glasses raised; they all drank; then it was over.

'Oh, King Lappin!' she cried as they went home together in the fog. 'If your nose hadn't twitched just at that moment, I should have been trapped!'

'But you're safe,' said King Lappin, pressing her paw.

'Quite safe,' she answered, pressing his too.

And they drove back through the Park, King and Queen of the marsh, of the mist, of the gorse-scented moor.

Thus time passed; one year; two years of time. And on a winter's night, which happened by a coincidence to be the anniversary of the golden-wedding party – but Mrs Reginald Thorburn was dead; the house was to let; and there was only a caretaker in residence – Ernest came home from the office. They had a nice little home; half a house above a saddler's shop in South Kensington, not far from the tube station. It was cold, with fog in the air, and Rosalind was sitting over the fire, sewing.

'What d'you think happened to me to-day?' she began as soon as he had settled himself down with his legs stretched to the blaze. 'I was crossing the stream when –'

'What stream?' Ernest interrupted her.

'The stream at the bottom, where our wood meets the black wood,' she explained.

Ernest looked completely blank for a moment.

'What the deuce are you talking about?' he asked.

'My dear Ernest!' she cried in dismay. 'King Lappin,' she added, dangling her little front paws in the firelight. But his nose did not twitch. Her hands – they turned to hands – clutched the stuff she was holding; her eyes popped half out of her head. It took him five minutes at least to change from Ernest Thorburn to King Lappin; and while she waited she felt a load on the back of her neck, as if somebody were about to wring it. At last he changed to King Lappin; his nose twitched; and they spent the evening roaming the woods much as usual.

But she slept badly. In the middle of the night she woke, feeling as if something strange had happened to her. She was stiff and cold.

At last she turned on the light and looked at Ernest lying beside her. He was sound asleep. He snored. But even though he snored, his nose remained perfectly still. It looked as if it had never twitched at all. Was it possible that he was really Ernest; and that she was really married to Ernest? A vision of her mother-in-law's dining-room came before her; and there they sat, she and Ernest, grown old, under the engravings, in front of the sideboard . . . It was their golden-wedding day. She could not bear it.

'Lappin, King Lappin!' she whispered, and for a moment his nose seemed to twitch of its own accord. But he still slept. 'Wake up, Lappin, wake up!' she cried.

Ernest woke; and, seeing her sitting bolt upright beside him, he asked:

'What's the matter?'

'I thought my rabbit was dead!' she whimpered. Ernest was angry.

'Don't talk such rubbish, Rosalind,' he said. 'Lie down and go to sleep.'

He turned over. In another moment he was sound asleep and snoring.

But she could not sleep. She lay curled up on her side of the bed, like a hare in its form. She had turned out the light, but the street-lamp lit the ceiling faintly, and the trees outside made a lacy network over it as if there were a shadowy grove on the ceiling in which she wandered, turning, twisting, in and out, round and round, hunting, being hunted, hearing the bay of hounds, and horns blowing . . . until the maid drew the blinds and brought their early tea.

Next day she could settle to nothing. She seemed to have lost something. She felt as if her body had shrunk; it had grown small, and black and hard. Her joints seemed stiff too, and when she looked in the glass, which she did several times as she wandered about the flat, her eyes seemed to burst out of her head, like currants in a bun. The rooms also seemed to have shrunk. Large pieces of furniture jutted out at odd angles and she found herself knocking against them. At last she put on her hat and went out. She walked along the Cromwell Road; and every room she passed and peered into seemed to be a dining-room where people sat eating under steel engravings, with thick yellow lace curtains, and mahogany sideboards. At last she reached the Natural History Museum; she used to like it when she was a child. But the first thing she saw when she went in was a stuffed hare standing on sham snow with pink glass eyes. Somehow it made her shiver all over. Perhaps it would be better when dusk fell. She went home and sat over the fire, without a light, and tried to imagine that she was out alone on a moor: and there was a stream rushing; and beyond the stream a dark wood. But she could get no farther than the stream. At last she squatted down on the bank on the wet grass, and sat crouched in her chair, with her hands dangling empty, and her eyes glazed, like glass eyes, in the firelight. Then there was the crack of a gun . . . She started as if she had been shot. It was only Ernest turning his key in the door. She waited, trembling. He came in and switched on the light. There he stood tall, handsome, rubbing his hands that were red with cold.

'Sitting in the dark?' he said.

'Oh, Ernest, Ernest!' she cried starting up in her chair.

'Well, what's up now?' he asked briskly, warming his hands at the fire.

'It's Lapinova . . .' she faltered, glancing wildly at him out of her great startled eyes. 'She's gone, Ernest. I've lost her!'

Ernest frowned. He pressed his lips tight together. 'Oh, that's what's up, is it?' he said, smiling rather grimly at his wife. For ten seconds he stood there, silent; and she waited, feeling hands tightening at the back of her neck.

'Yes,' he said at length. 'Poor Lapinova . . .' He straightened his tie at the looking-glass.

'Caught in a trap,' he said. 'Killed,' and sat down and read the newspaper.

So that was the end of that marriage.

ALASDAIR GRAY
Pillow Talk

Wakening he turned his head and saw she was still reading.
After a moment he said,
'About that e-mail you sent.'
'I never sent you an e-mail,' she said, eyes still on the book.
'Not before today, perhaps, but this afternoon you e-mailed me and said –'
'I repeat,' she interrupted, looking hard at him, 'I have never sent you or anyone else an e-mail in my life.'
'But you did send one to the office this afternoon. I remember it perfectly – the heading stating it was from you to me and everyone else in the firm. Why did you have to tell *them*? You must have sent it from a friend's computer or one in the public library.'
'You're still drunk.'
'If you mean I was drunk when we came to bed you are wrong. We had only one bottle of wine with the evening meal and I drank only one more glass of it than you. I'm glad you're sorry you sent that message but you'll never persuade me you didn't.'
'You're hallucinating. What am I supposed to have said?'
'That you want to leave me. Five words – *I want to leave you* – just that.' She stared at him, shut the book and said bitterly, 'Oh, very clever. Cruel, but clever.'
'Do you want to leave me?'
'Yes, but I never told you so. I've never told anyone that – they think ours is such a *solid* marriage. You must have noticed it's a farce and this is your bloody cunning way of blaming me for something I never said and was never going to say.'
'Blethers!' he cried, 'I am *never* cunning, *never* cruel. I remember these words coming up very clear and distinct on the computer screen: *I want to leave you*.'
'Then why didn't you mention it when you came home? Why didn't you mention it over dinner? Are you going to pretend you were brooding over it before we came to bed?' He thought hard for a

while then said, 'You're right. I must have dreamed it before I woke a moment ago.'

'I'm glad you've sobered up,' she said and resumed reading.

After a while he said, 'But you want to leave me.'

She sighed and said nothing.

'When will you do it?'

'I don't suppose I'll ever do it,' she murmured, still appearing to read, 'I haven't the courage to live alone. You're an alcoholic bore but not violent and I'm too old to find anyone better.'

'I'm glad!' he said loudly. 'I don't want you ever to leave because I love you. My life will be a misery if you leave me.'

'Then you're luckier than I am. Go back to sleep.'

He turned away from her and tried to sleep. About half an hour later he heard her shut the book and switch off the bedside lamp. He got up and went to a room next door where he had hidden a bottle of whisky for this sort of emergency.

ANDREY PLATONOV

The Return

Aleksey Alekseyevich Ivanov, a Guards captain, had been demobi-
lized and was leaving the army. His unit, in which he had served all
through the war, gave him a send-off, as was fitting, with regret,
love and respect, with music and with wine. His close friends and
comrades accompanied him to the railway station and, after saying
their final goodbyes, left him there on his own. But the train had
been delayed for hours; and, after those long hours had passed, it
went on being even more delayed. A cold autumn night was already
beginning; the station building had been destroyed in the war and
there was nowhere to spend the night, so Ivanov got a lift from a
car going his way and returned to his unit. The following day Ivanov's
fellow-servicemen gave him another send-off; once again they sang
songs and embraced the departing man to show their eternal friendship, but this time they expended their feelings more briefly and the
party was just a group of close friends.

Then Ivanov set out for the station a second time; at the station
he learned that yesterday's train had still not arrived, so he could
indeed have gone back to his unit for one more night. But it would
have been awkward to be seen off a third time and cause his comrades
more trouble, and Ivanov stayed, ready for a long wait on the deserted
asphalt of the platform.

Near the points just beyond the station stood a pointsman's hut
which had survived the war. A woman in a padded jacket and a warm
headscarf was sitting on a bench beside the hut; she had been there
with her luggage the day before, and she was still sitting there, waiting
for the train. The day before, as he left to spend the night with his
unit, Ivanov had wondered whether to invite this lone woman back
with him: she could sleep in the warm with the nurses; why leave
her to freeze all night? – there was no knowing if she would ever get
warm in the pointsman's hut. But while he was wondering, the car
had begun to move and Ivanov had forgotten about the woman.

Now the woman was still there, still motionless and in the same
place as before. Such constancy and patience showed the loyalty and

immutability of a woman's heart – at least in relation to her possessions and her home, to which the woman was most likely returning. Ivanov went up to her: maybe she too would find it less dull to have company than to be on her own.

The woman turned her face towards Ivanov and he recognized her. It was a young woman they had called 'Masha the bathhouse-attendant's daughter' because this was what she had once called herself – she really was the daughter of someone who had worked in a bathhouse. Ivanov had come across her now and then during the war, on his visits to an Airfield Service Battalion where this bathhouse Masha worked as a civilian assistant to the canteen cook.

The autumn countryside around them felt gloomy and forlorn at this hour. The train which was to take both Masha and Ivanov to their homes was somewhere far off in grey space. There was nothing to divert or comfort a human heart except another human heart.

Ivanov got into conversation with Masha and began to feel better. Masha was a straightforward and good-looking girl, and there was a kindness in her large worker's hands and her healthy young body. She too was returning home and wondering what it would be like to start living a new civilian life; she had got used to the airforce women, and to the pilots who loved her like an elder sister, gave her chocolate and called her 'Big Masha' because of her height and the way she had room in her heart for all her brothers at once, like a real sister, and not just for one of them in particular. It was unaccustomed and strange, and even frightening, to be going home to relatives she was no longer used to.

Ivanov and Masha felt orphaned now without the army, but Ivanov could never stay sad or despondent for long; if he did, he would feel as if someone were laughing at him from a distance and being happy instead of him, while all he did was scowl like a half-wit. So he would always turn back quickly to the business of living; he would find something to be interested in or consoled by, some simple makeshift pleasure, as he put it himself, and would thus escape his depression.

He moved up closer to Masha and asked her to let him give her a comradely kiss on the cheek. 'Just a tiny one,' he said, 'because the train's late and it's so boring waiting for it.'

'Only because the train's late?' asked Masha, looking intently at Ivanov's face.

The ex-captain looked about thirty-five; the skin of his face was brown, wind-beaten and sunburnt; his grey eyes looked at Masha modestly, even shyly, and his speech, though direct, was tactful and courteous. Masha liked the hoarse, husky voice of this older man, his rough dark face and the expression it had of strength and defence-lessness. Ivanov put out his pipe with a thumb that was inured to the smouldering heat, and sighed as he waited for permission. Masha drew away from Ivanov. He smelt strongly of tobacco and dry toast, with a hint of wine – pure substances that come from fire or else can give birth to fire. It was as if Ivanov fed solely on tobacco, rusks, beer and wine.

He repeated his request. 'I'll be careful, Masha, just a surface kiss . . . Imagine I'm your uncle.'

'I already have. Only not my uncle – my father.'

'Splendid. So you'll let me?'

'Fathers don't ask for permission,' Masha laughed.

Ivanov was to say to himself later that Masha's hair smelt of autumn leaves fallen in the forest, and he was never able to forget it . . . He walked away from the railway line and lit a small fire to fry some eggs for his and Masha's supper.

In the night the train arrived and carried Ivanov and Masha away, towards their homes. They travelled together for two days, and on the third day they reached the town where Masha had been born twenty years before. She collected her things together in the carriage and asked Ivanov to settle the bag more comfortably on her back, but Ivanov took her bag on his own shoulders and followed Masha out of the carriage, even though he had more than a day's journey still ahead of him.

Masha was surprised and touched by Ivanov's considerateness. She was afraid of finding herself suddenly alone in the town she had been born in, and had lived in, but which was now almost a foreign country to her. Her mother and father had been deported by the Germans and had died in some unknown place; now Masha had only a cousin and two aunts in her home town, people to whom she felt no real attachment.

Ivanov arranged with the station commandant to break his journey, and stayed with Masha. Really he should have hurried on to his own home, where his wife and two children, whom he had not seen for four years, were waiting for him. But Ivanov was putting off the joyful and anxious moment of reunion with his family. He was not sure why he was doing this – perhaps he wanted to enjoy his freedom a little longer.

Masha did not know Ivanov's family circumstances, and girlish shyness prevented her from asking. She trusted herself to him in the goodness of her heart, with no thought beyond the moment.

Two days later Ivanov resumed his journey home. Masha saw him off at the station. He kissed her in a habitual way and promised courteously to remember her image for ever.

Masha smiled in reply and said, 'Why remember me for ever? There's no need – and anyway you won't . . . I'm not asking you for anything. Forget me.'

'My dear Masha! Where were you before? Why didn't I meet you long, long ago?'

'Before the war I was at school, and long long ago I didn't exist at all.'

The train arrived and they said goodbye. Ivanov departed and did not see how Masha, left on her own, began to cry because she could not forget any friend or comrade, or anyone at all whose path had even once crossed hers.

Ivanov looked out of the carriage window at the small houses of the little town they were passing and which he was unlikely ever to see again in his life, and reflected that in a house just like one of these, though in another town, his wife Lyuba lived with their children, Petya and Nastya, and that they were expecting him; he had sent his wife a telegram when he was still with his unit, saying he was coming home without delay and that he longed to embrace her and the children as soon as he possibly could.

For the last three days Lyubov Vasilyevna, Ivanov's wife, had been to meet all the trains coming from the west. She took time off work, failed to fulfil her norm, and was unable to sleep at night for joy, listening instead to the slow indifferent movement of the pendulum of the wall-clock. On the fourth day Lyubov Vasilyevna sent Petya and Nastya to the station – to meet their father if he came during the day – but once again went to meet the night train herself.

Ivanov arrived on the sixth day. He was met by his son Petya. Petya was now getting on for twelve, and the father did not immediately recognize his son in this serious lad who seemed older than his years. The father saw that Petya was a thin, undersized little boy, but with a large head, a broad forehead and a calm face that seemed already accustomed to life's cares, while his small brown eyes looked at the world around him morosely and disapprovingly, as if all they saw everywhere was disorder. Petya was neatly dressed and shod: his boots were worn but still had some use in them, his trousers and jacket were old, cut down from his father's civilian clothing, but there were no holes in them, they had been darned and patched where necessary; all in all Petya was like a little peasant who had no money to spare but who took care of his clothes. His father was surprised, and he sighed.

'So you're my father, are you?' asked Petya, when Ivanov lifted him up and hugged and kissed him. 'You must be!'

'Yes, I am. Hello, Pyotr Alekseyevich!'

'Hello. Why have you been so long? We've been waiting and waiting.'

'It was the train, Petya. It was very slow. How are your mother and Nastya? Alive and well?'

'They're fine,' said Petya. 'How many decorations have you got?'

'Two, Petya, and three medals.'

'And mother and I thought your chest would be covered with them. Mother has two medals as well. She got them for good service . . . Why haven't you got any more luggage – just a bag?'

'I don't need any more.'

'I suppose a travelling trunk gets in the way when you're fighting?' asked the son.

'Yes,' the father agreed. 'It's easier with just a bag. No one there uses a trunk.'

'And I thought you all did. I'd keep my things in a trunk – in a bag things get crumpled and broken.'

Petya took the bag and carried it home while his father walked along behind him.

The mother met them on the porch; she had asked for time off work again, as if she had sensed in her heart that her husband would arrive that day. She had gone straight home from the factory, meaning to go on from there to the station. She was afraid: had Semyon Yevseyevich turned up at the house? He liked to drop in sometimes during the day; turning up in the afternoon and sitting with Petya and five-year-old Nastya had become a habit of his. True, Semyon Yevseyevich never came empty-handed, he always brought something for the children – sweets or sugar, a small loaf of white bread or a coupon for shoes and clothing. Lyubov Vasilyevna had never had anything to reproach Semyon Yevseyevich for; all these two years they had known each other he had been good to her, and he had been like a father to the children, kinder, in fact, than many a father. But Lyubov Vasilyevna did not want her husband to see Semyon Yevseyevich today; she tidied up the kitchen and the living room, wanting the house to be clean, with nothing that did not belong there. Later, tomorrow, or the next day, she herself would tell her husband everything, all that had happened. Fortunately, Semyon Yevseyevich had not come that day.

Ivanov went up to his wife, put his arms round her and stood there with her, not moving away, feeling the forgotten and familiar warmth of someone he loved.

Little Nastya came out of the house and, after looking at the father she did not remember, started pushing at his leg, trying to separate him from her mother; then she burst out crying. Petya stood silently beside his father and mother, with his father's bag on his back; after waiting a while, he said: 'That's enough, you two – Nastya's crying, she doesn't understand.'

The father moved away from the mother and picked Nastya up. She was crying from fear.

'Nastya!' Petya called to her. 'Calm down, I tell you! This is our father, he's one of the family.'

Once inside the house, the father had a wash and sat down at the table. He stretched out his legs, closed his eyes and felt a quiet joy in his heart, a peaceful satisfaction. The war was over. During it his feet had walked thousands of miles. Lines of tiredness lay on his face, and his eyes felt a stabbing pain beneath their closed lids – they wanted to rest now in twilight or darkness.

While he sat there, the whole family bustled about in the living room and in the kitchen, preparing a celebration meal. Ivanov examined, one after another, all the objects around the house – the clock, the crockery cupboard, the wall thermometer, the chairs, the flowers on the windowsills, the Russian kitchen-stove. They had lived here a long time without him, and they had missed him. Now he had come back and he was looking at them, getting to know each one of them again, as if they were relatives whose lives had been poor and lonely without him. He breathed in the familiar, unchanging smell of the house – smouldering wood, warmth from his children's bodies, a burning smell from the grate. This smell had been just the same four years ago, it had not dispersed or changed in his absence. Nowhere else had Ivanov ever smelt this smell, although in the course of the war he had been in several countries and hundreds of homes; the smells there had been different, always lacking the special quality of his own home. Ivanov also recalled the smell of Masha, the scent of her hair; but that had been a smell of leaves in a forest, of some overgrown path he did not know, a smell not of home but once again of unsettled life. What was she doing now and how was she coping with civilian life, Masha the bathhouse-attendant's daughter? God be with her . . .

Ivanov could see that the busiest person around the house was Petya. Not only did he work hard himself, but he also told his mother and Nastya what to do and what not to do, and how to do everything properly. Nastya was obeying Petya meekly and was no longer afraid of her stranger-father; she had the alert and attentive face of a child who did everything in life seriously and truthfully, and she surely had a kind heart too, since she did not mind Petya.

'Nastya, empty the potato peelings out of the mug, I need it.'

Nastya obediently emptied the mug and washed it. Meanwhile their mother was quickly making a spur-of-the-moment pie, without yeast, to put in the stove; Petya had already got the fire going.

'Come on, Mother, get a move on!' Petya commanded. 'You can see I've got the stove ready. You're not much of a Stakhanovite, you're a dawdler!'

'Just a minute, Petya, I'm nearly there,' said his mother obediently. 'I'll just put some raisins in and it'll be done. It must be a long time since your father had raisins. I've been saving them for ages.'

'He's had raisins all right,' said Petya. 'Our troops get raisins. Just look at their fat faces – they get enough food all right. Nastya, why are you sitting down – think you're a guest here? Go on, peel some potatoes, we're going to fry some for supper. You can't feed a whole family on nothing but pie!'

While his mother was making the pie, Petya took the large oven-fork and put a cast-iron pot of cabbage soup in the oven, so the heat would not go to waste; as he did this, he even admonished the fire:

'Why are you burning so messily, jumping about all over the place? Just burn evenly, and stay under the food – what do you think the trees in the forest grew up to make firewood for? And you, Nastya, why have you shoved the kindling into the stove just any old how? You should have laid it the way I taught you. And you're peeling too much off the potatoes again, you should peel them thinly and not dig out the flesh – that's how our food gets wasted! How many times do I have to tell you? This is the last time – do it again and you'll get a clout round the head!'

'Petya, why keep getting at Nastya?' their mother said gently. 'Just think for a moment! How can she peel so many potatoes, and do them all just as you want them, like a barber never nicking the flesh? Father's come home, and all you can do is find fault!'

'I'm not finding fault, I'm talking sense. Father needs feeding, he's just back from the war, and you two are wasting good food. Think how much we've wasted in potato peelings in a whole year! If we'd had a sow, we could have fed her all year on potato peelings alone, then taken her to the show and been given a medal. Just imagine it! But you don't understand.'

Ivanov had not known that his son had turned out like this; he sat and marvelled at his cleverness. But he preferred gentle little Nastya, who was also working away at household tasks. Her little hands were quick and deft – they must have had a lot of practice.

'Lyuba,' Ivanov said to his wife, 'why aren't you saying anything to me? Tell me how you've got on without me. How's your health been? And what work do you do?'

Lyubov Vasilyevna felt shy of her husband now, like a young bride; she was not used to him any more. She even blushed when he spoke to her and, just as in her youth, her face took on the timid, scared expression which Ivanov found so attractive.

'We've been all right, Alyosha. The children haven't been ill too often. I've taken care of them. The bad thing is that I've only been here with them at night. I work at the brick factory, at the press. It's a long way on foot.'

'Where do you work?' said Ivanov, not understanding.

'At the brick factory, at the press. I had no qualifications, of course, so at first I just did odd jobs outside. Then they gave me some training and put me on the press. It's been good to be working – only the children have been alone all the time. You can see how they've turned out. They know how to do everything themselves, they're like grown-ups,' Lyubov Vasilyevna said quietly. 'Whether that's a good thing, Alyosha, I just don't know.'

'We shall see, Lyuba . . . We'll all be living together now. There'll be time enough to work out what's good and what's bad.'

'Everything will be better now you're here. When I'm on my own I don't know what's right and what's wrong, and I've been afraid. Now it's for you to think about how to bring up the children.'

Ivanov stood up and paced about the room.

'So, all in all, you've kept in good spirits, have you?'

'It's been all right, Alyosha, and it's over now, we've stuck it out. Only we missed you dreadfully and we were afraid you'd never come back to us. We were afraid you'd die there, like others have . . .'

She began to cry over the pie, which she had already placed in its iron mould, and her tears dropped onto the dough. She had smeared the top of the pie with beaten egg and was still smoothing it with her palm, now smearing the festive pie with her tears.

Nastya gripped her mother's leg in her arms, pressed her face into her skirt and stared up at her father sternly from beneath her brows.

Her father bent down to her. 'What's the matter, Nastya, what's wrong? Are you cross with me?'

He gathered her up in his arms and stroked her head. 'What's the matter, little daughter? You've completely forgotten me, haven't you? You were tiny when I went away to the war.'

Nastya laid her head on her father's shoulder and she too began to cry.

'What is it, little Nastyenka?'

'Mummy's crying, so I'm crying too.'

Petya, who was standing in front of the stove, was bewildered and annoyed.

'What's the matter with you all? While you're all being moody, the heat's going to waste. Do you want the stove heated up all over again? Who'll give us coupons for more wood? We've used up the last lot, there's just a tiny bit left in the shed – about ten logs, and it's only aspen. Give me the dough, mother, before the heat all gets lost.'

Petya took out the big iron pot of cabbage soup and raked the embers on the floor of the stove, and Lyubov Vasilyevna, as if trying to please Petya, hurriedly put the two pies in, forgetting to brush the second one with egg.

Ivanov was finding his own home strange and rather hard to understand. His wife was the same, with her sweet, shy, though now deeply exhausted face, and the children were the same ones that had been born to him, except that they had grown older during the war, as was to be expected. But something was stopping Ivanov from feeling wholehearted joy at being back home – no doubt he was simply not used to family life any more and so was unable to understand even those nearest and dearest to him. Looking at Petya, his firstborn, now so grown up, listening as Petya gave commands and instructions to his mother and little sister, watching his worried, serious face, Ivanov confessed to himself with a sense of shame that he did not feel fatherly enough towards this boy, that he did not feel drawn to his own son. Ivanov was all the more ashamed of this lack of fatherly feeling because he was aware that Petya needed love and care more than the others did, for it was painful to look at him. Ivanov did not know in any detail how his family had lived while he was away, and he could not yet grasp at all clearly why Petya had come to be like this.

Sitting at the table, among his family, Ivanov realized what he had to do. He must get to work as soon as he could – he had to find a job and earn money, and help his wife bring up the children properly; then everything would gradually get better, and Petya would start running about with other children or sitting with a book, not standing at the stove with an oven-fork in his hands and giving orders.

During the meal Petya ate less than anyone else, but he scooped up all the crumbs and tipped them into his mouth.

'What are you doing, Petya?' his father asked him. 'Why are you eating crumbs when you haven't finished your pie? Eat it up and your mother will cut you another piece.'

'I could eat it all up,' Petya said with a frown. 'But I've had enough.'

'He's afraid that if he starts eating a lot, then Nastya will copy him and eat a lot too,' Lyubov Vasilyevna explained straightforwardly. 'And that worries him.'

'You two don't worry about anything,' said Petya unemotionally. 'I just want there to be more for you.'

Father and mother glanced at each other and shivered at their son's words.

'Well, and why aren't you eating?' the father asked little Nastya. 'Are you copying Petya? Eat up, or you won't grow up to be a big girl.'

'I am a big girl,' said Nastya.

She ate a small piece of pie, but pushed away another, bigger piece and covered it with a napkin.

'What are you doing?' her mother asked. 'Shall I put some butter on it for you?'

'No, I'm full up.'

'Well eat it like that then. Why've you pushed it away?'

'Because Uncle Semyon might come. I'm leaving it for him. It's not your pie, it's my pie I'm not eating. I'm putting it under my pillow so it doesn't get cold.'

Nastya got down from her chair; she took the pie wrapped up in a napkin over to her bed, and put it under the pillow.

Her mother remembered how she herself had once laid pillows over a pie she had baked for May Day, to keep it warm for Semyon Yevseyevich.

'Who is this Uncle Semyon?' Ivanov asked his wife.

Lyubov Vasilyevna did not know what to say. 'I don't know who he is,' she said. 'He comes on his own to see the children. His wife and his own children were killed by the Germans, he's grown fond of our two and he comes to play with them.'

'To play with them?' said Ivanov in surprise. 'What games do they play when he comes? How old is he?'

Petya looked quickly at his mother, then at his father; his mother did not answer his father's question, she only looked at Nastya with sad eyes. The father smiled unpleasantly, got up from his chair, lit a cigarette and then asked Petya, 'Where are the toys you and this Uncle Semyon play with?'

Nastya got down from her chair, climbed up onto another chair by the chest of drawers, took out some books and brought them to her father. 'They're book-toys,' she said. 'Uncle Semyon reads them out loud to me. Look what a funny teddy bear, he's a toy and he's a book too . . .'

Ivanov took the book-toys his daughter handed him: about Misha the Bear, and a toy cannon, and the little house where Granny Domna lived, spinning flax with her granddaughter . . .

Petya remembered it was time to close the damper in the

stovepipe, so the warmth would not escape from the house. After closing the damper, he said to his father, 'Semyon Yevseyevich is older than you . . . He helps us out, leave him in peace.'

Glancing out of the window just in case, Petya noticed that the clouds in the sky were not the right kind of clouds for September. 'Look at those clouds,' he said. 'They're the colour of lead – they must be full of snow. Don't say winter's going to set in tomorrow! What will we do? We haven't dug up the potatoes yet, we haven't stocked up on food. What a situation to be in!'

Ivanov looked at his son, listened to him talking and realized he felt shy of him. He would have liked to ask his wife more about this Semyon Yevseyevich who had been coming to visit for the last two years, and whether it was Nastya this man came to see or his good-looking wife, but Petya distracted Lyubov Vasilyevna by talking about household matters: 'Mother, give me tomorrow's bread-coupons and the registration cards, and give me the paraffin coupons as well – tomorrow's the last day and we must get our charcoal, oh but you've lost the sack, they won't give us any charcoal without one, you must have a good look for the sack right now, or else sew a new one out of rags, how can we manage without a sack? And tell Nastya not to let anyone into our yard tomorrow for water – they take too much from the well; with winter coming the water will drop and our rope's not long enough to let the bucket down lower, and we don't want to have to eat snow, anyway we'd need firewood to thaw it out.'

As he said all this, Petya swept up around the stove and sorted out the kitchen utensils. Then he took the pot of soup out of the oven.

'We've had some pie and now we're having some cabbage-and-meat soup, with bread,' Petya announced. 'And you, father, must go first thing tomorrow to the District Soviet and the Military Commissariat. Then you'll be put on the list straight away and we'll get ration cards for you more quickly.'

'All right,' said the father obediently.

'Yes, and mind you don't oversleep and forget.'

'I won't,' the father promised.

Their first shared meal after the war – soup with meat – was eaten by the family in silence, with even Petya sitting there calmly; it was as if father and mother and children were afraid of destroying, through some chance word, the quiet happiness of a family sitting together.

Then Ivanov asked his wife, 'How have you managed for clothes, Lyuba? Is everything worn out?'

'We've been wearing all old things, but now we can buy something new,' Lyubov Vasilyevna smiled. 'I had to mend the children's clothes while they stood up in them. Then I cut down your suit, your two pairs of trousers and all your underclothes. There was no money to spare, you see, and the children had to wear something.'

'You did right,' said Ivanov. 'Children shouldn't have to go without.'

'They haven't had to. I even sold the coat you bought me. Now I wear my padded jacket.'

'Her jacket's too short. She could catch cold in it,' commented Petya. 'I'll go and work as a stoker at the bathhouse. I'll earn some money and get her a coat. People bring clothes to sell at the market, I've had a look and checked the prices. Some of the coats are all right.'

'We can get by without you and your wages,' said the father.

After dinner Nastya put a large pair of glasses on her nose and sat by the window to darn the little knitted mittens her mother now wore at the factory inside her work-mittens. It was already autumn; the weather had turned cold.

Petya glanced across at his sister and began to scold her: 'What are you up to now? Why have you got Uncle Semyon's glasses on?'

'I'm not looking through them, I'm looking over them.'

'Oh really! . . . I can see what you're doing! You'll ruin your eyesight and go blind, then you'll be on a pension and be a burden for the rest of your life. Take the glasses off this minute, I tell you, and stop darning those mittens, mother will darn them, or I'll do them myself as soon as I have a moment. Get out your exercise book and practise your writing – goodness knows when you last did any!'

'Does Nastya go to school then?' asked the father.

Their mother replied that Nastya was not yet big enough for school, but that Petya made her do lessons every day; he had bought her an exercise book, and she practised drawing the strokes for letters. Petya was also teaching his sister to do sums, adding and subtracting pumpkin seeds in front of her, while Lyubov Vasilyevna was herself teaching Nastya to read.

Nastya put down the mitten and took an exercise book and a pen and nib out of the chest of drawers, while Petya, satisfied that everything was being done properly, put on his mother's padded jacket and went outside to chop wood for the next day; he usually brought the firewood into the house at night and laid it behind the stove to dry out, so it would give out more heat and be more efficient.

In the evening Lyubov Vasilyevna got supper ready early. She wanted the children to go to sleep in good time so that she and her husband could sit together and talk. But the children did not fall asleep until long after supper; Nastya, lying on the wooden couch, kept watching her father from under the blanket, while Petya, who had lain down on the Russian stove he always slept on, winter and summer alike, tossed and turned, grunting and whispering something, and it was quite some time before he quietened down. But the night wore on, and Nastya closed her eyes that were tired from looking, while Petya started to snore on the stove.

Petya always slept lightly and on his guard: he was afraid something might happen in the night and he would not hear – a fire, or robbers breaking in, or his mother might forget to latch the door and it would come open during the night and all the warmth would escape. This time it was the troubled voices of his parents that woke him; they were talking in the room next to the kitchen. What time it was – midnight or nearly morning – he did not know, but his father and mother were not asleep.

'Alyosha, don't make so much noise, the children will wake up,' his mother was saying quietly. 'You mustn't say bad things about him, he's a good man, and he's loved your children . . .'

'We don't need his love,' said the father. 'I love my children myself. Loving other people's children – I like that! I sent you certificates regularly and you had your job – what did you need this Semyon Yevseyevich for? Still hot-blooded, are you? Oh Lyuba, Lyuba! You're not the woman I thought you were . . . You've made a fool of me.'

The father fell silent, then struck a match to light his pipe.

'What are you saying, Alyosha? How can you?' the mother burst out. 'When I've brought up the children and they've hardly ever been ill and they've got plenty of flesh on them.'

'So what?' said the father. 'Some women were left with four children, but they managed all right, and their kids are no worse than ours. And as for Petya and the way you've brought him up – he carries on like an old man, but it wouldn't surprise me if he's forgotten how to read.'

From his place on the stove Petya sighed and then pretended to snore, so he could go on listening. 'All right,' he thought, 'maybe I am an old man, but it was all very well for you – you didn't have to worry where your next meal was coming from!'

'Yes, but he's learnt some of life's hardest lessons!' said the mother. 'And he doesn't fall behind in his schoolwork.'

'Who is this Semyon of yours?' said the father angrily. 'Stop leading me up the garden path.'

'He's a good man.'

'You love him, do you?'

'Alyosha, I'm the mother of your children.'

'Go on, give me a straight answer.'

'I love you, Alyosha. I'm a mother. It's a long time since I was a woman, and that was only ever with you. I can't even remember when it was.'

The father said nothing, smoking his pipe in the darkness.

'I've missed you, Alyosha. Of course I had the children, but that's not the same as having you. I was waiting for you all the time, all those long terrible years. Often I was afraid to wake up in the morning.'

'What's his job, where does he work?'

'He works at our factory, in the supplies section.'

'I see, a swindler.'

'He isn't a swindler. I don't know . . . His whole family were killed in Mogilyov. There were three children, the daughter was already grown up.'

'Doesn't matter. He found himself another family, ready-made, and a woman who's still quite young, and good-looking – so he's got things nice and cosy again.'

The mother did not reply. There was a silence, but soon Petya could hear his mother crying.

'He talked to the children about you, Alyosha,' she began, and Petya could tell that big tears were hovering in her eyes. 'He told the children how you were fighting for us and how you were suffering. They'd ask why, and he'd say because you're a good man.'

The father gave a laugh and knocked the ash out of his pipe.

'So that's the kind of man he is, your Semyon Yevseyevich! Never even seen me, yet he sings my praises. Quite a character!'

'No, he's never seen you. He made things up, so the children would go on loving you, so they wouldn't lose touch with their father.'

'But why? Why was he doing it? Because he wanted you and he was in a hurry? Go on, tell me, what was he after?'

'Maybe he just has a kind heart, Alyosha, maybe that's why. Why shouldn't it be?'

'I'm sorry, Lyuba, but you're a fool. No one does things for nothing!'

'But Semyon Yevseyevich often brought things for the children. He always brings something – sweets, white flour, sugar. Not long ago he brought Nastya some felt boots, only they were no good, they were too small. And he's never asked for anything from us. We didn't need anything either, Alyosha, we could have managed without his presents, we'd got used to the way we were living, but Semyon Yevseyevich says he feels better when he's doing something for other people, it stops him missing his dead family so badly. It really isn't what you think – you'll see when you meet him.'

'You're talking nonsense!' said the father. 'Stop trying to trick me . . . I'm fed up with you, Lyuba. And I still want to enjoy life.'

'Enjoy life with us, Alyosha.'

'While you're carrying on with Semyon Yevseyevich?'

'I won't, Alyosha. He'll never come here again. I'll tell him to stop coming.'

'So something has been happening, if it's going to stop? Oh Lyuba, how could you? You women are all the same.'

'And what about you men?' the mother said in a hurt voice. 'What do you mean – we're all the same? I'm not the same. I've been working day and night, we've been making linings for locomotive fireboxes. I've grown thin in the face and horrible-looking, no one recognizes me, beggars don't even ask me for money. I've had a hard time too, and the children were alone at home. I'd get back from work – and there was the stove to light, the supper to cook, it was dark, and the children were miserable. They couldn't help round the house like they do now, even Petya was still little. And it was then that Semyon Yevseyevich started calling on us. He'd come round – and just sit with the children. He lives all on his own, you see. "Can I come and visit you sometimes," he asked, "so I can warm up a bit?" I told him our house was cold too, and the firewood was damp, but he said, "It's my soul that's chilled to the marrow. Just let me sit near your children, you don't need to heat up the stove for me." "All right," I said, "come round then. With you here the children won't be so frightened." Then I got used to his visits too. We all began to feel better when he came. I'd look at him and think of you, I'd remember we had you . . . It was so sad without you, it was awful. Why not let someone come round? I thought. Time will pass quicker, we won't be so miserable. What use is time to us when you're not here?'

'Well go on, what happened after that?' said the father impatiently.

'Nothing happened after that. Now you're back, Alyosha.'

'Well, all right then, if that's the truth,' said the father. 'It's time to get some sleep.'

'Stay up a bit longer,' the mother begged. 'Let's talk, I'm so happy to be with you.'

'Will they never quieten down?' thought Petya, lying on the stove. 'They've made it up – what more do they want? Mother's got to get up early for work, but she's still wide awake. A fine time to cheer up and stop crying!'

'And did this Semyon love you?' asked the father.

'Wait a minute. I'll go and tuck Nastya in, she gets uncovered in her sleep and she'll be cold.'

The mother covered Nastya up with the blanket, went into the kitchen and paused by the stove to check whether Petya was asleep. Petya knew what she was up to and started to snore. Then she went back and he heard her voice again.

'I dare say he did love me. I saw him looking at me affectionately – and I'm not much to look at now, am I? Life's been hard on him, Alyosha, and he had to love somebody.'

'You might at least have given him a kiss then, if that's the way things were,' said the father in a nice voice.

'Don't be silly! He did kiss me, twice, but I didn't want him to.'

'Why did he do it then, if you didn't want him to?'

'I don't know. He said he just lost his head, and that he was thinking of his wife, and I look a bit like her.'

'And does he look like me?'

'No, he doesn't. No one's like you, Alyosha, you're the only one who's like you.'

'The only one? Counting starts with one: first one, then two.'

'He only kissed me on the cheek, not on the lips.'

'Makes no difference where.'

'Alyosha, it does make a difference. And what do you know about how things have been for us?'

'What do you mean? I've fought through the whole war, I've been closer to death than I am to you at this moment.'

'While you were fighting, I was dying of worry. My hands were shaking from grief, but I had to keep working cheerfully. I had to feed the children and help our State against the Fascist enemy.'

She was talking calmly, but her heart was heavy, and Petya was sorry for his mother; he knew that she had learnt to mend shoes for all three of them, not to have to pay a lot of money to the cobbler, and that she had repaired electric cooking rings for their neighbours in return for potatoes.

'I couldn't go on like that, longing for you,' said the mother. 'And if I had, it would have been the end of me, I know it would, and there were the children to think of. I needed to feel something else, Alyosha, some sort of happiness, just to get some rest. There was a man who said he loved me, and he was gentle to me, like you used to be long ago.'

'You mean this Semyon Yevsey of yours?'

'No, someone else. He works as an instructor for our trade union district committee, he's an evacuee.'

'To hell with who the man is! So what happened? Did he console you?'

Petya knew nothing about this instructor, and this surprised him. 'So our mother's been naughty too,' he whispered to himself. 'Fancy that!'

'I got nothing from him, no joy at all,' the mother replied. 'Afterwards I felt even worse. My soul had been drawn to him because it was dying, but when he was close to me, really close, I felt nothing. All I thought about was household things, and I wished

I hadn't let him be close. I realized I could only be calm and happy with you and that I'd only rest when you were close to me again. I'm lost without you, I can't even keep myself going for the children. Stay with us, Alyosha, we'll have a good life.'

Petya heard his father get up from the bed without speaking, light his pipe and sit down on the stool.

'How many times did you meet him and be really close?' asked the father.

'Only once,' said the mother. 'It never happened again. How many times should I have?'

'As many times as you like, that's your business,' declared the father. 'So why say you're the mother of our children, and that you've only been a woman with me, a long time ago?'

'It's the truth, Alyosha.'

'How can it be? What kind of truth? You were a woman with him too, weren't you?'

'No, I wasn't a woman with him, I wanted to be, but I couldn't. I felt I couldn't go on without you. I just needed someone to be with me, I was so worn out, my heart had gone all dark, I couldn't love my children any more, and you know I'd go through anything for them, I'd give the very bones from my body!'

'Just a minute,' said the father. 'You say you made a mistake with this second Semyon of yours. You didn't get any happiness from him – and yet here you are, you're still in one piece.'

'Yes,' whispered the mother. 'I'm still alive.'

'So you're lying to me again! So much for your truth!'

'I don't know,' whispered the mother. 'I don't know very much at all.'

'All right, but I know a lot, I've been through more than you have,' said the father. 'You're a whore, that's what you are.'

The mother was silent. The father's breathing was fast and laboured.

'So here I am, home at last,' he said. 'The war's over, and now you've wounded me in the heart . . . All right, you go and live with your Semyons. You've made a fool of me, you've turned me into a laughingstock. But I'm not a plaything, I'm a human being.'

In the dark the father began putting on his clothes and his shoes. Then he lit the paraffin lamp, sat down at the table, and wound up his watch.

'Four o'clock,' he said to himself. 'Still dark. It's true what they say: women aplenty, but not a wife to be found.'

It grew quiet in the house. Nastya was breathing evenly, asleep on the wooden couch. Up on the warm stove, Petya pressed his face into the pillow and forgot he was meant to be snoring.

'Alyosha,' said the mother in a gentle voice. 'Alyosha, forgive me.'

Petya heard his father groan, and then heard the sound of breaking glass; through a gap in the curtain he could see it had got darker in the other room, though a light was still burning. 'He's crushed the glass,' Petya guessed. 'And there's no lamp-glass to be got anywhere.'

'You've cut your hand,' said the mother. 'You're bleeding. Take a towel from the chest of drawers.'

'Shut up!' the father shouted at her. 'I can't stand the sound of your voice. Wake the children! Wake them up this very minute! Wake them, do you hear? I'll tell them what sort of mother they've got! I want them to know.'

Nastya cried out in fear and woke up.

'Mummy!' she called out. 'Can I get into bed with you?'

Nastya liked getting into bed with her mother in the night, to lie under the blanket with her and get warm.

Petya sat up on the stove, swung his legs over the edge, and said to everyone: 'Go to sleep! Why have you woken me up? It's not day yet, it's still dark outside! Why are you making such a noise? Why is the lamp burning?'

'Go to sleep, Nastya, go back to sleep, it's still early, I'll come to you in a minute,' the mother answered. 'And you lie down, Petya, and don't talk any more.'

'Why are you talking then?' said Petya. 'And what does Father want?'

'What's that to do with you?' the father replied. 'A right sergeant-major you are!'

'And why have you smashed the lamp-glass? Why are you frightening Mother? She's thin enough as it is. She eats her potatoes without any butter, she gives all the butter to Nastya.'

'And do you know what your mother's been up to here, do you know what she's been playing at?' the father cried plaintively, like a little boy.

'Alyosha!' Lyubov Vasilyevna said softly to her husband.

'Yes, I do, I know everything!' said Petya. 'Mother's been crying for you, she's been waiting for you, and now you've come back home – and she's still crying! You're the one who doesn't know!'

'You don't understand anything yet!' said the father furiously. 'A fine son we've produced!'

'I understand everything perfectly,' Petya answered from the stove. 'It's you who don't understand. There's work to do, we have to go on living, and you two are quarrelling like stupid fools.'

Petya stopped. He lay down on his pillow; and silently, without meaning to, he began to cry.

'You've had things too much your own way in this house,' said the father. 'But it's all the same now. You can carry on being the boss.'

Petya wiped away his tears and answered: 'Some father you are, saying things like that, and you a grown-up who's been through the war! You should go to the war-invalids' co-op tomorrow – you'll find Uncle Khariton there, behind the counter, he cuts the bread and he never cheats anyone. He's been in the war too and come back. Go and ask him – he tells everyone, he laughs about it, I've heard him myself. He's got a wife, Anyuta, she learnt to drive and now she delivers the bread, and she's a good woman, she doesn't steal any of it. Anyuta had a friend too, and she used to visit him and they'd have a drink and something to eat. This friend of hers has a decoration, he's lost an arm and he's in charge of the shop where you take your coupons to get clothes.'

'Stop talking nonsense and go to sleep,' said his mother. 'It'll soon be light.'

'Well, you two are stopping me sleeping . . . And it won't soon be light . . . This man with no arm made friends with Anyuta, life got better for them, but Khariton still lived at the war . . . Then Khariton comes back and starts cursing Anyuta. He curses her all day long and at night he has some vodka and something to eat, but Anyuta just cries and doesn't eat at all. He curses and curses, till he's tired out, then he stops tormenting Anyuta and says, "You fool of a woman, having only one man – and a man with only one arm at that! When I was away on my own I had Glashka and I had Aproska, and then there was Maruska and Anyushka your namesake, and then I had Magdalinka into the bargain!" And he laughs. And

Anyuta laughs too. And she starts boasting about her Khariton: what a fine man he is, no better man anywhere, he killed Fascists and he had so many women after him he couldn't ward them off . . . Uncle Khariton tells us all this in the shop, he's taking in the loaves of bread one by one . . . And now they're quite peaceful, they have a good life . . . And Uncle Khariton laughs again and says, "But I deceived my Anyuta – I hadn't had anyone. No Glashka, no Nyushka, no Aproska, and no Magdalinka into the bargain. A soldier's the son of the Fatherland, he's got no time to fool around, his heart is levelled against the enemy. I just made all that up to give Anyuta a scare." Go to bed, father, put the light out – without the glass it just smokes!'

Ivanov listened in amazement to this story told by his son. 'What a devil!' he said to himself. 'I kept thinking he'd start talking about my Masha.'

Petya was exhausted and he began snoring; this time he really was asleep.

When he woke up it was broad daylight, and he was frightened to find he had slept so long and not yet done anything in the house.

No one was at home except Nastya. She was sitting on the floor turning the pages of a picture book her mother had bought her a long time ago. She looked through this book every day, because she had no other books, and traced the words with her finger, as if she were reading.

'Why are you messing up your book already?' Petya said to his sister. 'Put it away. Where's mother? Has she gone to work?'

'Yes,' answered Nastya quietly, closing the book.

'And where's father got to?' Petya looked round the house, in the kitchen and in the living room. 'Has he taken his bag?'

'Yes, he has,' said Nastya.

'What did he say to you?'

'Nothing. He kissed my mouth and my eyes.'

'Did he?' said Petya, and began to think.

'Get up off the floor,' he ordered his sister. 'I'll give you a proper wash and get you dressed, we're going out.'

At that moment their father was sitting in the station. He had already drunk a large glass of vodka and had got himself a hot meal with his travel voucher. In the night he had made up his mind once and for all to take the train to the town where he had left Masha and to meet up with her there again, perhaps never to part from her. A pity he was so much older than this bathhouse-attendant's daughter whose hair smelt of the countryside. But you can never tell – there's no knowing the future. All the same Ivanov hoped Masha would be at least a little bit glad to see him again; that would be enough, it would mean he too had a new and close friend, one, moreover, who was beautiful and cheerful and kind. You never can tell!

Soon the train arrived, going in the direction Ivanov had come from only yesterday. He took his kitbag and went on to the platform. 'Masha isn't expecting me,' he thought. 'She told me I'd forget her, whatever I said, and that we'd never meet again; yet here I am, on my way to her for ever.'

He got into a carriage and stood at the end of it, so that when the train pulled out he could look for a last time at the little town where he had lived before the war and where his children had been born. He wanted to look one more time at the house he had left; it could be seen from the train – the street it stood on led to the level crossing, and the train had to go over the crossing.

The train started, and went slowly over the points and out into the empty autumn fields. Ivanov took hold of the handrail and looked out from the carriage at what had been his hometown – at the little houses, the bigger buildings, the sheds, the lookout tower of the fire-station . . . In the distance he recognized two tall chimneys: one was the soap factory, the other was the brick factory – Lyuba would be working there now at the press. Let her live her own life now, and he would live his. Maybe he could forgive her, but what difference would that make? His heart had hardened against her now and there was no forgiveness in it for a woman who had kissed another man and lived with him just so that the war, and separation from her husband, would not make her so lonely and miserable. And the fact that it was the hardness of her life, and the torment of need and yearning, that had driven Lyuba to her Semyon or her Yevsey was no excuse; it was simply proof of her feelings. All love comes from need and yearning; if human beings never felt need or yearning, they would never love.

Ivanov was about to enter a compartment, to lie down and sleep; he no longer wanted a last look at the house where he had lived and

where his children still did live: why torment oneself to no purpose?
He looked out to see how far it was to the crossing – and there it
was in front of him. It was here the railway crossed the track that
led into the town; on this track lay wisps of straw and hay that had
fallen off carts, and willow twigs and horse dung. There was rarely
anyone on the track, except on the two market days of the week;
just occasionally there would be a peasant on his way to the town
with a full cart of hay, or on the way back to his village. That was
how it was now: the track was deserted. All he could see, in the
distance, running down the street that led into the track, were two
children. One of them was bigger and one smaller, and the big one
had taken the smaller one by the hand and was hurrying it along,
but the small one, no matter how fast it tried to move its little legs,
could not keep up with the bigger one. Then the bigger one began
to drag the smaller one. They stopped at the last house of the town
and looked towards the station, evidently wondering whether or not
to go that way. Then they looked at the passenger train going over
the crossing and began to run down the cart track, straight towards
the train, as if suddenly wanting to reach it before it passed by.

Ivanov's carriage had passed the crossing. Ivanov picked up his
bag, meaning to go through into the carriage and lie down for a
sleep on the upper bunk where other passengers would not disturb
him. But what about those two children? Had they managed to reach
the train before the last carriage went by? Ivanov leaned out and
looked back.

The two children, hand in hand, were still running along the
track towards the crossing. They both fell down together, got up
and ran on. The bigger one raised his one free hand and, turning
his face towards Ivanov as the train passed by, began to beckon to
someone, as if calling them to come back to him. Then they both
fell down again. Ivanov could see that the bigger child had a felt
boot on one foot and a rubber galosh on the other, which was why
he kept falling.

Ivanov closed his eyes, not wanting to see and feel the pain of
the exhausted children now lying on the ground, and then felt a
kind of heat in his chest, as if the heart imprisoned and pining
within him had been beating long and in vain all his life and had
only now beaten its way to freedom, filling his entire being with
warmth and awe. He suddenly recognized everything he had ever

known before, but much more precisely and more truthfully. Previously, he had sensed the life of others through a barrier of pride and self-interest, but now, all of a sudden, he had touched another life with his naked heart.

Once more, from the carriage steps, he looked down the train towards the distant children. He knew now that they were his own children, Petya and Nastya. They must have seen him when the train was going over the crossing, and Petya had beckoned him home to their mother, but he had paid no attention, he had been thinking of something else and had not recognized his own children.

Now Petya and Nastya were a long way behind, running along the sandy path beside the rails; Petya was still holding little Nastya by the hand and dragging her along behind him when she was unable to move her legs quickly enough.

Ivanov threw his kitbag out of the carriage onto the ground, and then climbed down to the bottom step and got off the train, onto the sandy path along which his children were running after him.

Translated from the Russian by Robert and Elizabeth Chandler
and Angela Livingstone

A. M. HOMES

Do Not Disturb

My wife, the doctor, is not well. In the end she could be dead. It started suddenly, on a country weekend, a movie with friends, a pizza, and then pain. 'I liked the part where he lunged at the woman with a knife,' Eric says.

'She deserved it,' Enid says.

'Excuse me,' my wife says, getting up from the table.

A few minutes later I find her doubled over on the sidewalk. 'Something is ripping me from the inside out.'

'Should I get the check?' She looks at me like I am an idiot.

'My wife is not well,' I announce, returning to the table. 'We have to go.'

'What do you mean – is she all right?'

Eric and Enid hurry out while I wait for the check. They drive us home. As I open the front door, my wife pushes past me and goes running for the bathroom. Eric, Enid, and I stand in the living room, waiting.

'Are you all right in there?' I call out.

'No,' she says.

'Maybe she should go to the hospital,' Enid says.

'Doctors don't go to the hospital,' I say.

She lies on the bathroom floor, her cheek against the white tile. 'I keep thinking it will pass.'

'Call us if you need us,' Eric and Enid say, leaving.

I tuck the bath mat under her head and sneak away. From the kitchen I call a doctor friend. I stand in the dark, whispering, 'She's just lying there on the floor, what do I do?'

'Don't do anything,' the doctor says, half-insulted by the thought that there is something to do. 'Observe her. Either it will go away, or something more will happen. You watch and you wait.'

Watch and wait. I am thinking about our relationship. We haven't been getting along. The situation has become oxygenless and addictive, a suffocating annihilation, each staying to see how far it will go.

I sit on the edge of the tub, looking at her. 'I'm worried.'

'Don't worry,' she says. 'And don't just sit there staring.'

Earlier in the afternoon we were fighting, I don't remember about what. I only know – I called her a bitch.

'I was a bitch before I met you and I'll be a bitch long after you're gone. Surprise me,' she said. 'Tell me something new.'

I wanted to say, I'm leaving. I wanted to say, I know you think I never will and that's why you treat me like you do. But I'm going. I wanted to get in the car, drive off, and call it a day.

The fight ended with the clock. She glanced at it. 'It's six-thirty, we're meeting Eric and Enid at seven; put on a clean shirt.'

She is lying on the bathroom floor, the print of the bath mat making an impression on her cheek. 'Are you comfortable?' I ask.

She looks surprised, as though she's just realized she's on the floor.

'Help me,' she says, struggling to get up.

Her lips are white and thin.

'Bring me a trash can, a plastic bag, a thermometer, some Tylenol, and a glass of water.'

'Are you going to throw up?'

'I want to be prepared,' she says.

We are always prepared. We have flare guns and fire extinguishers, walkie talkies, a rubber raft, a hundred batteries in assorted shapes and sizes, a thousand bucks in dollar bills, enough toilet paper and bottled water to get us through six months. When we travel we have smoke hoods in our carry-on bags, protein bars, water purification tablets, and a king-sized bag of M&Ms. We are ready and waiting.

She slips the digital thermometer under her tongue; the numbers move up the scale – each beep is a tenth of a degree.

'A hundred and one point four,' I announce.

'I have a fever?' she says in disbelief.

'I wish things between us weren't so bad.'

'It's not as bad as you think,' she says. 'Expect less and you won't be disappointed.'

We try to sleep; she is hot, she is cold, she is mumbling something about having 'a surgical belly', something about 'guarding and rebound'. I don't know if she's talking about herself or the NBA.

'This is incredible.' She sits bolt upright and folds over again, writhing. 'Something is struggling inside me. It's like one of those alien movies, like I'm going to burst open and something's going to spew out, like I'm erupting.' She pauses, takes a breath. 'And then it stops. Who would ever have thought this would happen to me – and on a Saturday night?'

'Is it your appendix?'

'That's the one thought I have, but I'm not sure. I don't have the classic symptoms. I don't have anorexia or diarrhea. When I was eating that pizza, I was hungry.'

'Is it an ovary? Women have lots of ovaries.'

'Women have two ovaries,' she says. 'It did occur to me that it could be Mittelschmertz.'

'Mittelschmertz?'

'The launching of the egg, the middle of the cycle.'

At five in the morning her temperature is one hundred and three. She is alternately sweating and shivering.

'Should I drive you back to the city or to the hospital out here?'

'I don't want to be the doctor who goes to the ER with gas.'

'Fine.'

I am dressing myself, packing, thinking of what I will need in the waiting room: cell phone, notebook, pen, something to read, something to eat, my wallet, her insurance card.

We are in the car, hurrying. There is an urgency to the situation, the unmistakable sense that something bad is happening. I am driving seventy miles an hour.

She is not a doctor now. She is lost, inside herself.

'I think I'm dying,' she says.

I pull up to the emergency entrance and half-carry her in, leaving the car doors open, the engine running; I have the impulse to drop her off and walk away.

The emergency room is empty. There is a bell on the check-in desk. I ring it twice.

A woman appears. 'Can I help you?'

'My wife is not well,' I say. 'She is a doctor.'

The woman sits at her computer. She takes my wife's name. She takes her insurance card and then she takes her temperature and blood pressure. 'Are you in a lot of pain?'

'Yes,' my wife says.

Within minutes a doctor is there, pressing on my wife. 'It's got to come out,' he says.

'What?' I ask.

'Appendix. Do you want some Demerol?'

She shakes her head. 'I'm working tomorrow and I'm on call.'

In the cubicle next to her, someone vomits.

The nurse comes to take blood. 'They called Barry Manilow – he's a very good surgeon.' She ties off my wife's arm. 'We call him Barry Manilow because he looks like Barry Manilow.'

'I want to do right by you,' Barry Manilow says, as he's feeling my wife's belly. 'I'm not sure it's your appendix, not sure it's your gall bladder either. I'm going to call the radiologist and let him scan it. How's that sound?' She nods.

I take the surgeon aside. 'Should she be staying here? Is this the place to do this?'

'It's not a kidney transplant,' he says.

The nurse brings me a cold drink. She offers me a chair. I sit close to the gurney where my wife lies. 'Do you want me to get you out of here? I could hire a car and have us driven to the city. I could have you medevaced home.'

'I don't want to go anywhere,' she says. She is on the wrong side of it now.

Back in the cubicle, Barry Manilow is talking to her. 'It's not your appendix. It's your ovary. It's a hemmorhagic cyst; you're bleeding and your hematocrit is falling. We have to operate. I've called a gynecologist and the anesthesiologist – I'm just waiting for them to arrive. We're going to take you upstairs very soon.'

'Just do it,' she says.

I stop Barry Manilow in the hall. 'Can you try and save the ovary, she very much wants to have children. It's just something she hasn't gotten around to yet – first she had her career, then me, and now this.'

'We'll do everything we can,' he says, disappearing through the door marked 'Authorized Personnel Only'.

I am the only one in the surgical waiting room, flipping through copies of *Field and Stream, Highlights for Children*, a pamphlet on colon cancer. Less than an hour later, Barry Manilow comes to find me. 'We saved the ovary. We took out something the size of a lemon.'

'The size of a lemon?'

He makes a fist and holds it up – 'A lemon,' he says. 'It looked a little funny. We sent it to Pathology.' He shrugs.

A lemon, a bleeding lemon, like a blood orange, a lemon souring in her. Why is fruit used as the universal medical measurement?

'She should be upstairs in about an hour.'

When I get to her room she is asleep. A tube poking out from under the covers drains urine into a bag. She is hooked up to oxygen and an IV.

I put my hand on her forehead. Her eyes open.

'A little fresh air,' she says, pulling at the oxygen tube. 'I always wondered what all this felt like.'

She has a morphine drip, the kind she can control herself. She keeps the clicker in hand. She never pushes the button.

I feed her ice chips and climb into the bed next to her. In the middle of the night I go home. In the morning she calls, waking me up.

'Flowers have been arriving like crazy,' she says, 'from the hospital, from the ER, from the clinic.'

Doctors are like firemen. When one of their own is down they go crazy.

'They took the catheter out, I'm sitting up in a chair. I already had some juice and took myself to the bathroom,' she says proudly. 'They couldn't be nicer. But, of course, I'm a very good patient.'

I interrupt her. 'Do you want anything from the house?'

'Clean socks, a pair of sweat pants, my hairbrush, some toothpaste, my face soap, a radio, maybe a can of Diet Coke.'

'You're only going to be there a couple of days.'

'You asked if I needed anything. Don't forget to feed the dog.'

Five minutes later she calls back, crying. 'I have ovarian cancer.'

I run out the door. When I get there the room is empty. I'm expecting a big romantic scene, expecting her to cling to me, to tell me how much she loves me, how she's sorry we've been having such a hard time, how much she needs me, wants me, now more than ever. The bed is empty. For a moment I think she's died, jumped out the window, escaped. Her absence is terrifying.

In the bathroom, the toilet flushes. 'I want to go home,' she says, stepping out, fully dressed.

'Do you want to take the flowers?'

'They're mine, aren't they? Do you think all the nurses know I have cancer? I don't want anyone to know.'

The nurse comes with a wheelchair; she takes us down to the lobby. 'Good luck,' she says, loading the flowers into the car.

'She knows,' my wife says.

We are on the Long Island Expressway. I am dialing and driving. I call my wife's doctor in New York.

'She has to see Kibbowitz immediately,' the doctor says.

'Do you think I'll lose my ovary?'

She will lose everything – instinctively I know that.

We are home. She is on the bed with the dog on her lap. She peeks beneath the gauze; her incision is crooked, the lack of precision an incredible insult. 'Do you think they can fix it?'

In the morning we go to Kibbowitz. She is again on a table, her feet in the stirrups, in launch position, waiting. Before the doctor arrives she is interviewed and examined by seven medical students. I hate them. I hate them for talking to her, for touching her, for wasting her time. I hate Kibbowitz for keeping her on the table for more than an hour, waiting.

And she is angry with me for being annoyed. 'They're just doing their job.'

Kibbowitz arrives. He is enormous, like a hockey player, a brute and a bully. It is hard to understand how a man gets gynecologic oncology as his calling. I can tell immediately that she likes him. She will do anything he says.

'Scootch down a little closer to me,' he says, settling himself on a stool between her legs. She lifts her ass and slides down. He examines her. He looks under the gauze – 'Crooked,' he says. 'Get dressed and meet me in my office.'

'I want a number,' she says. 'A survival rate.'

'I don't deal in numbers,' he says.

'I need a number.'

He shrugs. 'How's seventy percent?'

'Seventy percent what?'

'Seventy percent live five years.'

'And then what?' I ask.

'And then some don't,' he says.

'What has to come out?' she asks.

'What do you want to keep?'

'I wanted to have a child.'

This is a delicate negotiation; they talk parts. 'I could take just the one ovary,' he says. 'And then after the chemo you could try and get pregnant and then after you had a child we could go in and get the rest.'

'Can you really get pregnant after chemo?' I ask.

The doctor shrugs. 'Miracles happen all the time,' he says. 'The problem is you can't raise a child if you're dead. You don't have to decide now, let me know in a day or two. Meanwhile I'll book the operating room for Friday morning. Nice meeting you,' he says, shaking my hand.

'I want to have a baby,' she says.

'I want to have you,' I say.

Beyond that I say nothing. Whatever I say she will do the opposite. We are at that point – spite, blame, and fault. I don't want to be held responsible. She opens the door of the consulting room. 'Doctor,' she shouts, hurrying down the hall after him, clutching her belly, her incision, her wound. 'Take it,' she screams. 'Take it all the hell out.'

He is standing outside another examination room, chart in hand.

He nods. 'We'll take it through your vagina. We'll take the ovaries, the uterus, cervix, omentum, and your appendix, if they didn't already get it in Southampton. And then we'll put a port in your chest and sign you up for chemotherapy – eight rounds should do it.'

She nods.

'See you Friday.'

We leave. I am holding her hand, holding her pocketbook on my shoulder, trying to be as good as anyone can be.

'Why don't they just say "eviscerate"? Why don't they just come out and say, on Friday at nine we're going to eviscerate you – be ready.'

'Do you want a little lunch? Some soup? There's a lovely restaurant near here.'

She looks flushed. I put my hand to her forehead. She's burning up. 'You have a fever. Did you mention that to the doctor?'

'It's not relevant.'

Later, when we are home, I ask, 'Do you remember our third date? Do you remember asking – how would you kill yourself if you had to do it with bare hands? I said I would break my nose and shove it up into my brain, and you said you would reach up with your bare hands and rip your uterus out through your vagina and throw it across the room.'

'What's your point?'

'No point – I just suddenly remembered it. Isn't Kibbowitz taking your uterus out through your vagina?'

'I doubt he's going to throw it across the room,' she says. There is a pause. 'You don't have to stay with me now that I have cancer. I don't need you. I don't need anyone. I don't need anything.'

'If I left, I wouldn't be leaving because you have cancer. But I would look like an ass, everyone would think I couldn't take it.'

'I would make sure they knew it was me, that I was a monster, a cold steely monster, that I drove you away.'

'They wouldn't believe you.'

She suddenly farts and runs, embarrassed, into the bathroom – as though this is the first time she's farted in her life. 'My life is ruined,' she yells, slamming the door.

'Farting is the least of it.'

When she comes out she is calmer, she crawls into bed next to me, wrung out, shivering.

I hold her. 'Do you want to make love?'

'You mean one last time before I'm not a woman, before I'm a dried old husk?'

Instead of fucking we fight. It's the same sort of thing, dramatic, draining. When we're done, I roll over and sleep in a tight knot on my side of the bed.

'Surgical menopause,' she says. 'That sounds so final.' I turn toward her. She runs her hand over her pubic hair. 'Do you think they'll shave me?'

I am not going to be able to leave the woman with cancer. I am not the kind of person who leaves the woman with cancer, but I don't know what you do when the woman with cancer is a bitch. Do you hope that the cancer prompts the woman to reevaluate herself, to take it as an opportunity, a signal for change? As far as she's concerned there is no such thing as the mind–body connection; there is science and there is law. There is fact and everything else is bullshit.

Friday morning, while she is in the hospital registration area waiting for her number to be called, she makes another list out loud: 'My will is in the top left drawer of the dresser. If anything goes wrong, pull the plug. No heroic measures. I want to be cremated. Donate my organs. Give it away, all of it, every last drop.' She stops. 'I guess no one will want me now that I'm contaminated.' She says the word 'contaminated' filled with disgust, disappointment, as though she has failed, soiled herself.

It is nearly eight p.m. when Kibbowitz comes out to tell me he's done. 'Everything was stuck together like macaroni and cheese. It took longer than I expected. I found some in the fallopian tube and some on the wall of her abdomen. We cleaned everything out.'

She is wheeled back to her room, sad, agitated, angry.

'Why didn't you come and see me?' she asks accusatorily.

'I was right there the whole time, on the other side of the door, waiting for word.'

She acts as though she doesn't believe me, as though I screwed with a secretary from the patient services office while she was on the table.

'How're you feeling?'

'Like I've taken a trip to another country and my suitcases are lost.'

She is writhing. I adjust her pillow, the position of the bed.

'What hurts?'

'What doesn't hurt? Everything hurts. Breathing hurts.'

Because she is a doctor, because she did her residency at this hospital, they give me a small folding cot to set up in the corner of the room. Bending to unfold it, something happens in my back, a hot searing pain spreads across and down. I lower myself to the floor, grabbing the blanket as I go.

Luckily she is sleeping.

The nurse who comes to check her vital signs sees me. 'Are you in trouble?'

'It's happened before,' I say. 'I'll just lie here and see where it goes.'

She brings me a pillow and covers me with the blanket.

Eric and Enid arrive. My wife is asleep and I am still on the floor. Eric stands over me.

'We're sorry,' Eric whispers. 'We didn't get your message until today. We were at Enid's parents' – upstate.'

'It's shocking, it's sudden, it's so out of the blue.' Enid moves to look at my wife. 'She looks like she's in a really bad mood, her brow is furrowed. Is she in pain?'

'I assume so.'

'If there's anything we can do, let us know,' Eric says.

'Actually, could you walk the dog?' I pull the keys out of my pocket and hold them in the air. 'He's been home alone all day.'

'Walk the dog – I think we can do that,' Eric says, looking at Enid for confirmation.

'We'll check on you in the morning,' Enid says.

'Before you go; there's a bottle of Percoset in her purse – give me two.'

During the night she wakes up. 'Where are you?' she asks.

'I'm right here.'

She is sufficiently drugged that she doesn't ask for details. At around six she opens her eyes and sees me on the floor.

'Your back?'

'Yep.'

'Cancer beats back,' she says and falls back to sleep.

When the cleaning man comes with the damp mop, I pry myself off the floor. I'm fine as long as I'm standing.

'You're walking like you have a rod up your ass,' my wife says.

'Is there anything I can do for you?' I ask, trying to be solicitous.

'Can you have cancer for me?'

The pain management team arrives to check on my wife's level of comfort.

'On a scale of one to ten, how do you feel?' the pain fellow asks.

'Five,' my wife says.

'She lies,' I say.

'Are you lying?'

'How can you tell?'

The specialist arrives. 'I know you,' he says, seeing my wife in the bed. 'We went to school together.'

My wife tries to smile.

'You were the smartest one in the class and now look,' he reads my wife's chart. 'Ovarian cancer and you, that's horrible.'

My wife is sitting up high in her hospital bed, puking her guts into a metal bucket, like a poisoned pet monkey. She is throwing up bright green like an alien. Ted, her boss, stares at her, mesmerized.

The room is filled with people – people I don't know, medical people, people she went to school with, people she did her residency with, a man whose fingers she sewed back on, relatives I've not met. I don't understand why they don't excuse themselves, why they don't step out of the room. I don't understand why there is no privacy. They're all watching her like they've never seen anyone throw up before – riveted.

She is not sleeping. She is not eating. She is not getting up and walking around. She is afraid to leave her bed, afraid to leave her bucket.

I make a sign for the door. I borrow a black Magic Marker from the charge nurse and print in large black letters, DO NOT DISTURB.

They push the door open. They come bearing gifts, flowers, food, books. 'I saw the sign, I assumed it was for someone else.'

I am wiping green spittle from her lips.

'Do you want me to get rid of everyone?' I ask.

I want to get rid of everyone. The idea that these people have some claim to her, some right to entertain, distract, bother her more than I, drives me up the wall. 'Should I tell them to go?'

She shakes her head. 'Just the flowers, the flowers nauseate me.'

An hour later, I empty the bucket again. The room remains overcrowded. I am on my knees by the side of her hospital bed, whispering, 'I'm leaving.'

'Are you coming back?' she whispers.

'No.'

She looks at me strangely. 'Where are you going?'

'Away.'

'Bring me a Diet Coke.'

She has missed the point.

It is heartbreaking seeing her in a stained gown, in the middle of a bed, unable to tell everyone to go home, unable to turn it off. Her pager is clipped to her hospital gown, several times it goes off. She returns the calls. She always returns the calls. I imagine her saying, 'What the hell are you bothering me for – I'm busy, I'm having cancer.'

Later, I am on the edge of the bed, looking at her. She is increasingly beautiful, more vulnerable, female.

'Honey?'

'What?' Her intonation is like a pissy caged bird – *cawww*. 'What? What are you looking at? What do you want?' *Cawww*.

'Nothing.'

I am washing her with a cool washcloth.

'You're tickling me,' she complains.

'Make sure you tell her you still find her attractive,' a man in the hall tells me. 'Husbands of women who have mastectomies need to keep reminding their wives that they are beautiful.'

'She had a hysterectomy,' I say.

'Same thing.'

Two days later, they remove the packing. I am in the room when the resident comes with a long tweezers like tongs and pulls yards of material from her vagina, wads of cotton, and gauze, stained battlefield red. It's like a magic trick gone awry, one of those jokes about how many people you can fit in a telephone booth, more and more keeps coming out.

'Is there anything left in there?' she asks.

The resident shakes his head. 'Your vagina now just comes to a stop, it's a stump, an unconnected sleeve. Don't be surprised if you bleed, if you pop a stitch or two.' He checks her chart and signs her out. 'Kibbowitz has you on pelvic rest for six weeks.'

'Pelvic rest?' I ask.

'No fucking,' she says.

Not a problem.

Home. She watches forty-eight hours of Holocaust films on cable TV. Although she claims to compartmentalize everything, suddenly she identifies with the bald, starving prisoners of war. She sees herself as a victim. She points to the naked corpse of a woman. 'That's me,' she says. 'That's exactly how I feel.'

'She's dead,' I say.

'Exactly.'

Her notorious vigilance is gone. As I'm fluffing her pillows, her billy club rolls out from under the bed. 'Put it in the closet,' she says.

'Why?' I ask, rolling it back under the bed.

'Why sleep with a billy club under the bed? Why do anything when you have cancer?'

During a break between *Shoah* and *The Sorrow and the Pity*, she taps me. 'I'm missing my parts,' she says. 'Maybe one of those lost eggs was someone special, someone who would have cured something, someone who would have invented something wonderful. You never know who was in there. They are my lost children.'

'I'm sorry.'

'For what?' she looks at me accusingly.

'Everything.'

'Thirty-eight-year-olds don't get cancer, they get Lyme disease, maybe they have appendicitis, on rare occasions in some other parts of the world they have Siamese twins, but that's it.'

In the middle of the night she wakes up, she throws the covers off. 'I can't breathe, I'm burning up. Open the window, I'm hot, I'm so hot.'

'Do you know what's happening to you?'

'What are you talking about?'

'You're having hot flashes.'

'I am not,' she says, as though I've insulted her. 'They don't start so soon.'

They do.

'Get away from me, get away,' she yells. 'Just being near you makes me uncomfortable, it makes my temperature unstable.'

On Monday she starts chemotherapy.

'Will I go bald?' she asks the nurse.

I cannot imagine my wife bald.

'Most women buy a wig before it happens,' the nurse says, plugging her into the magic potion.

One of the other women, her head wrapped in a red turban, leans over and whispers, 'My husband says I look like a porno star.' She winks. She has no eyebrows, no eyelashes, nothing.

We shop for a wig. She tries on every style, every shape and color. She looks like a man in drag, like she's wearing a bad Halloween costume, like it's all a horrible joke.

'Maybe my hair won't fall out?' she says.

'It's okay,' the woman in the wig shop says. 'Insurance covers it. Ask your doctor to write a prescription for a cranial prosthesis.'

'I'm a doctor,' my wife says.

The wig woman looks confused. 'It's okay,' she says, putting another wig on my wife's head.

She buys a wig. I never see it. She brings it home and immediately puts it in the closet. 'It looks like Linda Evans, like someone on *Dynasty*. I just can't do it,' she says.

Her scalp begins to tingle. Her hair hurts. 'It's as though someone grabbed my hair and is pulling as hard as they can.'

'It's getting ready to go,' I say. 'It's like a time bomb. It ticks and then it blows.'

'What are you, a doctor? Suddenly you know everything about cancer, about menopause, about everything?'

In the morning her hair is falling out. It is all over the pillow, all over the shower floor.

'Your hair's not really falling out,' Enid says when we meet them for dinner. Enid reaches and touches her hair, sweeps her hand through it, as if to be comforting. She ends up with a handful of hair; she has pulled my wife's hair out. She tries to put it back, she furiously pats it back in place.

'Forget that I was worried about them shaving my pubic hair, how 'bout it all just went down the drain.'

She looks like a rat, like something that's been chewed on and spit out, like something that someone tried to electrocute and failed. In four days she is eighty percent bald.

She stands before me naked. 'Document me.'

I take pictures. I take the film to one of those special stores that has a sign in the window – we don't censor.

I give her a baseball cap to wear to work. Every day she goes to work, she will not miss a day, no matter what.

I, on the other hand, can't work. Since this happened, my work has been nonexistent. I spend my day as the holder of the feelings, the keeper of sensation.

'It's not my fault,' she says. 'What the hell do you do all day while I'm at the hospital?'

Recuperate.

She wears the baseball cap for a week and then takes a razor, shaves the few scraggly hairs that remain, and goes to work bald, without a hat, without a wig – starkers.

There's something both admirable and aggressive about her baldness, as if she's saying to everyone – I have cancer and you have to deal with it.

'How do you feel?' I ask at night when she comes home from the hospital.

'I feel nothing.'

'How can you feel nothing?'

'I am made of steel and wood,' she says happily.

As we're falling asleep she tells me a story. 'It's true, it happened as I was walking to the hospital. I accidentally bumped into someone on the sidewalk. Excuse me, I said and continued on. He ran after me. "Excuse me, boy. Excuse me, boy. You knocked my comb out of my hand and I want you to go back and pick it up." I turned around – we bumped into each other, I said excuse me, and that will have to suffice. "You knocked it out of my hand on purpose, white boy." I said, I am not a boy. "Then what are you – Cancer Man? Or are you just a bitch? A bald fucking bitch." I wheeled around and chased him. You fucking crazy ass, I screamed. You fucking crazy ass. I screamed it about four times. He's lucky I didn't fucking kill him,' she says.

I am thinking she's lost her mind. I'm thinking she's lucky he didn't kill her.

She stands up on the bed – naked. She strikes a pose like a body builder. 'Cancer Man,' she says, flexing her muscles, creating a new superhero. 'Cancer Man!'

Luckily she has good insurance. The bill for the surgery comes – it's itemized. They charge per part removed. Ovary $7,000, appendix $5,000, the total is $72,000 dollars. 'It's all in a day's work,' she says.

We are lying in bed. I am lying next to her, reading the paper.

'I want to go to a desert island, alone. I don't want to come back until this is finished,' she says.

'You are on a desert island, but unfortunately you have taken me with you.'

She looks at me. 'It will never be finished – do you know that? I'm not going to have children and I'm going to die.'

'Do you really think you're going to die?'

'Yes.'

I reach for her.

'Don't,' she says. 'Don't go looking for trouble.'

'I wasn't. I was trying to be loving.'

'I don't feel loving,' she says. 'I don't feel physically bonded to anyone right now, including myself.'

'You're pushing me away.'

'I'm recovering,' she says.

'It's been eighteen weeks.'

Her blood counts are low. Every night for five nights, I inject her with Nupagen to increase the white blood cells. She teaches me how to prepare the injection, how to push the needle into the muscle of her leg. Every time I inject her, I apologize.

'For what?' she asks.

'Hurting you.'

'Forget it,' she says, disposing of the needle.

'Could I have a hug?' I ask.

She glares at me. 'Why do you persist? Why do you keep asking me for things I can't do, things I can't give?'

'A hug?'

'I can't give you one.'

'Anyone can give a hug. I can get a hug from the doorman.'

'Then do,' she says. 'I need to be married to someone who is like a potted plant, someone who needs nothing.'

'Water?'

'Very little, someone who is like a cactus or an orchid.'

'It's like you're refusing to be human,' I tell her.

'I have no interest in being human.'

This is information I should be paying attention to. She is telling me something and I'm not listening. I don't believe what she is saying.

I go to dinner with Eric and Enid alone.

'It's strange,' they say. 'You'd think the cancer would soften her, make her more appreciative. You'd think it would make her stop and think about what she wants to do with the rest of her life. When you ask her, what does she say?' Eric and Enid want to know.

'Nothing. She says she wants nothing, she has no needs or desires. She says she has nothing to give.'

Eric and Enid shake their heads. 'What are you going to do?'

I shrug. None of this is new, none of this is just because she has cancer – that's important to keep in mind, this is exactly the way she always was, only more so.

A few days later a woman calls; she and her husband are people we see occasionally.

'Hi, how are you, how's Tom?' I ask.

'He's a fucking asshole,' she says. 'Haven't you heard? He left me.'

'When?'

'About two weeks ago. I thought you would have known.'

'I'm a little out of it.'

'Anyway, I'm calling to see if you'd like to have lunch.'

'Lunch, sure. Lunch would be good.'

At lunch she is a little flirty, which is fine, it's nice actually, it's been a long time since someone flirted with me. In the end, when we're having coffee, she spills the beans. 'So I guess you're wondering why I called you?'

'I guess,' I say, although I'm perfectly pleased to be having lunch, to be listening to someone else's troubles.

'I heard your wife was sick, I figured you're not getting a lot of sex, and I thought we could have an affair.'

I don't know which part is worse, the complete lack of seduction, the fact that she mentions my wife not being well, the idea that my wife's illness would make me want to sleep with her, her stun gun bluntness – it's all too much.

'What do you think? Am I repulsive? Thoroughly disgusting? Is it the craziest thing you ever heard?'

'I'm very busy,' I say, not knowing what to say, not wanting to be offensive, or seem to have taken offense. 'I'm just very busy.'

My wife comes home from work. 'Someone came in today – he reminded me of you.'

'What was his problem?'

'He jumped out the window.'

'Dead?'

'Yes,' she says, washing her hands in the kitchen sink.

'Was he dead when he got to you?' There's something in her tone that makes me wonder, did she kill him?

'Pretty much.'

'What part reminded you of me?'

'He was having an argument with his wife,' she says. 'Imagine her standing in the living room, in the middle of a sentence, and out the window he goes. Imagine her not having a chance to finish her thought?'

'Yes, imagine, not being able to have the last word. Did she try to stop him?' I ask.

'I don't know,' my wife says. 'I didn't get to read the police report.
I just thought you'd find it interesting.'

'What do you want for dinner?'

'Nothing,' she says. 'I'm not hungry.'

'You have to eat something.'

'Why? I have cancer. I can do whatever I want.'

Something has to happen.

I buy tickets to Paris. 'We have to go.' I invoke the magic word,
'It's an *emergency*.'

'It's not like I get a day off. It's not like I come home at the end
of the day and I don't have cancer. It goes everywhere with me. It
doesn't matter where I am, it's still me – it's me with cancer. In
Paris I'll have cancer.'

I dig out the maps, the guide books, everything we did on our
last trip is marked with fluorescent highlighter. I am acting as
though I believe that if we retrace our steps, if we return to a place
where things were good, there will be an automatic correction, a
psychic chiropractic event, which will put everything into
alignment.

I gather provisions for the plane, fresh fruit, water, magazines,
the smoke hoods. It's a little-known fact, smoke inhalation is a major
cause of death on airplanes.

'What's the point,' she says, throwing a few things into a suitcase.
'You can do everything and think you're prepared, but you don't
know what's going to happen. You don't see what's coming until it
hits you in the face.'

She points at someone outside. 'See that idiot crossing the street
in front of the truck – why doesn't he have cancer?'

She lifts her suitcase – too heavy. She takes things out. She leaves
her smoke hood on the bed. 'If the plane fills with smoke, I'm going
to be so happy,' she says. 'I'm going to breathe deeply, I'm going
to be the first to die.'

I stuff the smoke hood into my suitcase, along with her raincoat,
her extra shoes, and vitamin C drops. I lift the suitcases, I feel like
a pack animal, a sherpa.

In France, the customs people are not used to seeing bald women.
They call her 'sir'.

'Sir, you're next, sir. Sir, please step over here, sir.'

My wife is my husband. She loves it. She smiles. She catches my eye and strikes a subdued version of the super hero/body builder pose, flexing. 'Cancer Man,' she says.

'And what is the purpose of your visit to France?' the inspector asks. 'Business or pleasure?'

'Reconciliation,' I say, watching her – Cancer Man.

'Business or pleasure?'

'Pleasure.'

Paris is my fantasy, my last-ditch effort to reclaim my marriage, myself, my wife.

As we are checking into the hotel, I remind her of our previous visit – the chef cut himself, his finger was severed, she saved it, and they were able to reattach it. 'You made medical history. Remember the beautiful dinner they threw in your honor.'

'It was supposed to be a vacation,' she says.

The bellman takes us to our room – there's a big basket of fruit, bottles of Champagne and Evian with a note from the concierge welcoming us.

'It's not as nice as it used to be,' she says, already disappointed. She opens the Evian and drinks. Her lips curl. 'Even the water tastes bad.'

'Maybe it's you. Maybe the water is fine. Is it possible you're wrong?'

'We see things differently,' she says, meaning she's right, I'm wrong.

'Are you in an especially bad mood, or is it just the cancer?' I ask.

'Maybe it's you?' she says.

We walk, across the river and down by the Louvre. There could be nothing better, nothing more perfect, and yet I am suddenly hating Paris – the beauty, the fineness of it is dwarfed by her foul humor. I realize there will be no saving it, no moment of reconciliation, redemption. Everything is irredeemably awful and getting worse.

'If you're so unhappy, why don't you leave?' I ask her.

'I keep thinking you'll change.'

'If I changed any more I can't imagine who I'd be.'

'Well, if I'm such a bitch, why do you stay?'

'It's my job, it's my calling to stay with you, to soften you.'

'I absolutely do not want to be softer, I don't want to give another inch.'

She trips on a cobblestone, I reach for her elbow, to steady her, and instead unbalance myself. She fails to catch me. I fall and recover quickly.

'Imagine how I feel,' she says. 'I am a doctor and I can't fix it. I can't fix me, I can't fix you – what a lousy doctor.'

'I'm losing you,' I say.

'I've lost myself. Look at me – do I look like me?'

'You act like yourself.'

'I act like myself because I have to, because people are counting on me.'

'I'm counting on you.'

'Stop counting.'

All along the Tuileries there are Ferris wheels – the world's largest Ferris wheel is set up in the middle.

'Let's go,' I say, taking her hand and pulling her toward them.

'I don't like rides.'

'It's not much of a ride. It's like a carousel, only vertical. Live a little.'

She gets on. There are no seat belts, no safety bars. I say nothing. I am hoping she won't notice.

'How is it going to end?' I ask while we're waiting for the wheel to spin.

'I die in the end.'

The ride takes off, climbing, pulling us up and over. We are flying, soaring; the city unfolds. It is breathtaking and higher than I thought. And faster. There is always a moment on any ride when you think it is too fast, too high, too far, too wide, and that you will not survive. And then there is the exhilaration of surviving, the thrill of having lived through it and immediately you want to go around again.

'I have never been so unhappy in my life,' my wife says when we're near the top. 'It's not just the cancer, I was unhappy before the cancer. We were having a very hard time. We don't get along, we're a bad match. Do you agree?'

'Yes,' I say. 'We're a really bad match, but we're such a good bad match it seems impossible to let it go.'

'We're stuck,' she says.

'You bet,' I say.

'No. I mean the ride, the ride isn't moving.'

'It's not stuck, it's just stopped. It stops along the way.'

She begins to cry. 'It's all your fault. I hate you. And I still have to deal with you. Every day I have to look at you.'

'No, you don't. You don't have to deal with me if you don't want to.'

She stops crying and looks at me. 'What are you going to do, jump?'

'The rest of your life, or my life, however long or short, should not be miserable. It can't go on this way.'

'We could both kill ourselves,' she says.

'How about we separate?'

I am being more grown-up than I am capable of being. I am terrified of being without her, but either way, it's death.

The ride lurches forward.

I came to Paris wanting to pull things together and suddenly I am desperate to be away from her. If this doesn't stop now, it will never stop, it will go on forever. She will be dying of her cancer and we will still be fighting. I begin to panic, to feel I can't breathe. I am suffocating; I have to get away.

'Where does it end?'

'How about we say good-bye?'

'And then what? We have opera tickets.'

I cannot tell her I am going. I have to sneak away, to tip-toe out backwards. I have to make my own arrangements.

We stop talking. We're hanging in mid-air, suspended. We have run out of things to say. When the ride circles down, the silence becomes more definitive.

I begin to make my plan. In truth, I have no idea what I am doing. All afternoon, everywhere we go, I cash traveler's checks, I get cash advances, I have about five thousand dollars' worth of francs stuffed in my pocket. I want to be able to leave without a trace, I want to be able to buy myself out of whatever trouble I get into. I am hysterical and giddy all at once.

We are having an early dinner on our way to the opera.

I time my break for just after the coffee comes. 'Oops,' I say, feeling my pockets. 'I forgot my opera glasses.'

'Really?' she says. 'I thought you had them when we went out.'

'They must be at the hotel. You go on ahead, I'll run back. You know I hate not being able to see.'

She takes her ticket. 'Hurry,' she says. 'I hate it when you're late.'

This is the bravest thing I have ever done. I go back to the hotel and pack my bag. I am going to get out. I am going to fly away. I may never come back. I will begin again, as someone else – unrecognizable.

I move to lift the bag off the bed, I pull it up and my knee goes out. I start to fall but catch myself. I pull at the bag and take a step – too heavy. I will have to go without it. I will have to leave everything behind. I drop the bag, but still I am falling, folding, collapsing. There is pain, searing, spreading, pouring, hot and cold, like water down my back, down my legs.

I am lying on the floor, thinking that if I stay calm, if I can just find my breath, and follow my breath, it will pass. I lie there waiting for the paralysis to recede.

I am afraid of it being over and yet she has given me no choice, she has systematically withdrawn life support: sex and conversation. The problem is that, despite this, she is the one I want.

There is a knock at the door. I know it is not her, it is too soon for it to be her.

'*Entrez,*' I call out.

The maid opens the door, she holds the DO NOT DISTURB sign in her hand. 'Oooff,' she says, seeing me on the floor. 'Do you need the doctor?'

I am not sure if she means my wife or a doctor other than my wife.

'No.'

She takes a towel from her cart and props it under my head. She takes a spare blanket from the closet and covers me with it. She opens the Champagne and pours me a glass, tilting my head up so I can sip. She goes to her cart and gets a stack of night chocolates and sits beside me, feeding me Champagne and chocolate, stroking my forehead.

The phone in the room rings, we ignore it. She refills my glass. She takes my socks off and rubs my feet. She unbuttons my shirt and rubs my chest. I am getting a little drunk. I am just beginning to relax and then there is another knock, a knock my body recognizes before I am fully awake. Everything tightens. My back pulls tighter still, any sensation below my knees drops off.

'I thought something horrible happened to you, I've been calling and calling the room, why haven't you answered? I thought you'd killed yourself.'

The maid excuses herself. She goes into the bathroom and gets me a cool washcloth.

'What are you doing?' my wife asks.

There is nothing I can say.

'Knock off the mummy routine. What exactly are you doing? Were you trying to run away and then you chickened out? Say something.'

To talk would be to continue; for the moment I am silenced. I am a potted plant, and still that is not good enough for her.

'He is paralyzed,' the maid says.

'He is not paralyzed. I am his wife, I am a doctor. I would know if there was something really wrong.'

JACKIE KAY

You Go When You Can No Longer Stay

It is not so much that we are splitting up that is really worrying me, it is the fact that she keeps quoting Martin Amis. The other day we were in our bedroom having a silly argument about where things hang in the wardrobe when she said to me, 'Like Martin Amis says, you go when you can no longer stay.' It seemed odd to me. I looked outside the window into our street and saw Mr Davies post a letter. I saw three down's white cat walk daintily along our wall, and then jump off. I often say nothing at all when she says something that is perturbing. It seemed odd to me, because here we are two very long-term lesbians, who have been in it so long we look as if we could have knitted each other up, been in it so long we have grown to look the same, wear similar clothes and have almost identical expressions on our plain faces, that Martin Amis should be coming into our lives in this way.

I hadn't even realized she was so keen on him until she made that remark; the one thing we don't share is books. It is the only area of our lives where we are truly different. I read thrillers and human-interest books, about somebody who has done something that I am not likely to do, or somebody who is interested in something that I know nothing about. She reads novels and then she re-reads the novels she has read. And sometimes she reads slim volumes of poetry which always look a little sinister and have very peculiar titles. We are not the kind of couple that share a book, one after the other, which is maybe a shame and maybe if we had been that kind of couple we wouldn't be splitting up now. It seems to me from the amount that she has started quoting Martin Amis that she's had a secret passion for him all along.

We were in the kitchen the other day arguing again about sex. It is a sore point between us. A kind of Achilles heel. 'All marriage turns into a sibling relationship,' she said terrifically confidently. 'Who said that?' I asked with a sickening, sinking heart. She paused, stirring her coffee. 'Do you want a coffee?' she said. 'No, thank you,' I said. 'Don't tell me it was Martin Amis.' 'Yes,' she said defensively. 'He's quite right. You just don't fancy each other after a while.'

'I fancy you,' I said, then instantly regretted it.

'No you don't, you think you do,' she said, adding a big splash of milk into the coffee mug. 'Sure you don't want a cup?' she said. 'All right, then,' I said. And she quite gleefully got another mug out of the kitchen cupboard. I think I bought the mug but I can't be sure. She smiled at me. When she smiles at me, I remember who she is. Then she said, 'You become far too similar, especially two women. It's like looking in the mirror. You need a bit of difference to feel real passion.' 'Oh,' I said and sipped at my coffee anxiously. 'Life is too short not to feel passion,' she said. I knew where it was all going, but I didn't want her to tell me. I actually wanted to hide. I wanted to run up the stairs and hide in the airing cupboard. I couldn't stop thinking about my eighty-two-year-old mother, who was even fonder of Hilary than she was of me, who had taken years to accept our relationship and then had finally totally embraced it. My old mother would be devastated. I felt edgy just thinking about it.

'Do you want a Jaffa with your coffee?' she asked me, as if a Jaffa could be the answer to all my troubles, as if a Jaffa could truly console. 'Yes, please,' I said. I'd got into the habit of saying yes to as many things as possible, thinking that if I said yes enough she might stop saying no. She put three Jaffas on my plate but I noticed she took none for herself. 'Aren't you having any?' I asked her, a bit alarmed. 'No,' she said. 'Why not?' I said. 'Oh, for goodness' sake, Ruth, stop trying to control me. After a while all relationships turn into power struggles,' she said. 'Would you ask that same question to a friend?'

'I'm just wondering why you put three on a plate for me if you're not having any yourself,' I said suspiciously. I was becoming very suspicious of her because she had started to change all of her habits and it was very worrying to me. 'Do you know something?' she said, very nastily. 'I think you are going mad.'

'Does Martin Amis say that?' I said furiously. 'Does he say one person in a couple during a break-up will always accuse the other of going mad?'

She sighed and shook her head. She was actually looking quite beautiful these days. The person I didn't want to hear about was clearly making her feel good about herself. 'I'm just trying to have a cup of coffee with you, that's all. If I can't have a cup of coffee with you without fighting, we will have to put the house on the market even sooner than we said. As Martin Amis says, you go when you can no longer stay,' she said, standing up in the kitchen and drinking her coffee. She wouldn't sit down these days. There it was again, that bloody awful quote. It was deliberate then. She knew it was agitating me; she'd started to repeat it at random in whatever corner of our house we found ourselves in. I could even hear it in my sleep.

She left the room, coffee in hand, and I heard her playing music up the stairs. She'd taken to playing music a lot recently, another big change for her. This was a thin voice I didn't much like, one of those new English jazz singers with a very insipid style. I preferred the Dinah Washingtons of this world. I got up from the table and put two of the Jaffa cakes in the bin. I gave the third to our dog. I saw what she was up to. She was trying to fatten me up as she lost weight. Well, we were both a little on the generous side. I was about three stone overweight and Hilary was at least two. Whenever we went out to a big lesbian do, I noticed that we weren't the only long-term couple that was overweight. I used to think that was happiness, being fat together, rolling about from one side of the big double bed to the other. Most of our old relationship revolved around food. Our idea of a super day used to be a day when we were both off work. (Now I notice her days off don't coincide with mine any more.) Hilary didn't have to go into the council, which was depressing her, and I didn't have to go into the tax office, which was depressing me. We'd get into our big bed with lots of treats – a couple of Chow Mein Pot Noodles, a big plate of chocolate biscuits, a big pot of cookies-and-cream Häagen-Dazs. Bliss. And we'd watch *The Maltese Falcon* for the umpteenth time or *Now, Voyager* or *All About Eve*. Heaven. A day like that was even nicer if it was raining outside. At the end of *Now, Voyager*, we'd both say that line together, 'Oh, Jerry, don't let's ask for the moon, we have the stars,' and clutch at each other as if we were frightened of losing everything.

A lot of the people who know us often get us mixed up as though we were identical twins. Some people call me Hilary and Hilary Ruth. It's a bit silly because we don't really look all that alike. Admittedly we do both buy similar-looking clothes in Marks and

Spencer. Our casual-clothes days and smart-clothes days are always the same. But recently Hilary has started to shop in Harvey Nichols. I went in there one day on my own and took a look at some of the prices. They actually made me feel quite ill and I felt terribly worried. That night I said to Hilary, 'I don't think shopping at Harvey Nichols on your salary is very sensible.' She was reading the new Martin Amis at the time, *Yellow Dog*. 'This is about a man who suddenly becomes very violent,' she said quite menacingly. I said, 'I feel as if I'm living with a gambler. You have run up massive bills on our joint Visa.'

'I told you we should never have had a joint account,' Hilary said and got up and opened a bottle of red wine, which was another curious thing, because we only usually have a nice bottle of white, a Chardonnay, at the weekend. Now Hilary has taken to red wines, big heavy reds like Cabernet Sauvignons and Riojas and she's taken to drinking them during the week. She slurped her wine. I noticed that she'd lost quite a bit of weight. 'Anyway, I think you should be a bit more careful,' I said, trying to sound calm. 'I think you should stop being a control freak,' she said. Then she got up and left the room again, taking her glass and the bottle with her. I heard the music go on up the stairs. She was playing it really quite loud. This time it was Otis Redding. We haven't played Otis Redding for years. She came running back down the stairs. I thought she was going to apologize, but she just picked up *Yellow Dog* without a word and went back up stairs. I could hear Otis singing 'Sitting on the Dock of the Bay'.

I was annoyed at myself. I started clearing away the remains of our meal. I noticed that Hilary had left all of her rice. She'd eaten her salad, though. I didn't know quite what to do with myself because we usually watched *Frost* on the TV together or *Miss Marple* or *Midsomer Murders*. But lately Hilary had said, 'That isn't me, watching *Frost*. That's you.' She'd started saying this a lot recently. 'I'm not the kind of person who does such and such or who says such and such or who watches such and such.' I wondered furiously if Martin Amis had put her up to that too. Perhaps there was something in one of his books that advised people in long-term relationships to stop doing everything that they used to enjoy doing. Perhaps he, being so resolutely heterosexual, so smug with his roll-ups, was trying to destroy the lesbian relationship. I suddenly had a brainwave. If she was reading him, the only thing I could do to read her was read him too. I rushed into Waterstone's in town and bought everything they had by him. I hid the books under the spare-room bed, the spare room which I have now been consigned to. Hilary needs space to think about what we should do, she has said. She needs space and calm. I have stopped reading my murder mysteries for the moment. Hilary always looked down upon them. Of course she thinks she is much cleverer than me. 'It's always the woman that gets it,' she'd say whenever I picked up another thriller.

I've started to feel very odd within my own life. It's most peculiar to feel lonely inside your own life. It's a secret, of course, because nobody would know and all of our friends still think everything is fine between us, though I must say they have all taken to admiring Hilary recently and saying things like, 'You're looking great.' This morning we had breakfast together, which was a nice change. Sunday breakfast. Hilary had bacon and egg but no toast and no newspapers. She has even given up the Sunday papers; I'm not sure why. When I asked her about it, she said, 'Do I have to explain everything to you?' Then when she saw my slightly hurt face, she said, 'I'm engrossed in *Yellow Dog* and newspapers are a huge waste of time.'

I suggested we go out for a Sunday walk or a run in the car in the afternoon. Hilary said yes, good idea. I felt very pleased about this because it seemed to me that if we could go out for a walk in some beautiful countryside normal life might return, encouraged by the light on the hills or a gushing waterfall. 'Shall we go to Coniston Water or Derwent Water and then go for Sunday lunch in a pub somewhere?' I said excitedly. 'No, I don't want to make a big production out of it,' Hilary said. 'Let's just go to the park with Orlando. I've got other things I want to do today.' The dog was wagging her tail as Hilary fetched the lead, wagging her tail frantically.

It was a freezing-cold day. I had my scarf tied firmly around my neck. Hilary looked a bit bare but I daren't suggest she put a scarf on. I rather like the winter cold if I am well wrapped up. We were walking side by side, with our dog Orlando running on happily in front of us, when Hilary suddenly said to me, 'I thought it best that we talk about this outside of the house rather than in. You know I have not been happy for some time.'

'I didn't know that,' I said, hurt.

'Oh, come on. You did, darling,' Hilary said, quite gently. I shook my head and put my hands in my pockets. Our dog ran back towards us. I picked up her stick and threw it again really quite far. It was truly an astonishingly beautiful winter day; even the clouds were lit up from behind as if they had highlights in their hair. 'Isn't it lovely light today?' I said. 'Isn't it absolutely gorgeous?'

'Why won't you let me talk about this?' Hilary said.

'Don't spoil our walk, darling,' I said, picking up the stick again and throwing it. It was the coldest it had been yet. Freezing bitter cold, but still very beautiful, beautiful in an icy, frosty way. The ducks and the geese were sitting on top of the ice on the pond as if they were on holiday. Hilary sighed beside me. I could tell she was about to try again. 'I know that you are finding this hard, that's only natural. I know that we thought we'd be together forever. But stuff happens; life changes. We have to move on.'

I walked beside her. At least she hadn't quoted again from Martin Amis, nor had she told me her name. I presumed it was a she, anyway. I didn't want to know her name; I didn't want to know what she looked like; I didn't want to know anything about her. 'Could you at least do me one favour?' I asked Hilary. 'Could you tell me nothing about her, nothing at all?'

'That's silly,' Hilary said. 'I'm not buying into that. I've done nothing to be ashamed of.'

'You've stopped loving me,' I said, quietly.

'We weren't good for each other any more,' she said. I looked at her and suddenly noticed that she'd lost at least three stone. 'How have you lost all this weight?' I asked her. 'I don't want to tell you,' she said. 'I don't want you copying that too. You copy everything. If you hadn't copied everything, we might still have been lovers.'

'What do I copy?' I said, feeling extremely alarmed.

'Nothing,' she said. 'Never mind.' We walked round the pond in silence. I noted a few things I think about the geese but I can't remember what they were.

I noticed that Hilary was sweating quite profusely even though it was sub-zero temperatures. I sneaked a look at her. She had that mad look on her face, eyebrows knitted together, quite unappealing if I am honest. It occurred to me that she might be having her menopause and that all of these changes of behaviour were actually the change of life. She had after all been behaving very erratically recently, flying off the handle at the slightest thing. 'Are you having a hot flush?' I asked her.

'No I certainly am not!' she said.

But it was out and now I knew. Hilary was having her menopause and keeping it secret from me. That explained everything: it explained why she no longer wanted to share the double bed. The sheets were probably soaking in the middle of the night! It explained the temper tantrums and the outbursts. 'Why didn't you just tell me? For goodness' sake, we are both lesbians,' I said. 'You might describe yourself like that. You know I don't,' she said. 'Well, whatever, why didn't you tell me you were having hot flushes?' Hilary is three years younger than I am and I could tell she was fuming, absolutely fuming, about getting her change of life first. 'It can happen at any age,' I said. 'I've just been lucky I haven't had mine yet. I was a late starter with my periods. When you start late, you apparently have your menopause later. Did you start yours early?'

'Don't do this,' Hilary was beside herself now. 'I am not having my menopause. I don't know how many times I have to say this,' she said, tired. 'This is typical of you. You are in denial. I am in love. This is a love story of all the strange things happening to me so late in the goddamned day.' She wasn't going to get me this time with that Martin Amis. I said, 'When I come in the door I go tee hee hee. The place kills me.'

She said, 'Have you been reading him?'

'Yes,' I said, quite pleased.

'See, I told you, you always had to copy me,' she said, apoplectic with rage now. 'And now you've gone out and bought him. Nothing's sacred.'

I smiled. I shouted, '*Or-lan-do*,' my voice going up and down merrily. 'Who is going to have the dog?' I said. 'I am,' Hilary said. 'I'm much fonder of Orlando than you are. Orlando is my dog.'

'She is not,' I said indignantly.

'I don't think I want to do this,' Hilary said.

'Do what?' I said, still like a fool feeling a little hopeful.

'Have these silly fights. We are two grown-ups. We have to be able to sort this out amicably. It's not like we have kids.'

'Having a dog is like having a kid,' I said.

'It is not. Don't be stupid.'

We walked in silence then round the pond for the third time. I couldn't count the amount of times we have walked round and round and round that pond. I thought of all the walks over our twenty-five years together. Our walking books are the only books we truly share, tiny leaflet-sized books that tell us of lengths and grades of difficulty in Strathglass and surrounding glens. I thought of our favourite walk from just below Beinn Mhor, and the lovely waterfall in the woods up the hill from the old sheep fanks. And the odd little cemetery you come across as you reach the end of the walk. Rumour has it that once a burial party arrived there from Tomich village minus the coffin. I thought of all the walks over all the years – off the beaten track and out of breath. Parts of the country, we used to believe, truly belonged to us: the Lakes, the Highlands, the Peak District. I couldn't bear to think of Hilary anywhere, in any of these places with some other love, her dark fleece zipped up, her walking boots thick with mud, and a map in her hand. I looked at Hilary. I couldn't imagine her even wearing a fleece in the future. She looked so slim now; she looked like somebody else, oddly focused and deliberate-looking as if the resolve to do this had made her quite certain of herself. I couldn't quite believe it. Hilary had slimmed her way out of my hands. When we got inside our cream kitchen, I thought she might have a cup of tea and a scone and jam for old times' sake. 'Scones are a thing of the past,' Hilary said and I had the impression that she wasn't quoting from Martin Amis this time.

It seemed to me that Hilary wanted to consign our whole life to the past. The other day I arrived home, very excited, with a classic copy of the *Dandy* – December the 30th, 1972. Hilary and I have collected comics for over ten years and have spent many a happy hour laughing over the antics of Dennis the Menace or Desperate Dan or Beryl the Peril. I said triumphantly, 'Look what I've just found!' thinking that Hilary would remember our love through Beryl the Peril's impersonation of an Abominable Snowman. But Hilary just stared at it a little disdainfully and said, 'You can have the comic collection, that was always more your thing. I'll have the CDs.'

I put the kettle on and got out a fresh jar of rhubarb-and-ginger jam. I pulled the little bit of tracing paper off the top. I opened our cake tin and took out one of yesterday's homemade scones, a nice batch that had risen properly. I buttered my scone quite thickly and spread the nippy jam over it. I made a fresh pot of tea and put the cosy on. I sat down alone at the table. I poured us both a mug of tea. Hilary watched me eat my scone with some satisfaction, sipping at her mug of tea, standing, leaning against the fridge. She said nothing. She eyed me eating my scone. I wasn't the least bit bothered. I thought ahead to night-time in the spare room. I said to myself secretly another Martin Amis line: 'Jesus Christ, if I could make it into bed and get my eyes shut without seeing a mirror.' She smiled at me and I smiled back at her and both of our faces looked the same. We both had his tight, cool grin.

No Regrets?

Love means never having to say you're sorry.

Erich Segal

D. H. LAWRENCE
Two Blue Birds

There was a woman who loved her husband, but she could not live with him. The husband, on his side, was sincerely attached to his wife, yet he could not live with her. They were both under forty, both handsome, and both attractive. They had the most sincere regard for one another, and felt, in some odd way, eternally married to one another. They knew each other more intimately than they knew anybody else, they felt more known to one another than to any other person.

Yet they could not live together. Usually, they kept a thousand miles apart, geographically. But when he sat in the greyness of England, at the back of his mind, with a certain grim fidelity, he was aware of his wife, her strange yearning to be loyal and faithful, having her gallant affairs away in the sun, in the south. And she, as she drank her cocktail on the terrace over the sea, and turned her grey, sardonic eyes on the heavy dark face of her admirer, whom she really liked quite a lot, she was actually preoccupied with the clear cut features of her handsome young husband, thinking of how he would be asking his secretary to do something for him: asking in that good-natured, confident voice of a man who knows that his request will be only too gladly fulfilled.

The secretary of course adored him. She was *very* competent, quite young, and quite good looking. She adored him. But then all his servants always did: particularly his woman-servants. His men-servants were likely to swindle him.

When a man has an adoring secretary, and you are the man's wife, what are you to do? Not that there was anything 'wrong' – if you know what I mean! – between them. Nothing you could call adultery, to come down to brass tacks. No no! They were just the young master and his secretary. He dictated to her, she slaved for him and adored him, and the whole thing went on wheels.

He didn't 'adore' her. A man doesn't need to adore his secretary. But he depended on her. 'I simply rely on Miss Wrexall.' Whereas he could never rely on his wife. The one thing he knew finally about *her*, was that she didn't intend to be relied on.

So they remained friends, in the awful unspoken intimacy of the once married. Usually each year they went away together for a holiday, and if they had not been man and wife, they would have found a great deal of fun and stimulation in one another. The fact that they *were* married, had been married for the last dozen years, and couldn't live together for the last three or four, spoilt them for one another. Each had a private feeling of bitterness about the other.

However, they were awfully kind. He was the soul of generosity, and held her in real tender esteem, no matter how many gallant affairs she had. Her gallant affairs were part of her modern necessity. 'After all, I've got to *live*. I can't turn into a pillar of salt in five minutes, just because you and I can't live together! It takes years for a woman like me to turn into a pillar of salt. At least I hope so!'

'Quite!' he replied. 'Quite! By all means put them in pickle, make pickled cucumbers of them, before you crystallize out. That's my advice.'

He was like that: so awfully clever and enigmatic. She could more or less fathom the idea of the pickled cucumbers, but the 'crystallizing out,' what did that signify?

And did he mean to suggest that he himself had been well pickled, and that further immersion was for him unnecessary, would spoil his flavour? Was that what he meant? And herself, was she the brine and the vale of tears?

You never knew how catty a man was being, when he was really clever and enigmatic, withal a bit whimsical. He was adorably whimsical, with a twist of his flexible, vain mouth, that had a long upper lip so fraught with vanity! But then a handsome, clear-cut, histrionic young man like that, how could he help being vain? The women made him so.

Ah, the women! How nice men would be if there were no other women!

And how nice the women would be if there were no other men! That's the best of a secretary. She may have a husband, but a husband is the mere shred of a man, compared to a boss, a chief, a man who dictates to you and whose words you faithfully write down and then transcribe? Imagine a wife writing down anything her husband said to her! – But a secretary! Every *and* and *but* of his she preserves forever. What are candied violets in comparison!

Now it is all very well having gallant affairs under the southern sun; when you know there is a husband whom you adore dictating to a secretary whom you are too scornful to hate yet whom you rather despise, though you allow, she has her good points, away north in the place you ought to regard as home. A gallant affair isn't much good when you've got a bit of grit in your eye, or something at the back of your mind.

What's to be done? The husband, of course, did not send his wife away.

'You've got your secretary and your work,' she said. 'There's no room for me.'

'There's a bedroom and a sitting-room exclusively for you,' he replied. 'And a garden and half a motor-car. But please yourself entirely. Do what gives you most pleasure.'

'In that case,' she said, 'I'll just go south for the winter.'

'Yes, do!' he said. 'You always enjoy it.'

'I always do,' she replied.

They parted with a certain relentlessness, that had a touch of wistful sentiment behind it. Off she went to her gallant affairs, that were like the curate's egg, palatable in parts. And he settled down to work. He said he hated working, but he never did anything else. Ten or eleven hours a day. That's what it is to be your own master!

So the winter wore away, and it was spring, when the swallows homeward fly: or northward, in this case. This winter, one of a series similar, had been rather hard to get through. The bit of grit in the gallant lady's eye had worked deeper in, the more she blinked. Dark faces might be dark, and icy cocktails might lend a glow, she blinked her hardest, to blink that bit of grit away, without success. Under the spicy balls of the mimosa, she thought of that husband of hers, in his library, and of that neat, competent but *common* little secretary of his, forever taking down what he said!

'How a man can *stand* it! how *she* can stand it, common little thing as she is, I don't know!' the wife cried to herself.

She meant this dictating business, this ten hours a day intercourse, à deux, with nothing but a pencil between them: and a flow of words.

What was to be done? Matters, instead of improving, had grown worse. The little secretary had brought her mother and sister into the establishment. The mother was a sort of cook-housekeeper, the sister was a sort of upper maid: she did the fine laundry, and looked after 'his' clothes; and valeted him beautifully. It was really an excellent arrangement. The old mother was a splendid plain cook, the sister was all that could be desired as a valet-de-chambre, a fine laundress, an upper parlour-maid, and a table-waiter. And all economical to a degree. They knew his affairs by heart. His secretary flew to town when a creditor became dangerous, and she *always* smoothed over the financial crisis.

'He', of course, had debts, and he was working to pay them off. And if he had been a fairy prince who could call the ants to help him, he would not have been more wonderful than in securing this secretary and her family. They took hardly any wages. And they seemed to perform the miracle of loaves and fishes daily.

'She', of course, the wife who loved her husband, had helped him into debt, and she still was an expensive item. Yet when she appeared at her 'home', the secretarial family received her with most elaborate attentions and deference. The knight returning from the crusades didn't create a greater stir. She felt like Queen Elizabeth at Kenilworth, a sovereign paying a visit to her faithful subjects. But perhaps there lurked always this hair in her soup: Won't they be glad to be rid of me again!

But they protested No! No! They had been waiting and hoping and praying she would come. They had been pining for her to be there, in charge: the mistress, 'his' wife. Ah, 'his' wife!

'His' wife! His halo was like a bucket over her head.

The cook-mother was 'of the people', so it was the upper-maid daughter who came for orders.

'What will you order for tomorrow's lunch and dinner, Mrs Gee?'

'Well, what do you usually have?'

'Oh, we want *you* to say.'

'No, what do you *usually* have?'

'We don't have anything fixed. Mother goes out and chooses the best she can find, that is nice and fresh. But she thought you would tell her now what to get.'

'Oh, I don't know! I'm not very good at that sort of thing. Ask her to go on just the same, I'm sure she knows best.'

'Perhaps you'd like to suggest a sweet?'

'No, I don't care for sweets – and you know Mr Gee doesn't. So don't make one for me.'

Could anything be more impossible! They had the house spotless and running like a dream: how could an incompetent and extravagant wife dare to interfere, when she saw their amazing and almost inspired economy! But they ran the place on simply nothing! Simply marvellous people! And the way they strewed palm-branches under her feet!

But that only made her feel ridiculous, as if she were the ass, and the Crucifixion was next week.

'Don't you think the family manage very well?' he asked her tentatively.

'Awfully well! Almost romantically well!' she replied. 'And I suppose you're perfectly happy?'

'I'm perfectly comfortable,' he replied.

'I can see you are,' she replied. 'Amazingly so! I never knew such comfort! Are you sure it isn't bad for you?'

She eyed him stealthily. He looked very well, and extremely handsome, in his histrionic way. He was shockingly well-dressed and valeted. And he had that air of easy aplomb and good-humour which is so becoming to a man, and which he only acquires when he is cock of his own little walk, made much of by his own hens.

'No!' he said, taking his pipe from his mouth and smiling whimsically round at her. 'Do I look as if it were bad for me?'

'No, you don't,' she replied promptly: thinking naturally, as a woman is supposed to think nowadays, of his health and comfort, the foundation, apparently, of all happiness.

Then, of course, away she went on the backwash.

'Perhaps for your work, though, it's not so good as it is for *you*,' she said, in a rather small voice. She knew he couldn't bear it if she mocked at his work for one moment. – And he knew that rather small voice of hers.

'In what way?' he said, bristles rising.

'Oh, I don't know,' she answered indifferently. 'Perhaps it's not good for a man's work if he is too comfortable.'

'I don't know about *that*!' he said, taking a dramatic turn round the library and drawing at his pipe. 'Considering I work, actually, by the clock, for twelve hours a day, and for ten hours when it's a short day, I don't think you can say I am deteriorating from easy comfort.'

'No, I suppose not,' she admitted.

Yet she did think it, nevertheless. His comfortableness didn't consist so much in good food and a soft bed, as in having nobody, absolutely nobody and nothing, to contradict him. 'I do like to think he's got nothing to aggravate him,' the secretary had said to the wife.

'Nothing to aggravate him!' – what a position for a man! Fostered by women who would let nothing 'aggravate' him. If anything would aggravate his wounded vanity, this would!

So thought the wife. But what was to be done about it? In the silence of midnight she heard his voice in the distance dictating away, like the voice of God to Samuel, alone and monotone, and she imagined the little figure of the secretary busily scribbling shorthand. Then in the sunny hours of morning, while he was still in bed – he never rose till noon – from another distance came that sharp insect-noise of the typewriter, like some immense grasshopper chirping and rattling. It was the secretary, poor thing, typing out his notes.

That girl – she was only twenty eight – really slaved herself to skin and bone. She was small and neat, but she was actually worn out. She did far more work than he did, for she had not only to take down all those words he uttered, she had to type them out, make three copies, while he was still resting.

'What on earth she gets out of it,' thought the wife, 'I don't know. She's simply worn to the bone: for a very poor salary, and he's never kissed her, and never will, if I know anything about him.'

Whether his never kissing her – the secretary, that is – made it worse or better, the wife did not decide. He never kissed anybody. Whether she herself – the wife, that is – wanted to be kissed by him, even that she was not clear about. She rather thought she didn't.

What on earth did she want then? She was his wife. What on earth did she want of him.

She certainly didn't want to take him down in shorthand, and type out again all those words. And she didn't really want him to kiss her: she knew him too well. Yes, she knew him too well. If you know a man too well, you don't want him to kiss you.

What then? What did she want? Why had she such an extra-ordinary hang-over about him? Just because she was his wife? Why did she rather 'enjoy' other men – and she was relentless about enjoyment – without ever taking them seriously? And why must she take him so damn seriously, when she never really 'enjoyed' him?

Of course she *had* had good times with him, in the past, before – ah! before a thousand things, all amounting really to nothing. But she enjoyed him no more. She never even enjoyed being with him. There was a silent ceaseless tension between them, that never broke, even when they were a thousand miles apart.

Awful! That's what you call being married! What's to be done about it? Ridiculous, to know it all and not do anything about it!

She came back once more, and there she was, in her own house, a sort of super-guest, even to him. And the secretarial family devoting their lives to him.

Devoting their lives to him! But actually! Three women pouring out their lives for him day and night! And what did they get in return? Not one kiss! Very little money, because they knew all about his debts and had made it their life-business to get them paid off! No expectations! Twelve hours work a day! Comparative isolation, for he saw nobody!

And beyond that? – nothing! Perhaps a sense of uplift and importance because they saw his name and photograph in the newspapers sometimes. But would anybody believe that it was good enough?

Yet they adored it! They seemed to get a deep satisfaction out of it, like people with a mission. Extraordinary!

Well, if they did, let them. They were of course rather common, 'of the people', there might be a sort of glamour in it for them.

But it was bad for him. No doubt about it. His work was getting diffuse and poor in quality – and what wonder! His whole tone was going down, becoming commoner. Of course it was bad for him.

Being his wife, she felt she ought to do something to save him. But how could she. That perfectly devoted, marvellous secretarial family, how could she make an attack on them? – Yet she'd love to sweep them into oblivion. Of course they were bad for him: ruining his work, ruining his reputation as a writer, ruining his life. Ruining him with their slavish service.

Of course she ought to make an onslaught on them! But how *could* she! Such devotion! And what had she herself to offer in their place? Certainly not slavish devotion to him, nor to his flow of words! Certainly not!

She imagined him stripped once more naked of secretary and

secretarial family, and she shuddered. It was like throwing the naked baby in the dust bin. Couldn't do that!

Yet something must be done. She felt it. She was almost tempted to get into debt for another thousand pounds, and send in the bill, or have it sent in to him, as usual.

But no! Something more drastic!

Something more drastic, or perhaps more gentle. She wavered between the two. And wavering, she just did nothing, came to no decision, dragged vacantly on from day to day, waiting for sufficient energy to take her departure once more.

It was spring! What a fool she had been to come up in spring! And she was forty! What an idiot of a woman, to go and be forty!

She went down the garden in the warm afternoon, when birds were whistling loudly from the cover, the sky being low and warm, and she had nothing to do. The garden was full of flowers: he loved them for their theatrical display. Lilac and snow-ball bushes, and laburnum and red may, tulips and anemones and coloured daisies. Lots of flowers! Borders of forget-me-nots! Bachelor's buttons! What absurd names flowers had! She would have called them blue dots and yellow blobs and white frills. Not so much sentiment, after all!

There is a certain nonsense, something showy and stagey about spring, with its pushing leaves and chorus-girl flowers, unless you have something corresponding inside you. Which she hadn't.

Oh heaven! Beyond the hedge she heard a voice: a steady, rather theatrical voice. Oh heaven! – he was dictating to his secretary in the garden. Good God, was there nowhere to get away from it!

She looked around: there was indeed plenty of escape. But what was the good of escaping? He would go on and on. She went quietly towards the hedge, and listened.

He was dictating a magazine article about the modern novel. 'What the modern novel lacks is architecture –' Good God! Architecture! He might just as well say: What the modern novel lacks is whalebone, or a teaspoon, or a tooth stopped.

Yet the secretary took it down, took it down, took it down! No, this could not go on! It was more than flesh and blood could bear.

She went quietly along the hedge, somewhat wolf-like in her prowl, a broad, strong woman in an expensive mustard-coloured silk jersey and cream-coloured pleated skirt. Her legs were long and shapely, and her shoes were expensive.

With a curious wolf-like stealth she turned the hedge and looked across at the small, shaded lawn where the daisies grew impertinently. 'He' was reclining in a coloured hammock under the pink-flowering horse-chestnut tree, dressed in white serge with a fine yellow-coloured linen shirt. His elegant hand dropped over the side of the hammock and beat a sort of vague rhythm to his words. At a little wicker table, the little secretary, in a green knitted frock, bent her dark head over her note-book, and diligently made those awful short-hand marks. He was not difficult to take down, as he dictated slowly, and kept a sort of rhythm, beating time with his dangling hand.

'In every novel there must be one outstanding character with which we always sympathize – with *whom* we always sympathize – even though we recognize its – even when we are most aware of the human frailties –'

Every man his own hero, thought the wife grimly, forgetting that every woman is intensely her own heroine.

But what did startle her was a blue bird dashing about near the feet of the absorbed, shorthand scribbling little secretary. At least it was a blue-tit, blue with grey and some yellow. But to the wife it seemed blue, that juicy spring day, in the translucent afternoon. The blue bird, fluttering round the pretty but rather *common* little feet of the little secretary.

The blue bird! The blue bird of happiness! Well I'm blest! – thought the wife. Well I'm blest!

And as she was being blest, appeared another blue bird, that is, another blue-tit, and began to wrestle with the first blue-tit. A couple of blue birds of happiness, having a fight over it! Well I'm blest!

She was more or less out of sight of the human pre-occupied pair. But 'he' was disturbed by the fighting blue birds, whose little feathers began to float loose.

'Get out!' he said to them mildly, waving a dark-yellow handkerchief at them. 'Fight your little fight, and settle your private affairs elsewhere, my dear little gentlemen.'

The little secretary looked up quickly, for she had already begun to write it down. He smiled at her his twisted whimsical smile.

'No, don't take that down,' he said affectionately. 'Did you see those two tits laying into one another?'

'No!' said the little secretary, gazing brightly round, her eyes half blinded with work.

And she saw the queer, powerful, elegant, wolf-like figure of the wife, behind her, and terror came into her eyes.

'I did!' said the wife, stepping forward with those curious shapely, she-wolf legs of hers, under the very short skirt.

'Aren't they extraordinarily vicious little beasts?' said he.

'Extraordinarily!' she re-echoed, stooping and picking up a little yellow breast-feather. 'Extraordinarily! See how the feathers fly!'

And she got the feather on the tip of her finger, and looked at it. Then she looked at the secretary, then she looked at him. She had a queer, werewolf expression between her brows.

'I think,' he began, 'these are the loveliest afternoons, when there's no direct sun, but all the sounds and the colours and the scents are sort of dissolved, don't you know, in the air, and the whole thing is steeped, steeped in spring. It's like being on the inside, you know how I mean, like being inside the egg and just ready to chip the shell.'

'Quite like that!' she assented, without conviction.

There was a little pause. The secretary said nothing. They were waiting for the wife to depart again.

'I suppose,' said the latter, 'you're awfully busy, as usual?'

'Just about the same,' he said, pursing his mouth deprecatingly.

Again the blank pause, in which he waited for her to go away again.

'I know I'm interrupting you,' she said.

'As a matter of fact,' he said, 'I was just watching those two blue-tits.'

'Pair of little demons!' said the wife, blowing away the yellow feather from her finger-tip.

'Absolutely!' he said.

'Well, I'd better go, and let you get on with your work,' she said.

'No hurry!' he said, with benevolent nonchalance. 'As a matter of fact, I don't think it's a great success, working out of doors.'

'What made you try it?' said the wife. 'You know you never could do it.'

'Miss Wrexall suggested it might make a change. But I don't think it altogether helps, do you, Miss Wrexall?'

'I'm sorry,' said the little secretary.

'Why should *you* be sorry?' said the wife, looking down at her as a wolf might look down half benignly at a little black-and-tan mongrel. 'You only suggested it for his good, I'm sure!'

'I thought the air might be good for him,' the secretary admitted.

'Why do people like you never think about yourselves?' the wife asked.

The secretary looked her in the eye.

'I suppose we do, in a different way,' she said.

'A *very* different way!' said the wife ironically. 'Why don't you make *him* think about *you*,' she added, slowly, with a sort of drawl. 'On a soft spring afternoon like this, you ought to have him dictating poems to you, about the blue birds of happiness fluttering round your dainty little feet. – I know *I* would, if I were his secretary.'

There was a dead pause. The wife stood immobile and statuesque, in an attitude characteristic of her, half turning back to the little secretary, half averted. She half turned her back on everything.

The secretary looked at him.

'As a matter of fact,' he said, 'I was doing an article on the Future of the Novel.'

'I know that,' said the wife. 'That's what's so awful! Why not something lively in the life of the novelist?'

There was a prolonged silence, in which he looked pained and somewhat remote, statuesque. The little secretary hung her head. The wife sauntered slowly away.

'Just where were we, Miss Wrexall?' came the sound of his voice.

The little secretary started. She was feeling profoundly indignant. Their beautiful relationship, his and hers, to be so insulted!

But soon she was veering downstream on the flow of his words, too busy to have any feelings, except one of elation at being so busy.

Teatime came: the sister brought out the tea-tray into the garden. And immediately, the wife appeared. She had changed, and was wearing a chicory-blue dress of fine cloth. The little secretary had gathered up her papers and was departing, on rather high heels.

'Don't go, Miss Wrexall,' said the wife.

The little secretary stopped short, then hesitated.

'Mother will be expecting me,' she said.

'Tell her you're not coming. And ask your sister to bring another cup. I want you to have tea with us.'

Miss Wrexall looked at the man, who was reared on one elbow in the hammock, and was looking enigmatical, Hamletish.

He glanced at her quickly, then pursed his mouth in a boyish nonchalance.

'Yes, stay and have tea with us for once,' he said. 'I see strawberries, and I know you're the bird for them.'

She glanced at him, smiled wanly, and hurried away to tell her mother. She even stayed long enough to slip on a silk dress.

'Why how smart you are!' said the wife, when the little secretary reappeared on the lawn, in chicory-blue silk.

'Oh, don't look at my dress, compared to yours!' said Miss Wrexall. – They were of the same colour, indeed!

'At least you earned yours, which is more than I did mine,' said the wife, as she poured tea. 'You like it strong?'

She looked with her heavy eyes at the smallish, birdy, blue-clad, overworked young woman, and her eyes seemed to speak many inexplicable dark volumes.

'Oh, as it comes, thank you,' said Miss Wrexall, leaning nervously forward.

'It's coming pretty black, if you want to ruin your digestion,' said the wife.

'Oh, I'll have some water in it then.'

'Better, I should say.'

'How'd the work go, all right?' asked the wife, as they drank tea, and the two women looked at each other's blue dresses.

'Oh!' he said. 'As well as you can expect. It was a piece of pure flummery. But it's what they want. – Awful rot, wasn't it Miss Wrexall?'

Miss Wrexall moved uneasily on her chair.

'It interested me,' she said. 'Though not so much as the novel.'

'The novel? Which novel?' said the wife. 'Is there another new one?'

Miss Wrexall looked at him. Not for worlds would she give away any of his literary activities.

'Oh, I was just sketching out an idea, to Miss Wrexall,' he said.

'Tell us about it!' said the wife. 'Miss Wrexall, *you* tell us what it's about.'

She turned on her chair, and fixed the little secretary.

'I'm afraid –' Miss Wrexall squirmed – 'I haven't got it very clearly myself, yet.'

'Oh, go along! Tell us what you *have* got then!'

Miss Wrexall sat dumb and very vexed. She felt she was being baited. She looked at the blue pleatings of her skirt.

'I'm afraid I can't,' she said.

'Why are you afraid you can't? You're so *very* competent. I'm sure you've got it all at your finger-ends. I expect you write a good deal of Mr Gee's books for him, really. He gives you the hint, and you fill it all in. Isn't that how you do it?' She spoke ironically, and as if she were teasing a child. And then she glanced down at the fine pleatings of her own bluey skirt, very fine and expensive.

'Of course you're not speaking seriously?' said Miss Wrexall, rising on her mettle.

'Of course I am! I've suspected for a long time – at least, for some time – that you write a good deal of Mr Gee's books for him, from his hints.'

It was said in a tone of raillery, but it was cruel.

'I should be *terribly* flattered,' said Miss Wrexall, straightening herself, 'if I didn't know you were only trying to make me feel a fool.'

'Make you feel a fool? – my dear child! – why nothing could be further from me! You're twice as clever, and a million times as competent as I am. Why my dear child, I've the greatest admiration for you! I wouldn't do what you do, not for all the pearls in India. I *couldn't*, anyhow –'

Miss Wrexall closed up and was silent.

'Do you mean to say my books read as if –' he began, rearing up and speaking in a narrowed voice.

'I do!' said his wife. '*Just* as if Miss Wrexall had written them from your hints. I *honestly* thought she did – when you were too busy –'

'How very clever of you!' he said.

'Very!' she cried. 'Especially if I was wrong!'

'Which you were,' he said.

'How very extraordinary!' she cried. – 'Well, I am once more mistaken!'

There was a complete pause.

It was broken by Miss Wrexall, who was nervously twisting her fingers.

'You want to spoil what there is between me and him, I can see that,' she said bitterly.

'My dear, but what *is* there between you and him?' asked the wife.

'I was *happy* working with him, working for him! I was *happy* working for him!' cried Miss Wrexall, tears of indignant anger and chagrin in her eyes.

'My dear child!' cried the wife, with simulated excitement, 'go *on* being happy working with him, go on being happy while you can! If it makes you happy, why then, enjoy it! Of course! Do you think I'd be so cruel as to want to take it away from you? – working with him? *I* can't do shorthand and typewriting and double-entrance book-keeping, or whatever it's called. I tell you, I'm utterly incompetent. I never earn anything. I'm the parasite on the British oak, like the mistletoe. The blue bird doesn't flutter round my feet. Perhaps they're too big and trampling.'

She looked down at her expensive shoes.

'If I *did* have a word of criticism to offer,' she said, turning to her husband, 'it would be to you, Cameron, for taking so much from her and giving her nothing.'

'But he gives me everything, everything!' cried Miss Wrexall. 'He gives me everything!'

'What do you mean by everything,' said the wife, turning on her sternly.

Miss Wrexall pulled up short. There was a snap in the air, and a change of currents.

'I mean nothing that *you* need begrudge me,' said the little secretary rather haughtily. 'I've never made myself cheap.'

There was a blank pause.

'My God!' said the wife. 'You don't call that being cheap? Why, I should say you got nothing out of him at all, you only give! And if you don't call that making yourself cheap – my God! –'

'You see we see things different,' said the secretary.

'I should say we do! – *thank God*!' rejoined the wife.

'On whose behalf are you thanking God?' he asked sarcastically.

'Everybody's, I suppose! Yours, because you get everything for nothing, and Miss Wrexall's, because she seems to like it, and mine because I'm well out of it all.'

'You *needn't* be out of it all,' cried Miss Wrexall magnanimously, 'if you didn't *put* yourself out of it all.'

'Thank you, my dear, for your offer,' said the wife rising. 'But I'm afraid no man can expect *two* blue birds of happiness to flutter round his feet: tearing out their little feathers! —'

With which she walked away.

After a tense and desperate interim, Miss Wrexall cried:

'And *really*, need any woman be jealous of *me*!'

'Quite!' he said.

And that was all he did say.

FRANCES GAPPER

Pink and Blue

The first time you visited my house, I remember how pretty you looked sitting on my sofa – your blue skin against my pink cushions. You were my first blue affair, I was your first pink person, although you'd once had a green experience. I asked you, what was green like? Fey, you said, and vain. And jealous. I wasn't any of those things, I was pink. I felt glad to be pink, excited by blue.

Twiddling open my pink Venetian blinds, I introduced you to my garden – rhododendrons Pink Pearl and Sugar Pink, roses, clematis, lilies, hibiscus, pinks. Of course, not all were in flower. You politely didn't mention the green. We conspired not to admit green's existence. But you asked me, why no fuchsia (why no future?). Because, I explained, fuchsias are rarely pure pink. More often part-red or semi-purple.

You only had a window-box, in which you grew morning glories . . .

Then I ushered you into my boudoir: the essence of pinkness with its valanced bed and dressing-table, its frilly pillows. You gasped – in admiration, I thought at first. Then, unforgivably, you laughed. Oh, very Barbara Cartland, you said.

I am in fact a distant cousin of that lady. Until you spoke, I'd been proud of the connection, the extra pink credentials it gave me. Now I shrank from your cold blue laughter. As my pinkness faded to the merest tinge, you looked a bit concerned. I mean, you said hastily, this room doesn't seem to entertain the possibility of being blue, of blueness.

Looking at you then, I saw as if for the first time how blue you were, how blue. Me pink, you blue. How strange you were to me, how utterly different from myself. Afraid and longing, I asked, what does blue mean.

We stared at each other. In your blue eyes, I saw oceans and eternities. In my pink ones, you saw I don't know what.

It means, you said. But then our lips touched – yours chilly, mine lipsticked – and from then on we spoke love, not philosophy.

I found making love to blue quite frightening. Parts of me

disappeared into you and I wasn't sure if I'd ever get them back. Blue had hidden wet bits, pockets of slippery-slidiness, jelly or spawn. Like *Blue Planet*, which pink people weren't supposed to watch, but I had, and was dismayed by it. The lobster scenes were most unnerving, though filmed in a Welsh aquarium. I prefer my lobster cooked and served up to table.

The bed looked as though we'd squashed grapes in our rolling around, but I was fresh enough in love to find that delightful. The bedroom smelled richly purple, I myself like that unpleasant whiff of stale wine you get from bottle banks.

Pink was surprisingly warm and furry, you said. Like making love to a novelty hot-water-bottle. Although this didn't sound very romantic, I continued to snuggle against you, thinking sweet pink thoughts. How well pink and blue go together, the contrast highlighting our uniqueness, et cetera.

That night I dreamed in more than one colour.

You departed with airy grace. Pink nets twitched – pink shock! – as you walked down the street.

Blue, my family cried, we don't like blue. People like us don't associate with blue, or marry into it. There's nothing *wrong* with blue, they added, doubtfully. It's just not fashionable.

Lavender, lilac, violet, aubergine, buddleia and plum. My children, I thought.

But looking up at the sky, I heard my family whisper – blue is such a common colour. It's just everywhere!

One day, quite unthinkingly, I put some of your washing in with mine. The danger of colours bleeding, I didn't understand. Always wash colours separately, I'd never been advised. Oh my poor clothes, all streaky and blotched! Poor compromised me!

'I'm altered, too,' you said. 'Regrettably.'

'But you've absorbed me – see, I don't show . . .'

'You are so self-obsessed!'

This was so not true. I worried about many things that weren't myself exactly. Coral reefs destroyed by pesticides running off the land. Factory-farmed salmon.

I loved to watch sunsets. 'They kill me!' you cried. 'Pink pollutes the air.'

You refused to eat pink, I found the taste of blue repellent. We stopped having sex.

You called me fey and vain. You were jealous.

So we faded out of each others' lives. I took a pink china heart you'd given me and threw it against the wall. It shattered. It wasn't pink all through, of course, but white under a glaze. I felt doubt in my own heart – was I pink all through and forever? Or did I, like white, contain the possibility of being any colour?

Part 2
Black for train, bus and street, white my office uniform. On colour Fridays, held every two months for charity, I wore grey. They didn't know I'd been pink, once. I never blushed.

Part 3
Ill. Doctor's certificate. Lay in bed. Long time.

Part 4
A bee collecting pollen in my garden. Hanging upside down from or creeping inside a flower's narrow bell, it whined instead of buzzed. Ants performed huge tasks, shifting bits of twig and carrying seeds or crumbs or fellow ants, dead ones. The smells of rain, leaves, wet earth. Convalescence. Would I do or be anything ever again.

Part 5
A new outdoors love returned me to colour. Pale green lichen blew in tufts on thorn twigs or scaled mossy trunks. I felt as though you, green, had always been my leafy partner, the stalk upon which I flower. Yet so different!

We had an ex-lover in common. Blue, you said, was fey and vain. And jealous. Your emerald face inspired me to wonder. You showed me the pinkness of trees under their bark. Pink exists in nature, you said, it need not be anxiously cultivated. Pink balsam and spindle-berries and the occasional pink leaf – oh look! you cried. Look!

WILLIAM TREVOR
Access to the Children

Malcolmson, a fair, tallish man in a green tweed suit that required pressing, banged the driver's door of his ten-year-old Volvo and walked quickly away from the car, jangling the keys. He entered a block of flats that was titled – gold engraved letters on a granite slab – The Quadrant.

It was a Sunday afternoon in late October. Yellow-brown leaves patterned grass that was not for walking on. Some scurried on the steps that led to the building's glass entrance doors. Rain was about, Malcolmson considered.

At three o'clock precisely he rang the bell of his ex-wife's flat on the third floor. In response he heard at once the voices of his children and the sound of their running in the hall. 'Hullo,' he said when one of them, Deirdre, opened the door. 'Ready?'

They went with him, two little girls, Deirdre seven and Susie five. In the lift they told him that a foreign person, the day before, had been trapped in the lift from eleven o'clock in the morning until teatime. Food and cups of tea had been poked through a grating to this person, a Japanese businessman who occupied a flat at the top of the block. 'He didn't get the hang of an English lift,' said Deirdre. 'He could have died there,' said Susie.

In the Volvo he asked them if they'd like to go to the Zoo and they shook their heads firmly. On the last two Sundays he'd taken them to the Zoo, Susie reminded him in her specially polite, very quiet voice: you got tired of the Zoo, walking round and round, looking at all the same animals. She smiled at him to show she wasn't being ungrateful. She suggested that in a little while, after a month or so, they could go to the Zoo again, because there might be some new animals. Deirdre said that there wouldn't be, not after a month or so: why should there be? 'Some old animals might have died,' said Susie.

Malcolmson drove down the Edgware Road, with Hyde Park in mind.

'What have you done?' he asked.

261

'Only school,' said Susie.

'And the news cinema,' said Deirdre. 'Mummy took us to a news cinema. We saw a film about how they make wire.'

'A man kept talking to Mummy. He said she had nice hair.'

'The usherette told him to be quiet. He bought us ice-creams, but Mummy said we couldn't accept them.'

'He wanted to take Mummy to a dance.'

'We had to move to other seats.'

'What else have you done?'

'Only school,' said Susie. 'A boy was sick on Miss Bawden's desk.'

'After school stew.'

'It's raining,' said Susie.

He turned the windscreen-wipers on. He wondered if he should simply bring the girls to his flat and spend the afternoon watching television. He tried to remember what the Sunday film was. There often was something suitable for children on Sunday afternoons, old films with Deanna Durbin or Nelson Eddy and Jeanette MacDonald.

'Where're we going?' Susie asked.

'Where d'you want to go?'

'A Hundred and One Dalmatians.'

'Oh, please,' said Susie.

'But we've seen it. We've seen it five times.'

'Please, Daddy.'

He stopped the Volvo and bought a *What's On*. While he leafed through it they sat quietly, willing him to discover a cinema, anywhere in London, that was showing the film. He shook his head and started the Volvo again.

'Nothing else?' Deirdre asked.

'Nothing suitable.'

At Speakers' Corner they listened to a Jehovah's Witness and then to a woman talking about vivisection. 'How horrid,' said Deirdre. 'Is that true, Daddy?' He made a face. 'I suppose so,' he said.

In the drizzle they played a game among the trees, hiding and chasing one another. Once when they'd been playing this game a woman had brought a policeman up to him. She'd seen him approaching the girls, she said; the girls had been playing alone and he'd joined in. 'He's our daddy,' Susie had said, but the woman had still argued, claiming that he'd given them sweets so that they'd say that. 'Look at him,' the woman had insultingly said. 'He needs a shave.' Then she'd gone away, and the policeman had apologized.

'The boy who was sick was Nicholas Barnet,' Susie said. 'I think he could have died.'

A year and a half ago Malcolmson's wife, Elizabeth, had said he must choose between her and Diana. For weeks they had talked about it; she knowing that he was in love with Diana and was having some kind of an affair with her, he caught between the two of them, attempting the impossible in his effort not to hurt anyone. She had given him a chance to get over Diana, as she put it, but she couldn't go on for ever giving him a chance, no woman could. In the end, after the shock and the tears and the period of reasonableness, she became bitter. He didn't blame her: they'd been in the middle of a happy marriage, nothing was wrong, nothing was lacking.

He'd met Diana on a train; he'd sat with her, talking for a long time, and after that his marriage didn't seem the same. In her bitterness Elizabeth said he was stupidly infatuated: he was behaving like a murderer: there was neither dignity nor humanity left in him. Diana she described as a flat-chested American nymphomaniac and predator, the worst type of woman in the world. She was beautiful herself, more beautiful than Diana, more gracious, warmer, and funnier: there was a sting of truth in what she said; he couldn't understand himself. In the very end, after they'd been morosely drinking gin and lime-juice, she'd suddenly shouted at him that he'd better pack his bags. He sat unhappily, gazing at the green bottle of Gordon's gin on the carpet between his chair and hers. She screamed; tears poured in a torrent from her eyes. 'For God's sake go away!' she cried, on her feet, turning away from him. She shook her head in a wild gesture, causing her long fair hair to move like a horse's mane. Her hands, clenched into fists, beat at his cheeks, making bruises that Diana afterwards tended.

For months after that he saw neither Elizabeth nor his children. He tried not to think about them. He and Diana took a flat in Barnes, near the river, and in time he became used to the absence of the children's noise in the mornings, and to Diana's cooking and her quick efficiency in little things, and the way she always remembered to pass on telephone messages, which was something that Elizabeth had always forgotten to do.

Then one day, a week or so before the divorce was due, Diana said she didn't think there was anything left between them. It hadn't worked, she said; nothing was quite right. Amazed and bewildered, he argued with her. He frowned at her, his eyes screwed up as though he couldn't properly see her. She was very poised, in a black dress, with a necklace at her throat, her hair pulled smooth and neatly tied. She'd met a man called Abbotforth, she said, and she went on talking about that, still standing.

'We could go to the Natural History Museum,' Deirdre said. 'Would you like to, Susie?'

'Certainly not,' said Susie.

They were sitting on a bench, watching a bird that Susie said was a yellow-hammer. Deirdre disagreed: at this time of year, she said, there were no yellow-hammers in England, she'd read it in a book. 'It's a little baby yellow-hammer,' said Susie. 'Miss Bawden said you see lots of them.'

The bird flew away. A man in a raincoat was approaching them, singing quietly. They began to giggle. '*Sure, maybe some day I'll go back to Ireland,*' sang the man, '*if it's only at the closing of my day.*' He stopped, noticing that they were watching him.

'Were you ever in Ireland?' he asked. The girls, still giggling, shook their heads. 'It's a great place,' said the man. He took a bottle of VP wine from his raincoat pocket and drank from it.

'Would you care for a swig, sir?' he said to Malcolmson, and Malcolmson thanked him and said he wouldn't. 'It would do the little misses no harm,' suggested the man. 'It's good, pure stuff.' Malcolmson shook his head. 'I was born in County Clare,' said the man, 'in 1928, the year of the Big Strike.' The girls, red in the face from containing their laughter, poked at one another with their elbows. 'Aren't they the great little misses?' said the man. 'Aren't they the fine credit to you, sir?'

In the Volvo on the way to Barnes they kept repeating that he was the funniest man they'd ever met. He was nicer than the man in the news cinema, Susie said. He was quite like him, though, Deirdre maintained: he was looking for company in just the same way, you could see it in his eyes. 'He was staggering,' Susie said. 'I thought he was going to die.'

Before the divorce he had telephoned Elizabeth, telling her that Diana had gone. She hadn't said anything, and she'd put the receiver down before he could say anything else. Then the divorce came through and the arrangement was that the children should remain with Elizabeth and that he should have reasonable access to them. It was an extraordinary expression, he considered: reasonable access.

The Sunday afternoons had begun then, the ringing of a doorbell that had once been his own doorbell, the children in the hall, the lift, the Volvo, tea in the flat where he and Diana had lived and where now he lived on his own. Sometimes, when he was collecting them, Elizabeth spoke to him, saying in a matter-of-fact way that Susie had a cold and should not be outside too much, or that Deirdre was being bad about practising her clarinet and would he please speak to her. He loved Elizabeth again; he said to himself that he had never not loved her; he wanted to say to her that she'd been right about Diana. But he didn't say anything, knowing that wounds had to heal.

Every week he longed more for Sunday to arrive. Occasionally he invented reasons for talking to her at the door of the flat, after the children had gone in. He asked questions about their progress at school, he wondered if there were ways in which he could help. It seemed unfair, he said, that she should have to bring them up single-handed like this; he made her promise to telephone him if a difficulty arose; and if ever she wanted to go out in the evenings and couldn't find a babysitter, he'd willingly drive over. He always hoped that if he talked for long enough the girls would become so noisy in their room that she'd be forced to ask him in so that she could quieten them, but the ploy never worked.

In the lift on the way down every Sunday evening he thought she was more beautiful than any woman he'd ever seen, and he thought it was amazing that once she should have been his wife and should have borne him children, that once they had lain together and loved, and that he had let her go. Three weeks ago she had smiled at him in a way that was like the old way. He'd been sure of it, positive, in the lift on the way down.

He drove over Hammersmith Bridge, along Castelnau and into Barnes High Street. No one was about on the pavements; buses crept sluggishly through the damp afternoon.

'Miss Bawden's got a black boyfriend,' Susie said, 'called Eric Mantilla.'

'You should see Miss Bawden,' murmured Deirdre. 'She hasn't any breasts.'

'She has lovely breasts,' shouted Susie, 'and lovely jumpers and lovely skirts. She has a pair of earrings that once belonged to an Egyptian empress.'

'Flat as a pancake,' said Deirdre.

After Diana had gone he'd found it hard to concentrate. The managing director of the firm where he worked, a man with a stout red face called Sir Gerald Travers, had been sympathetic. He'd told him not to worry. Personal troubles, Sir Gerald had said, must naturally affect professional life; no one would be human if that didn't happen. But six months later, to Malcolmson's surprise, Sir Gerald had suddenly suggested to him that perhaps it would be better if he made a move. 'It's often so,' Sir Gerald had said, a soft smile gleaming between chubby cheeks. 'Professional life can be affected by the private side of things. You understand me, Malcolmson?' They valued him immensely, Sir Gerald said, and they'd be generous when the moment of departure came. A change was a tonic; Sir Gerald advised a little jaunt somewhere.

In reply to all that Malcolmson said that the upset in his private life was now over; nor did he feel, he added, in need of recuperation. 'You'll easily find another berth,' Sir Gerald Travers replied, with a wide, confident smile. 'I think it would be better.'

Malcolmson had sought about for another job, but had not been immediately successful: there was a recession, people said. Soon it would be better, they added, and because of Sir Gerald's promised generosity Malcolmson found himself in a position to wait until things seemed brighter. It was always better, in any case, not to seem in a hurry.

He spent the mornings in the Red Lion, in Barnes, playing dominoes with an old-age pensioner, and when the pensioner didn't turn up owing to bronchial trouble Malcolmson would borrow a newspaper from the landlord. He slept in the afternoons and returned to the Red Lion later. Occasionally when he'd had a few drinks he'd find himself thinking about his children and their mother. He always found it pleasant then, thinking of them with a couple of drinks inside him.

'It's *The Last of the Mohicans*,' said Deirdre in the flat, and he guessed that she must have looked at the *Radio Times* earlier in the day. She'd known they'd end up like that, watching television. Were they bored on Sundays? he often wondered.

'Can't we have *The Golden Shot*?' demanded Susie, and Deirdre pointed out that it wasn't on yet. He left them watching Randolph Scott and Binnie Barnes, and went to prepare their tea in the kitchen.

On Saturdays he bought meringues and brandy-snaps in Frith's Patisserie. The elderly assistant smiled at him in a way that made him wonder if she knew what he wanted them for; it occurred to him once that she felt sorry for him. On Sunday mornings, listening to the omnibus edition of *The Archers*, he made Marmite sandwiches with brown bread and tomato sandwiches with white. They loved sandwiches, which was something he remembered from the past. He remembered parties, Deirdre's friends sitting around a table, small and silent, eating crisps and cheese puffs and leaving all the cake.

When *The Last of the Mohicans* came to an end they watched *Going for a Song* for five minutes before changing the channel for *The Golden Shot*. Then Deirdre turned the television off and they went to the kitchen to have tea. 'Wash your hands,' said Susie, and he heard her add that if a germ got into your food you could easily die. 'She kept referring to death,' he would say to Elizabeth when he left them back. 'D'you think she's worried about anything?' He imagined Elizabeth giving the smile she had given three weeks ago and then saying he'd better come in to discuss the matter.

'Goody,' said Susie, sitting down.

'I'd like to marry a man like that man in the park,' said Deirdre. 'It'd be much more interesting, married to a bloke like that.'

'He'd be always drunk.'

'He wasn't drunk, Susie. That's not being drunk.'

'He was drinking out of a bottle –'

'He was putting on a bit of flash, drinking out of a bottle and singing his little song. No harm in that, Susie.'

'I'd like to be married to Daddy.'

'You couldn't be married to Daddy.'

'Well, Richard then.'

'Ribena, Daddy. Please.'

He poured drops of Ribena into two mugs and filled them up with warm water. He had a definite feeling that today she'd ask him in, both of them pretending a worry over Susie's obsession with death. They'd sit together while the children splashed about in the bathroom; she'd offer him gin and lime-juice, their favourite drink, a drink known as a Gimlet, as once he'd told her. They'd drink it out of the green glasses they'd bought, years ago, in Italy. The girls would dry themselves and come to say good-night. They'd go to bed. He might tell them a story, or she would. 'Stay to supper,' she would say, and while she made risotto he would go to her and kiss her hair.

'I like his eyes,' said Susie. 'One's higher than another.'

'It couldn't be.'

'It is.'

'He couldn't see, Susie, if his eyes were like that. Everyone's eyes are –'

'He isn't always drunk like the man in the park.'

'Who?' he asked.

'Richard,' they said together, and Susie added: 'Irishmen are always drunk.'

'Daddy's an Irishman and Daddy's not always –'

'Who's Richard?'

'He's Susie's boyfriend.'

'I don't mind,' said Susie. 'I like him.'

'If he's there tonight, Susie, you're not to climb all over him.'

He left the kitchen and in the sitting-room he poured himself some whisky. He sat with the glass cold between his hands, staring at the grey television screen. 'Sure, maybe some day I'll go back to Ireland,' Deirdre sang in the kitchen, and Susie laughed shrilly.

He imagined a dark-haired man, a cheerful man, intelligent and subtle, a man who came often to the flat, whom his children knew well and were already fond of. He imagined him as he had imagined himself ten minutes before, sitting with Elizabeth, drinking Gimlets from the green Italian glasses. 'Say good-night to Richard,' Elizabeth would say, and the girls would go to him and kiss him good-night.

'Who's Richard?' he asked, standing in the kitchen doorway.

'A friend,' said Deirdre, 'of Mummy's.'

'A nice friend?'

'Oh, yes.'

'I love him,' said Susie.

He returned to the sitting-room and quickly poured himself more whisky. Both of his hands were shaking. He drank quickly, and then poured and drank some more. On the pale carpet, close to the television set, there was a stain where Diana had spilt a cup of coffee. He hated now this memory of her, he hated her voice when it came back to him, and the memory of her body and her mind. And yet once he had been rendered lunatic with the passion of his love for her. He had loved her more than Elizabeth, and in his madness he had spoilt everything.

'Wash your hands,' said Susie, close to him. He hadn't heard them come into the room. He asked them, mechanically, if they'd had enough to eat. 'She hasn't washed her hands,' Susie said. 'I washed mine in the sink.'

He turned the television on. It was the girl ventriloquist Shari Lewis, with Lamb Chop and Charley Horse.

Well, he thought under the influence of the whisky, he had had his fling. He had played the pins with a flat-chested American nymphomaniac and predator, and he had lost all there was to lose. Now it was Elizabeth's turn: why shouldn't she have, for a time, the dark-haired Richard who took another man's children on to his knee and kissed them good-night? Wasn't it better that the score should be even before they all came together again?

He sat on the floor with his daughters on either side of him, his arms about them. In front of him was his glass of whisky. They laughed at Lamb Chop and Charley Horse, and when the programme came to an end and the news came on he didn't want to let his daughters go. An electric fire glowed cosily. Wind blew the rain against the windows, the autumn evening was dark already.

He turned the television off. He finished the whisky in his glass and poured some more. 'Shall I tell you,' he said, 'about when Mummy and I were married?'

They listened while he did so. He told them about meeting Elizabeth in the first place, at somebody else's wedding, and of the days they had spent walking about together, and about the wet, cold afternoon on which they'd been married.

'February the 24th,' Deirdre said.

'Yes.'

'I'm going to be married in summer-time,' Susie said, 'when the roses are out.'

His birthday and Elizabeth's were on the same day, April 21st. He reminded the girls of that; he told them of the time he and

Elizabeth had discovered they shared the date, a date shared also with Hitler and the Queen. They listened quite politely, but somehow didn't seem much interested.

They watched *What's in a Game?* He drank a little more. He wouldn't be able to drive them back. He'd pretend he couldn't start the Volvo and then he'd telephone for a taxi. It had happened once before that in a depression he'd begun to drink when they were with him on a Sunday afternoon. They'd been to Madame Tussaud's and the Planetarium, which Susie had said frightened her. In the flat, just as this time, while they were eating their sandwiches, he'd been overcome with the longing that they should all be together again. He'd begun to drink and in the end, while they watched television, he'd drunk quite a lot. When the time came to go he'd said that he couldn't find the keys of the Volvo and that they'd have to have a taxi. He'd spent five minutes brushing his teeth so that Elizabeth wouldn't smell the alcohol when she opened the door. He'd smiled at her with his well-brushed teeth but she, not then being over her bitterness, hadn't smiled back.

The girls put their coats on. Deirdre drank some Ribena; he had another small tot of whisky. And then, as they were leaving the flat, he suddenly felt he couldn't go through the farce of walking to the Volvo, putting the girls into it and then pretending he couldn't start it. 'I'm tired,' he said instead. 'Let's have a taxi.'

They watched the Penrhyn Male Voice Choir in *Songs of Praise* while they waited for it to arrive. He poured himself another drink, drank it slowly, and then went to the bathroom to brush his teeth. He remembered the time Deirdre had been born, in a maternity home in the country because they'd lived in the country then. Elizabeth had been concerned because she'd thought one of Deirdre's fingers was bent and had kept showing it to nurses who said they couldn't see anything the matter. He hadn't been able to see anything the matter either, nor had the doctor. 'She'll never be as beautiful as you,' he'd said and quite soon after that she'd stopped talking about the finger and had said he was nice to her. Susie had been born at home, very quickly, very easily.

The taxi arrived. 'Soon be Christmas,' said the taxi man. 'You chaps looking forward to Santa Claus?' They giggled because he had called them chaps. 'Fifty-six more days,' said Susie.

He imagined them on Christmas Day, with the dark-haired

Richard explaining the rules of a game he'd bought them. He imagined all four of them sitting down at Christmas dinner, and Richard asking the girls which they liked, the white or the brown of the turkey, and then cutting them small slices. He'd have brought, perhaps, champagne, because he was that kind of person. Deirdre would sip from his glass, not liking the taste. Susie would love it.

He counted in his mind: if Richard had been visiting the flat for, say, six weeks already and assuming that his love affair with Elizabeth had begun two weeks before his first visit, that left another four months to go, allowing the affair ran an average course of six months. It would therefore come to an end at the beginning of March. His own affair with Diana had lasted from April until September. 'Oh darling,' said Diana, suddenly in his mind, and his own voice replied to her, caressing her with words. He remembered the first time they had made love and the guilt that had hammered at him and the passion there had been between them. He imagined Elizabeth naked in Richard's naked arms, her eyes open, looking at him, her fingers touching the side of his face, her lips slightly smiling. He reached forward and pulled down the glass shutter. 'I need cigarettes,' he said. 'There's a pub in Shepherd's Bush Road, the Laurie Arms.'

He drank two large measures of whisky. He bought cigarettes and lit one, rolling the smoke around in his mouth to disguise the smell of the alcohol. As he returned to the taxi, he slipped on the wet pavement and almost lost his balance. He felt very drunk all of a sudden. Deirdre and Susie were telling the taxi man about the man in Hyde Park.

He was aware that he walked unsteadily when they left the taxi and moved across the forecourt of the block of flats. In the hall, before they got into the lift, he lit another cigarette, rolling the smoke about his mouth. 'That poor Japanese man,' said Deirdre.

He rang the bell, and when Elizabeth opened the door the girls turned to him and thanked him. He took the cigarette from his mouth and kissed them. Elizabeth was smiling: if only she'd ask him in and give him a drink he wouldn't have to worry about the alcohol on his breath. He swore to himself that she was smiling as she'd smiled three weeks ago. 'Can I come in?' he asked, unable to keep the words back.

'In?' The smile was still there. She was looking at him quite closely. He released the smoke from his mouth. He tried to remember what it was he'd planned to say, and then it came to him.

'I'm worried about Susie,' he said in a quiet voice. 'She talked about death all the time.'

'Death?'

'Yes.'

'There's someone here actually,' she said, stepping back into the hall. 'But come in, certainly.'

In the sitting-room she introduced him to Richard who was, as he'd imagined, a dark-haired man. The sitting-room was much the same as it always had been. 'Have a drink,' Richard offered.

'D'you mind if we talk about Susie?' Elizabeth asked Richard. He said he'd put them to bed if she liked. She nodded. Richard went away.

'Well?'

He stood with the familiar green glass in his hand, gazing at her. He said:

'I haven't had gin and lime-juice since –'

'Yes. Look, I shouldn't worry about Susie. Children of that age often say odd things, you know –'

'I don't mind about Richard, Elizabeth, I think it's your due. I worked it out in the taxi. It's the end of October now –'

'My due?'

'Assuming your affair has been going on already for six weeks –'

'You're drunk.'

He closed one eye, focusing. He felt his body swaying and he said to himself that he must not fall now, that no matter what his body did his feet must remain firm on the carpet. He sipped from the green glass. She wasn't, he noticed, smiling any more.

'I'm actually not drunk,' he said. 'I'm actually sober. By the time our birthday comes round, Elizabeth, it'll all be over. On April the 21st we could have family tea.'

'What the hell are you talking about?'

'The future, Elizabeth. Of you and me and our children.'

'How much have you had to drink?'

'We tried to go to *A Hundred and One Dalmatians*, but it wasn't on anywhere.'

'So you drank instead. While the children –'

'We came here in a taxi-cab. They've had their usual tea, they've watched a bit of *The Last of the Mohicans* and a bit of *Going for a Song* and all of *The Golden Shot* and *The Shari Lewis Show* and –'

'You see them for a few hours and you have to go and get drunk –'

'I am not drunk, Elizabeth.'

He crossed the room as steadily as he could. He looked aggressively at her. He poured gin and lime-juice. He said:

'You have a right to your affair with Richard, I recognize that.'

'A *right*?'

'I love you, Elizabeth.'

'You loved Diana.'

'I have never not loved you. Diana was nothing – nothing, nothing at all.'

'She broke our marriage up.'

'No.'

'We're divorced.'

'I love you, Elizabeth.'

'Now listen to me –'

'I live from Sunday to Sunday. We're a family, Elizabeth; you and me and them. It's ridiculous, all this. It's ridiculous making Marmite sandwiches with brown bread and tomato sandwiches with white. It's ridiculous buying meringues and going five times to *A Hundred and One Dalmatians* and going up the Post Office Tower until we're sick of the sight of it, and watching drunks in Hyde Park and poking about at the Zoo –'

'You have reasonable access –'

'Reasonable access, my God!' His voice rose. He felt sweat on his forehead. Reasonable access, he shouted, was utterly no good to him; reasonable access was meaningless and stupid; a day would come when they wouldn't want to go with him on Sunday afternoons, when there was nowhere left in London that wasn't an unholy bore. What about reasonable access then?

'Please be quiet.'

He sat down in the armchair that he had always sat in. She said:

'You might marry again. And have other children.'

'I don't want other children. I have children already. I want us all to live together as we used to –'

'Please listen to me –'

'I get a pain in my stomach in the middle of the night. Then I wake up and can't go back to sleep. The children will grow up and I'll grow old. I couldn't begin a whole new thing all over again: I haven't the courage. Not after Diana. A mistake like that alters everything.'

'I'm going to marry Richard.'

'Three weeks ago,' he said, as though he hadn't heard her, 'you smiled at me.'

'Smiled?'

'Like you used to, Elizabeth. Before —'

'You made a mistake,' she said, softly. 'I'm sorry.'

'I'm not saying don't go on with your affair with this man. I'm not saying that, because I think in the circumstances it'd be a cheek. D'you understand me, Elizabeth?'

'Yes, I do. And I think you and I can be perfectly good friends. I don't feel sour about it any more: perhaps that's what you saw in my smile.'

'Have a six-month affair —'

'I'm in love with Richard.'

'That'll all pass into the atmosphere. It'll be nothing at all in a year's time —'

'No.'

'I love you, Elizabeth.'

They stood facing one another, not close. His body was still swaying. The liquid in his glass moved gently, slopping to the rim and then settling back again. Her eyes were on his face: it was thinner, she was thinking. Her fingers played with the edge of a cushion on the back of the sofa.

'On Saturdays,' he said, 'I buy the meringues and the brandy-snaps in Frith's Patisserie. On Sunday morning I make the sandwiches. Then I cook sausages and potatoes for my lunch, and after that I come over here.'

'Yes, yes —'

'I look forward all week to Sunday.'

'The children enjoy their outings, too.'

'Will you think about it?'

'About what?'

'About all being together again.'

'Oh, for heaven's sake!' She turned away from him. 'I wish you'd go now,' she said.

'Will you come out with me on our birthday?'

'I've told you.' Her voice was loud and angry, her cheeks were flushed. 'Can't you understand? I'm going to marry Richard. We'll be married within a month, when the girls have had time to get to know him a little better. By Christmas we'll be married.'

He shook his head in a way that annoyed her, seeming in his drunkenness to deny the truth of what she was saying. He tried to light a cigarette; matches dropped to the floor at his feet. He left them there.

It enraged her that he was sitting in an armchair in her flat with his eyelids drooping through drink and an unlighted cigarette in his hand and his matches spilt all over the floor. They were his children, but she wasn't his wife: he'd destroyed her as a wife, he'd insulted her, he'd left her to bleed and she had called him a murderer.

'Our birthday,' he said, smiling at her as though already she had agreed to join him on that day. 'And Hitler's and the Queen's.'

'On our birthday if I go out with anyone it'll be Richard.'

'Our birthday is beyond the time –'

'For God's sake, there is no beyond the time. I'm in love with another man –'

'No.'

'On our birthday,' she shouted at him, 'on the night of our birthday Richard will make love to me in the bed you slept in for nine years. You have access to the children. You can demand no more.'

He bent down and picked up a match. He struck it on the side of the empty box. The cigarette was bent. He lit it with a wobbling flame and dropped the used match on to the carpet. The dark-haired man, he saw, was in the room again. He'd come in, hearing her shouting like that. He was asking her if she was all right. She told him to go away. Her face was hard; bitterness was there again. She said, not looking at him:

'Everything was so happy. We had a happy marriage. For nine years we had a perfectly happy marriage.'

'We could –'

'Not ever.'

Again he shook his head in disagreement. Cigarette ash fell on to the green tweed of his suit. His eyes were narrowed, watching her, seemingly suspicious.

'We had a happy marriage,' she repeated, whispering the words, speaking to herself, still not looking at him. 'You met a woman on a train and that was that: you murdered our marriage. You left me to plead, as I am leaving you to now. You have your Sunday access. There is that legality between us. Nothing more.'

'Please, Elizabeth –'

'Oh for God's sake, stop.' Her rage was all in her face now. Her lips quivered as though in an effort to hold back words that would not be denied. They came from her, more quietly but with greater bitterness. Her eyes roved over the green tweed suit of the man who once had been her husband, over his thin face and his hair that seemed, that day, not to have been brushed.

'You've gone to seed,' she said, hating herself for saying that, unable to prevent herself. 'You've gone to seed because you've lost your self-respect. I've watched you, week by week. The woman you met on a train took her toll of you and now in your seediness you want to creep back. Don't you know you're not the man I married?'

'Elizabeth –'

'You didn't have cigarette burns all over your clothes. You didn't smell of toothpaste when you should have smelt of drink. You stand there, pathetically, Sunday after Sunday, trying to keep a conversation going. D'you know what I feel?'

'I love –'

'I feel sorry for you.'

He shook his head. There was no need to feel sorry for him, he said, remembering suddenly the elderly assistant in Frith's Patisserie and remembering also, for some reason, the woman in Hyde Park who peculiarly had said that he wasn't shaved. He looked down at his clothes and saw the burn marks she had mentioned. 'We think it would be better', said the voice of Sir Gerald Travers unexpectedly in his mind.

'I'll make some coffee,' said Elizabeth.

She left him. He had been cruel, and then Diana had been cruel, and now Elizabeth was cruel because it was her right and her instinct to be so. He recalled with vividness Diana's face in those first moments on the train, her eyes looking at him, her voice. 'You have lost all dignity,' Elizabeth had whispered, in the darkness, at night. 'I despise you for that.' He tried to stand up but found the effort beyond him. He raised the green glass to his lips. His eyes closed and when he opened them again he thought for a drunken moment that he was back in the past, in the middle of his happy marriage. He wiped at his face with a handkerchief.

He saw across the room the bottle of Gordon's gin so nicely matching the green glasses, and the lime-juice, a lighter shade of green. He made the journey, his legs striking the arms of chairs. There wasn't much gin in the bottle. He poured it all out; he added lime-juice, and drank it.

In the hall he could hear voices, his children's voices in the bathroom, Elizabeth and the man speaking quietly in the kitchen. 'Poor wretch,' Elizabeth was saying. He left the flat and descended to the ground floor.

The rain was falling heavily. He walked through it, thinking that it was better to go, quietly and without fuss. It would all work out; he knew it; he felt it definitely in his bones. He'd arrive on Sunday, a month or so before their birthday, and something in Elizabeth's face would tell him that the dark-haired man had gone for ever, as Diana had gone. By then he'd be established again, with better prospects than the red-faced Sir Gerald Travers had ever offered him. On their birthday they'd both apologize to one another, wiping the slate clean: they'd start again. As he crossed the Edgware Road to the public house in which he always spent an hour or so on Sunday nights, he heard his own voice murmuring that it was understandable that she should have taken it out on him, that she should have tried to hurt him by saying he'd gone to seed. Naturally, she'd say a thing like that; who could blame her after all she'd been through? At night in the flat in Barnes he watched television until the programmes closed down. He usually had a few drinks, and as often as not he dropped off to sleep with a cigarette between his fingers: that was how the burns occurred on his clothes.

He nodded to himself as he entered the saloon bar, thinking he'd been wise not to mention any of that to Elizabeth. It would only have annoyed her, having to listen to a lot of stuff about late-night television and cigarettes. Monday, Tuesday, Wednesday, he thought, Thursday, Friday. On Saturday he'd buy the meringues and brandy-snaps, and then it would be Sunday. He'd make the sandwiches listening to *The Archers*, and at three o'clock he'd ring the bell of the flat. He smiled in the saloon bar, thinking of that, seeing in his mind the faces of his children and the beautiful face of their mother. He'd planted an idea in Elizabeth's mind and even though she'd been a bit shirty she'd see when she thought about it that it was what she wanted, too.

He went on drinking gin and lime-juice, quietly laughing over being so upset when the children had first mentioned the dark-haired man who took them on to his knee. Gin and lime-juice was a Gimlet, he told the barmaid. She smiled at him. He was celebrating, he said, a day that was to come. It was ridiculous, he told her, that a woman casually met on a train should have created havoc, that now, at the end of it all, he should week by week butter bread for Marmite and tomato sandwiches. 'D'you understand me?' he drunkenly asked the barmaid. 'It's *too* ridiculous to be true – that man will go because none of it makes sense the way it is.' The barmaid smiled again and nodded. He bought her a glass of beer, which was something he did every Sunday night. He wept as he paid for it, and touched his cheeks with the tips of his fingers to wipe away the tears. Every Sunday he wept, at the end of the day, after he'd had his access. The barmaid raised her glass, as always she did. They drank to the day that was to come, when the error he had made would be wiped away, when the happy marriage could continue. 'Ridiculous,' he said. 'Of course it is.'

COLETTE

A Letter

My Dear Valentine,

I received your postcard. I was able to make out – from the few lines covering the view of the Lac du Bourget like a network of fine hairs – what faithful friendliness and affectionate concern there is in it.

We parted somewhat coolly, and you write to me, circumspect: 'Abominable weather, impossible excursions, we're thinking of going back home . . . And what about you, what are you doing?'

That's enough; it's not hard to translate: 'I'm afraid I've made you very angry . . . Don't forget me, don't hold it against me; we don't share two ideas in common, but I'm very fond of you. I don't know why; I like you just as you are, with all your faults. I'm upset about you: put my mind at ease.'

Don't blush, my friend Valentine – it'll make your face powder cake! – and understand right away that I am still your friend.

I've followed your travels in the newspapers. *Figaro* assured me of your presence in Trouville, and I don't know which fashionable women's paper it was that depicted you in the most surprising terms: you were attributed with an 'impeccable navy-blue Louis XV suit, with a twisted Guayaquil pompadour . . .' A twisted Guayaquil pompadour! Really! As a friend by the name of Claudine used to say to me, 'I don't know what it is, but it must be beautiful!'

Because I'm living in a desert of golden sand – sixty square kilometers of beach, without a single strand of greenery, without one bald pebble – I am surprised, honestly, that there still are ladies who wear hats, tight-fitting dresses, boned collars, long corsets, and perilously high heels. How can I admit to you that, for the season, I have put away my dresses and shoes, and that beneath the indifferent and calloused soles of my feet I walk on the varnished seaweed, the sharp-edged shells, and the gray, salty furze that breaks through the sand? How dare I paint myself to you, dark as I am, my nose peeling a little from too much sun, my arms gloved in a deep shade of reddish brown? Thank God, the gulls and the delightful curlews are the only ones frightened by my riding outfit: knickers which at one time were blue, and a coarse knitted jersey. Add to that blue cycling stockings, rubber shoes, a soft cap, and the whole thing perched on top of a big nag of a bay horse – and you'll have a little equestrian group you wouldn't want to run into in the Bois de Boulogne.

At least let me congratulate you! *Femina* prints a picture of you, in your tennis clothes, among those of the 'best rackets' in Deauville . . . this Joan of Arc cuirass of white serge, which cuts across the pleated skirt at mid-thigh, is charming. You look like a little warrior in it, not the least bit athletic, but so endearing!

You see, we're not angry with each other at all. You're so unbearable, Valentine my friend! And I'm so impossible! I can still see us, very dignified, exchanging courteous and theatrical goodbyes. You had asked me what I was doing this summer and I'd answered, 'Well . . . first of all I'm going to do "Flesh" in Marseille.' To which you said, 'Again!'

Me: 'What do you mean "again"?'

You: 'That horrid thing again!'

Me: 'It's not horrid, it's a "sensational mime-drama"!'

You: 'It's perfectly horrid! Isn't that the one where you tear off your dress and appear . . .'

Me: 'Undressed, precisely.'

You: 'And it doesn't matter to you?'

Me: 'What do you mean, "it"?'

You: 'To show yourself off in public in an outfit, in a costume . . . well . . . It's beyond me! When I think that you stand there, in front of the whole world . . . oh . . . !'

Seized by an irresistible shudder of modesty, you covered your face with your hands and your whole body cringed, so that your dress, clinging to you, outlined you for an instant worse than naked: your little breasts crushed by the maillot corset, your stomach elongated and flat, ending in a mysterious fold, your round thighs pressed together, your delicate knees, bent slightly, every detail of your graceful body appeared to me so clearly beneath the crepe de Chine that it embarrassed me.

But you were already uncovering your incensed eyes.

'I have never seen . . . recklessness like yours, Colette!'

To which I responded, with witless rudeness, 'My dear, you bore me. You're neither my mother nor my lover: therefore . . .'

An exasperated sigh, a stiff handshake, that's all there was to our goodbye. Now, alone, I laugh to myself when I think of your special modesty, which shelters a slight body beneath vast, high hats, a body whose every step reveals, underneath a short, tight tunic, the movement of the hips, the protruding and rolling of the tight buttocks, and even the pink and amber color of your arms, shoulders, and back beneath the lace of the sleeves and the bodice. I'd really like to give you a good dressing down . . . you who – not content to appear in the light of day in this getup that a little Tanagra nymph would have found just barely adequate – come out of the water at Trouville with your nipples showing under your tight silk bathing suit glistening like a wet fish . . .

There's one thing, Valentine my friend, that you will never teach me, and that is that the skin on my lower back or my hips can be more tempting and more secret than the skin on my hand or my calf, and it's this 'recklessness', as you call it, this savage serenity, which makes all your indignation, your whole display of petty – do I dare say – local virtue, of your modesty by the square centimeter, pointless.

Do you remember the legal proceedings, still notorious, against nudity in the music hall? One little walk-on was cruelly upset at the time. She was playing two roles in a year-end review: in one she appeared nude, chaste, and silent, motionless on a cardboard cloud, with a bow in her hand. Two tableaux later, she came back onstage with 'Feminine Undergarments', dressed in a lace teddy and a pair of half hose: her naked little knees would quiver, as she sang a little song with indistinct words, and the flowers of her breasts would show mauve beneath the sheer linen. She looked sweet in it, slightly ridiculous, and perfectly indecent; well, one of her roles was cut: you understand that that meant she gave up the bow of Artemis and kept her sheer lace.

Does that seem perfectly natural to you? I was sure it did.

O infernal little woman! There are still moments when I am weak enough to want to make you understand me, to grab that hard little head of yours by its golden hair – real or false – and give it a good hard knock, to shake loose all its prejudices, all the bits and pieces of ideas, the debris of principles which, all together, make such an immoral fuss inside it.

Yes, immoral, you little dolt! Immoral, you ninny! Immoral, you nitwit! (And I'm still using polite language!) I don't care about your wide eyes and gaping mouth. You will never know all the bad things I think of you, you who look at me because I broke off with my husband, as though I had contracted an embarrassing disease, hard to hide and hard to admit. You will laugh, as though it were an easy paradox, if I try to explain to you that the married state appears preposterous and quite abnormal to me, you who have a husband – a husband in automobiles! – and who forget, when you're in his arms, about infidelity and the flight of a first lover . . .

Haven't you ever thought long and hard about that man, your husband? Don't answer me wittily and evasively: 'Yes, since I started cheating on him!' Remember back, without laughing, to the time when you didn't cheat on him. Wasn't there a day in your life when, faithful, loving, even in love, you suddenly looked at him and shrank back in astonishment: 'What is this man doing in my house with me? Why, in fact, am I living with this man here in my bedroom? I married him, fine! I've gone to bed with him, fine! – all that doesn't change the fact that this is *a man*, a man like any other, who is here in my bedroom, in my bed, in my life. He comes in, into my bathroom, after asking, "Am I bothering you, darling?" I reply, "No, my love!" but that doesn't change the fact that *this man* is here, in my bedroom, and that his face, the shape of his back, the way he strokes his mustache, suddenly strike me as strange, shocking, out of place . . . All my life, then, I'll live like this *with a man*, who will have the right to see how awful I look in the morning, to walk in on me while I'm drinking my laxative tisane, who'll ask about awkward dates in my little lady's calendar, and walk around in his shorts in my bathroom! There he is in my life, for the rest of my life! Why? The fact is, I don't know why. I love him . . . but that's another matter. Love has nothing to do with living together – on the contrary, most of the time it dies from it.'

Admit it, my friend: it is simply not possible that your married state has not appeared to you – for an hour, for an instant – in all its ludicrous crudeness! And who's to say that your husband, in his modesty, hasn't suffered from it too, with a man's modesty which is nearly always more delicate, more sincere than ours? I mean your husband, my husband, the husbands of all these ladies . . . One morning he'll wake up in a sullen mood, absorbed in his thoughts, hardly saying a word, eyes downcast. To your concerned 'What's

the matter, darling?,' he'll reply, 'Nothing . . . a little migraine . . .'
And after swallowing the headache powder offered by your affectionate
hand, he'll remain silent, with the look of a man to whom something
has happened.

What has happened to him is the same thing that has happened to
you! He doesn't recognize you. He steals glances at you, over his
newspaper, stunned and revolted, to discover you suddenly, to examine,
with a cold and lucid eye, *this woman* who is there in his home, who
sings as she pushes the tortoiseshell hairpins into her chignon, rings
for the maid, gives orders, makes decisions, arranges things . . . I swear
to you, my friend, that in these fugitive moments there are looks, from
lover to mistress, from wife to husband, which are frightening . . .

I remember a delightful remark my mother made one day, as she
was being upbraided by my father.

'I forbid you,' she said, 'to speak to me that way: you're not even
related to me!'

My childish ears remembered this singular remark and I have
thought about it often since.

At this moment, you little pest, you're quite capable of reading
this with a pretty, wicked little smile which means: 'You can understand why she bad-mouths marriage, she who . . .' I who *what*? I
who never had any reason to congratulate myself for it? What of it!
I won't let you sidestep the question in a ladylike way. I will quote
for you, as I remember it, the little sermon my mother gave me the
night before I married the man I loved, and who loved me.

'So, my poor little *toutou*, you're going to go away and leave me?
You're going away, and with who?'

'But, Mama, with the man I love!'

'I know perfectly well that you love him, and that's not the worst
part of this whole business. Believe me, it would be much better if
you loved him less. And afterward?'

'Afterward? Well, that's all!'

'That's all. A lot of good it'll do you! What I see most clearly is
that you're going off with some man, and I don't find that very
pretty, my daughter going off with some man.'

'But, Mama, he'll be my husband!'

'Him being your husband doesn't mean a thing to me. I myself
have had two husbands and I'm none the prouder for it . . . A man
whom you don't even know!'

'Oh, but I do, Mama, I do know him!'

'You do not know him, you silly little thing, because you love him! You are going to go away, all alone, with a man, and we'll watch you leave, your brothers and I, with long, sad faces. It's disgusting that things like this are allowed.'

'Oh really, Mama, you're extraordinary! What do you want me to do?'

'Whatever you want, naturally. But it's not right. The whole thing's set up so badly. Look at it for a minute! He tells you he loves you, and since you love him too, there you are in his arms, ready to follow him to the ends of the earth. But let him tell you all of a sudden, "I don't love you anymore," and he looks different to you! You discover he has the short nose of people who lack judgment and balance, the short, thick neck of those who kill in a fit of anger, the subtle and seductive voice of a liar, the weak and sensual chin of a woman . . . My darling little *toutou*, don't cry! I'm just an old killjoy. What can I do? I always say outrageous things, but the truth is that you'd have to marry your own brother if you wanted to marry with full knowledge of the facts, and even then! All this strange blood that comes into a family, and makes you look at your own son and say, "Where does he get those eyes, and that forehead, and his wild fits of anger, and his talent for lying?" Ah, my poor darling *toutou*, I'm not trying to explain, or to make the world over, as they say, but the whole thing's set up so badly!'

Forgive me, my friend. I'm letting myself get carried away by memories which might be lacking in happiness. I'm not trying to change what exists any more than my charming, crazy mother. Solitude, an intoxicating sense of freedom, and the absence of corsets has, as you can see, quickly turned me into a preacher of the worst sort. I only wanted to moralize a little, in my turn, purely as a tease.

And I bring to the game a lamentable conviction. It seems as if I can see, ten years or so from now, an old, dried-up, quibbling Colette, with hair like a Russian schoolgirl, in a reformist dress, who'll go into the towns advocating free love, proud loneliness, and *patatipatata*, and a whole pile of nonsense! Brrrr! But what demon shows me the image, still more terrible, of a forty-year-old Colette, burning with a new love, ripe and soft beneath her makeup, combative and desperate? With both arms outstretched I push both phantoms away from me, and I look for a sheltered narrow path between the two of them, where a friendly hand guides me.

Goodbye, my dear Valentine. I am afraid you won't like this letter. We will never understand one another, my friend. And I hope each of us will search, all our lives, for the other, with aggressive, unselfish tenderness. You no longer hope to 'bring me back to the fold'; I don't count on ever converting you. It provides our conversations with an artificial and inoffensive warmth, which gives us comfort and no illusions.

Goodbye! Go back to your tennis, in your Joan of Arc cuirass. I am going fishing for flatfish, which you find under your bare feet, in the deep holes left by the low tide. There's a strong wind up, the sand is blowing in long, swift streams which run parallel to the horizon, and their rippling locomotion is dizzying. Beneath the low sky, the beach is an endless desert, the color of ash, and the pale dunes smoke in the wind which scatters them. You would perish from desolation here, my dear, and yet it pleases me . . . I hug and kiss you; come back very beautiful and very happy.

Your friend,
Colette Willy

Translated from the French by Matthew Ward

ALAN SILLITOE
The Fishing-boat Picture

I've been a postman for twenty-eight years. Take that first sentence: because it's written in a simple way may make the fact of my having been a postman for so long seem important, but I realize that such a fact has no significance whatever. After all, it's not my fault that it may seem as if it has to some people just because I wrote it down plain; I wouldn't know how to do it any other way. If I started using long and complicated words that I'd searched for in the dictionary I'd use them too many times, the same ones over and over again, with only a few sentences – if that – between each one; so I'd rather not make what I'm going to write look foolish by using dictionary words.

It's also twenty-eight years since I got married. That statement is very important no matter how you write it or in what way you look at it. It so happened that I married my wife as soon as I got a permanent job, and the first good one I landed was with the Post Office (before that I'd been errand-boy and mash-lad). I had to marry her as soon as I got a job because I'd promised her I would, and she wasn't the sort of person to let me forget it.

When my first pay night came I called for her and asked: 'What about a walk up Snakey Wood?' I was cheeky-daft and on top of the world, and because I'd forgotten about our arrangement I didn't think it strange at all when she said: 'Yes, all right.' It was late autumn I remember and the leaves were as high as snow, crisp on top but soggy underneath. In the full moon and light wind we walked over the Cherry Orchard, happy and arm-in-arm. Suddenly she stopped and turned to me, a big-boned girl yet with a good figure and a nice enough face: 'Do you want to go into the wood?'

What a thing to ask! I laughed: 'You know I do. Don't you?'

We walked on, and a minute later she said: 'Yes, I do; but you know what we're to do now you've got a steady job, don't you?'

I wondered what it was all about. Yet I knew right enough. 'Get married,' I admitted, adding on second thoughts: 'I don't have much of a wage to be wed on, you know.'

'It's enough, as far as I'm concerned,' she answered.

And that was that. She gave me the best kiss I'd ever had, and then we went into the wood.

She was never happy about our life together, right from the start. And neither was I, because it didn't take her long to begin telling me that all her friends – her family most of all – said time and time again that our marriage wouldn't last five minutes. I could never say much back to this, knowing after the first few months how right everybody would be. Not that it bothered me though, because I was always the sort of bloke that doesn't get ruffled at anything. If you want to know the truth – the sort of thing I don't suppose many blokes would be ready to admit – the bare fact of my getting married meant only that I changed one house and one mother for another house and a different mother. It was as simple as that. Even my wage-packet didn't alter its course: I handed it over every Friday night and got five shillings back for tobacco and a visit to the pictures. It was the sort of wedding where the cost of the ceremony and reception go as a down payment, and you then continue dishing-out your wages every week for life. Which is where I suppose they got this hire purchase idea from.

But our marriage lasted for more than the five minutes everybody prophesied: it went on for six years; she left me when I was thirty, and when she was thirty-four. The trouble was that when we had a row – and they were rows, swearing, hurling pots: the lot – it was too much like suffering, and in the middle of them it seemed to me as if we'd done nothing but row and suffer like this from the moment we set eyes on each other, with not a moment's break, and that it would go on like this for as long as we stayed together. The truth was, as I see it now – and even saw it sometimes then – that a lot of our time was bloody enjoyable.

I'd had an idea before she went that our time as man and wife was about up, because one day we had the worst fight of them all. We were sitting at home one evening after tea, one at each end of the table, plates empty and bellies full so that there was no excuse for what followed. My head was in a book, and Kathy just sat there.

Suddenly she said: 'I do love you, Harry.' I didn't hear the words for some time, as is often the case when you're reading a book. Then: 'Harry, look at me.'

My face came up, smiled, and went down again to my reading. Maybe I was in the wrong, and should have said something, but the book was too good.

'I'm sure all that reading's bad for your eyes,' she commented, prising me again from the hot possessive world of India.

'It ain't,' I denied, not looking up. She was young and still fair-faced, a passionate loose-limbed thirty-odd that wouldn't let me sidestep either her obstinacy or anger. 'My dad used to say that on'y fools read books, because they'd such a lot to learn.'

The words hit me and sank in, so that I couldn't resist coming back with, still not looking up: 'He on'y said that because he didn't know how to read. He was jealous, if you ask me.'

'No need to be jealous of the rammel you stuff your big head with,' she said, slowly to make sure I knew she meant every word. The print wouldn't stick any more; the storm was too close.

'Look, why don't *you* get a book, duck?' But she never would, hated them like poison.

She sneered: 'I've got more sense; and too much to do.'

Then I blew up, in a mild way because I still hoped she wouldn't take on, that I'd be able to finish my chapter. 'Well let me read, anyway, wain't you? It's an interesting book, and I'm tired.'

But such a plea only gave her another opening. 'Tired? You're allus tired.' She laughed out loud: 'Tired Tim! You ought to do some real work for a change instead of walking the streets with that daft post bag.'

I won't go on, spinning it out word for word. In any case not many more passed before she snatched the book out of my hands. 'You booky bastard,' she screamed, 'nowt but books, books, books, you bleddy dead-'ead' – and threw the book on the heaped-up coals, working it further and further into their blazing middle with the poker.

This annoyed me, so I clocked her one, not very hard, but I did. It was a good reading-book, and what's more it belonged to the library. I'd have to pay for a new one. She slammed out of the house, and I didn't see her until next day.

I didn't think to break my heart very much when she skipped off. I'd had enough. All I can say is that it was a stroke of God's luck we never had any kids. She was confined once or twice, but it never came to anything; each time it dragged more bitterness out of her than we could absorb in the few peaceful months that came between. It might have been better if she'd had kids though; you never know.

A month after burning the book she ran off with a housepainter. It was all done very nicely. There was no shouting or knocking each other about or breaking up the happy home. I just came back from work one day and found a note waiting for me. 'I am going away and not coming back' – propped on the mantelpiece in front of the clock. No tear stains on the paper, just eight words in pencil on a page of the insurance book – I've still got it in the back of my wallet, though God knows why.

The housepainter she went with had lived in a house on his own, across the terrace. He'd been on the dole for a few months and suddenly got a job at a place twenty miles away I was later told. The neighbours seemed almost eager to let me know – after they'd gone, naturally – that they'd been knocking-on together for about a year. No one knew where they'd skipped off to exactly, probably imagining that I wanted to chase after them. But the idea never occurred to me. In any case what was I to do? Knock him flat and drag Kathy back by the hair? Not likely.

Even now it's no use trying to tell myself that I wasn't disturbed by this change in my life. You miss a woman when she's been living with you in the same house for six years, no matter what sort of cat-and-dog life you led together – though we had our moments, that I will say. After her sudden departure there was something different about the house, about the walls, ceiling and every object in it. And something altered inside me as well – though I tried to tell myself that all was just the same and that Kathy's leaving me wouldn't make a blind bit of difference. Nevertheless time crawled at first, and I felt like a man just learning to pull himself along with a clubfoot; but then the endless evenings of summer came and I was happy almost against my will, too happy anyway to hang on to such torments as sadness and loneliness. The world was moving and, I felt, so was I.

In other words I succeeded in making the best of things, which as much as anything else meant eating a good meal at the canteen every midday. I boiled an egg for breakfast (fried with bacon on Sundays) and had something cold but solid for my tea every night. As things went, it wasn't a bad life. It might have been a bit lonely, but at least it was peaceful, and it got as I didn't mind it, one way or the other. I even lost the feeling of loneliness that had set me thinking a bit too much just after she'd gone. And then I didn't dwell on it any more. I saw enough people on my rounds during the day to last me through the evenings and at week-ends. Sometimes I played draughts at the club, or went out for a slow half pint to the pub up the street.

Things went on like this for ten years. From what I gathered later Kathy had been living in Leicester with her housepainter. Then she came back to Nottingham. She came to see me one Friday evening, payday. From her point of view, as it turned out, she couldn't have come at a better time.

I was leaning on my gate in the backyard smoking a pipe of tobacco. I'd had a busy day on my rounds, an irritating time of it – being handed back letters all along the line, hearing that people had left and that no one had any idea where they'd moved to; and other people taking as much as ten minutes to get out of bed and sign for a registered letter – and now I felt twice as peaceful because I was at home, smoking my pipe in the backyard at the fag-end of an autumn day. The sky was a clear yellow, going green above the housetops and wireless aerials. Chimneys were just beginning to send out evening smoke, and most of the factory motors had been switched off. The noise of kids scooting around lamp-posts and the barking of dogs came from what sounded a long way off. I was about to knock my pipe out, to go back into the house and carry on reading a book about Brazil I'd left off the night before.

As soon as she came around the corner and started walking up the yard I knew her. It gave me a funny feeling, though: ten years ain't enough to change anybody so's you don't recognize them, but it's long enough to make you have to look twice before you're sure. And that split second in between is like a kick in the stomach. She didn't walk with her usual gait, as though she owned the terrace and everybody in it. She was a bit slower than when I'd seen her last, as if she'd bumped into a wall during the last ten years through walking in the cock o' the walk way she'd always had. She didn't seem so sure of herself and was fatter now, wearing a frock left over from the summer and an open winter coat, and her hair had been dyed fair whereas it used to be a nice shade of brown.

I was neither glad nor unhappy to see her, but maybe that's what shock does, because I was surprised, that I will say. Not that I never expected to see her again, but you know how it is, I'd just forgotten her somehow. The longer she was away our married life shrunk to a year, a month, a day, a split second of sparking light I'd met in the black darkness before getting-up time. The memory had drawn itself too far back, even in ten years, to remain as anything much more than a dream. For as soon as I got used to living alone I forgot her.

Even though her walk had altered I still expected her to say something sarky like: 'Didn't expect to see me back at the scene of the crime so soon, did you, Harry?' Or: 'You thought it wasn't true that a bad penny always turns up again, didn't you?'

But she just stood. 'Hello, Harry' – waited for me to lean up off the gate so's she could get in. 'It's been a long time since we saw each other, hasn't it?'

I opened the gate, slipping my empty pipe away. 'Hello, Kathy,' I said, and walked down the yard so that she could come behind me. She buttoned her coat as we went into the kitchen, as though she were leaving the house instead of just going in. 'How are you getting on then?' I asked, standing near the fireplace.

Her back was to the wireless, and it didn't seem as if she wanted to look at me. Maybe I was a bit upset after all at her sudden visit, and it's possible I showed it without knowing it at the time, because I filled my pipe up straightaway, a thing I never normally do. I always let one pipe cool down before lighting the next.

'I'm fine,' was all she'd say.

'Why don't you sit down then, Kath? I'll get you a bit of a fire soon.'

She kept her eyes to herself still, as if not daring to look at the old things around her, which were much as they'd been when she left. However she'd seen enough to remark: 'You look after yourself all right.'

'What did you expect?' I said, though not in a sarcastic way. She wore lipstick, I noticed, which I'd never seen on her before, and rouge, maybe powder as well, making her look old in a different way, I supposed, than if she'd had nothing on her face at all. It was a thin disguise, yet sufficient to mask from me – and maybe her – the person she'd been ten years ago.

'I hear there's a war coming on,' she said, for the sake of talking.

I pulled a chair away from the table. 'Come on, sit down, Kathy. Get that weight off your legs' – an old phrase we'd used though I don't know why I brought it out at that moment. 'No, I wouldn't be a bit surprised. That bloke Hitler wants a bullet in his brain – like a good many Germans.' I looked up and caught her staring at the picture of a fishing boat on the wall: brown and rusty with sails half spread in a bleak sunrise, not far from the beach along which a woman walked bearing a basket of fish on her shoulder. It was one of a set that Kathy's brother had given us as a wedding present, the other two having been smashed up in another argument we'd had. She liked it a lot, this remaining fishing-boat picture. The last of the fleet, we used to call it, in our brighter moments. 'How are you getting on?' I wanted to know. 'Living all right?'

'All right,' she answered. I still couldn't get over the fact that she wasn't as talkative as she had been, that her voice was softer and flatter, with no more bite in it. But perhaps she felt strange at seeing me in the old house again after all this time, with everything just as she'd left it. I had a wireless now, that was the only difference.

'Got a job?' I asked. She seemed afraid to take the chair I'd offered her.

'At Hoskins,' she told me, 'on Ambergate. The lace factory. It pays forty-two bob a week, which isn't bad.' She sat down and did up the remaining button of her coat. I saw she was looking at the fishing-boat picture again. The last of the fleet.

'It ain't good either. They never paid owt but starvation wages and never will I suppose. Where are you living, Kathy?'

Straightening her hair – a trace of grey near the roots – she said: 'I've got a house at Sneinton. Little, but it's only seven and six a week. It's noisy as well, but I like it that way. I was always one for a bit of life, you know that. "A pint of beer and a quart of noise" was what you used to say, didn't you?'

I smiled. 'Fancy you remembering that.' But she didn't look as though she had much of a life. Her eyes lacked that spark of humour that often soared up into the bonfire of a laugh. The lines around them now served only as an indication of age and passing time. 'I'm glad to hear you're taking care of yourself.'

She met my eyes for the first time. 'You was never very excitable, was you, Harry?'

'No,' I replied truthfully, 'not all that much.'

'You should have been,' she said, though in an empty sort of way, 'then we might have hit it off a bit better.'

'Too late now,' I put in, getting the full blow-through of my words. 'I was never one for rows and trouble, you know that. Peace is more my line.'

She made a joke at which we both laughed. 'Like that bloke Chamberlain!' – then moved a plate to the middle of the table and laid her elbows on the cloth. 'I've been looking after myself for the last three years.'

It may be one of my faults, but I get a bit curious sometimes. 'What's happened to that housepainter of yours then?' I asked this question quite naturally though, because I didn't feel I had anything to reproach her with. She'd gone away, and that was that. She hadn't left me in the lurch with a mountain of debts or any such thing. I'd always let her do what she liked.

'I see you've got a lot of books,' she remarked, noticing one propped against the sauce bottle, and two more on the sideboard.

'They pass the time on,' I replied, striking a match because my pipe had gone out. 'I like reading.'

She didn't say anything for a while. Three minutes I remember, because I was looking across at the clock on the dresser. The news would have been on the wireless, and I'd missed the best part of it. It was getting interesting because of the coming war. I didn't have anything else to do but think this while I was waiting for her to speak. 'He died of lead-poisoning,' she told me. 'He did suffer a lot, and he was only forty-two. They took him away to the hospital a week before he died.'

I couldn't say I was sorry, though it was impossible to hold much against him. I just didn't know the chap. 'I don't think I've got a fag in the place to offer you,' I said, looking on the mantelpiece in case I might find one, though knowing I wouldn't. She moved when I passed her on my search, scraping her chair along the floor. 'No, don't bother to shift. I can get by.'

'It's all right,' she said. 'I've got some here' – feeling in her pocket and bringing out a crumpled five-packet. 'Have one, Harry?'

'No thanks. I haven't smoked a fag in twenty years. You know that. Don't you remember how I started smoking a pipe? When we were courting. You gave me one once for my birthday and told me to start smoking it because it would make me look more distinguished! So I've smoked one ever since. I got used to it quick enough, and I like it now. I'd never be without it in fact.'

As if it were yesterday! But maybe I was talking too much, for she seemed a bit nervous while lighting her fag. I don't know why it was, because she didn't need to be in my house. 'You know, Harry,' she began, looking at the fishing-boat picture, nodding her head towards it, 'I'd like to have that' – as though she'd never wanted anything so much in her life.

'Not a bad picture, is it?' I remember saying. 'It's nice to have pictures on the wall, not to look at especially, but they're company. Even when you're not looking at them you know they're there. But you can take it if you like.'

'Do you mean that?' she asked, in such a tone that I felt sorry for her for the first time.

'Of course. Take it. I've got no use for it. In any case I can get another picture if I want one, or put a war map up.' It was the only picture on that wall, except for the wedding photo on the sideboard below. But I didn't want to remind her of the wedding picture for fear it would bring back memories she didn't like. I hadn't kept it there for sentimental reasons, so perhaps I should have dished it. 'Did you have any kids?'

'No,' she said, as if not interested. 'But I don't like taking your picture, and I'd rather not if you think all that much of it.' We sat looking over each other's shoulder for a long time. I wondered what had happened during these ten years to make her talk so sadly about the picture. It was getting dark outside. Why didn't she shut up about it, just take the bloody thing? So I offered it to her again, and to settle the issue unhooked it, dusted the back with a cloth, wrapped it up in brown paper, and tied the parcel with the best post-office string. 'There you are,' I said, brushing the pots aside, laying it on the table at her elbows.

'You're very good to me, Harry.'

'Good! I like that. What does a picture more or less in the house matter? And what does it mean to me, anyway?' I can see now that we were giving each other hard knocks in a way we'd never learned to do when living together. I switched on the electric light. As she seemed uneasy when it showed everything up clearly in the room, I offered to switch it off again.

'No, don't bother' – standing to pick up her parcel. 'I think I'll be going now. Happen I'll see you some other time.'

'Drop in whenever you feel like it.' Why not? We weren't enemies. She undid two buttons of her coat, as though having them loose would make her look more at her ease and happy in her clothes, then waved to me. 'So long.'

'Good night, Kathy.' It struck me that she hadn't smiled or laughed once the whole time she'd been there, so I smiled to her as she turned for the door, and what came back wasn't the bare-faced cheeky grin I once knew, but a wry parting of the lips moving more for exercise than humour. She must have been through it, I thought, and she's above forty now.

So she went. But it didn't take me long to get back to my book.

A few mornings later I was walking up St Ann's Well Road delivering letters. My round was taking a long time, for I had to stop at almost every shop. It was raining, a fair drizzle, and water rolled off my cape, soaking my trousers below the knees so that I was looking forward to a mug of tea back in the canteen and hoping they'd kept the stove going. If I hadn't been so late on my round I'd have dropped into a café for a cup.

I'd just taken a pack of letters into a grocer's and, coming out, saw the fishing-boat picture in the next-door pawnshop window, the one I'd given Kathy a few days ago. There was no mistaking it, leaning back against ancient spirit-levels, bladeless planes, rusty hammers, trowels, and a violin case with the strap broken. I recognized a chip in the gold-painted woodwork near the bottom left corner of its frame.

For half a minute I couldn't believe it, was unable to make out how it had got there, then saw the first day of my married life and a sideboard loaded with presents, prominent among them this surviving triplet of a picture looking at me from the wreckage of other lives. And here it is, I thought, come down to a bloody nothing. She must have sold it that night before going home, pawnshops always keeping open late on a Friday so that women could get their husbands' suits out of pop for the week-end. Or maybe she'd sold it this morning, and I was only half an hour behind her on my round. Must have been really hard up. Poor Kathy, I thought. Why hadn't she asked me to let her have a bob or two?

I didn't think much about what I was going to do next. I never do, but went inside and stood at the shop counter waiting for a grey-haired doddering skinflint to sort out the popped bundles of two thin-faced women hovering to make sure he knew they were pawning the best of stuff. I was impatient. The place stank of old clothes and mildewed junk after coming out of fresh rain, and besides I was later than ever now on my round. The canteen would be closed before I got back, and I'd miss my morning tea.

The old man shuffled over at last, his hand out. 'Got any letters?'

'Nowt like that, feyther. I'd just like to have a look at that picture you've got in your window, the one with a ship on it.' The women went out counting what few shillings he'd given them, stuffing pawn-tickets in their purses, and the old man came back carrying the picture as if it was worth five quid.

Shock told me she'd sold it right enough, but belief lagged a long way behind, so I looked at it well to make sure it really was the one. A price marked on the back wasn't plain enough to read. 'How much do you want for it?'

'You can have it for four bob.'

Generosity itself. But I'm not one for bargaining. I could have got it for less, but I'd rather pay an extra bob than go through five minutes of chinning. So I handed the money over, and said I'd call back for the picture later.

Four measly bob, I said to myself as I sloshed on through the rain. The robbing bastard. He must have given poor Kathy about one and six for it. Three pints of beer for the fishing-boat picture.

I don't know why, but I was expecting her to call again the following week. She came on Thursday, at the same time, and was dressed in the usual way: summer frock showing through her brown winter coat whose buttons she couldn't leave alone, telling me how nervous she was. She'd had a drink or two on her way, and before coming into the house stopped off at the lavatory outside. I'd been late back from work, and hadn't quite finished my tea, asked her if she could do with a cup. 'I don't feel like it,' came the answer. 'I had one not long ago.'

I emptied the coal scuttle on the fire. 'Sit down nearer the warmth. It's a bit nippy tonight.'

She agreed that it was, then looked up at the fishing-boat picture on the wall. I'd been waiting for this, wondered what she'd say when she did, but there was no surprise at seeing it back in the old place, which made me feel a bit disappointed. 'I won't be staying long tonight,' was all she said. 'I've got to see somebody at eight.'

Not a word about the picture. 'That's all right. How's your work going?'

'Putrid,' she answered nonchalantly, as though my question had been out of place. 'I got the sack, for telling the forewoman where to get off.'

'Oh,' I said, getting always to say 'Oh' when I wanted to hide my feelings, though it was a safe bet that whenever I did say 'Oh' there wasn't much else to come out with.

I had an idea she might want to live in my house again seeing she'd lost her job. If she wanted to she could. And she wouldn't be afraid to ask, even now. But I wasn't going to mention it first. Maybe that was my mistake, though I'll never know. 'A pity you got the sack,' I put in.

Her eyes were on the picture again, until she asked: 'Can you lend me half-a-crown?'

'Of course I can' – emptied my trouser pocket, sorted out half-a-crown, and passed it across to her. Five pints. She couldn't think of anything to say, shuffled her feet to some soundless tune in her mind. 'Thanks very much.'

'Don't mention it,' I said with a smile. I remembered buying a packet of fags in case she'd want one, which shows how much I'd expected her back. 'Have a smoke?' – and she took one, struck a match on the sole of her shoe before I could get her a light myself.

'I'll give you the half-crown next week, when I get paid.' That's funny, I thought. 'I got a job as soon as I lost the other one,' she added, reading my mind before I had time to speak. 'It didn't take long. There's plenty of war work now. Better money as well.'

'I suppose all the firms'll be changing over soon.' It occurred to me that she could claim some sort of allowance from me – for we were still legally married – instead of coming to borrow half-a-crown. It was her right, and I didn't need to remind her; I wouldn't be all that much put out if she took me up on it. I'd been single – as you might say – for so many years that I hadn't been able to stop myself putting a few quid by. 'I'll be going now,' she said, standing up to fasten her coat.

'Sure you won't have a cup of tea?'

'No thanks. Want to catch the trolley back to Sneinton.' I said I'd show her to the door. 'Don't bother. I'll be all right.' She stood waiting for me, looking at the picture on the wall above the sideboard. 'It's a nice picture you've got up there. I always liked it a lot.'

I made the old joke: 'Yes, but it's the last of the fleet.'

'That's why I like it.' Not a word about having sold it for eighteen pence.

I showed her out, mystified.

She came to see me every week, all through the war, always on Thursday night at about the same time. We talked a bit, about the weather, the war, her job and my job, never anything important. Often we'd sit for a long time looking into the fire from our different stations in the room, me by the hearth and Kathy a bit further away at the table as if she'd just finished a meal, both of us silent yet not uneasy in it. Sometimes I made a cup of tea, sometimes not. I suppose now that I think of it I could have got a pint of beer in for when she came, but it never occurred to me. Not that I think she felt the lack of it, for it wasn't the sort of thing she expected to see in my house anyway.

She never missed coming once, even though she often had a cold in the winter and would have been better off in bed. The blackout and shrapnel didn't stop her either. In a quiet off-handed sort of way we got to enjoy ourselves and looked forward to seeing each other again, and maybe they were the best times we ever had together in our lives. They certainly helped us through the long monotonous dead evenings of the war.

She was always dressed in the same brown coat, growing shabbier and shabbier. And she wouldn't leave without borrowing a few shillings. Stood up: 'Er . . . lend's half-a-dollar, Harry.' Given, sometimes with a joke: 'Don't get too drunk on it, will you?' – never responded to, as if it were bad manners to joke about a thing like that. I didn't get anything back of course, but then, I didn't miss such a dole either. So I wouldn't say no when she asked me, and as the price of beer went up she increased the amount to three bob then to three-and-six and, finally, just before she died, to four bob. It was a pleasure to be able to help her. Besides, I told myself, she has no one else. I never asked questions as to where she was living, though she did mention a time or two that it was still up Sneinton way. Neither did I at any time see her outside at a pub or picture house; Nottingham is a big town in many ways.

On every visit she would glance from time to time at the fishing-boat picture, the last of the fleet, hanging on the wall above the sideboard. She often mentioned how beautiful she thought it was, and how I should never part with it, how the sunrise and the ship and the woman and the sea were just right. Then a few minutes later she'd hint to me how nice it would be if she had it, but knowing it would end up in the pawnshop I didn't take her hints. I'd rather have lent her five bob instead of half-a-crown so that she wouldn't take the picture, but she never seemed to want more than half-a-crown in those first years. I once mentioned to her she could have more if she liked, but she didn't answer me. I don't think she wanted the picture especially to sell and get money, or to hang in her own house; only to have the pleasure of pawning it, to have someone else buy it so that it wouldn't belong to either of us any more.

But she finally did ask me directly, and I saw no reason to refuse when she put it like that. Just as I had done six years before, when she first came to see me, I dusted it, wrapped it up carefully in several layers of brown paper, tied it with post-office string, and gave it to her. She seemed happy with it under her arm, couldn't get out of the house quick enough, it seemed.

It was the same old story though, for a few days later I saw it again in the pawnshop window, among all the old junk that had been there for years. This time I didn't go in and try to get it back. In a way I wish I had, because then Kathy might not have had the accident that came a few days later. Though you never know. If it hadn't been that, it would have been something else.

I didn't get to her before she died. She'd been run down by a lorry at six o'clock in the evening, and by the time the police had taken me to the General Hospital she was dead. She'd been knocked all to bits, and had practically bled to death even before they'd got her to the hospital. The doctor told me she'd not been quite sober when she was knocked down. Among the things of hers they showed me was the fishing-boat picture, but it was so broken up and smeared with blood that I hardly recognized it. I burned it in the roaring flames of the firegrate late that night.

When her two brothers, their wives and children had left and taken with them the air of blame they attached to me for Kathy's accident I stood at the graveside thinking I was alone, hoping I would end up crying my eyes out. No such luck. Holding my head up suddenly I noticed a man I hadn't seen before. It was a sunny afternoon of winter, but bitter cold, and the only thing at first able to take my mind off Kathy was the thought of some poor bloke having to break the bone-hard soil and dig this hole she was now lying in. Now there was this stranger. Tears were running down his cheeks, a man in his middle fifties wearing a good suit, grey though but with a black band around his arm, who moved only when the fed-up sexton touched his shoulder – and then mine – to say it was all over.

I felt no need to ask who he was. And I was right. When I got to Kathy's house (it had also been his) he was packing his things, and left a while later in a taxi without saying a word. But the neighbours, who always know everything, told me he and Kathy had been living together for the last six years. Would you believe it? I only wished he'd made her happier than she'd been.

Time has passed now and I haven't bothered to get another picture for the wall. Maybe a war map would do it; the wall gets too blank, for I'm sure some government will oblige soon. But it doesn't really need anything at the moment, to tell you the truth. That part of the room is filled up by the sideboard, on which is still the wedding picture, that she never thought to ask for.

And looking at these few old pictures stacked in the back of my mind I began to realize that I should never have let them go, and that I shouldn't have let Kathy go either. Something told me I'd been daft and dead to do it, and as my rotten luck would have it it was the word dead more than daft that stuck in my mind, and still sticks there like the spinebone of a cod or conger eel, driving me potty sometimes when I lay of a night in bed thinking.

I began to believe there was no point in my life – became even too far gone to turn religious or go on the booze. Why had I lived? I wondered. I can't see anything for it. What was the point of it all? And yet at the worst minutes of my midnight emptiness I'd think less of myself and more of Kathy, see her as suffering in a far rottener way than ever I'd done, and it would come to me – though working only as long as an aspirin pitted against an incurable headache – that the object of my having been alive was that in some small way I'd helped Kathy through her life.

I was born dead, I keep telling myself. Everybody's dead, I answer. So they are, I maintain, but then most of them never know it like I'm beginning to do, and it's a bloody shame that this has come to me at last when I could least do with it, and when it's too bloody late to get anything but bad from it.

Then optimism rides out of the darkness like a knight in armour. If you loved her . . . (of course I bloody-well did) . . . then you both did the only thing possible if it was to be remembered as love. Now didn't you? Knight in armour goes back into blackness. Yes, I cry, but neither of us *did anything about it*, and that's the trouble.

GRACE PALEY
Wants

I saw my ex-husband in the street. I was sitting on the steps of the new library.

Hello, my life, I said. We had once been married for twenty-seven years, so I felt justified.

He said, What? What life? No life of mine.

I said, OK. I don't argue when there's real disagreement. I got up and went into the library to see how much I owed them.

The librarian said $32 even and you've owed it for eighteen years. I didn't deny anything. Because I don't understand how time passes. I have had those books. I have often thought of them. The library is only two blocks away.

My ex-husband followed me to the Books Returned desk. He interrupted the librarian, who had more to tell. In many ways, he said, as I look back, I attribute the dissolution of our marriage to the fact that you never invited the Bertrams to dinner.

That's possible, I said. But really, if you remember: first, my father was sick that Friday, then the children were born, then I had those Tuesday-night meetings, then the war began. Then we didn't seem to know them anymore. But you're right. I should have had them to dinner.

I gave the librarian a check for $32. Immediately she trusted me, put my past behind her, wiped the record clean, which is just what most other municipal and/or state bureaucracies will not do.

I checked out the two Edith Wharton books I had just returned because I'd read them so long ago and they are more apropos now than ever. They were *The House of Mirth* and *The Children*, which is about how life in the United States in New York changed in twenty-seven years fifty years ago.

A nice thing I do remember is breakfast, my ex-husband said. I was surprised. All we ever had was coffee. Then I remembered there was a hole in the back of the kitchen closet which opened into the apartment next door. There, they always ate sugar-cured smoked bacon. It gave us a very grand feeling about breakfast, but we never got stuffed and sluggish.

That was when we were poor, I said.

When were we ever rich? he asked.

Oh, as time went on, as our responsibilities increased, we didn't go in need. You took adequate financial care, I reminded him. The children went to camp four weeks a year and in decent ponchos with sleeping bags and boots, just like everyone else. They looked very nice. Our place was warm in winter, and we had nice red pillows and things.

I wanted a sailboat, he said. But you didn't want anything.

Don't be bitter, I said. It's never too late.

No, he said with a great deal of bitterness. I may get a sailboat. As a matter of fact I have money down on an eighteen-foot two-rigger. I'm doing well this year and can look forward to better. But as for you, it's too late. You'll always want nothing.

He had had a habit throughout the twenty-seven years of making a narrow remark which, like a plumber's snake, could work its way through the ear down the throat, halfway to my heart. He would then disappear, leaving me choking with equipment. What I mean is, I sat down on the library steps and he went away.

I looked through *The House of Mirth*, but lost interest. I felt extremely accused. Now, it's true, I'm short of requests and absolute requirements. But I do want *something*.

I want, for instance, to be a different person. I want to be the woman who brings these two books back in two weeks. I want to be the effective citizen who changes the school system and addresses the Board of Estimate on the troubles of this dear urban center.

I *had* promised my children to end the war before they grew up.

I wanted to have been married forever to one person, my ex-husband or my present one. Either has enough character for a whole life, which as it turns out is really not such a long time. You couldn't exhaust either man's qualities or get under the rock of his reasons in one short life.

Just this morning I looked out the window to watch the street for a while and saw that the little sycamores the city had dreamily planted a couple of years before the kids were born had come that day to the prime of their lives.

Well! I decided to bring those two books back to the library. Which proves that when a person or an event comes along to jolt or appraise me I *can* take some appropriate action, although I am better known for my hospitable remarks.

Permissions

Penguin Modern Classics

THE HEART IS A LONELY HUNTER
CARSON MCCULLERS

'She has examined the heart of man with an understanding that no other writer …
can hope to surpass' Tennessee Williams

Carson McCullers's prodigious first novel was published to instant acclaim when
she was just twenty-three. Set in a small town in the middle of the deep South, it is
the story of John Singer, a lonely deaf-mute, and a disparate group of people who
are drawn towards his kind, sympathetic nature. The owner of the café where Singer
eats every day, a young girl desperate to grow up, an angry drunkard, a frustrated
black doctor: each pours their heart out to Singer, their silent confidant and he in turn
changes their disenchanted lives in ways they could never imagine …

Moving, sensitive and deeply humane, *The Heart is a Lonely Hunter* explores
loneliness, the human need for understanding and our search for love.

PENGUIN MODERN CLASSICS

THE MORTGAGED HEART
CARSON MCCULLERS

'An exquisite talent' *Sunday Times*

Few writers have expressed the search for love and the need for human understanding with such power and poetic sensibility as Carson McCullers. *The Mortgaged Heart* contains some of the landmarks in the literary career that would see her become one of the twentieth century's great American writers: 'Wunderkind', her first published story, 'The Mute', her outline of what was to become her great first novel *The Heart is a Lonely Hunter*, as well as her haunting poetry, and essays and articles on subjects ranging from her neighbourhood of Brooklyn to life in wartime, from Christmas to the art of writing.

'A kind of literary biography … one sees the style and perception developing and expressing a unique sensibility' Paul Theroux, *Guardian*

PENGUIN MODERN CLASSICS

THE COLLECTED DOROTHY PARKER
DOROTHY PARKER

'She managed to express her real feelings in stanzas which snap and glitter like a Chanel handbag' Peter Ackroyd, *The Times*

Dorothy Parker was the most talked-about woman of her day, notorious as the hard-drinking bad girl with a talent for stinging repartée and endlessly quotable one-liners. In the bitingly witty poems and stories collected here, along with her articles and reviews, she brilliantly captures the spirit of the decadent Jazz Age in New York, exposing both the dazzle and the darkness. But beneath the sharp perceptions and the acidic humour, much of her work poignantly expresses the deep vulnerability of a troubled, self-destructive woman who, in the words of philosopher Irwin Edman, 'could combine a heartbreak with a wisecrack'.

Penguin Modern Classics

THE COLLECTED SHORT STORIES
F. SCOTT FITZGERALD

'His talent was as natural as the pattern that was made by the dust on a butterfly's wings' Ernest Hemingway

Encompassing the very best of F. Scott Fitzgerald's short fiction, this collection spans his career, from the early stories of the glittering Jazz Age, through the lost hopes of thirties, to the last, twilight decade of his life. It brings together his most famous stories, including 'The Diamond as Big as the Ritz', a fairytale of unlimited wealth; the sad and hilarious stories of Hollywood hack Pat Hobby; and 'The Lost Decade', written in Fitzgerald's last years.

Concerned with the dreams of youth, the power of money and the ravages of success, these are unforgettable stories that defined a generation.

PENGUIN MODERN CLASSICS

WINTER'S TALES
ISAK DINESEN (KAREN BLIXEN)

'Tales as delicate as Venetian glass' *The New York Times*

After the huge success of her autobiography *Out of Africa*, Isak Dinesen returned to a European setting in these exquisite, rapturous tales of rebirth and redemption.

Beginning with a sailor boy's bold progression into manhood, these stories are full of longing, a theme often mirrored in the desire to escape to sea, as in 'The Young Man with the Carnation' and 'Peter and Rosa'. This collection also includes 'Snow-Acre', a modern rendition of a folk-tale in which old ideals clash with the new order, and is considered by many to be one of her finest stories. Full of psychological insights, these luminous tales reveal the mystery and unexpectedness of human behaviour.

PENGUIN MODERN CLASSICS

FORTY STORIES
DONALD BARTHELME

'A magical gift of deadpan incongruity' John Updike

In *Forty Stories*, Donald Barthelme invented a random universe in which time, reality, meaning and language are turned exuberantly upside-down. He describes a startling array of occurrences – a lumberjack falls in love with a tree nymph; the poet Goethe becomes a loveable buffoon, spouting such eccentric aphorisms as 'Music is the frozen tapioca in the ice chest of History'; St Anthony's reclusive behaviour causes consternation among his friends and neighbours; and a vast swarm of porcupines, about to descend upon a university to enrol, forces the Dean to turn wrangler to herd them away. Tangling with the ludicrous and challenging the familiar, these small masterpieces provide piercing and hilarious insights into human idiosyncrasies.

'Among the leading innovative writers of modern fiction' *The New York Times*

With an Introduction by Dave Eggers

He just wanted a decent book to read ...

Not too much to ask, is it? It was in 1935 when Allen Lane, Managing Director of Bodley Head Publishers, stood on a platform at Exeter railway station looking for something good to read on his journey back to London. His choice was limited to popular magazines and poor-quality paperbacks – the same choice faced every day by the vast majority of readers, few of whom could afford hardbacks. Lane's disappointment and subsequent anger at the range of books generally available led him to found a company – and change the world.

'We believed in the existence in this country of a vast reading public for intelligent books at a low price, and staked everything on it'
Sir Allen Lane, 1902–1970, founder of Penguin Books

The quality paperback had arrived – and not just in bookshops. Lane was adamant that his Penguins should appear in chain stores and tobacconists, and should cost no more than a packet of cigarettes.

Reading habits (and cigarette prices) have changed since 1935, but Penguin still believes in publishing the best books for everybody to enjoy. We still believe that good design costs no more than bad design, and we still believe that quality books published passionately and responsibly make the world a better place.

So wherever you see the little bird – whether it's on a piece of prize-winning literary fiction or a celebrity autobiography, political tour de force or historical masterpiece, a serial-killer thriller, reference book, world classic or a piece of pure escapism – you can bet that it represents the very best that the genre has to offer.

Whatever you like to read – trust Penguin.